RIFLE SEASON

RIFLE
SEASON

A NOVEL

PAT KELLY

EMILY BESTLER BOOKS

ATRIA

NEW YORK AMSTERDAM/ANTWERP LONDON
TORONTO SYDNEY/MELBOURNE NEW DELHI

EMILY BESTLER BOOKS

ATRIA

An Imprint of Simon & Schuster, LLC
1230 Avenue of the Americas
New York, NY 10020

Simon & Schuster strongly believes in freedom of expression and stands against censorship in all its forms. For more information, visit BooksBelong.com.

For information about special discounts for bulk purchases, please contact Simon & Schuster Special Sales at 1-866-506-1949 or business@simonandschuster.com.

The Simon & Schuster Speakers Bureau can bring authors to your live event. For more information or to book an event, contact the Simon & Schuster Speakers Bureau at 1-866-248-3049 or visit our website at www.simonspeakers.com.

Interior design by Esther Paradelo

Manufactured in the United States of America

1   3   5   7   9   10   8   6   4   2

The Library of Congress Cataloging-in-Publication Data has been applied for.

ISBN 978-1-6680-9820-2
ISBN 978-1-6680-9822-6 (ebook)

Let's stay in touch! Scan here to get book recommendations, exclusive offers, and more delivered to your inbox.

Dedicated to Laverne Kelly,
teacher, mother and shining example

PROLOGUE

They were concealed in a pocket of aspen, frigid wind sheering off a blizzard of gold and scattering their scent. The client was prone, eyes behind the scope, trying to slow his pounding heart, but the altitude and his girth made that difficult. Mace was crouched beside him, lean as a Spartan, Leica 10×42 binos pinned on the behemoth munching wheatgrass across the canyon.

Both men were in camo under dayglow-orange vests and caps. The shot itself was through a gap in timber and understory, cake for the customized Winchester M70 with the right operator but still a keyhole at 350 yards. The elk's atypical rack was flat massive.

Mace counted nine antler points on the left beam and twelve on the right. The headgear resembled an immense brown spider lying on its back. He put the gross score at a rarified 450.

"Boone and Crockett, here we come," said the giddy shooter, a balding directional driller from Tulsa named Hodges who had paid dearly to be lying in that dirt.

"Keep that safety on and lower your damn voice," whispered Mace with an edge that didn't suffer hubris. His shaggy black hair and runaway Fu Manchu were lifted from an Allman Brothers cover but the spot-on resemblance to a frontier gunslinger was due entirely to his eyes. They were dark and narrow and wouldn't look misplaced in the sockets of a raptor. He was six feet even and thirty-three years old. His religion was attention to detail and he was bothered by a patch of foliage beyond the animal because it didn't move enough with the breeze.

Probably a trick of scudding clouds and sun but his gut wouldn't let the aberration go. Best be certain before that round exited the barrel at 2,950 feet per second and plowed through anything living or dead until inert. He glassed downrange one more time with excruciating care. No innocent critters were visible, nor any of the five hundred square inches of gaudy fluorescence required by Colorado on the outer garment of rifle hunters. Nothing but every shooter's wet dream there for the taking.

Mace glanced at his meal ticket, suddenly irked by the man's sloth compared to the chiseled creation they were about to execute. Odd. The cut of his clients had never bothered him so intensely. But a week of scouting this epic specimen so Hodges could emerge from his bourbon and rib-eye stocked tent to pull the trigger had grated on him. The unearned part, no different than driving a pack-a-day slob to the finish line of a marathon.

It wasn't just that, of course. It was a larger, ineluctable truth that simmered beneath the façade of his occupation. An occupation that paid a shitload of bills and kept his butt on a comfy pedestal in big-game circles. Bottom line, he was in demand because he delivered trophies rain or shine.

Mace smothered the rising buzz of his misgivings, put the Sig Sauer rangefinder on target and double-checked the distance. "Get ready," he said.

Hodges settled his jowl into the stock and slid the safety off. On cue, the bull stopped grazing and raised its head, senses strummed. Mace could feel the shot unraveling. All that fat-boy babysitting and one more trophy in the books with his name listed as guide about to evaporate.

Then the wind quit and the ballistic vagaries of air pressure and humidity aligned with a destiny neither man could conjure in their darkest imagination. "Send it," said Mace.

No sooner had the words cleared the roof of his mouth than Hodges fired and Mace saw the camo-clad apparition with a compound bow at full draw and roared like he was stabbed. The bull was already galvanized, leaping away from this specter when the .225-gram short-mag shattered the right side of its rack. The kinetic wallop briefly put the animal down before it lurched up and bolted away. Then the gunshot faded into silence and the flutter of dead leaves reconvened.

"Fuck you yelling about?" asked Hodges, clueless and squinting. "I hit him, didn't I?"

Mace jumped to his feet with a tremendous ringing in his ears despite impulse plugs in both to minimize the muzzle blast. He whipped the glasses up and scoured the area where the bull was standing but the bowhunter had vanished.

"Hey," said Hodges, cycling the bolt and cranking his head around. "I asked you a question."

Mace saw his mouth moving but couldn't hear him. Couldn't hear anything but his own adrenaline-cut blood thundering through his skull.

He snagged his pack off the ground because it had a basic trauma kit and took the fall line, crashing down through Gambel oak and slewing over slabs of granite. He splashed across a creek and sprinted up the other side of the drainage, struck by the throbbing clarity of everything before him.

He could have spotted a needle in a stadium but nearly tripped over the man sprawled face-down on his weapon with its cams and carbon-fiber arrow still nocked in the polyethylene string. Not that the guy would have cared. The slug had tumbled after hitting the antler, entering his chest and departing his back in a ruby blast that glazed the larkspur he was lying on.

Mace dug a pack of QuikClot from his ruck, ripped it open and stuffed the gauze into the exit wound, seeking the arterial breach. Blood soaked through instantly. He tore open another pack, stuffed that in the hole and applied pressure with both hands reminding himself there was no cell service so not to waste the motion. The body settled under his palms as if he were forcing it back into the earth.

Then Hodges blundered into the clearing and saw what he'd shot. His knees went funky and he dropped his rifle and staggered sideways with the heels of his hands mashed into his sockets.

Mace didn't notice. He was too busy staring at the bowhunter's half-turned face under the mossy-oak buff. He was young, mid-twenties at most. Only his brown eyes were visible. They were wide open and angled up to his left, as if there were something amazing lurking in the clouds.

ONE

A year had come and gone since Mace ignored his vaunted gut and demolished his life from the foundation up. It was early on a Monday morning and he was bagging trash on the shoulder of Highway 62 west of Ridgway sporting a yellow safety vest and a noticeable weave to his step. Off to the south, an October storm had left the summit of Mount Sneffels laser-white and hanging in a cobalt sky that beggared description but he was immune to the spectacle. Just kept snagging litter with his county-supplied grabber stick and working on a pint of Tito's with a nifty sleight of hand.

His beard had gone biblical and his chore jacket couldn't hide the belly he'd tacked on over the previous winter. His eyes had dulled along with his figure. They no longer cut glass, which didn't matter because he was done getting people in killing range of wary animals for a living. This diminishment, combined with a maintenance dose of vodka and weed, caused him to step on the dead mule deer before he saw it. The carcass was the same brown as the grass and his boot sank in putrefied organs as easy as pie. His cell rang from somewhere on his person but he didn't notice.

Disposing of roadkill was outside Mace's purview so he wiped his footwear on a post and kept working his way up Dallas Divide. The joint trial had been held in Montrose District Court and Hodges fainted during the autopsy exhibits. The DA accused Mace and his client of being more focused on success than safety but Hodges's lawyer was first-rate. Both men ducked the involuntary-manslaughter charge. Hodges reached a financial settlement with the dead man's family and changed his hunting venue to Utah. Mace, being the person who explicitly authorized the misbegotten shot, was sentenced to three hundred hours of community service and open-ended pariah status.

When he got even with Dallas Park Cemetery, Mace studied the burial ground. Seeing no visitors, he dropped the garbage bag and crossed the road. He found the headstone of the guy killed by his blip of inattention in the newer section of graves and laid his hand on the white marble with a practiced motion. Robert R. Martinez had been a lance corporal in the Marine Corps, hence the scarlet flag with the eagle and anchor flapping in the wind. Next to that was a vase of wilted columbine. According to the words in stone, he lived almost twenty-seven years and the anniversary of his passing would fall on Saturday, a date now in everlasting lockstep with the dawn of rifle season.

Ridgway had a bunch of cliques for a puny town and the vets were easily the most empathetic. They went out of their way to exonerate Mace, saying Martinez did his time in the sandbox and came back broken and reckless and maybe that was true. But it didn't absolve Mace of anything or begin to heal the runny gash in his soul. That wound had a mind of its own.

Mace never met the person boxed beneath his feet until he was too busy dying to chat. Saw him drinking with hermetic indifference at the True Grit Café but had no occasion to exchange pleasantries. Now he visited the same man's grave with furtive regularity, communing with all that was mortgaged in that split second of shit judgment. Only dumb luck and bleary vigilance had kept him from bumping into Martinez's parents since the broad-daylight nightmare of the funeral.

Mace drained the pint, hearing his dad hold forth on cut corners, magic meteorological thinking and lapses in situational awareness when rounds were chambered. All the slipshod urges capable of turning the most meticulous hunt into the disaster he now personified. So he didn't register the brown Subaru Outback with the Semper Fi decal parking behind him until the driver emerged and shut the door. The sound made him turn and the sight of the trim woman with the graying ponytail and bright brown eyes shoved him backward. The Tito's bottle shattered at his feet.

Anna Martinez, mom of the dead bowhunter, was fifty-nine years old and assumed the man in the safety vest was a cemetery worker. When she recognized her son's de facto killer, she yanked the door open and got back behind the wheel but couldn't for the life of her get the key into the ignition. Her husband Gabriel was slumped in the front seat with a hollowed-out mien and paid the panic attack no mind. His hair was thick and white, his body brittle in repose. When her hands stopped shaking, Anna grabbed the fresh-cut columbine off the back seat and got out, eyes on the ground.

She switched out the flowers, tossed the broken bottle in a trash can and walked up to Mace with her jaw set and a tornado of livid grief roaring through her head. Then she got a good long look at the wrecked soul standing next to her son's marker. And what came out of her mouth surprised even her. "Did you know Robert loved guns before he joined the Marines?"

"No, ma'am," said Mace, staring at her nose to maintain his balance.

"Got his first rifle when he was ten. And after that, opening day was his Christmas Day. Didn't matter if it was rabbits or deer or elk. Shot anything he could eat. I heard you were a lot like that."

She waited for Mace to acknowledge that statement but he had his hands full just standing there so she focused on the jagged sweep of peaks behind his head and kept unpacking her point.

"Two tours over there changed everything. He came back hating guns. Then summer before last he got into bowhunting. Started disappearing for days at a time. Never took anyone with him. Never told us where he was going. He was so quiet and different, we were scared to death he'd kill himself up there. But we were wrong. Face paint and camo became his magic medicine. He loved being invisible. Loved seeing how close he could get to a big buck or bull. And when he talked about it, his eyes would light up and he'd be our sweet boy all over again."

Mace cleared his throat. "He ever harvest any of those animals?"

"Never shot a living thing with that bow. I asked him why. Know what he said?"

She gave Mace a ten-second chance to answer like it was a pop quiz. He shook his head and her eyes drifted down to the grave. "Just because it wasn't stupid easy like pulling a trigger didn't make it right. Anyway, here's the thing I want you to take with you. The main thing. Nobody on earth would have known Robert was there that day. Nobody. Not even you. Mason Winters."

Then they heard the metallic creak. Anna turned and Mace looked past her. A frail hand was pushing the Subaru's passenger door open. "Don't do this to him," she whispered. "Please."

Mace ducked his head and cut toward the highway, not stopping until he was a mile down the shoulder next to a brush-strafed black Tundra with an empty gun rack and a toolbox in the bed. He got in, dug a tallboy from the console and drank it, staring through a windshield so scummy with bug juice and dope smoke the world looked sepia. Then he twirled the FM dial until "Far Away Eyes" sucked him into a twangy daydream and off he went sans seat belt. A bit later, the six-thousand-pound Tundra slipped the leash and mowed down a split-rail fence before coming to a debris-decorated halt in the ditch on the right. His face punctuated the impact by bouncing off the steering wheel.

Deputy Glenn Frazier was driving a blue Tahoe with a light bar down Dallas Divide dwelling on the buffalo cheeseburger at the Grit he intended to devour for lunch. A double with sweet-potato fries. Some darker things were messing with his head, like his paycheck being inhaled by a raft of bad decisions made in concert with his dick but that's what made hunger so fun. It was easy to fix. Glenn was a red-haired, six-four bruiser with a passing resemblance to a supersize Russell Crowe. He played defensive tackle at Mesa University in Grand Junction until ACL tears sank the dream. He'd added some girth but could still wreak havoc in a hurry if pissed. He was thirty-five years old and rocked the tan slacks, chocolate shirt and gray Stetson of the Ouray County Sheriff's Department.

When he saw the black Tundra churning dirt in the ditch full of busted railing, he pulled over ten yards back and studied the shit show. After determining the driver was more interested in digging a giant hole than getting clear of the ditch, he dismounted and rapped hard on the truck's window. Mace gave the cop a hostile appraisal before rolling the glass down.

"Fuck you want?" he said curtly, left eye slit to nothing under a purple golf ball–size knob.

"How about you turn that engine off and exit the vehicle," suggested Glenn.

"Watch your feet," said Mace, gunning the V8 and rocking the gears between drive and reverse.

Glenn hopped on the running board, shot his arm into the cab and snagged the keys. Then he hauled Mace out the window, slipping punches aimed at his face and threw him on the ground. When the cuffs clicked, he tossed Mace in the caged back seat of the Tahoe, deftly jimmied the Tundra out of the ditch, parked it on the far side of the road and wiped the debris off the hood. Satisfied with his handiwork, he got in the Tahoe, made a U and headed west back up the Divide.

After cresting the summit and dropping into San Miguel County, Glenn checked the rearview and saw his prisoner lying face-down, arms bent behind his back. "Don't be drooling on that seat."

Mace sat up and looked around, accepting his situation like he'd been there before. "Shouldn't you be out chasing homegrown terrorists with high-capacity magazines?"

"Bagged one yesterday," said Glenn. "Came out of Mountain Annie's smelling like sativa and shoutin' about the Second Amendment in Texan." Then he snapped his fingers. "Hey. Whatever happened to that sweet Sako 85 the fat cat from Odessa gave you? Had all that checkered walnut. Shot a .30-06 Springfield. Had your initials engraved on the receiver."

Mace frowned at the floor and dredged up the answer. "Sold it at a swap meet down in Cortez."

"You're shitting me. A fine personalized firearm like that?"

"Didn't need it."

Glenn traced the rim of the Uncompahgre Plateau with a pained expression because that's where he and Mace had hunted since they were runts. He'd stopped reminding Mace he wasn't the guy who shot the stoner bowhunter lurking in camo on the first day of rifle season. Stopped trying to reason with him about any damn thing because it turned out self-loathing was tougher than Kevlar.

After turning right on 60X Road, they climbed the flank of the plateau then headed west through broad parks and forested moraines. On a gravel straightaway a dirt bike bore down on them at terrific speed. The machine was green and white. The guy on board was brawny and wore a black helmet with a mirrored visor. He flashed a peace sign as he screamed by. Mace twisted around and saw an American flag plastered across the rider's back before he disappeared in a plume of dust.

"Future donor," said Glenn, eyes on the side mirror.

Three miles later, Glenn turned onto Clanton Road and shortly thereafter drove through a gate onto the track that ran into Mace's 160-acre parcel. It ended at a pretty two-story log home with a steep tin roof and covered porch. A squat barn rose beyond that, weathered gray and set against a meadow. Next to the barn was a woodshed and a fenced garden gone woolly with inattention.

Glenn parked in the yard, yanked Mace out, uncuffed him and blithely scratched the head of the sizable German shepherd that charged up, tail wagging. "Good boy, Vince. Good boy."

Then he threw Mace the Tundra keys and punched a thick finger into his chest, rocking him backward like the wobbly drunk he was. "No more next time."

Mace watched Glenn drive off, rubbing his wrists where the cuffs cut his skin, dug a roach from his pants and torched it. After that he went up the steps and into the house with the shepherd trotting at his heels, not bothering to close the front door. He was halfway across the living room when a Kodachrome snap of his parents drew him over to the mantel. Randy and Kay Winters were young and strong and standing on the porch of the same log home on a pure blue June day in 1983.

Randy was a legendary zero-nonsense outfitter and spitting image of their son. He was squinting at the photographer like his pocket was being picked. Kay Winters was dark-haired and raw-boned pretty. She wore a work shirt with the cuffs rolled over sunburned arms. An axe was slung over her shoulder. Her smile was serene. Kay taught English at Ouray High, ran the food bank and was considered a saint shacked up with cordial savages. One week before Mace's twenty-first birthday, an asshole in a hurry would pass on a blind curve outside the Gunnison and kill them both. Kay bequeathed her boy a curious, open-minded world view. Randy planted decades of hunting insight in his son's skull. The latter now hibernated in Mace's hippocampus like the Dead Sea Scrolls.

Mace stopped wondering what his folks would think of the dreary mess he'd made of his life and shifted his gaze to the arrowhead collection mounted over the fireplace in three sixteen-by-sixteen frames. Seventy-two complete points from Middle Archaic to Ute, all plucked from the deep past with his own hands. But his passion had waned and now his mind drifted toward booze and food.

He went into the kitchen, grabbed a rib eye from the fridge, dropped it in a skillet with a slab of butter and cranked up the burner. He downed three shots of Hornitos and watched the meat fry until a nagging detail sent him back into the living room. He stood before the fireplace a minute before spotting the unbelievable. There was a blank space in the dead center of his arrowhead collection. The crown jewel of his assemblage, a four-thousand-year-old Mount Albion point in green jasper was missing.

Which was about as inexplicable as a thing could get. He searched the floor and under furniture knowing he wouldn't find it because he'd never leave such a superb projectile point lying around. Then it occurred to him that never was an obsolete concept. He could have used the point to open a bottle of red. Or taken it from the frame intending to saw his wrists open and blacked out first. Relieved by the wealth of pathetic possibilities, he torched another pre-roll. Took him a minute to isolate Vince's barking in the numbing roar of his high. Then a bit longer to notice the oily smoke crawling along the ceiling and the dancing radiance coming from the kitchen.

He ran at the fiery fat arcing from the skillet thinking smoke inhalation wasn't a bad idea. The curtains over the sink and the pine cupboards were burning nicely. The Braun coffee maker was dripping blue flame. He'd be dead in short order. Then it dawned on him that Vince would drag him clear or die trying. He grabbed dish towels, sopped them under the faucet and beat the conflagration into smoldering submission. Then the greasy particulate and liquor ganged up on him and the floor heaved. He made it to the sofa in front of the fireplace and pitched face-first into nothing.

Jamie Winters drove her olive-green Rubicon through the gate and up to the house. The sun had set but no lights were on and no truck or dog was in the yard. The front door was wide open. She grabbed pepper spray and a maglite from the glove box and was about to punch 911 when Vince came flying out in a state of maximum agitation. When he saw Jamie behind the high beams, he turned on a dime and led her into the meat-fire stink. She was leggy and fast and wore blue scrubs.

She checked Mace's vitals and hit the lights. Found the charred-to-hell kitchen and stood there, jaws clamped, fighting heartbreak and volcanic anger simultaneously. Her chestnut hair was cut mannish short and her eyes dark brown. She was thirty-one years old and could still spike a volleyball through a wall. To say she was swan-necked and beautiful wasn't wrong but her poise dominated. It kept people on their toes. Then Vince planted his paws on her chest and reminded her dogs were put on earth to shortcut self-pity. She kissed him between the eyes. "You're right, big man."

She grabbed the extinguisher from the closet and blasted the embers. After that she flushed all the booze and pot she could find down the toilet. She was standing over Mace pondering life without him when his cell rang. She dug it from his pants as it went to voicemail and saw ten missed calls coming from the same guy. She stabbed redial and a gruff male voice answered.

"Figured you were incarcerated or dead," said Will.

Jamie looked down at her comatose husband. Realized he reeked of roadkill. "Not quite."

TWO

Tuesday's dawn was blazing through the windows when Mace opened his eyes and found Vince licking his face with languid concentration. He eased the dog's snout away and sat up wondering if the sun was rising or setting. Then Jamie came down the stairs with wet hair, name tag bouncing on fresh scrubs. Her cell was on speaker and a colleague was bringing her up to speed on ER intake at Montrose Memorial. She ended the call and gauged her spouse's condition with a clinical stare. He was still wearing his safety vest and gut-caked boots. "Where's your truck?" she asked.

Mace pictured the Tundra in a ditch then zoomed out. "East side of the Divide."

"Got your wallet?"

He patted himself down and held it up with sickly grin. "Yes ma'am."

"Great. You got five minutes to shower and get dressed."

"What's the rush?"

"You got a job interview. Comes with free breakfast at the Grit."

Mace wobbled to his feet wondering why his left eye was hot and half-shut. "For what?"

"Doesn't matter. You're going. Or I'm going."

He chewed on that last part, alarm piercing his hangover. "Going where?"

"About as far as I can get from you."

Mace raised his sooty hands even with his shoulders like a cornered criminal showing he was unarmed. "Can we make some coffee. Talk things over a second?"

"Absolutely."

She went into the kitchen, came out with the melted coffee maker and winged it at his head like she meant to kill him. He deflected the machine but it bruised his elbow down to bone.

"Fucking motherfuck!" he screamed, clutching his arm.

"Four minutes," said Jamie, walking out the door.

Jamie dropped man and shepherd at the Tundra and drove away. Mace yelled and ran after her waving his arms. He wore clean jeans and a fleece jacket. She didn't want to but she stopped.

"Gonna tell me who the hell I'm supposed to meet down there?" he said, catching his breath.

"Will Stoddard," said Jamie.

"Why?"

"Who cares. Season's three days off. Maybe he wants to pick what's left of your brain."

Mace considered this. Made no sense. "No way. He's been leasing ground out by Cottonwood Creek forever. North Fork. Same place you and I sacked the cutthroat couple summers ago."

"So what?" said Jamie.

Mace shut his eyes. Dying for a drink. "Calls it his trophy hole. Doesn't need shit from me."

"I don't care if it's wiping his butt and washing his truck. I'd jump on it if I were you."

He watched her speed off then dropped the tailgate of the Tundra so Vince could jump in the bed. After climbing behind the wheel, he dug a beer from the console and drank it slowly, marveling at the slack he swam in. He used to be booked three years out by oil-and-gas types who considered him as indispensable as a custom gun. They still called offering crazy money but it didn't matter. His state outfitter license was suspended and his liability insurance was canceled. He was about to pop another brew when he remembered the whole point of being up so goddamn early. He tossed the empty onto the shoulder he'd cleaned twenty-four hours previous and headed downhill.

Ridgway sat at the juncture of two highways and the Uncompahgre River. One road linked Ouray and Montrose while the other ran up to Telluride making a fetching chokepoint. Skiers, hikers and hunters passed through like spawning salmon and the town stayed local. Then a flood tide of virus refugees killed all things genuine and priced out the natives. But the True Grit Café abided.

Mace parked in front of the joint named after the John Wayne flick shot in town and glanced at the WELCOME-HUNTERS banner hanging from the roof. He left Vince in the bed, pushed inside and slid into a booth opposite a man with crewcut, salt-and-pepper hair and a walnut tan. Will Stoddard wore a jean jacket over a white T-shirt and was drill-instructor lean at sixty-four years of age. He stayed poker-faced while a waitress poured coffee and took Mace's order of banana pancakes and bacon. Then he dredged sausage through syrup, thinking good intentions surely paved the road to hell.

"Happened to your eye?"

"Steering wheel," said Mace, slamming the java and catching several people staring at him like his hair was on fire. "Got your money bulls spotted?"

"Couple nice racks on the back side of unit sixty-one. But you know how it is. Leaves turn and they get jumpy. Could be halfway to Moab by now."

"Don't sandbag me, Will. I'm not the competition anymore."

"That's for sure. How's the trash business?"

"Steady," said Mace. "Why?"

"Had some work to swing your way but you were too busy drunk driving to return my call."

"So what am I doing here?"

"Your wife took advantage of my advancing years and poor judgment."

Mace wondered how that happened but drew a blank. "Spit it out anytime you're ready."

"Couple from Phoenix called me a few days ago. Hot-shot realtors. Long story short, they're serious camera buffs who'll pay through the nose for a picture of a mountain lion."

"A live cat running around feeding and fornicating out in the world?"

"That's the deal," said Will. "And no hounds."

Mace's food came and he dove in. "Tall order unless you got one tranquilized somewhere."

"That's why I told them the odds of pulling that off were crap to none and the only guy I knew who could put it in the crap column would need eight hundred a day, hit or miss."

"How'd they find you?" asked Mace.

Will gave a dismissive wave. "Social media or some shit."

"How come you're not taking their money?"

"Because I'm a chooser not a beggar and I don't have beer on my breath before breakfast."

Mace sucked up his anger and kept eating instead of spitting on the lifeline. After the carbs hit his blood he felt a fire rekindle. The chemical siren call of the chase surprised him. "Lucky you."

"We're not talking about me. We're talking about you babysitting tourists in rough country."

"You want me to grovel you might as well order lunch."

"I want your word you won't make me regret this outbreak of sentimentality."

Mace had a moment of guilt that didn't stick. "I can do it. I know I can and so do you."

"You can find 'em a lion or stay off the bottle and the dope long enough to try?"

"Both," said Mace, wrapping his last piece of bacon in a napkin. "When they want to go?"

"Tomorrow's the only day they got. They're staying over in Telluride."

Mace looked around. Caught a guy side-eyeing him. "What else did you tell them about me?"

"Nothing beyond you being able to sneak up on anything there is when you were in the mood."

They shook hands outside and Will left in a red F-350 with Stoddard Guide Service on the door. There was a Winchester Model 94 in the rear window and a bumper sticker that said WELCOME-TO-COLORADO-NOW-GET-YOUR-WEED-AND-GET-OUT. Mace went to his truck, gave Vince the bacon and popped another beer praying the couple from Phoenix were obese smokers with bad knees.

THREE

After leaving Mace and the dog at the truck, Jamie got coffee to go in Ridgway then cut north on Highway 550 toward Montrose. She was passing the reservoir when she spotted Glenn's Tahoe tucked in tall brush on the right waylaying speeders. She skidded onto the shoulder, backed up until she was alongside the cop and lobbed a smile. "How's the highway robbery going?"

He tossed his radar gun on the dash, got out and walked over. "Cooking along until now."

"Nice of you to bring my man home in one piece."

"Wasn't that bad. Least he wasn't dragging forty feet of barbwire like last time."

"Trust me," said Jamie. "He made up for it."

Glenn laid his hand on her shoulder and just like that she was a crying hot mess and rummaging in the glove box for Kleenex. There weren't any. He offered the starched sleeve of his uniform. She grabbed it and smeared glassy tears and snot from elbow to wrist. "Thanks."

"Your tax dollars at work," said Glenn.

Jamie stared straight ahead, hands on the wheel. "How long you think he'll last like this?"

"You mean until he turns the corner?"

"How about kills himself."

Glenn planted his mitts on the roof of the Jeep and shook his head. "Come on. If he was gonna do that he woulda done it. Our boy's not the suicide type. Too much pain-in-the-butt backbone."

"You saw him plow through another fence and moved his truck and drove him home like he was fucking royalty. Gonna do that when he head-ons into a family of four?"

Glenn hitched his service belt like she was pelting him with trivialities. "Find you some faith, girl. Sooner than later he'll touch bottom and swim for the surface. We just gotta wait him out."

Jamie shut her eyes thinking best friends made shitty psychologists. "Earth to Glenn. Sooner than later has come and gone."

He squinted at her. Given pause by the flatness in her voice. "You thinking about taking a break? Go see your mom or something?"

Jamie looked up into his face. It was shaded by the Stetson and his features were stony and alert in a way she'd never seen before. Bolting to her mom's in Grand Junction had crossed her mind more than once. A half measure in the scheme of Mace's doom loop but a start. "Something."

"Do what you need to do but I'd appreciate you letting me know if he's gonna be on his own."

"Why? Gonna lock him up?"

Glenn gave that serious consideration and let it go. "More like dart and tranquilize."

A logging truck roared by and he tracked it south. The bed was stacked with beetle kill the diameter of telephone poles. Steel cables meant to hold the timber in place were loose and scything the wind. He slid behind the wheel of the Tahoe and leaned out the window. "Hang in there."

Jamie watched the blue-and-red bubbles accelerate from view then caught a gap in northbound traffic and headed for Montrose. She drove several miles lost in bad thoughts before checking the rearview. There was a Ford pickup with a camper behind her so she couldn't see the green-and-white dirt bike behind that. Or how the rider wearing the black helmet with the mirrored visor kept nicking the centerline like he was about to pass but never did even when he had plenty of road.

FOUR

Ten minutes before sunrise on Wednesday found Mace and Vince on the porch watching Clanton Road to the east and Dave Wood to the south. The dog was doing all the work because Mace had sampled the vodka and dope he kept stashed in the woodpile. Now he couldn't take his eyes off the pearly incandescence seeping over the horizon. Never crossed his mind how pungent those substances would be to the 225 million scent receptors in the shepherd's nose. Or how Vince had come to associate those smells with trouble. Hence the dog's red-alert status regarding the pickups prowling along the plateau's gravel roads with their lights off like steel megafauna.

Mace didn't pay the vehicles any mind because this was the leading edge of the amateur-hour army that invaded every fall and he knew the ilk of the occupants in granular detail. They had scoped rifles between the seats and thermoses between their thighs. The guns were made by Ruger or Browning or Remington and they were scouting with binos from Cabelas. Same place they got scent eliminator and field dressing kits. Their blood pressure was spiking because Saturday was opening day and unless they knew where elk were holding they might as well be packing BB guns.

The weekend warriors loved meat but they were praying for a huge rack to worship in their man cave. This quest was hardwired and inexpressible because they were ignorant of those who came before. Hunters armed with nothing but spears tipped with exquisite stone points designed to skewer the lungs of eight-ton mammoths. Once the mountain of protein was down in a pond of blood, the hunters had to fight off gargantuan lions and bears made fearless by the gore. Heinous death and injury were routine. Failure to secure the prize was punishable by starvation.

Mace burned thousands of adolescent hours imagining the nerve required to run a six-inch projectile point into the chest cavity of a pissed critter standing fourteen feet at the shoulder. Named after a seminal kill site in New Mexico, the lethality of the Clovis point allowed the Paleo-

Indians to cull the bottomless herds of megafauna grazing the future American West to extinction. A cautionary archeological truth that reduced the men in their comfy heated rides to poodles claiming to be dire wolves on their father's side. And Mace collaborated with that sham to the bitter end.

Beneath that residual shame was a baffled unease about his missing arrowhead. The green jasper point. Its disappearance was a tiny, inexplicable tear in the world.

He was about to dump his coffee and call the cat chase a bust when a pair of headlights came into view, slaloming around the pickups with casual finesse. The vehicle turned west, hung a left through the gate and glided up to the porch. The driver cut the lights and Mace saw a black BMW X5 with Arizona plates. "Sit tight, big man," he said to Vince and walked toward the car.

The guy behind the wheel climbed out and came around the hood. He had longish blond hair under a black Arizona Cardinals cap. He wore a moss-green down jacket, Patagonia rock pants and synthetic gray gloves that fit like a second skin. He was two inches taller than Mace and oozed a grating vitality. "I'm gonna presume you're Mason Winters," he said, flashing fantastic teeth.

"Mace'll do," said Mace and the guy kept coming with a swaggering, carefree gait. They shook hands and Mace felt the angular power of his frame and gauged his true calling as tight end. He put his age in the ballpark of his own and braced himself for humiliation. This ripped son of a bitch could carry him up a fourteen-thousand-foot peak slung over his shoulder like a goat and not break a sweat.

"Clay Brewer," said the man, hazel eyes sliding over the landscape and buildings. "Sick spread you got here. Freaking classic in the truest sense of the word. How much acreage comes with it?"

Mace listened for an accent, a habit no different than looking for tracks but Clay's enunciation was that of a news anchor's clean slate. "Since it's not for sale, I wouldn't worry about it."

"No problem," said Clay, handing over a business card. "But if you ever change your mind, I've got some rapacious clients down in the desert who'd snap this up as is."

"As is?"

Clay framed the property with both hands like a director setting up a shot. "Without the main house, tennis courts and helipad."

Mace gave him a buzzed frown, missing the joke and feeling worn out before they started.

Clay popped him on the shoulder. "Just messing with you, bro. I'd put in a bitchin' infinity pool to capture the totality of the panorama but otherwise this place is the double-D tits."

"Good to know," said Mace.

Then he tucked the card away and studied the woman in the passenger seat of the Beamer. She was texting, full lips and perfect button nose lit by the screen. When she finished, she shoved the door open and went straight at the men. She was a compact five eight and wore a red Nebraska Cornhuskers cap pulled low. Her face was unreadable in the predawn light.

Mace saw the legs of a downhill racer and an upper body built for javelin. She wore the same gloves and outerwear as Clay in different but equally subdued hues. Her shoulder-length hair was shiny and black as obsidian. When she got close, he saw she was a Latina with olive skin and russet eyes with amber pigmentation. He put their acuity at extreme and revised her sport to biathlon. She was almost too formidable to be pretty until she smiled and became a heartbreaker in the mold of Lindsey Vonn. She offered her hand and he felt the marble grip of a gym rat.

"Vanessa Delgado," she said with a clean and velvety Chicana accent.

"Mace."

"And who's that beauty on the porch?" she said, looking at the dog.

Mace was about to make a come motion but the shepherd read his mind and was on Clay like a torpedo. He stuck his hand out and Vince inhaled its essence, eyes locked on the stranger's face. After a tense interval, the dog turned his attention to Vanessa. She knelt without warning, clamped her hands on the shepherd's head and murmured sweet nothings at close range. Mace twitched, one hand going for the dog's collar but Vince had already dissolved into wagging mush.

"What a beast," she said. "Bet he's a great watchdog."

"Watchdog and warhead rolled into one," said Mace. "That's Vince."

"Where'd he get that name?" said Vanessa, nuzzling jaws that could render in a blink.

Mace noted her implacable chill and wondered where it came from. "My grandad."

"And what's back in there?" she said, pointing into the dense fir and aspen beyond the meadow.

Mace following her gaze, struck by her inhalation of detail. "Why?"

"I see an old path," she said.

She was right. It was a forty-year-old track leading to a two-room cabin where Mace's parents lived before the house went up. They built it out of the wind and out of sight. How she spotted the overgrown trail in the predawn gloom was a weird feat of pattern recognition.

"There's a little cabin past those trees," said Mace. "My mom and dad put it up back when."

"Just making sure I wasn't seeing things."

"You're not."

Then she stood up, checked her chunky polymer watch and shot her guide a look. "Let's roll."

"Good idea," said Mace, hiding his annoyance that she'd taken the lead while he stood there thumb up his ass. He watched them grab Camel-Baks and Canon EOS 5Ds with fat zooms from the BMW and realized this might be his future. Guiding nature lovers on species-specific hikes. Then he brushed that hellish vision aside and pointed at the cameras. "Those make any noise?"

Clay held up his Canon. "Not when they're on silent mode."

"Then that's the mode they stay on. Everybody set on food and water? Gonna be a long day."

"Bring it," said Clay, gaze flicking to the house.

Jamie stood on the porch, dressed for work. She gave a little wave. "Morning."

Mace cleared his throat. "Jamie, this is Clay and Vanessa."

"Beautiful home you have," said Vanessa.

"Thank you," said Jamie. "I'd invite you in for coffee but our kitchen burned down."

"Bummer," said Clay, blatantly eyeing a great bod in scrubs. "You a nurse?"

Jamie dissected the pair's bougie veneer. Will said they were real estate agents and the cocky rock-jawed jock was prototypical but the woman was something else. Absurdly fit and openly pleasant with an uncanny stare that had nothing to do with her smile. They struck her as creepy colleagues not spouses. Then again, closet psychopaths would make excellent realtors.

"ER doc," she said.

"Didn't know there was a hospital around here," said Clay.

"There isn't. I work down in Montrose."

"You must stay busy in a place this wild," said Vanessa.

"It can definitely hurt people. But nobody knows this country like my husband."

"That's what we hear," said Vanessa. Then she pointed at the Tundra. "That our ride?"

"That's it," said Mace, watching the pair cross to his truck.

Clay took shotgun and Vanessa got in the back. Their boots made a nasty racket against the empty beer cans on the floor. Mace heard the noise and wished he'd cleaned out the cab and bought some air freshener to negate the stink of torched fatties but too late now. He mounted the steps hoping for some kind of truce and went to kiss Jamie on the mouth. She stiff-armed him backward.

"I saw you out by the woodpile filling that pink Nalgene with vodka."

Mace looked like a kid caught shoplifting. "It's just in case."

"Of what?"

He glanced at the Tundra, wondering if they were watching. "In case I need it."

"You hear the new you talking? The alcoholic asshole about to drive tourists into wild-as-hell county."

Mace couldn't meet her eyes. "Yea. I hear it. But I gotta go."

Jamie stared past him at the rugged countryside she called home. It was breathtaking as ever but suddenly meaningless. Grief and regret had knee-capped her man. Blinded him with self-loathing. And setting the house on fire was just a warm-up. Mace was gonna drag her and everything they had down a black hole of shit and razor blades before he was dead or done.

"Your coulda-shoulda cancer killed us," she said. "You know that, right?"

Mace was mumbling a lame response when she turned and disappeared into the house. He watched the door slam then climbed in his truck and drove out under a cloudless pink sky. Vince paced the Tundra to the gate, jumped up and planted his paws on the driver's door. Mace cupped his muzzle through the window. "Go home, big man. Watch over your mom till I get back."

He watched the shepherd lope for the house then drove into the sun for two miles before turning west onto a dirt track paved with tire-killing rocks that made no impression on his ten-ply rubber. The track followed a tiny creek hemmed in by thick alder and aspen. Clay couldn't resist remarking on the astoundingly filthy windshield. "Jesus. When's the last time you cleaned this glass?"

"Why would I do that?" said Mace.

"Maybe see where you're going."

"I know where I'm going," said Mace. Then he glanced in the rearview and found Vanessa's eyes waiting for him, agile and sharp.

"Your wife must be handy to have around when things get ugly," she said.

"Way handier than me."

"Got kids?" she asked.

"Not yet," said Mace, trying to remember if Will said they were married. Different last names didn't mean there weren't wedding bands under those gloves.

"Just like us," said Vanessa, landing a thudding punch on Clay's shoulder.

"What brought you guys to Telluride?" asked Mace.

"We did the Imogine Pass Run. Stayed for the color to try out the Canons."

"Got some crazy aspen shots," said Clay. "But wanted to go mega bodacious on our last day."

Mace did his best to rein in the sarcasm. "Going from leaves to lions is pretty ambitious."

"What do you mean?" said Vanessa.

"You could hike around up here for a year and never see one in the flesh."

"So it's a waste of time."

"Lemme put it this way," said Mace. "If not getting a puma picture before dark means the day's shit-canned, yea. But if doing something most people wouldn't even try without dogs or a game camera strapped to a tree then no. Let's hit it hard and enjoy the chase."

"Damn," said Vanessa. "Book by its cover."

"Meaning what?"

"I like the way you think."

Mace checked the rearview again like she knew he would and held his gaze with a calm but blunt sexuality. Then Clay was grabbing the steering wheel and yanking it hard right so the truck grazed the large aspen lying across the track instead of punching in the grille and hood. Mace slammed on the brakes and Clay eye-fucked him like a man comfortable with up-close violence.

"See something you like, bro?" he asked. "You up for a spousal time-share, just say the word."

Vanessa kicked Clay's seat hard enough to break a lesser man's clavicle. "Down goddammit."

Clay didn't blink until Mace's expression made him nearly piss himself laughing. Then Mace punched the door open and grabbed a chain saw from the bed. He wanted to cut Clay in half but settled for sawing the tree up and kicking it off the road. After that, they drove west past colossal stumps of ponderosa logged in a frenzy during World War II. Few miles later they left the quilt of second-home parcels and entered the realm of ranches and national forest, a boundary marked by gated barbwire. A NO-TRESPASSING sign made of steel and stamped with the number 95 hung on the top strand. Mace opened the gate, shut it and kept grinding up the grade and gaining altitude.

"Can we stop?" asked Vanessa, spotting at a roofless cabin set in a stand of Englemann spruce.

"Long as you know every minute you sightsee is a minute less to find a cat," said Mace.

She nodded, grabbed her camera and hopped out. Clay found a shred of signal and got fully absorbed texting. Then Vanessa playfully jerked her head for Mace to tag along and he did.

They reached the homestead and saw the interior was overrun by bramble and juniper. The log walls were being erased by insects and weather. Odd chunks of rusted iron littered the ground. Vanessa snapped a few photos then took in the sheer isolation. The sunlight was overwhelming.

"Must have been lonely."

Mace could feel her proximity like a warm magnet. "No lonely people in Phoenix?"

"Who knows. Too hot to go outside half the year."

Mace pointed at the old-growth timber shielding the site from the north. "Only reason this one held up is because it had a windbreak. Got one on my place you'd never know existed."

"How do you know it did?"

"My dad showed me where it was. Bought me a metal detector for my birthday and turned me loose. Found a Union cavalry buckle a foot down. Dug halfway to China looking for his rifle."

"Wow. What do you think happened to the guy?"

"Smallpox. Yellow fever. Busted leg hunting meat on a minus-twenty-degree day. Take your pick. Any of those things would put you on the wrong side of the grass back then."

He saw a shiny cylindrical object in the ruins, picked it up and surveyed the drainage below. Saw how dawn would come up behind him. How the log cubicle formed a perfect blind. Then he scoured the ground again. One shot only. The hunter must have made it count.

Vanessa squinted at the thing then plucked it from Mace's hand, fingertips brushing across his palm. A sensual jolt ran up his arm and down his belly where it fanned out like warm jelly.

"What'd you find?" she asked innocently.

Mace touched the dent in the cartridge where the firing pin struck the primer sending the slug on its faster-than-sound passage. "Spent rifle shell. Someone shot elk from here last year."

She held it up to the light. "What a beautiful bullet."

"Bullet's gone," said Mace. "That's just the casing."

She closed her fist and savored the shell's hard perfection and purpose. "Can I keep it?"

Mace nodded. She stuck it in her pocket and studied the rugged vista again.

"The people who built this place, what were they doing out here?" she asked.

"Cattle or prospecting was the only way to make a living a hundred and forty years ago. This damn sure wasn't a ranch back then and I've never seen tailings up here. So they were after something else."

"Like what?"

Mace looked at the humble log home. The one window no bigger than a textbook. The disintegrating stove hauled up from Denver by mule. The endless, oxygen-starved isolation must have driven more than a few out of their minds. "Seeing what they were made of."

That remark hung in the air until Clay tapped the horn and motioned them to hurry up. By the time Mace and Vanessa got back he was standing by the tailgate, taking a piss and enjoying the scenery. He'd put on sleek sunglasses. He gave Vanessa a long look, unreadable behind the shades.

"What was that ninety-five thing on the fence back there?" he asked, taking his time zipping up.

"Means we're on the Ninety-Five Ranch," said Mace.

"Catchy name. How big is it?"

"Most everything you're looking at for a good ways."

Clay whistled. "Hedge-fund candy, bro. Baubles of the ruling class."

Mace gave Vanessa a look. "Hell's he talking about?"

"Billionaire bait," she said. "They love things you can see from space."

"Well, there's the man to talk to," said Mace. He gave Clay his binos and pointed at the battered Willys easing down the slope opposite a mile away. "His great-grandad started the spread in 1895."

Clay snugged the binos to his eyes and saw a white-haired guy wearing a dingy yellow cowboy hat and bib overalls driving the ancient Jeep. A brown-and-black border collie rode shotgun. A bolt-action rifle was clamped on the metal dash. Man and dog were staring back with interest.

"Dude owns a jillion acres and drives a junkyard Jeep?" asked Clay.

"Apparently," said Mace.

"Do we have to ask his permission to be here?"

Mace gave the rancher a wave that he returned before disappearing into timber. "Just did."

Then he took his binos back and climbed in the truck. Clay hopped in the bed and Vanessa took shotgun and they bounced up the back side of a sharp ridge. At the first hairpin, Mace stopped and glassed Horsefly Peak to the south. The summit had a dusting of snow but its lower reaches were dry and thick with chokecherry. Ten mule deer grazed in plain view across a wide glade.

"Jesus," said Clay, jumping out, camera up. "Look at that congregation of elk over there."

"Deer," said Mace, grabbing the rangefinder from the glove box then catching himself. He was unarmed. Range was irrelevant. He stuck the device between his legs. "Also known as cat food."

"Great," said Vanessa. "Now what?"

Mace checked the sun. "Lions feed at dusk and dawn. Rest of the day they hold in cover. No way in the world to walk up on 'em. Which gives us eight hours to find a fresh kill and get positioned so the cat doesn't see us or smell us like neon signs dunked in cow shit."

"Find the snack bar and the lion comes to us."

"In theory. But they're very good at hiding groceries. And careful beyond all else."

"Yo, Mace," yelled Clay, pointing at the deer. "Could you make that shot back in the day?"

Mace felt heat scoot up his neck. Back in what fucking day? He looked at Clay but he'd gone back to snapping the animals as if an answer wasn't the point. Or he knew the answer.

"I guess he thinks you're retired from the whole hunting thing," said Vanessa.

"Why would he think that?"

"Maybe your friend Will mentioned it."

Mace studied the mule deer again, running the trigonometry of elevation and bullet drop by muscle memory. "Depends on the wind. That's a good four hundred and fifty yards."

Vanessa reached between his legs, brushing his crotch before snagging the rangefinder and putting it on the deer like she'd used one before. "Wow," she said. "Four forty."

Mace shrugged, mouth dry. "Lucky guess."

"Bullshit. And you didn't answer his question."

Mace took his time turning to her. "Back in the day, I could make that shot in the dark."

They were still eye to eye when Clay got in and shut the door. "What'd I miss?"

"First-date stuff," said Vanessa, sticking the rangefinder back in the glove box.

Mace drove across Horsefly Creek then turned uphill on a track so clogged by brush their passage sounded like fingernails on a blackboard. After gaining a thousand feet in altitude, he stopped and took three dayglow-orange vests and caps from the bed. He put one set on, clipped bear spray to his belt and set the rest of the orange gear on the tailgate. "One size fits all," he said.

"Wait a sec," said Clay. "Won't that stuff make it easier for the mountain lions to see us?"

"They don't see color the way we do," said Mace. "They're looking for shape and movement."

"Then what's the point?" asked Vanessa.

"Muzzle-loading season just ended and rifle season starts Saturday. Some hunters don't pay attention to dates. So the last thing you want to do is look like an elk in sunglasses."

"Shit," said Clay, getting into his safety gear in a hurry.

"You mean muzzle loading like those goofy Civil War reenactor clubs?" asked Vanessa.

"Kinda," said Mace. "Gun has to be unrifled and use black powder. Cuts down on velocity and range and accuracy. So placing a knockdown round is harder."

Vanessa tossed her Nebraska Cornhuskers hat in the bed, put the orange one on, checked her reflection in the side mirror then slipped into her vest. "Just to make it all more fake sporting?"

Mace was surprised by the casual animosity. "Probably. Never guided any muzzle loaders."

"Why not?"

"Hunting is hard enough on these animals," said Mace. "If you can't kill 'em clean and quick don't take the shot." Then he spread a topo map and tapped a narrow escarpment three miles away at an elevation of nine thousand feet. "That's where we're headed."

"What's there?" asked Clay.

"View of this saddle to the south where we might find a fresh kill. Watch where I step and keep your head down. And no talk unless I start it. You got a question give me a hand signal."

Then he put the map away, shouldered his pack and took off feeling a buzz from being back in charge. Clay and Vanessa pulled their gear on watching his speed and gait like coaches at a tryout. After he disappeared around a bend in the trail they trotted after him. Half a mile later Mace was huffing like a dying steam engine and his clients were bunched up on his heels, Clay in the lead.

"Yo, bro," he said. "What's the hand signal for CPR?"

Mace glanced back at him, too gassed to come up with a retort.

Clay kept poking. "How about where's my oxygen and wheelchair and drool-proof blanky?"

Vanessa slapped the orange cap off his head. "Shut the fuck up."

After another mile, they hit a flat stretch pocked with scrub oak and Mace saw coyotes loping away with no more noise than socks on carpet. He veered over to the carcass splayed in the tall grass and watched the realtors circle the mess. The doe's front legs were wrenched off and its stomach torn open. The rump had been violently devoured. "That's how coyotes feed," he said.

"Poor thing," whispered Vanessa, picturing the deer's final moments of numb horror.

"They get the animal down and have a tug-o'-war," said Mace. "Then eat ass-first."

Clay squinted at the shiny mangle of organs, steroidal vocabulary stalling out. "Dang."

The couple started snapping pictures but Mace kept moving. He reached a shady band of spruce, puked his scrambled egg breakfast and planted his butt on a log. His quads were on fire and his heart was about to claw out his chest and run off. He pulled the eighty-proof pink Nalgene bottle, took a gulp and replaced the cap just as Vanessa and Clay jogged up, perky and oblivious to the altitude.

She jerked a thumb back down the trail. "Why not stake out that kill?"

"Lions are picky," wheezed Mace. "They don't eat off other people's plates."

Clay gobbled a protein bar and appraised their guide. "Tell you what. This might not fly."

Mace licked his lips thinking about the joint in his pocket. "What might not fly?"

"You," said Vanessa.

Mace lurched to his feet, face slick with sweat. "Just knocking off a little rust."

"Rust my ass," said Clay. "You're decrepit and enfeebled."

Vanessa winced. "Bought him a thesaurus to enhance his agent-speak. Big mistake obviously."

But what he said was true as hell, thought Mace. He pulled out the blunt, took two massive hits and lapsed into a coughing fit that made his eyes bug and water. Then tucked the roach away like it was made of gold leaf. "Called a sabbatical."

The couple exchanged a look. Mace thought it had meaning beyond finding a cat but his O_2 deficit clouded any conclusion. He did wonder why they weren't mad. Maybe eight hundred dollars a day was pocket change. Or they were about to fire him. "Ready to cut me loose?" he asked.

"Not yet," said Vanessa. "Just don't stroke out on us." Then she pointed at the nick in the ridge above and to their right. "That has to be the notch we're headed for."

"That's it," said Mace, thinking she could sure read a map. Then he saw the dark-legged front nosing in from the northwest. Looked like monsoon weather but it was too late in the year. On the other hand, best believe your eyes not the calendar. Few inches of July-like rain would translate into two feet of October snow. Mace knew that was his father talking but figured it didn't matter. The front seemed to be moving east. And he was on a tourist lark, not a three-day bighorn hunt.

"How about we wait for you up there?" said Vanessa.

Mace dug out a Red Bull and drank it pondering his customers. The vomiting and booze and weed had cleared his head. "How 'bout you two fall in behind me and keep your mouths shut."

They reached the ridgeline in an hour. Mace was wobbly enough to call it quits right there but didn't have the wind to say so. He shed his pack, flopped prone behind the sandstone fin and snugged the Leicas into his sockets. Then glassed the topography below thinking the odds of finding the proverbial fresh lion kill were still crap to none. Talk the talk, take the money and go home.

The ground he scoured was slung between two promontories, dropped off sharply on either side and resembled a five-hundred-acre saddle covered with pinion and manzanita. Clay slid up next to Mace and followed the slow weave of his binoculars with impatient disinterest. Vanessa rolled onto her back and followed a pair of red-tail hawks riding the thermals directly overhead. They were commiserating in soft shrieks and banking in tight spirals, wingtips almost touching. Long ago she read they mated for life and never forgot. Her eyes softened as she admired the perfect predator romance borne on thin air. Then she rolled over and watched her guide ply his trade.

Mace combed the saddle for another chunk of time then started over again without a word. Twenty minutes after that he froze and made an adjustment to the ocular. Clay broke out his Bushnell 10×42 binos and studied the ground holding Mace's attention but saw no dead deer.

"What are you looking at?" he whispered.

"Haven't decided yet," said Mace.

Vanessa got prone beside him, thighs sliding along his. "But it could be a lion kill."

"Could be," said Mace. "Could be a black bear kill. They take deer when they get a chance. If it's too much meat they cache it. But if I was dumb enough to bet, I'd put money on it being a cat."

Vanessa snagged the binos from Mace's hands. He let her because her touch felt good.

"Where am I looking?" she asked.

Mace pointed at the northern rim where the snow held longer and the vegetation was thicker. On the lip was a clearing littered with deadfall and bramble. A heavy stand of pine shaded it from casual discovery. "Left side. Just inside the trees."

Vanessa aimed the glass accordingly and adjusted the focus. "You mean that little mound with the branch sticking up with the pine cone at the end?"

"Yea. Except that's a foreleg and the cone is a hoof."

Her knuckles tensed and she exhaled sharply. "Holy shit. He's right."

Mace felt a drug-like surge of vindication but kept his mouth shut.

Clay put his glasses on the spot beneath the stand of pine he'd swept before and suddenly saw the deer leg clear as day. "Superlatives fail me," he murmured.

Mace took his binos from Vanessa and stowed them away. "Now comes the hard part."

He moved to the notch in the ridge and cased the eighty yards of twenty-degree grade salted with loose rock running down to the saddle then motioned the couple over and pointed at the slope.

"When you see me hit those trees at the bottom, wait ten minutes then come on down one at a time. Nice and easy. No rush and no damn noise.

Then find cover, stay put, stay low and do not move. I'll come back and find you. Understood?"

Vanessa nodded. Clay just stared, rubbed wrong by orders from a boozehound. Then Mace slid though the notch and down the incline. The couple watched his progress. His footwork wasn't bad.

"Might still have it," she said.

Clay shrugged. "Might at that."

After their guide disappeared, they waited ten minutes and slipped through the notch and down the grade with a liquid stealth not learned from showing open houses.

Mace was deep in the saddle when he stopped to check the treetops. Once he had the wind direction nailed, he started a wide, head-down recon. When he reached the western flank of the saddle he doubled back on a different course. In the heart of the brush, a small pine-needle-covered mound caught his eye. He leaned close but didn't touch what he saw and moved on.

After returning to where he started, he spotted Clay and Vanessa under a big pinion. He caught their eyes and they came over quick and quiet with excited expressions. Like kids on a field trip. Then he took off with them at his heels until he reached the same needle-covered mound.

"Cats are into delicacies," said Mace in a voice that didn't carry past their ears. He scraped the needles away to reveal a six-inch brown turd cut with hair and bone fragments. "They shave off the fur with their teeth and dissect out the stomach so the acid doesn't ruin the heart and liver. And they cover their scat. This one isn't that old. He might not get hungry again for days. We'll see."

"How do you know it's a male?" asked Vanessa, lips brushing his ear.

Mace pointed at a robust print in the dirt a yard away. "Paw size."

"What else?" she said with a grin.

Mace led them to a granite mound the size of a boxcar. It was downwind of the kill and covered with juniper. He made them wait while he scrambled up through branches to the far side of the rocks where he found a good blind with a clear view of the cache fifty yards away. Then he crawled back to where he left the couple and stopped in disbelief. They were gone.

He saw movement and rose to his knees. The two of them were on their feet, walking backward. Clay's right arm was extended. There was a Glock 45 in his hand. Mace followed the barrel and saw a black bear cub ambling toward them, flipping rocks and licking up ants. A yearling weighing about seventy pounds. Then the cub got a whiff of sweat and sunblock, saw the two humans and bawled for help. Then mom came crashing through the oak like an ursine cannonball.

Clay hauled Vanessa behind him and drew down on the bear seeing all the sketchy places he should have died and didn't pass before his eyes. Made being mauled to death in nowhere Colorado kinda quaint. He was deciding where to place the first round, head or chest, when a dayglow orange vest slid into his gunsights and stopped. Then the back of Mace's skull and his spread arms.

The 320-pound sow halted her charge eight paces from Mace, huffed explosively and slammed her forelegs into the ground. The cub wheeled and vanished. Mace had the bear spray in his right hand. His left was raised in casual greeting. His voice was soothing but firm. "It's all good darling. All good. Go get your baby and ignore the clown with the gun because he's not gonna shoot."

Clay glared down his right arm, weapon locked on Mace's back. Pissed at the stoner hayseed messing up his shot and telling him what he was or wasn't gonna do. "Why not?" he asked.

"She's bluffing," said Mace quietly. "She just wants the cub safe. Do not fire that weapon."

The bear made one more huge raging huff and galloped after her kid. Mace listened to her foliage-crashing passage thinking of all her kind he got killed or killed himself. "Sorry, momma."

"Talking to yourself now or that bear?" said Clay.

Mace turned around. Lightheaded with relief until he saw Clay's sidearm was still aimed in his direction. His stance was rock steady. "Lower that goddamn gun," snapped Mace.

Clay didn't. Just lowered the barrel slightly. Putting it on Mace's gut. "You got a death wish?"

Mace froze. Thumb easing the safety off on the bear spray. "I knew she didn't mean it."

"Fuck the bear. You looking to get shot is what I'm asking."

"If I'd known you were dumb enough to pack a pistol on a nature hike I wouldn't be here."

"But you saw it and ran downrange anyway. Put your spine in my sights. That's a death wish."

Vanessa stood beside her man and studied Mace with newfound appreciation. "Or maybe he was actually ready to die for that bear."

Clay smiled. "You mean for all the ones he made into rugs?"

"Yea."

"Still aberrant suicidal shit if you ask me."

Vanessa watched Mace another second. "But in a good way. Stow the pistol."

Clay holstered the piece under his jacket and zipped it up. Then Mace rolled into his face.

"What are you doing with a concealed weapon out here?"

"None of your business," said Clay.

"I can guarantee you it's my business to know when a client's carrying a sidearm."

"So now you know. Got an Arizona concealed carry in the Beamer."

"Fuck Arizona," said Mace. "This is my world."

"Maybe your world's a little safer than mine."

"That why you're pointing a semiautomatic at my back?"

Clay got nose to nose with Mace, eyes lit and ready. "You ran directly in front of my weapon."

Mace blinked. The asshole was right. Clay lived in a concrete shithole with a stupid crime rate. Where pistols were as common as cell phones and he'd never been charged by a bear before. His reaction was moronic but not crazy. He put the bear spray away and stepped back.

"I'm not an NRA nutjob," said Vanessa. "But tripping out over a handgun seems a little extreme for a guy who made his living with big bad rifles."

Mace looked at her, heart grinding, sweat trickling under his clothes. "Meaning what?"

"If you need an excuse to call it a day let's wrap it up right now and head home. Don't drag us into your sad-boy quitter bullshit for nothing."

Mace looked off. She'd read his mind. A perfect stranger. Hell yea he needed excuses. He was addicted to excuses. Had been for a year. They were the sucking white noise in his head and she'd handed him a beauty. *Screw this doomed goose chase. Go home and get mummified on the porch.* But then what. The deep end beckoned. The one with no bottom. The one where he burns the whole house down with him in it. He turned to Clay and stuck his hand out. "Give me the Glock."

Clay backed up a step, stance widening. "Why?"

"Simple. Safety first. Give me the gun or we're done. Up to you."

Clay glanced at Vanessa for guidance but she was watching the same two hawks with a dreamy expression because she already knew how this hormonal face-off would end. Sure enough, Clay opened his coat and surrendered the weapon butt-first. Mace released the magazine, ejected the chambered round, caught it on the fly and stuffed the gun and ammo in his coat. His brisk familiarity with a pistol wasn't lost on Clay.

"Know your way around a sidearm."

"Not exactly particle physics," said Mace.

Then he laid a finger across his lips and walked past them toward the granite mound with the view of the kill. They fell in behind him, quiet as mice. When they got situated in the juniper on the far end of the rock he motioned them to flatten out and get their cameras ready. Then he pointed at the verge of the saddle where the vegetation was a solid wall and spoke in the barest whisper.

"If I were him, I'd come through there."

When they were settled, Mace backed into the juniper until his silhouette was obliterated. Then time bled out and the sun dropped into the clouds piling up over Utah. The light got purple and brassy and the shadow of higher ground crept over their perch. The temp fell like an axe.

The aspen glow was down to a smudge when Mace shifted his gaze from the kill to the thicket for the hundredth time and felt a jolt of amazement. A man wearing face paint and camo was kneeling just inside the trees. His compound bow was raised, arrow at full draw, aimed at something off to the right. Even under the paint he seemed vaguely familiar. Mace looked at Vanessa thinking her hyperacuity would spot the guy right away but her expression was blank. As if entranced. He put the Leicas on the hunter and his heart stopped. It was Robert Martinez.

Mace lowered the binos and mashed his face into his hands. When he looked up again, Robert had set the bow aside and was down on hands and knees. His camo sloughed off like snakeskin and he grew huge paws, tan flanks and a lush, black-tipped tail. Then he became the biggest, finest mountain lion Mace had ever seen. After a vigilant pause, the puma glided into the open, lantern gaze freezing Clay and Vanessa in abject wonder. They almost had their cameras up when Mace rose to his feet, jaw hung, head shaking slowly in disbelief. The great cat saw him and vanished without seeming to move. The entire animal dissolving in a blink. A genuine act of magic.

It was 10 p.m. when the Tundra rolled into the yard and Mace got out. Vince mauled him with joy but he didn't notice. The house was lit up but Jamie's Rubicon was gone. A yawning numbness entered his body and left his legs and arms leaden. Then the truck's doors creaked and the couple was coming at him, gear slung over their shoulders. Vince lowered his head and snarled and they stopped in unison. Mace was about to reprimand the dog when his gut started humming like a wire in the wind. Somehow the Arizona realtors were no longer harmless visitors on a photo safari.

Vanessa made a pouty face. "Vince the valiant. What's wrong?"

Mace pointed at the porch. "Place."

The shepherd mounted the steps and sat smartly, eyes locked on the situation in the yard.

"Guess he changed his mind about something," said Mace.

Clay moved closer and stuck his hand out. "My weapon please."

Mace dug out the Glock then the magazine and the loose round and gave them all back.

Clay seated the magazine, holstered the pistol and held up eight hundred dollars in crispy C-notes. "When you're ready to sell this singular slab of paradise, you give me a call. And I'll make it rain money."

Mace didn't touch the cash. Too busy wondering why he wanted to kill this guy so bad for nothing more than being an obnoxious tool. And why neither of them took their skintight gloves off all day. Not once. For any reason whatsoever. "Sorry about messing up your photo shoot."

Clay took Mace's hand, pressed the bills into it and stepped back. "Here's the reality behind that self-effacing remark. We saw the mountain lion, bro. Saw it with our own eyes, not through some soulless chunk of technology. And that was a spiritually transcendent moment."

Then he gave Mace a bear hug that realigned his spine, hopped in the Beamer and fired it up. Mace was looking at the money when Vanessa touched his arm and gave him a carnal sigh that said in another life they would have fucked all day like bunnies on crank.

"Clay's right," she said. "Your conditioning was junk but your instincts were outstanding. You got us forty-five yards from a crazy-careful creature. And who could do that on a day's notice?"

Mace replayed the puma's position relative to their perch and also put the range at forty-five yards. And she did that calculation in extremely low light. A very interesting skill set.

"I told you we had to get stupid lucky," he said. "And that's exactly what happened."

She offered her hand and he took it. Her grip was softer. More human. Like there was nothing left to prove or discover. "Maybe. But I do have a question. Did you ever hunt mountain lions?"

Mace hesitated. "Why?"

"I heard you hunted everything."

"Yea. I hunted mountain lions."

"And killed them."

"Yea," said Mace, exhaustion giving way to fuck-it shame. "Quite a few as a matter-of-fact."

"And what were you thinking when you destroyed a creature that perfect for fun?"

Mace stared at the ground for the answer but nothing came to him because it was another person in another life who committed those atrocities. That was his excuse anyway. "Don't remember."

Vanessa shook her head. Amazed. "Which makes it even worse."

After the Beamer glided out the gate, Vince came off the porch and stood at Mace's side. They watched the machine accelerate east under a swarm of constellations, high beams slicing over open country. Jupiter levitated over the igneous peaks to the south and the horned owl living under the crown of the barn passed overhead without a molecule of sound. Then Mace went inside and found the handwritten note leaning against the salt and pepper on the kitchen table:

Running what I need up to my mom's.
Spending the night. I'll swing by tomorrow
after work and grab Vince. Think about how
much sense this makes before you lose your shit.
And how much I love you.

Mace wadded up the message, threw it in the trash, kicked the table over and smashed two chairs to kindling against the wall. He stood there staring at the mess for a minute. Then dug the note out of the garbage, smoothed it out and stuck it in his pocket. After that he put the table back in place, pulled up an intact chair, sat down and looked around. The sweetest, most perfect thing in the world was coming home and finding Jamie waiting. It was all he needed. Made him a man in good standing with the universe. And now he'd wrecked it. Wrecked it good and deep.

Vince stayed put in the yard, ignoring the ruckus in the house. His mission in life was protection and he'd heard enough furniture-wrecking tantrums to know they were harmless. His eyes were nailed on the precise spot where the BMW disappeared from view. And that's where they stayed.

FIVE

The Adobe Hills are called that because *adobe* means "mud brick" in Spanish. They're composed of clay and shale and shaped by eons of erosion into yellowish domes that are lunar in appearance. They're ideal for dirt biking and overlook Montrose Regional Airport. Which is why the rider on the green-and-white Suzuki SuperMoto was admiring the view. It was midmorning on Thursday.

He wore a black helmet with a mirrored visor and a replica Easy Rider jacket with an American flag across the back. His boots went to his shins and he disdained gloves, gripping the handlebars with big battered knuckles. He was six foot one and usefully bulked up like a middle linebacker.

Hazim Musovic removed his helmet and studied the swell of the Uncompahgre Plateau to the west. He had topaz-blue eyes and blond crewcut hair. His jut-jawed countenance belonged on a pedestal illustrating the purest of archetypes. He could have been a Visigoth wielding an axe against Roman centurions or a Red Army rifleman killing Germans in Stalingrad and the face of a soldier wouldn't change a whit. A welter of vivid scars made him look older than his forty-nine years. He couldn't get used to the scale of the American West. It was preposterous and magnetic.

He'd toured the tiny terminal earlier watching men retrieve rifle cases from the carousel as if the prospect of shooting a harmless herbivore was the height of masculinity. Having killed scores of heavily armed men with IEDs, bare hands and assault rifles, Hazim found this riskless hobby obscene. One group in particular, five loud fellows wearing large hats and pointed footwear, drew him over like a tiger to a pen of bleating goats. He rolled into their midst and hosed the lot with a rabid battlefield grin. The lethality cooking off the biker caused the pretend warriors to study their phones and murmur about the weather before filing meekly out of the terminal into an Escalade.

Hazim was replaying this incident and cursing himself for his childish lack of discipline when a soft roar made him check the sky to the north. A dazzling white jet was turning on final. The Gulfstream G700 touched down and taxied toward an apron south of the terminal. Hazim watched the wheels get chocked before pulling out a cell phone and sending a text, almost laughing at the way his hands trembled. But why wouldn't they? His dream had finally arrived. The culmination of all he'd become applied to one last conflict. The supremacy of right over might no matter the price. He strapped his helmet on and drove down to the service road that skirted the airport.

When he hit Townsend, he turned north past car dealerships and gas stations then right into the Hampton Inn. He curved around to the back and stopped behind a security fence with a clean view of the Gulfstream. He kept his helmet turned slightly, as if watching the United flight disgorging passengers onto the tarmac off to his left. But he could the see Gulfstream's door very clearly.

The jet's stairs unfolded and two men deplaned and fanned out. They wore jeans and parkas and moved with alert economy. Luka was thirty-three and tall with shaggy black hair and earbuds pumping Russian rap that made his body sway in sync with howling angst. A boyish grin creased his unlined face. Marko was forty-six and squat with a full head of gray hair and a beard to match. He wore a hard scowl that never quite faded. Hazim knew all about them. They were elite Serbian mercenaries with MP5K submachine guns under their parkas and ballistic vests under the weapons. They were experts in close-quarter and long-range work and had gained notoriety during Russia's 2014 annexation of Crimea by running a betting pool for the longest confirmed civilian kill regardless of age or sex. More often than not they won. Both lived and breathed the hired-gun ethos.

Once Luka and Marko were in position, a clean-shaven man in a good suit sans tie appeared in the plane's door. Stefan was thirty-eight and somewhat oily despite his tailored presentation. He had wavy brown hair, an MBA from Cambridge and an HK45 semiauto under his jacket. He was better with the pistol than he looked but close protection wasn't his primary task. His job was multilingual executive assistant. And truth be told, compared to the mercs, he was a labradoodle among wolves. When he got brisk all-clear nods from Luka and Marko, he ducked back into the Gulfstream.

A minute later, someone moved to the rim of the cabin door and stopped where they could see the terrain beyond without exposure. This was an animallike pause. That of a predator about to emerge from cover. Then David Petrovic stepped into the fierce Western Slope sun and Hazim's blood pressure exploded. A speedball of rage and hate that shook the machine between his legs.

Petrovic wore a white cashmere sweater that complemented his Croatian tan and carried a Negrini rifle case the way a pool shark carries a custom cue. His longish gray hair was swept into a ducktail and his waist had gone to seed but his upper body was bricked with muscle. Combined with the jutting chin and baleful sapphire eyes, there was more than a whiff of Brando. He lingered in the jet's door, drinking in the forested anticlines and picturing his majestic prey crumbling to its knees in the orange glow of his Swarovski scope. He couldn't recall a more heroic landscape.

Hazim studied Petrovic, visualizing emptying his Beretta M9 into the man's navel. A grouping that would let him to live long enough for Hazim to explain how they ended up at the same tiny American airport. But that would be suicide. The mercs would cut him down at three hundred meters. And their employer would vanish into the sky with another death-defying escape carved into legend.

Big-game hunting was the perfect encore career for Petrovic. It involved exotic travel and utilized the same cold-blooded acumen that built an outlet-store empire stretching from Sofia to Warsaw. But he was too good at it. The gaps in his bucket list of trophy animals had dwindled to a precious few and he was dreading the finish line. One of those gaps was the fabled Colorado elk.

This being his first trip to the Serengeti of John Wayne and Clint Eastwood, he'd decided to honor the occasion by dialing back his obsession with security from maniacal to bare essentials. In part because this was his dream hunt and in part because his baseline precautions were already in place. Including a ghost jet owned by an offshore entity and a flight plan filed for Seattle. There was another factor, of course. Father Time was murmuring in his ear, talking trash that could not be ignored any longer. So he was determined to savor the realm of the chase as much as the kill.

Embracing his own twilight with a seeking and uncluttered mind before darkness fell forever.

Still, Petrovic couldn't help noticing the biker beyond the fence because the pilot light of his paranoia was never off. The rider's hands were on the handlebars and he was staring at a commercial jet deplaning its load. But he kept the helmet with the silvery visor on. A nagging detail reminiscent of past unpleasantness. Then Petrovic reminded himself that he was 5,831 air miles from his estate on the Danube, in a country where the average person didn't know the Bosnian War from the Boston Celtics. So he descended the stairs toward a black Mercedes-AMG that shrugged off armor-piercing rounds like snowballs with a spring to his step. He was sixty-three years old and doing the only thing he truly loved. Recreational killing in stupendous natural settings.

When Petrovic and Stefan were tucked in the back seat and all the luggage and rifles and wine were loaded into the cargo hold, Luka took the wheel and Marko took the front passenger seat. Then they exited the airport with Petrovic's favorite aria, Handel's "Va tacito" filling the Benz with the drama of stealth and betrayal that swirled around Julius Caesar to the end of his days.

Hazim was already six miles south of the airport where Montrose falls away into pasture and hop farms. He turned east onto a paved road that flanked a golf course pocked with large identical homes before jumping the irrigation ditch on his right and dismounting behind a stack of hay bales. He had a noticeable limp, his left knee not fully bearing his weight. After concealing himself, he raised the Zeiss 20×60 binoculars he liberated from a corpse in Syria and put them on the Cape Cod compound across the road. The walled residence had three garages and multiple security cameras with overlapping fields of view. A tall and substantial steel gate guarded the motor court.

Ten minutes later, the gate rolled back and the black Mercedes disappeared into the middle garage. Thirty minutes after that, a red truck with an old lever-action carbine in the window pulled up to the gate. The driver pushed the intercom and the gate opened. Hazim knew this was the guide named Stoddard. Luka ran a mirror under the truck while Marko frisked the driver, which irritated him greatly. Then Stefan led Stoddard inside and Hazim punched a number on his cell phone. After three rings there was a beep and Hazim said, "The show is sold out."

Then he put the phone away and stared at his empty hands like they belonged to someone else. He couldn't detect the tiniest tremor. This made him smile. His fighting nerves had kicked in.

He mounted the bike, retraced his route north and cruised past Montrose Memorial Hospital. There was a farmers market in the park across the street. He dismounted and walked past stands of produce without removing his helmet. He took an apple from a woman wearing a Case Tractor cap and offered her a dollar. She laughed and indicated the apple was on the house. He nodded thanks, walked back to the bike and opened an app on his phone. A map appeared with a motionless blue car icon in the physicians' parking lot across the street. It had not moved since 6 a.m.

The person who drove the vehicle represented by the icon spent ninety minutes at Gold's Gym on Main every other day and looked extremely fit. This person never missed a workout but went at random times. He reminded himself not to underestimate their strength. This person also struck him as highly focused. A very dangerous combination. One slip in concentration could jeopardize everything. After verifying the vehicle was there with his own eyes, he drove to his motel.

The Alpine Inn was an L-shaped affair composed of a dozen shabby log cabins. A red, white and blue WELCOME-HUNTERS banner hung over the entrance like every other motel in town. The place was almost empty when Hazim checked in six days ago. Now there were pickups in front of every unit and Cody Jinks twanged from a communal boom box. Hazim eased the motorcycle past clots of blue-collar elk acolytes manning grills and ice chests on their annual pilgrimage to the holy land. The dress code was camo-centric mixed with NRA-, NFL- and NASCAR-themed outerwear.

He parked the Suzuki in front of the last cabin behind a burgundy Silverado with Colorado plates. There was a large toolbox and a cradle in the bed. He set a ramp on the bumper, gunned the bike into the cradle then hopped down and entered his unit. After locking the door and removing his helmet, he parted the curtains on the front window the width of his hand. Then he devoured the apple while studying the other guests closely. Nobody paid the slightest attention to his arrival. He didn't understand why they all looked so happy but they reminded him of World Cup fans. The communal exultance of true believers.

After making sure the blue car icon hadn't moved, he took a quick shower, put on a T-shirt and sweatpants and turned on the TV. He found a show about tornado chasers, turned up the volume and spread a burgundy-and-gold prayer rug on the floor. The same burgundy as his Silverado and the main reason he selected it from the flock of used pick-ups for sale in Grand Junction. Then he opened another app, one with an ornate compass. The needle settled on a thirty-two-degree bearing.

Hazim aligned the rug with Mecca, raised his hands even with his ears then crossed his wrists over his stomach. After dropping to his knees and pressing his forehead to the rug, he began to pray in Arabic. An ambulance wailed past the motel but it made no dent in his concentration.

SIX

The same ambulance deposited an obese white male howling in agony at Montrose Memorial's emergency room. Earlier in the day, the howler had enjoyed a fentanyl lozenge while cleaning his .444 Marlin, inadvertently feeding a round into the chamber with the muzzle resting on his boot. Drug-addled clumsiness ensued and the rifle discharged, sending a slug through his foot and the floor. Being a Level III trauma center, there was no general surgeon in-house so Jamie's primary task as ER doctor was frontline damage control until one arrived. It was midafternoon on Thursday.

"Kearny?" she asked, debriding minced tissue and cauterizing blasted open veins inside a cue-ball-size sinkhole. Everything but her darting eyes was obscured by a mask and loupes.

"Just parked," said a male nurse running IVs into both of the patient's arms.

Jamie irrigated the wound, flushing bits of leather and sock sucked into the cavity by the round's faster-than-sound passage and worried about projectile infection. "Move it with the Kefazol."

The muzzle gas had penetrated the subcutaneous tissue and blossomed outward, leaving soggy flaps of skin that reminded her of an orchid. The exit wound on the bottom of the foot was cherry mulch draped with pieces of yellowish tendon that resembled vermicelli. God how she loved the controlled calamity of it all. The speed and clarity required to save limbs and lives. The icy dexterity. And beneath that was a molten core of pride because she knew how good she was.

She was packing gauze in the wound and applying pressure when a hushed commotion erupted and Brian Kearny entered the exam room. He wore jeans and boots and a stockman's vest flecked with llama hair because he raised the animals just outside town. An ex–army doc with multiple forward combat deployments, he wore his gray hair in a ponytail and the weathered calm of a man in his element. Not unlike a seasoned frontline commander steeped in life-and-death decisions.

"Who's the DIY marksman?" he asked cheerfully as he scrubbed in and gowned up.

"Forty-one-year-old male positive for opiates with a contact wound on the right foot. Entry at the fifth metatarsal, exit through the plantar fascia. Said he used a three-hundred-grain soft point."

Kearny checked the patient's oxygen-masked face to get a bead on skin color then leaned over the table, moved the sooty flaps of skin aside and peered closely at Jamie's craftsmanship. Wet light leaked in from the exit wound. "Nice work. What else we got besides a foot with a view?"

"Diabetes, hypertension and uh, asthma," said Jamie, trailing off, suddenly fixated by the wall clock's spot-on resemblance to a time bomb. The sweep of the minute hand counting down to some catastrophe she could only guess at. Maybe she went too far by leaving Mace alone. He could be hanging from a rafter out in the barn, pulse feathering to nothing. Vince howling and jumping, unable to save him. The official time of death would be 3:48 p.m. Then she reminded herself of Mace's battered but rock-ribbed arrogance. He wasn't wired to kill himself. Not like that anyway.

The surgeon noted her rigid focus on the clock. "We cutting into your day?"

Jamie heard him and started to explain but a dizzying anger gripped her throat. She looked down at the exploded appendage realizing the refuge of her profession had finally been breached. Mace's self-immolation was in the room. His disease was fouling the air like a ruptured sewer line.

Kearny saw her sickness clear as day and all that down-home cordiality vaporized into a do-not-even-think-of-shitting-me stare. "Are you one hundred percent squared away, Ms. Winters?"

The question slapped her back into the beeping hyperreality of triage. "You bet," she said.

He graded her condition a few more seconds, head cocked, no stranger to the effects of fatigue and stress. "I'll need the stone-cold hot-shot version of you to save this foot."

"And you got it."

"Outstanding. Get him ready for the OR."

Jamie turned to with a vengeance. Channeling her rage into a laser focus that was invulnerable to anything less than an asteroid tearing out of the sky and killing half of Montrose.

SEVEN

Mace slept through Thursday morning and late into the afternoon. Would have kept right on snoozing if he hadn't heard the dog. He ran downstairs and saw the shepherd running from window to window. He looked outside but didn't see anything. He opened the front door and Vince ran out, right into the waiting arms of that same huge mountain lion. The cat eviscerating the dog from neck to nuts and ran for timber dragging its kill. Mace reached behind the door for his 12-gauge pump but it wasn't there. So he sprinted after the lion, bellowing in grief until he landed on the bedroom floor. Vince ran up the stairs and found him sprawled on his back sobbing at the ceiling.

After a thorough licking, the dog allowed the man to get to his feet, hobble over to his closet and get dressed. Then the two of them went down to the charred kitchen where Mace made cold instant coffee with a double dollop of vodka before retiring to the porch to assess his immediate future. The sun was fading, smearing the peaks with bands of magenta but Mace saw nothing pretty. The oncoming darkness was moving quicker than usual. Sliding toward him with great clawed hands. Running into town for a load of food and alcohol suddenly made urgent sense.

He considered taking the dog but the power of the nightmare made him leery of leaving Vince in the truck bed. The shepherd hated being cooped up in the cab and barked long and loud if he was. So Mace turned on every light and made sure every point of entry was secure then locked the front door on his way out, leaving Vince watching from a window. He drove through the gate, locked it behind him and stood there scrutinizing the world in every direction trying to isolate the source of his dread but nothing took shape. Then he headed out, one eye on the rearview.

After hitting the liquor store, he put the groaning box of booze in the truck and was about to dip when he saw a large man sitting in the Grit waving a thick middle finger his direction. Mace returned the bird, strolled into the café and sat opposite Glenn. It was full dark now.

"That your idea of community relations?"

"Depends on the citizen," said the deputy. He had a napkin tucked into the collar of his uniform and was eating meat loaf drenched in brown gravy. He did this without the tiniest spatter of goo. A copy of *Farm & Ranch* magazine was open next to his elbow. "How'd the photo safari go?"

"How'd you know about that?"

"Ran into Will at the Shell station. Bitching about some fancy pain-in-the-butt client. Said he hooked you up with a couple from Phoenix who wanted a cat pic. You get 'em one?"

"For about two seconds."

Glenn looked up from his food with a dreamy expression. "Remember those mountain-lion medallions in cream sauce I used to make?"

Mace wished he didn't. His eyes kept drifting over to the bar but he stayed put, counting the seconds until he could head home and dive into a substance-induced coma.

Glenn read his one-track concentration. "You know your wife's about to cut you loose?"

Mace snapped his head around and looked at his buddy. Saw him and Jamie talking behind his back. He wrestled his anger down, dug out his cell and made a call. Jamie's voice said to leave a message but he couldn't think of one and put the phone away. "Thanks for the news flash."

"She overdue?" said Glenn.

"Hard to be overdue after you moved out."

This got Glenn's attention in a new way. He squinted at Mace. "Up to her mom's?"

"Yep."

"For how long?"

"Coming back for Vince tonight."

"Probably just trying to scare you sober."

"Well," said Mace, lifting a fry off the cop's plate. "The scared part sure worked."

"Good," said Glenn. "Speaking of scared, Jamie still have that .38 Airweight?"

Mace frowned. The question was out of nowhere. "What?"

"The Smith & Wesson you got her after her friend got raped changing a tire."

Mace thought about that. The assault was three years ago and shook

Jamie to the core. She wanted a pistol so he bought her the revolver because it was safer and more reliable than a semiauto. "She got in some range time but I don't know where she keeps it. What do you care?"

"Last thing you need right now is a loaded firearm waiting for the wrong person to find it."

Mace couldn't stop a wistful grin. "Gun's a tool not a rattlesnake."

"That's your dad talking right there."

"Chapter and verse," said Mace, getting to his feet.

"Hold on," said Glenn, fork load of meat poised under his chin as he pointed at Mace's truck. It was parked under a streetlight, plates lit bright. "Your tags expired in March. It's October."

Mace stared at Glenn thinking he was paying a little too much attention to certain things but had no idea why. "I'll look into it," he said then left.

After he got outside the café, Mace glanced over his shoulder, saw Glenn was absorbed with chatting up his waitress and grabbed a fifth of vodka from the truck. Then he walked north past the post office and stopped in front of a small house with a brown Subaru in the driveway. He cut across the lawn until he was just steps from the picture window facing the street, cracked the bottle and took a slug. The curtains were pulled back revealing most of the ground floor. Martinez's mother was visible at the kitchen table in the back going through a pile of books. Newspaper and magazine cuttings feathered the pages. He moved closer and determined they were cookbooks.

She was going through the strips of paper one at a time, smoothing them out with her fingertips before reading. Mace wondered what she was looking for. Maybe one of her son's favorite dishes. Or something special for the man sitting on the couch in the living room holding a remote. His eyes were blank except for the glimmer emitted by a television.

Mace studied the framed photos of the man's son littering the tables and shelves like he always did. Only one featured Robert Martinez in full Marine Corps dress. The others were taken before the world engulfed the boy and spit him out. The nine-year-old with a spinning rod and a stringer of rainbows on the bank of Ridgway Reservoir. The middle school soccer player sitting in the bleachers with his teammates for the team picture. The grinning senior with his blushing prom date clutching her corsage. Later on, had Mace been asked how long he stood there gazing at the hell he created he would have absolutely no idea.

EIGHT

Kearney performed the three-hour procedure with Jamie assisting then shooed her starving and elated into the night. She hit the Sonic on Townsend right at closing and sat in the deserted parking lot devouring a bacon cheeseburger while watching greasy wrappers swirl by. She checked her phone and saw a missed call from Mace but no message and checked the sky. It was clogged with fast-moving clouds like real winter weather was coming. Then the last employee killed the drive-in's lights and she got the same inbound-disaster feeling. She turned on the heat and drove north through town faster than usual, hands at ten and two like something might run in front of her.

She caught a red light at main and sat there feeling watched. The highway to Grand Junction and her mom's lay straight ahead. Or she could turn left and head west. Get the dog as planned and get eyes on Mace. When the light went green she took the turn. Two miles later she cut over to Dave Wood Road and followed her normal route home. The backcountry quickly swallowed everything man-made on either side. Bats and coyotes darted through the high beams.

When cell service was about to die she pulled over at the same place she always did and called Mace. He didn't answer but service was spotty all over the plateau and maybe he was out running errands. She left the same message she always did despite herself. "Be there in twenty. Love you."

Then she took off. Not five minutes later, she was curving toward the bridge over Roubideau Creek when she came upon a body lying in the middle of the road.

She yanked the wheel left, stomped the brakes and skidded, missing the figure by inches. Then backed up to shield the victim from southbound traffic, hit her flashers and jumped out. Had to be a man by the size of his shoulders and hands. He was on his back, legs tangled, arms flung wide, head lolled to one side. Crossed her mind he was dead or paralyzed. A green-and-white motorcycle lay at the end of a long gouge in the gravel, still ticking with engine heat.

Jamie stuck an index finger under the black helmet with the cracked, silvery visor. His carotid was thumping nicely. His breathing was quick and shallow. "Can you hear me?" she asked.

The helmet quivered in her direction. She immediately stabilized it with both hands and spoke sharply. "Do not move your head. Do not move anything. Do you understand?"

"Yes," whispered the rider.

She squeezed his right leg above the knee. "Feel that?"

"Feel what?" he said.

"Shit," said Jamie. She looked around. Decided to run up the grade, gain some elevation and maybe snag a cell signal. "Do not move. Okay?"

"Okay," said the biker.

Jamie was turning away and rising to her feet when his hands clapped onto her shoulders, spun her around and set an arm bar across her neck with shocking speed and power. She managed a garbled scream before her windpipe crimped. Thinking she was done if she passed out, she kicked a knee out and slammed her heel into his balls. This caused a wheezing gasp of pain and a brief loosening of his arm. She twisted around, kneeing his groin and clawing his neck but it was like attacking marble. Then the biker smothered her arms, twirled her around like a rowdy child and reset the sleeper hold. She rag-dolled in seconds and he tossed her onto the back seat of the Rubicon.

Hazim grabbed her phone off the road feeling stupid, nuts burning. She was even stronger than he had thought. If that kick had been slightly more accurate she might have broken his grip and gotten away. He could only imagine chasing her through the forest running in all directions. The whole mission would have ended then and there. But it hadn't and for a reason. After sealing her cell inside a Faraday bag, he got in the Rubicon and turned the flashers off. Then he bashed the Jeep through the willows on the left side of the road. A hundred yards into pine and aspen, he parked it beside the Silverado, grabbed her pack and parka off the rear seat and tossed them in the pickup's cab. Then he zip-tied Jamie's hands and feet, cinched a hood over her head and lifted her out.

After wrapping a blanket around her body, he tucked her into the

Silverado's toolbox and put his ear close to her mouth. She was breathing slow and deep so he left her there and checked the Rubicon's cargo hold. There was a duffel bag with a parka and snow boots and a trauma kit the size of a carry-on bag. He popped the latter open and put a light on the contents. It was basically a combat surgery kit. Everything from chest seals and abdominal dressings to nasopharyngeal airways and IV antibiotics. He snapped the kit shut, grabbed the duffel and set both in the toolbox alongside Jamie. Then he padlocked the lid and jogged back to his Suzuki.

He gunned the bike through Roubideau Creek into a thicket of choke-berry, dropped the machine onto its side and covered it with debris. Then hurled his helmet into darkness. It thudded to earth and the night was silent save for a jet whispering toward Denver. He watched his breath frost and felt the wound that should have killed him come alive in the cold. Someone skilled with a Dragunov rifle put a slug through his right lung and dumped half his blood into the mud of Mostar twenty-three years ago. The sniper thought he was dead because there was no be-sure shot. His or her mistake and Hazim's good fortune. Then pain shot through his bruised nuts and he reminded himself the mission was in its infancy and he'd already committed a serious error. Underestimating the enemy's will to fight.

After dropping the Faraday bag with Jamie's cell in the creek and covering it with rocks, he jogged back to his truck and hauled camo netting from the bed. He draped it over the Rubicon and set a layer of limbs on top of the netting. It would be found eventually but not from the air. Then he climbed in the Silverado, doubled back into Montrose and drove south on Highway 550, letting a sense of elation sink into his racing heart. Surely, God would not allow him to come this far for nothing. Then he realized how presumptuous that was and asked for forgiveness.

He turned east on Buckhorn Road, crossed the Uncompahgre River, killed the lights and pulled on night-vision goggles. Then took a dirt track south, passing rusted combines and rotting cattle chutes. He was passing a ruined corral when a leggy wild dog with a sharp snout and hot yellow eyes crossed in front of his vehicle. A rabbit dangled limply from its mouth. The dog stopped and gave the truck a leisurely appraisal. Unnerved, Hazim tore off his goggles and hit the high beams. The canine seemed to smile at the blinding contraption, as in welcome to the party. Then it vanished like a thought. Hazim doused the lights and yanked his goggles back on.

Thirty minutes later, he reached a gate with a padlock. He opened it, drove through and locked it behind him. Then drove over a dry streambed and up an embankment into a stand of giant cottonwoods with an understory of greasewood and sumac. They were only sixteen miles south of the hospital where Jamie worked. On the verge of the trees was a derelict 1975 Winnebago Brave.

Hazim parked the Silverado in the heart of the grove and sat there listening to the trees creak in the blustery night. He'd never felt farther from home even though home had been annihilated long ago. Then he pulled the Beretta M9 from under his coat and walked around the scabby relic. The twenty-one-foot RV's tires were fossilized in place and plywood had been slapped over all the windows decades previous. Wind-dragged sage and trash were heaped against the fenders. A rusted out steel skirt meant to halt snow from creeping under the chassis was still in place. But a brand spanking new canvas tarp was nailed over the motor home's door to block light from escaping when opened.

NINE

Mace was driving over the summit of Dallas Divide when he saw the Big Dipper dimming behind a vast ceiling of cirrostratus clouds. By the time he turned onto 60X Road he'd made a vague mental note to check the oil in the generator and stack more wood on the porch off the kitchen. Vague because vodka was a foolish and disarming friend that didn't give a shit about blizzards.

He turned into the yard, saw no Jeep and no lights. His first thought was the power was out. He killed the engine, rolled the window down and listened for Vince but heard nothing. His second thought was Jamie had taken the dog and turned the lights off. He grabbed his phone, saw the missed call and played the hour-old message saying she was twenty minutes away. There it was. She snagged the pooch and ran. Probably relieved he wasn't around to grovel and whine. He called her but it went straight to voicemail. He looked at the pitch-black house again and something was so wrong it froze him where he sat. Then an alien sensation washed over him. That of being prey.

His arm flinched for the Ruger Mini-14 that used to live in the gun rack. But that rifle was long gone along with every other firearm he ever owned. He was reaching for the maglite under the seat when a presence slid up on his left. Then a Glock 9 snaked through the window and touched his temple.

"Did you know a person is a thousand times more likely to be struck by lightning than attacked by a mountain lion?" asked Vanessa. Her tone was easy and conversational. Her face relaxed.

When his brains didn't splatter all over the seats, Mace swallowed. "What do you want?"

She stepped away, weapon extended. Clay opened the door, grabbed the phone and the keys from the ignition then yanked Mace out and pushed him to the ground. After searching him and zip-tying his wrists behind his back he wiggled the phone. "Passcode," he said. "Pretty please."

Mace gave it. Clay unlocked the phone, burrowed into Mace's settings and toggled enough shit to kill the tracking. Then he marched Mace into the barn, Glock 45 against his spine. Vanessa trailed gun up, meticulously sweeping the night to their rear.

Once inside the barn, she slid the big door shut and flipped the shop light on over the workbench. The interior contained ATVs, a snowmobile, camping gear and a reloading table. Vince was lying on his side on the floor of a horse stall, eyes slit, tongue lolling. Lifeless.

Mace gagged on rage before looking at Vanessa. "You're dead. You're both fucking dead."

Clay punched Mace in the kidney. The blow was curt and precise and made him grunt in a key he didn't know he had. Then Clay grabbed his hair and ground the Glock 45's muzzle into his ear.

"Don't push it, mountain man. Or I'll stomp your guts out your ass."

Vanessa watched Mace closely. How he bore the pain. Looking for limits. She didn't speak until the color returned to his face. "Just his way of saying you need to integrate your thinking with ours right now. And that means suppressing some very understandable caveman shit to achieve a common goal. If that sounds workable, great. If not, speak up and we'll move on. No hard feelings."

No hard feelings and a bullet in the head thought Mace. "Sounds workable. Where's Jamie?"

"Relaxing. Which brings us to rules. Do what we say when we say it. Don't hesitate. Don't misconstrue. Don't get cute. Don't be brave. And don't forget the people with Jamie comcheck randomly. They don't receive an all-copacetic code within a set time she's dead. You turn rabbit she's dead. Signal for help she's dead. Fuck up your assignment, presto, you're both dead. Clear?"

Mace turned, staring at the finality of the shepherd's pose. "Clear."

Vanessa produced an Inmarsat satphone and held it close to his face. "Good. Say hi."

The device had a nice screen. On it was someone hog-tied on a mattress against a black drop cloth wearing a black hood. A white LED beam was the only illumination. A big scarred hand lifted the hood and there was Jamie. The beam stayed nailed between her eyes, keeping her blind.

"Jamie," said Mace, trying to sound normal and failing miserably.

She cocked violently toward her name. "Mace?"

"I'm right here. I'm okay. I can see you."

"What the hell is happening?" she asked, blinking furiously.

"Not sure yet. But I'm gonna do whatever they want. Just let me get it done."

"Maybe you should ask the shithead in charge if they're sure they have the right people."

A snippet of shrill noise bled in on Jamie's end. Mace listened to it dropping through metallic octaves. An aircraft descending. A jet. Hard to say how big.

"They seem pretty sure," he said.

Jamie tried to stare down the beam to see his face but it was hopeless. She ducked her head, squeezing tears that sparked in the light. "I love you. Don't let them hurt Vince. Okay?"

Then the hood was yanked down and the call cut. Vanessa graded Mace's reaction. Gauging his mettle at every turn. "Look on the bright side. You get to find out what you're made of."

Mace chewed on that. Letting his bloodlust simmer. "You and me both."

She grinned. Looked at Clay. "See? I told you this was gonna be fun."

"No you didn't," said Clay. "You said this would be as fun as we make it."

Vanessa turned back to Mace. Saw he was hunkered down now. All armored up inside. Dog dead and wifey ninety-nine percent totally screwed. Time to throw the curve. Toss him a bone.

"Tell him about the shepherd."

Clay didn't like that. "You sure?"

"Do it," she said.

"I darted your steadfast pooch with five milligrams of propofol," said Clay. "Go see."

Mace went in the stall, dropped to his knees and put his head on Vince's chest. There was a heartbeat. He tried not to cry but did. Just a tad. Then Clay hauled him over to Vanessa and spun him around. She cut the zip ties with a Gerber folding knife and let the blade dangle at her side.

"Look at me, great white hunter."

Mace turned slowly, rubbing his wrists, thinking she could cut his throat with her eyes shut.

"I know it's a shitty long-shot deal. But better than nothing."

Mace saw a USGS topographic map on the workbench behind her. "Where we headed?"

She went over and motioned him to follow. The map covered the plateau from Unaweep Canyon to Horsefly Peak. She tapped the center of it with the knifepoint. "We need to know exactly where your buddy Will Stoddard is taking his client on Saturday morning. Then you're gonna get us there first and in range before dawn. Sun at our backs, por favor."

Mace's gut jumped. "In range of who?"

"Not your problem."

He stared at the map. An immense hunk of rough ground he knew up, down and sideways.

"How am I supposed to know where Will's going?"

"Up to you. But if you think it's impossible now's the time to mention it."

Clay raised his weapon and slid left so a round passing through Mace's back would miss his partner. Drooling at the idea of their guide exsanguinating on the barn floor.

Mace looked over his shoulder into the pistol's fat bore thinking this was how it was gonna be for the duration. A short leash with a hair trigger. "How do you know I won't be lying?"

"We already covered that," said Vanessa.

Mace leaned over the map and pretended to study the hundred-some square miles of wild. Pretended because he didn't need to. He had a very good idea where Will was headed because he had his haunts like all top outfitters. But one in particular. The trophy hole he mentioned to Jamie not forty-eight hours ago. The North Fork of Cottonwood Creek. Keeping that knowledge a secret as long as possible might maximize his lifespan. Or shorten it. Had to play it as it lay and see.

Problem was that drainage was huge. Guessing exactly where Will would set up would be luck of the highest order. Guess wrong and he and Jamie were done. Guess right and he'd probably get Will killed in the bargain. Vanessa watched him stall out, brow knit. Misread it as pre-ops jitters.

"Looks like great white hunter needs a drink."

"Bet he wants the usual," said Clay. "Cheap vodka with a weed chaser."

Mace shut his eyes. They were not wrong. Then he saw Jamie kneeling on the mattress, black hood snapping down over her face. "Either shut the hell up and let me think or pull the trigger."

Clay kept his sidearm steady on Mace's spine. "What do you say honeybun?"

Vanessa checked her watch. Mace was a tactical advantage. Very much like a drone. Using him to get on target and out clean was too enticing to drop just yet. "Let him think."

Mace stared at the map replaying a phone call he had made the night before Martinez died. He called Will on opening-day eve as was his custom and his father's before him. They commiserated about bulls they'd scouted and wished each other luck. Will mentioned seeing a truly stupendous rack but said the bull was way wily. The next morning Mace's world ended with a single errant shot. Later on he learned Will's client bagged a 390-point bull that same morning. High-quality rack but nothing stupendous. So the odds of Will going after the animal with the epic headgear he glimpsed last year were good. But nowhere near definite. "I need a computer," he said.

"Why?" said Jamie.

"Need to see parcel maps for Montrose and San Miguel County."

"Why?"

"To have a rat's ass chance of doing what you want me to do."

Vanessa went over to a backpack, dug out a Getac B360 laptop, set it on the bench, popped it open and watched Mace type. Took him five minutes to find four large parcels in prime elk habitat. He narrowed those down to two then one. A two-thousand-acre rectangle hemmed in by wilderness on three sides and smack in the middle of Cottonwood Creek's north drainage. That was where Will was likely headed. But Mace circled a much, much larger area. "Somewhere in there. Maybe."

Vanessa took the comp and dropped a pin in the center of the vast swath of backcountry Mace just outlined. "Now show me a route in where we won't run into other hunters."

"No such thing," said Mace thinking the more wrenches he could throw in the works the better.

"Why not?"

"Opening day's a circus up here. The unwashed masses with rifles."

Clay whistled. Shook his head. "Our disgraced guide's a poet."

Vanessa stared at the screen. "Okay. Think of it as the route with the least chance of you getting more innocent people killed without pulling the trigger yourself."

Mace switched back to the topo map. Traced a thirty-some mile drive north to Old Highway 90 then west to Dry Park Draw. "It's county gravel to there. After that we walk about ten miles."

"Show me the walk," she said.

Mace drew his finger along a curving ridge that eventually formed the western rim of the basin holding the North Fork of Cottonwood Creek. Then he circled a chunk of hard country where you could hide a large herd of elephants much less one bull and a few careful men in camo.

"How will Stoddard and his client get there?" she asked.

Mace looked at the map. Traced a tiny broken line denoting a forest service trail that dropped into the basin from the east. "He's gonna drive his guy close as he can. Then maybe take that trail."

Vanessa nodded. Tapped Mace's ten-mile hike to the basin. "We got good cover on the way in?"

"Nothing but if you know what to look for."

She grinned at his self-serving response. "Understood. You foresee any problem getting there by oh-four-hundred Saturday?"

"Snow. Lots of it."

"Forecast says only five to six inches," said Clay.

"Not mine," said Mace.

"A poet and a meteorologist," said Clay.

Vanessa eyed Mace. Saw his forecast had teeth. "Good. Foul weather favors the attacker."

They let Mace pack his bugout pack under strict supervision then scoured the Tundra for weapons and phones before offloading the liquor and stowing their gear. They let him say goodbye to Vince and put bowls of food and water by the dog's head. After that, he drove out through the gate and used a spare lock to secure it. One with a combo only he knew. Last thing he needed was a neighbor dropping by and finding the house empty and the dog drugged senseless in the barn. For a second he wondered how long that old stall would hold Vince once he rebooted into search-and-protect mode. Then he'd have to get out of the barn. Be tough but the dog didn't know quit.

When he turned around he saw Vanessa waiting in the dark by the driver's door. He walked over thinking she had more instructions and stopped right in front of her. A faint smile crossed her lips. Then she rotated her shoulders and whipped the butt of her Glock across his left temple.

Mace staggered sideways and dropped to all fours, skin torn, blood gushing off his face. It was a skillful strike. Designed to inflict maximum nerve-ripping agony without material impact on his utility. She handed him gauze to staunch the bleeding then bent down close to his ear so she wouldn't have to raise her voice. "That's for the mountain lions."

TEN

Hazim opened the motor home's door, shut it behind him, locked the dead bolt and stood on the steps in the gloom behind the tarp. He wore a jacket and pants in woodland camo, a black beanie and a pack. The Zeiss glass hung around his neck and a scoped bolt-action rifle was slung over his shoulder. He listened intently for several seconds then pushed the tarp aside causing a covey of grouse to explode from under a toppled windmill. When he was done jumping out of his skin, he watched the birds bank over a ruined greenhouse and vanish into the honey-blue of Friday's dawn.

After scanning the perimeter, he walked toward the cottonwoods, weapon at low ready. He'd purchased the Kimber 84M and Vortex scope at a pawnshop in Delta six days ago along with six boxes of Winchester .270 ammo. The proprietor recorded the data on his bootleg Belgian passport and skipped the background check because of the faked language barrier and hard cash. Hazim sighted the rifle in at three hundred meters later that day and found the everyman elk gun to be very accurate.

As he entered the grove he spooked an animal from the undergrowth and whipped the rifle up but the creature vanished unseen. Then he looked back at the RV. Half a century of weather had sanded the brown and tangerine striping down to undercoat but the aluminum skin was solid. The front bumper had a Michigan plate with GREAT LAKE STATE embossed in rust. He imagined an American family driving across the vast country waving at cowboys. A Honda generator shimmied silently under the chassis. Most of the sky was clear but towering clouds loomed to the northwest.

He moved past the Silverado and out the far side of the grove then ducked low and limped up a cone-shaped hill. When he reached the top he went to work with the binos. Visibility was excellent in every direction. Several run-down-looking structures were visible, none closer than thirty-five hundred meters and none with vehicles nearby or curling smoke. A twin-engine plane descended lazily toward the north. Nine kilometers to the east, cars and trucks plied Highway 550. The normal world was attending to normal things, oblivious to the warfighter coiled in their midst.

Descending the hill, he came upon a lush patch of buffalo grass and prayed. When he was done, he wondered if he had made salah over the bones of the dope farmers the couple told him had lived in the RV long ago. In Bosnia, in places like Prijedor and Srebrenica, praying on verdant ground almost guaranteed an ossuary beneath the devout. And every skull would have a neat hole.

When he got back to the Winnebago he unlocked the door and entered a fake-walnut time capsule with green appliances, gold curtains and burnt-orange wallpaper. Rats had colonized the RV and the stench had been knifelike when he set up five days ago. He bought disinfectant and scrubbed the interior, dimming the odor to mildly disgusting. His captive sat on the mattress at the stern, hooded head turned expectantly. Her wrists were cuffed behind her back and her ankles were shackled. A chain ran from the shackles to a D-ring in the wall. A space heater pushed dust around. The tableau gave Hazim a stab of shame. A female noncombatant treated like a battle-hardened detainee at Guantánamo Bay. He reminded himself of the objective and the shame receded. He set his rifle by the door, slid into the breakfast nook, set his pistol on the table and took out his cell.

"Time to call in sick," he said.

Jamie processed the biker's accent again. English draped with Russian. Maybe. A guy who made the floor sag when he moved. The floor of a trailer out in the boonies given the rat shit. A place where she could be raped ad nauseam, left for dead and found years hence. But all the trouble applied to grabbing her and getting her stashed away uninjured meant she had some use for now.

"Okay," she said.

Hazim squatted in front of her. "You have the flu. You forgot to charge your phone and borrowed one. If they don't believe you, my friends kill your husband and I kill you. Understood?"

Jamie nodded, tongue frozen, hot panic flushing through her body. The son of a bitch was so matter-of-fact. Like he was reading items off a menu. No big deal either way. Hazim punched a number on his cell, put it on speaker and held it inches from her hooded mouth.

"Emergency room," said a tired voice submerged in ambient intake noise. "This is Shannon."

Jamie cleared her throat and coughed hard, praying it sounded real. "Shannon. It's Jamie."

"Jesus. You sound like shit."

"Hundred and one and a sore throat. Slept through the alarm. Can someone cover me?"

"No worries. Hydrate and hit the sack," said the nurse, hanging up even as she spoke.

Hazim watched the motionless person under the hood. He was a devout soldier not a kidnapper of women and he couldn't help admiring the way she stopped to offer aid then fought like a tiger. Made him want to explain himself. An absurd and dangerous idea.

"How was that?" asked Jamie, abruptly making conversation.

Hazim was thrown by the question. He stared at the hood. Saw the faint quiver. "Fine."

He got to his feet, eradicated the cell and SIM card with pliers and tossed the pieces in the weeds outside the door. After that, he set an Inmarsat satphone identical to Vanessa's on the table, sent a test and received a quick reply. Then he made coffee and tried to settle his swirling emotions.

In the planning phase, using the wife as a weapon seemed righteous given the endless sorrow inflicted by the Monster. But a week of recon had given him an annoying appreciation of her beauty and bearing. No doubt her husband would do anything to save her. Hence her value.

He hated not being the trigger-puller when the time came but he accepted the logic. Combat wear and tear had caught up. His mind wandered and his body hurt. He was a very good marksman but not in the elite class of the two Americans and their camouflage was impeccable. Just another fit couple roaming the American West. They didn't have the divine right of retribution but they had the résumé. And if it was Allah's will, they would be granted calm winds and a clean shot.

He had implored the assassins to avoid a bullet to the head if possible and go for the chest or stomach thereby allowing the Monster time to suffer the realization of his end. But they gave him no assurance because they were pragmatic in the extreme. Even so, the Monster's brains splattered in the pristine mountain light would be a blessing of nearly equal magnitude.

Hazim finished his drink and stared at the boarded-up window over the sink. His mind floated through the plywood into a primeval forest fertilized by a thousand years of warfare. Men of all ages sprinted by like rabbits. Shooting rippled in the distance. His father ran beside him, strapping and blond bearded and wearing a prayer cap embroidered in red and white. He saw his gangly teenage son's terror and pushed him under the trunk of a downed tree. After a sobbing hug he ran on, shouting a prayer to bait the killers away from his boy. Hazim burrowed under the trunk until he was tucked into a shallow grave and ate dirt to stop his teeth from chattering. In the lull that followed, birds sang and the trees swayed. Then he heard a defiant scream cut short by gunfire.

A bit later, men in camo passed meters from his hiding place, hunting stragglers. They carried assault rifles and were jubilantly sharing flasks of brandy. They were Serbs. Freshly minted arbiters of life and death. They saw the toppled trunk and literally sat down on top of the boy, bloody boots dangling in his face. They reminded Hazim of his mother's empty slippers. She was liquified by a mortar shell while standing in the door of their home, leaving nothing but the gory shoes as if she'd born wings. Then one of the soldiers tossed a bullet tattered scrap on the ground and they took turns pissing on it. It was Hazim's father's prayer cap. They couldn't stop laughing.

Their mirth hardened into the thud of a helicopter that yanked Hazim's eyes open. He grabbed the satphone, threw the RV door open and shoved the tarp aside. A blue-and-white helo was passing overhead but too high and too fast to be searching for a missing ER doc. Then the satphone vibrated. He checked the message, sent a reply, shut the door and opened the Yeti by the driver's seat. Inside the cooler were several Starbucks bags bulging with bottles of water, sandwiches and energy bars. He grabbed the bag, sat down at the table and after a minute addressed his captive.

"Are you hungry?" he asked. "I have food and water."

The question startled her. Food was the last thing on her mind. Dying in a rat hole and never seeing Mace again was front and center. But if she was ever gonna pull some tricky getaway she better fortify herself when she had the chance. Then her helpless anger got the best of her.

"Fuck off and die you chickenshit son of a bitch."

Hazim nodded, struck by her vulgar vitality. "Does that mean you're not hungry?"

She didn't respond so he grabbed a tuna sandwich and ate it in silence. Then another washed down by something called kombucha. "Starvation impairs judgment and will," he said finally.

Her head moved, lining up on her captor again. "You have a lot of experience in starvation?"

"Some."

"Then you need food way more than me," she said.

"Why is that?"

"Kidnapping may be the national sport in the shithole country you come from but not here. Might as well stick that pistol I keep hearing you set on the table in your mouth and pull the trigger. Because I can promise you that's how this is all gonna end."

Hazim sipped a bottle of water thinking Americans were the most dangerous people on the planet. And he had a PhD in dangerous people. "What about your national sport?" he said quietly.

"Which one?"

"Shooting little children huddled in classrooms."

Jamie became rigid under the hood. His hateful calm was her death knell. He would kill her without hesitation when the time came. Because she and everything she stood for was the enemy.

Hazim picked up his rifle and binoculars and went outside. To the west, the Uncompahgre Plateau rose like the back side of a titanic wave headed for shore. He had no idea it was the stump of a primordial range that would have lorded over the Himalayas. But he was certain his life was nothing more than a fleeting opportunity to become one with Allah's will. Then he looked at the crumbling greenhouse. He knew what was in there because the American couple was meticulous. But he hadn't seen it with his own eyes because he didn't want to, which suddenly struck him as weak. So he went inside. Amid the broken glass and weeds was a deep and narrow grave next to a neat mound of earth. The American woman's final resting place, just waiting for her remains.

After praying for strength, he went outside and put the binos on the great veins of golden trees lacing the plateau, knowing not one of those trillion leaves stirred without purpose. He also knew Jamie was right. He would die here and that was just. He'd lived far longer than he ever imagined.

ELEVEN

Mace's Tundra was parked thirty-two miles north of his home, hidden behind juniper and facing Old Highway 90. Mace and his clients stood in the bed watching vehicles go by. Mace wore a beanie covering the bandage on his temple. The truck was hidden because he figured Will might take Old 90 to make one last scout of the North Cottonwood Creek drainage to confirm the mega-bull was holding. *Might* being the key word. But if Will's red F-350 did blow by, that would at least confirm the big picture of where he was gonna hunt. It was 7 a.m. on Friday and concrete clouds were bulging down from the north. The air was dead still, waiting to be sucked into the oncoming front.

"Are they all hunters?" asked Vanessa, watching the steady trickle of vehicles.

"Most of 'em," said Mace. He knew some were headed to posh ranch hunts with cabins and hot grub while a bunch would park on public land, dine on jerky and sleep in their rides. He also knew deep pockets and custom guns wouldn't mean squat come tomorrow. Position and steady pressure on the trigger were all that counted to put animals down no matter how many legs they walked on.

He'd rehashed the sound of a descending jet at the end of Jamie's call for hours and come up with the same conclusion every time. Could be Grand Junction or Montrose or Telluride or Durango. Flight approaches that covered vast areas of terrain making it a wildly useless deduction.

Clay slapped the roof of the cab and pointed as Will's truck rolled by heading west. Mace exhaled. So far so good. Then a phone vibrated and Vanessa pulled his cell from her pocket.

She let it go to voicemail before holding it up for him to see. "Who's Glenn?"

"Ouray County deputy sheriff," said Mace.

She held his eyes a moment. Flat and calm. "And why would he be calling you?"

"Aside from being my buddy, he's probably checking on the Jamie situation."

"You tell your buddy about us hiring you to get a lion pic?"

"Didn't have to. He knew."

"How?"

"Small town."

She studied him another moment. "One more rule under the category of cute. If you try to send some coded message like a thousand idiotic movies and streaming junk, Clay will kill you. If Jamie tries it, the person at that location will kill her. On the spot. Okay?"

Mace nodded. "So what do I tell him?"

"A version of the truth. You're still on the payroll. We're going for a bull elk photo this time."

"That's nuts. He won't buy it."

"Keep it simple," said Clay. "Tell him we offered irresistible renumeration and you caved."

"Listen to me," said Mace. "Tomorrow is opening fucking day. He will know something is up."

Vanessa hit redial and handed him the phone. "You bet he will. Drug-addled screwups have shit judgment. So what else is new?"

The call rang forever. Mace was composing a message when Glenn picked up. Two-way radio chat crackled softly in the background. "Ouray County Morgue. Anthony Bourdain speaking."

"Hell is wrong with you?" said Mace.

"Jamie turn up?"

"For a minute," said Mace. "Then ran up to her mom's to think things over."

Glenn was silent a moment. "Well, shit. Do me a favor and don't kill yourself on my watch."

"How about I wait until Monday?"

"That works. You home?"

Mace looked at Vanessa and Clay. They stared back, as in your funeral.

"East of Norwood. That couple wanted elk pictures and they got green to burn so here I am."

"So you got 'em taking pictures of elk people are getting ready to shoot?"

"Relax. I got spots that don't get hunted."

"Damn. Guess all that booze and skunk made you clairvoyant."

"Safety first," said Mace. "Gotta go."

He hung up and handed the phone to Vanessa. She looked to their rear. Saw a buckling asphalt road curving west into a sandstone canyon. "What's down that way?" she asked.

"Abandoned mine," said Mace.

"Anyone hunt down there?"

"Nope."

"Why not?"

Mace drove down the road until a high steel fence cut across the pavement. Rising over the razor wire was a bullet-riddled sign that read: NO TRESPASSING—US DEPARTMENT OF ENERGY. Beyond the fence were abandoned barracks and ore bins and sidewalks choked with sagebrush.

"What was this place?" asked Vanessa.

"Uranium mine," said Mace. "Made plutonium for the Manhattan Project. Still kinda hot."

She checked her watch. "Hide our ride."

Mace reversed into timber and Vanessa took the keys from the ignition. Clay was already out of the truck, pack on his back, casing the fence line where tall brush ran up to it. Hadn't gone far when he found a yard-high slit at ground level. He glassed the structures on the other side, saw zero human activity and waved his companions over. Vanessa pulled on her pack, motioned Mace to move out and they all dipped through the wire. After a quick look around, they veered toward the steel-netted maw of a mine shaft with a large red sign in front: CAUTION RADIOACTIVE GAS.

The entrance was flanked by two yellow trefoil radiation symbols. There was a magenta circle in the center of each one about the size of a lemon. Vanessa pulled up a good distance from the tunnel and glanced at Mace. Her smile was breezy with anticipation. A kid in her sandbox.

"See those little yellow signs?" she asked. "I make that two hundred and ninety-three yards."

Mace squinted at the radiation symbols. "Two ninety-nine."

Clay raised his Bushnell glass and hit the range button. "Three hundred even," he said.

Then he opened his pack and dug out a rectangular composite case. Inside were two large telephoto lenses. He grabbed one, unscrewed the front end and removed a trigger assembly, bolt action and firing pin from the fake housing. He did likewise with the second telephoto, removing four five-round magazines loaded with .300 Win mags. After that, he pulled a thick-legged camera tripod from his pack, removed the base of the first leg and slid out a barrel and suppressor. The second held a folding polymer stock and Leupold scope. The third a forestock.

Mace watched Clay unifying the components with smooth dexterity and realized the majority of them belonged to a Remington Model 700 rifle. And ninety seconds later there it was, the Chevy Impala of elk guns customized into a sexy long-range nail driver. It was downright scary. These creeps knew their stuff and weren't relying on ostentatious equipment. They'd paired a reliable factory gun with a great scope and off-the-shelf loads. All hidden inside high-end camera gear. In qualified hands, the rifle's accuracy to 650 yards would be excellent. Inside four hundred yards, even in windy conditions, a freaking turkey shoot. Mace revised his odds of survival downward.

Clay mounted the scope, punched the magazine home and dropped prone facing the tunnel. He aligned the reticle, racked the bolt and welded his cheek into the stock. His right hand was on the firing grip, left cupped below the butt. Then he settled into the eye box. "Left-hand target."

The .300 Win mag left the muzzle at three thousand feet per second with a soft crack that dissipated like a cough. The round left a hole touching the rim of the magenta bull's-eye. Clay ejected the casing, adjusted windage and elevation and squeezed off another shot. A second hole appeared inside the circle, north of dead center. He tickled the elevation and emptied the magazine, cycling with silky precision. When he was done, a three-round group had blown out the core of the magenta circle.

"Remind me to bring a book next time," said Vanessa.

Clay got to his feet and picked up his brass. "Criticism is my protein shake."

Vanessa shrugged off her pack and removed another disarticulated Model 700 with the same modifications. Her assembly scheme was identical except her hand speed tricked the eye. The rifle materialized and she was prone and done adjusting the scope in a minute flat. "Right-hand target."

Her first round hit a smidge left of dead solid bull's-eye. She tweaked the windage and ran off the rest of the magazine. When the pulverized sandstone cleared, there were four dead-center hits with zero separation. The equivalent of hitting a quarter four times in a row at the far end of three football fields. She got up and gathered her spent shells with a contented expression.

"Exhibitionist," said Clay.

Mace was still staring at the targets as both guns were deconstructed with the same alacrity and reconcealed inside the photo gear. "We hunting all of Will's clients or just one?" he asked.

"Just one," said Vanessa. Then she indicated the way back to the truck. "After you."

Fifty yards from the fence they saw the white Dodge Ram with the bubble on the roof waiting on the other side. The man at the wheel was watching their approach closely. Vanessa and Clay picked up the pace and pulled even with Mace, flanking him with friendly expressions.

"What's this?" said Vanessa.

"Security guard," said Mace.

"He armed?" Clay asked.

"Probably."

"Just keep it mellow," said Vanessa. "We'll think of something."

Clay waved affably at the guard. "And pour on that pithy frontier charm."

The man dismounted the Dodge and stood by the slit in the fence. He wore a black fleece, a black Pyramid Energy cap and a Colt 45 ACP on his right hip. He was fifties and beefy and easy to picture busting skulls. The grin behind his Ray-Bans was ugly. "Cut that hole yourselves?"

"No sir," said Mace, moving right up to the fence. "Already there. Scrap hunters probably."

"Wasn't there yesterday."

"All I can tell you is we used it but we didn't cut it."

"And you couldn't read a giant sign that says no trespassing."

"Oh I read it," said Mace, grinning. "Doesn't mean my judgment doesn't suck on occasion."

This instantly rubbed the guard wrong. "You think messing around on DOE property is funny?"

"Hang on," said Mace, raising his hands. "That was a stupid joke. We didn't touch a thing in there. My friends wanted pictures of a World War Two uranium mine. That's all. Just pictures. They're big atomic bomb buffs. Came all the way from Chicago."

The man looked past Mace at Clay and Vanessa. "How come I don't see any cameras?"

Mace almost said look in their packs then stopped himself. The guy stayed locked on the couple.

"Your friends retarded or what?" he asked.

"Look," said Mace. "It was my idea. I screwed up, okay? Not their fault."

"Let's let the sheriff decide that," said the man, pulling out a cell phone.

The guard's forefinger was stabbing a number when a dark dot appeared above his left eye followed by a deafening slap of energy and a fan of pink beyond his head. He toppled backward with an alarmed expression, still gripping the phone. None of it made sense until Mace turned and saw Vanessa's Glock extended with both hands. She was saying something to Clay but Mace couldn't hear the words. Couldn't hear anything. Then they rushed past him and through the fence.

She pulverized the guy's phone and SIM card while Clay dragged the body out of the red gunk around the head and kicked dirt over a chunk of skull trailing curly dark hair. Then they spun around guns up because they'd momentarily forgotten about their guide. Mace was braced against the fence, face ashen. Clay looked bummed he didn't get a chance to plug him on the run. Vanessa motioned Mace over. He wobbled through the slit and she pointed at the open door of the Ram.

"Think quick. Why would he leave his truck up here and disappear?"

Mace looked in the cab. Saw a scoped rifle, dayglow cap and vest and a sleeping bag. A photo of the guard's two burly sons wearing Montrose High football uniforms was taped to the dash.

"He was gonna sleep in the truck. Hunt up here tomorrow."

Clay braced his legs against the mine entrance and pulled the steel netting back enough for Mace to drag the corpse into the shaft. When Mace couldn't see his hand in front of his face, he dropped the carcass and scurried back to the entrance. Clay handed him the empty Browning, dayglow gear and sleeping bag. Mace lugged the stuff into blackness, blinking sweat until he tripped over the body causing a squelching gurgle. Flailing to right himself, he stuck a hand deep in the dead guy's blown-out head. Felt like lukewarm dumplings. Then he ran like hell for the light.

When he and Clay came through the fence the Ram was gone and Vanessa was waiting. Mace looked around thinking the father of two probably wouldn't be missed until Sunday. Then months or years would pass before someone stumbled on a mummifying body with a rifle in a hot shaft.

Vanessa tossed Mace the keys and they all got in the Tundra. Clay clapped Mace on the shoulder from the back seat and laughed. "Atomic bomb buffs. That was some inspired fabulism, bro."

Mace turned the ignition and checked the rearview. A stiff wind was already erasing the boot and tire prints. Then the snow would come. The icing on the cake of a flawless random murder.

Mace got back on Highway 90 for a few miles then took a forest service road until Vanessa motioned him off into timber. He watched his hands shake while Vanessa got on her laptop then snuck a peek at the screen. Saw a prosperous-looking man step from a Mercedes onto a wide boulevard. The Eiffel Tower loomed in the distance. He wore a trench coat over a suit. Two hard men in windbreakers flanked him. They seemed keen on harming the photographer. Then Vanessa clicked the photo away and there was the map with the pin in the sprawling ground Mace outlined.

"I see two forks of Cottonwood Creek," she said. "North and south."

"Right."

"What fork are we focusing on?"

Mace was about to say north then didn't. Save his hole card a little longer. See if the uncertainty got them worried. Or caused a slip. Then he noticed he was cold, even in the truck. "Both."

"Except two forks is twice the ground."

"I'm sure about the drainage. Not which fork."

"Sounds hit-or-miss," she said. "Why not get the data firsthand?"

Took Mace a sec to get her drift. "As in call Stoddard and ask where he's hunting tomorrow?"

"Why not?" she said. "You don't want to ruin his hunt with the jerk-off realtors from Phoenix who decided they want a bull elk picture. You're worried about crossing paths is all."

Mace ran that chat through his head. Where he tells Will he's taking the same photographers out looking for racks on opening day. It was reckless nonsense. But Vanessa did have a point. Will might do him a favor out of pure pity. No different than helping a fool cross a busy street. And if Will did cough up where he was gonna hunt, it would make killing his customer way easier. And probably quicker, reducing his own lifespan accordingly. Then the logistics of staying useful long enough to turn the tables on these fuckers shorted his aching mind out. He punched the door open.

Clay and Vanessa got out and watched him walk away with the far envelope of pistol range in mind. Mace paused at twenty paces, sweating like a pig with hot and cold flashes. Then he had an idea. A proposal actually. He was walking back to the truck when a bar wrapper landed at his feet.

"Come on," said Clay, still chewing. "Show us some technique. Keep America beautiful."

Mace stared at the little piece of trash. The perfect symbol of his situation. "Beautiful is you crawling around lung shot begging for one last dick up your ass."

Clay charged. From standstill to sprint in two steps, knife flashing in his right hand. Mace got his arms up and feet spread figuring he was hamburger but might as well go down swinging.

"Knock it off," said Vanessa. Not loud but firm.

Clay stopped on a dime. Steam was coming out his ears but his voice was calm. "Speaking of dick, you ever wonder if the individual babysitting your wife is using protection? I'm kinda skeptical myself. I mean why would an inveterate psychopath fresh from a Texas prison bother. He's been living on cock and macaroni for twelve years. Probably forgot what a love glove looks like."

Mace offered a twitchy smile. Forehead all shiny. Eyes stinging with sweat. "Tell you what. Let's circle back to that when you're not busy being pussy-whipped."

Being a highly disciplined professional, Clay let his raging homicidal testosterone cleanse his thinking and put Mace's dismemberment aside for later. Like a tasty little snack. "Let's."

Mace walked around Clay over to Vanessa. "Here's the deal. Trophy animals aren't real estate. They wander. Even if Will tells me which fork that leaves a big chunk of ground to glass."

Vanessa noted his perspiration and dilated pupils. "You got a better idea?"

"You know where Will's base camp is. Do your guy tonight. He'll be sitting in front of a roaring fire lit up like a billboard, not prone at dawn with a rifle ready. And the range would be minimal."

"True," she said. "But there are three homes within four miles of his camp. Too many roads. Too many eyes. And the guy has two good operators. Mercs with a ton of experience and night vision. They'll have fields of fire all dialed in. We wouldn't know what we were walking into."

"Dirt-nap time," said Clay. "With you on point."

Mace was suddenly too wiped to think. Almost too wiped to stand. Vanessa noticed, handed him a bottle of water and watched him closely while he drank it. Then she kept talking.

"Tomorrow the target will be humping tough terrain full of armed friendlies. His people will get desensitized by random fire. We decide when and where to engage. Be over before they know what hit 'em. Then we evac like turistas with our quirky, unemployable hunting guide."

Mace processed that plan. Screw football and biathlon. The couple's calling was combat tactics. They were vets plying their skills in the private sector. Probably still had sand in their hair. And he was key to their plan A getaway. Until he wasn't. Best be useful. "You forgot spread out."

"What do you mean?" said Vanessa.

"No way a bunch of guys are gonna make that stalk," said Mace. "Will's gonna park those extra guns least a thousand yards back and tell 'em not to breathe. Be just him and the alpha dog when they post up on that bull. Only way Will would roll. But it doesn't mean those other guys won't be glassing everything in every direction right up until the shot. So we still need to get lucky."

"Careful, babe," said Clay. "He might be better at hunting people than he lets on."

Mace was praying Clay was right when a tremor flitted up his legs and through his chest. Withdrawal had arrived. He walked off a few yards, fighting a wave of nausea. Saw two cow elk not eighty yards away, standing side by side in full view. Robert Martinez stepped from timber and stood beside the animals like they were old pals. Then all three studied Mace with what he figured was pity and disgust. After that, Martinez smiled, shook his head and melted into nothing.

Vanessa followed Mace's gaze. Looked at the elk then her guide. A fine quiver afflicted his arms and his respiration was elevated. Otherwise he was toughing it out like she knew he would.

"Friends of yours?" she asked.

Mace kept staring at the spot where Martinez disappeared. "Not really."

Clay motioned her out of earshot.

"What'd I tell you?" he said. "This freak's broken."

She thought about that. "But he got us on top of that lion."

"Yea. Then cracked and gave us away. If that was real world we'd be bagged and tagged."

Vanessa weighed their desert-urban skill set against the alpine topography like she'd done ad nauseam since the gig solidified. Then threw in the funky ballistics and weather and the abundance of amateur guns. The math came out the same. He wasn't indispensable but he did provide an edge.

"We need him," she said.

"A doper and a drunk who has telepathic encounters with wildlife?"

"A functioning alcoholic. Juiced just enough. Not a detoxing mess."

Clay shook his head. "That's some thin fucking ice right there."

"You know another kind?"

Clay eyeballed Mace a second. "Guess not."

Then he took a lumbar pack from the truck and tossed it to her. Vanessa unzipped the pack, removed two plastic airline bottles of Tito's from two dozen and went over to Mace. He saw the booze lying in the palm of her hand and scooped it up with desperate, clumsy fingers. His dexterity was down to pathetic but he finally got the tops off and drained them both lickety-split no problem.

TWELVE

Will Stoddard was lying prone seventeen miles north of the mine where the dead guard was stashed, ascending sun warming his sore back. He rubbed his eyes and glassed the watershed fanning out below for the umpteenth time. It was locked in shadow and contained a meandering creek steeped with beaver ponds. After a bit, he saw a bull across the stream on the edge of timber grazing next to a pocket of cows. He scored the rack at just shy of 330 points. A more-than-respectable prize most hunters would convert to taxidermical shrines and revere for decades but not his new client. Respectable was crap in his book. It was midmorning on Friday.

Stifling his irritation that David Petrovic's standards were now his mission to fulfill, Will moved uphill to where a forest service trail topped the ridgeline and dropped into the drainage beyond. There he got prone and scoured ground all the way to the sheer granite massif that corked the top of the watershed. He was looking for the bull he glimpsed last year, a true six-by-six trophy with gorgeous symmetry. Headgear that would grace the ceiling of the record books for years to come.

He'd seen the animal last week but wanted to get eyes on it one more time to make sure it was holding. He was in the dead center of a massive parcel hunted solely by him for years so it was unlikely the bull would get pressured off. But still he worried about the whims of nature and the knuckleheaded trespassers opening day tended to spawn like cockroaches. He was still glassing an hour later and about to give up when he caught movement in the pines high on the watershed's western flank. Then the bull he was after crossed a narrow lane of open ground, head on a swivel, ears and eyes scanning continuously like it absolutely knew the guide was out there somewhere.

Will got a good glimpse and that was plenty. The bull was phenomenal. He lowered the binos, captivated by its permanent state of wariness and thinking the animal's death would be wasted on an asshole like Petrovic.

But he couldn't see a way out of it. He'd charged the foreigner a premium a year in advance hoping he'd find another guide because the man left a bad taste in his mouth even over the phone. But Petrovic knew what he wanted, waited patiently and that was that.

Will slid off the rim and walked five miles down the trail to the dead end of a seasonal park service road where he left his truck. There was a heavy chain to prevent motorized entry and a sign warning hikers and hunters to stay off private land. He got in his rig and headed down the park service dirt to Old Highway 90 and turned east. Eight miles later, he cut north on a track that ended at the eighty-acre parcel he bought before he got married. The terrain was dense with aspen and oak and cut by a tiny creek. Will had a rambling home and workshop outside Montrose where he lived with his wife Lucinda and raised two grown-and-gone kids but this ground was his forever office and den.

He parked his truck in a flat clearing next to a lifted '98 Explorer with Dunlop mud rovers that belonged to his cook, Jimmy Temple. Then went over to the coffeepot sitting on a propane stove on a worn-out picnic table and poured himself a cup. Around the clearing were four canvas wall tents with cedar plank floors. The two big ones were for clients to bunk and dine. The smaller ones were Will and Jimmy's digs. There was a spacious pine outhouse and a stone firepit. A sixty-kilowatt Kohler hummed from a hut. The generator was a nod to creature comfort and heated all four tents.

Beyond the camp was a range cut through oak. Steel plates no bigger than saucers hung from log stands on chains at 200, 350 and 500 yards. A sloping dirt berm on the back side kept rounds from zanging off into space. Normally there'd be horses tethered to cover more ground and pack out meat but Petrovic had no riding experience and declined the mounts. Except for the generator and the thousand-gallon propane tank, a person with a sense of Uncompahgre history might swear they'd stumbled on a cow camp from the bygone dark days of Ute elimination and sheep wars.

There was a racket from the chuck tent and Jimmy emerged, all five eight and 236 pounds of him. He was bald and bitter and sported a mustache that would choke a walrus but had a gourmet touch with ranch grub. He was forty-three and been cooking for Will since his catering service went belly-up five years ago due largely to his personality. "Where the fuck are these refugees?" he asked.

"If they're not here, they're on their way," said Will. "I'm just sorry they speak English."

"Why would you say that?"

"Because your mouth is dirtier than a badger's ass."

"You're lucky as shit I don't speak Russian."

Will squinted at him. "What gave you the idea they were Russian?"

"Guy's name is Petrovic, ain't it? You telling me that ain't Ruski?"

Will took his blood thinner and messaged his temples against an inbound headache. "They're from Serbia and they're paying top dollar to be here. And that's all you need to know."

The cook scowled. "Serbia? Where the hell is that?"

"Right by a bunch of other countries you couldn't find if they were bolted around your neck."

Jimmy huffed back into his kitchen and Will measured the march of clouds. He smelled a dump coming and heard the same opening-day mantra he muttered every year for more than he could remember. Next October you're hip-deep in the Gulf of Mexico throwing lures at tarpon and reds until your goddamn arm falls off. Almost had the ring of truth this time. Then a smooth rumble leaked through the trees. Jimmy came out of the tent trailing the perfume of baking biscuits and the two of them watched the black G-Wagon claw up the dirt track toward camp.

"Fucking Tiger tank," said the cook.

When the camp came into view, Luka stopped and Marko carefully glassed the people and structures. Then both removed the compact submachine guns from under their coats and handed them to Stefan in the back seat. He lifted the rear carpet on the floor and opened the safe welded into the chassis. Inside were two HK assault rifles and a pair of Walther pistols. He handed them to Luka and Marko. They seated magazines and got ready to work. Then Stefan locked the full-auto stuff away and they drove up the last hundred yards, parking beside the other vehicles.

Luka and Marko dismounted first, rifles at low ready, eyes quartering the camp like blood hounds fresh from their crates. Having never seen Jimmy before, Luka veered over immediately.

"Good morning," he said in fair English with a thick Serbian accent before frisking the cook.

Jimmy eyes widened, too afraid to move. Felt like he'd fallen into an episode of *Narcos*.

Finding nothing but love handles and a cell, Luka patted Jimmy on the head and joined Marko searching the tents. When they were done, they gave the all-clear wave and Petrovic bounded over to Will and hugged him like a long-lost brother even though they'd met yesterday.

"Tell me you found the biggest elk in Colorado and tied it to a fucking tree," he said. His English was superb and unhindered by the heavy Slavic intonation.

"Working on it," said Will, thrown by the fruity alcohol on Petrovic's breath. He indicated his cook. "This is Jimmy, Mr. Petrovic. Makes the best chicken-fried steak west of the Gunnison."

Petrovic's brow furrowed as he shook Jimmy's hand. "This steak is fried inside a chicken?"

"Christ, no," said Jimmy. "Just sounds that way. I'm making it for lunch if you wanna watch."

"I would be honored," said Petrovic, pulling a flask and offering it to Jimmy. "To the chef."

Jimmy took a swig and they ducked into the chuck tent. Will went after Luka and Marko.

When he caught up with them, he pointed at the HKs. "Those things better not be fully automatic."

"They are not," said Marko. "Semiauto only."

"For sure, *deda*," added Luka with a laugh because *deda* meant "grandfather" in Serbian.

Both mercs took full-immersion English when Petrovic purchased a hunting estate in Wales and loved practicing the language of the USA because it made them feel like they were in a movie.

"Mind if I take a look?" said Will.

Marko lifted his rifle so the receiver was in full view. "See? No fully automatic here."

Will squinted. There was a selector switch aft of the trigger with two modes. A white square for safety and a red square for semiauto. "Just checking," he said.

"Absolutely no problem," said Marko.

Will tapped the big curved magazine. "But that thing ain't legal for hunting elk. Semiautos can't hold more than six rounds. That looks like at least twenty to me."

"This is not for hunting."

"Then why'd you bring it?"

Marko's courteous demeanor dissolved into a flat stare. "Because it is my job."

"Is that right," said Will. "And what kinda job requires a twenty-round clip?"

Marko glanced at Luka and the absurdity of the question caused them to giggle until they lost control altogether, waving their hands apologetically at the mystified guide. Because he'd never seen a twenty-round clip become a teardrop in a tidal wave of incoming gunfire. Eventually Stefan came over and spoke quietly in Serbian to Marko and Luka. Both men nodded politely at the outfitter then fanned out and continued sweeping the far reaches of the clearing around the camp.

"What's so funny about carrying that kinda firepower?" asked Will.

"That would depend on one's life experience," said Stefan. His English was London-schooled. Clean and orderly. "But I can assure you those weapons are purely for security purposes."

"Here's the deal," said Will. "I don't need to know how you got Colorado trophy tags all the way over there in Europe. But I do need to know what you're so worried about. And if that's a problem then you and I have a problem."

"My job is worrying about everything," said Stefan.

"On the back side of nowhere, in the safest country on the planet?"

"Especially."

Will grinned. "Now that right there is what we call ten gallons of shit in a five-gallon hat."

"What's a five-gallon hat?" asked Stefan.

"Doesn't matter. Means you didn't answer my question."

Stefan sighed condescendingly. "Before Mr. Petrovic became an international developer, he was a high-ranking member of the Serbian judiciary deciding the fate of the most barbaric criminals imaginable. You would call them mafia or terrorists but in fact they were fanatical scum."

"So?" said Will.

"Many of these criminals were heavily armed and preferred death to

prison. They left brothers and sons with long memories and valid passports. Does that answer your question?"

A sinking feeling blossomed in Will's gut. Like he'd hit a patch of black
ice on a tight curve with no guardrails. "Your gun hands going hunting
with us?"

"Of course," said Stefan. Then he paused, squinting at the surrounding
forest as if it were transmitting a complex and foreboding message exclu-
sively for him. "We all are."

"Then they need to swap out those Rambo rigs for bolt-action rifles
right now."

"No problem," said Stefan, wondering what *Rambo rig* meant but not
asking.

He turned and shouted in Serbian at the two mercs. They stared sul-
lenly at Will a moment then headed toward the Benz. When Luka got
even with the range, he pivoted and splattered ten rounds on the two-
hundred-yard plate in nine seconds and kept walking. Stefan was grinning
in awe at the display of marksmanship when Will grabbed his arm and
spun him around.

"Next time someone discharges a firearm on my hunt without my permission, I'll shut this trip down so fast you'll think you got run over and
plowed under. You understand that?"

Stefan gaped and muttered before Will cut him off. "Yes or no."

"Yes."

"Good. Now go tell your boss what I said. And make damn sure he
understands it's a take-it-or-leave-it type deal."

Will watched him hurry off as his cell rang. He checked the caller ID and
picked up. "Figured you got those real estate agents mauled and skipped
town."

"No such luck," said Mace. "But I did find 'em a honker of a cat up on
the Ninety-Five."

"You owe me a twenty-ounce rib eye and a soak in Ouray."

"Done. So where you gonna be hunting?"

"Why?" asked Will. "You coming out of retirement?"

"Naw. That couple wants to snap a bull elk tomorrow. They're kinda
fascinated by the whole hunting thing. Just wanna stay out your way."

"You gotta be kidding me."

"I know," said Mace. "Little crazy but you got me into this."

"I didn't get you into acting like you have a runaway brain tumor."

"Would've gone this morning but Jamie's got a bad virus. If she's looking better tonight, I'll cover this couple in dayglow and get rolling at the crack."

"On goddamn day one of rifle season?" said Will, still straining to wrap his mind around this.

"They leave on Sunday, Will. And I need the money. Just don't want to mess up your hunt."

"Doesn't make it right."

"You saying I didn't learn my lesson?"

Will paused, picking his words carefully. "I'm saying I never heard you desperate before."

"That makes two of us. So tell me where you're headed or don't. I got my hands full here."

A tailgate slammed. Will turned as Luka and Marko slipped into the trees with scoped bolt-action Mausers. He knew the difference between soldiers and hunters and he was looking at it.

"Now you listen and you listen close," said Will. "We'll start west of Mailbox Branch toward Cottonwood Creek. That doesn't pan out, we'll work our way southeast to Telephone Draw."

"What fork of the Cottonwood?"

"North," said Will. "Below Blue Mud Spring."

"Jamie and I fished that stretch once," said Mace. "You got us permission, remember?"

"That's right. I did. But you stay the hell out of there tomorrow."

"Got it. How's your hunting party going?"

Will stared at the men occupying his camp. "*Sketchy* is the only word that comes to mind."

There was a stretch of silence. Mace started to say he was sorry but didn't. "Watch yourself."

"Likewise," said Will.

Mace handed his cell phone to Vanessa and watched her stow it inside her parka in a pocket right next to her holstered Glock. Both on her left side for a quick and easy snatch. Then she popped Mace playfully on the shoulder. "See how easy that was?"

Mace nodded thinking he'd just shoved Will in front of a bullet train. And if there was a purgatory for chickenshit traitors he'd just made his reservation.

By the time Will got back to his clients, a fire was blazing and Petrovic was hunched over the picnic table medicating his coffee with Croatian brandy and oiling a custom Weatherby Magnum. Will figured the rifle ran about seven grand, not counting the beautiful Swarovski scope. Stefan was working on a bottle of Haut-Brion and tapping on a MacBook Pro attached to a sat link.

Will checked his watch and saw it was barely noon. "Kinda early ain't it?"

"But always later than you think," said Petrovic, offering the bottle of booze with a steady hand.

Will declined but the remark registered. Then Stefan motioned him over to the laptop. There was a highly detailed topo map of the immediate area on the screen. Will leaned down and saw a blue pin blinking on the exact location of his camp along with a parcel number and his name. Hard not to admire the technology that made nothing secret or private anymore. "Nice toy," he said.

"Mind showing me where you intend to take us tomorrow?" asked Stefan.

"Why?"

"Because my job includes knowing where Mr. Petrovic is going to be before he gets there."

"For those security purposes you mentioned."

Stefan smiled patiently. "There's no reason we both can't do our jobs, is there?"

Will stabbed a forefinger into the screen, smudging a remote valley to the northwest.

Stefan clicked to satellite and zoomed in on a dirt road ending at a small parking area. A trail climbed from there into the drainage Will indicated. "And this is where we leave your truck?"

"That's the plan."

"How far to where the elk will be?"

"That's up to them. Anything else?"

Stefan shook his head. Will looked over at Petrovic. He was still oiling the Weatherby.

"Wouldn't lube a rifle like that up here. Gets cold enough the oil can gum up the action. Same thing goes for taking a gun from hot to cold. Frozen condensation can cause a misfire."

Petrovic nodded sagely and continued oiling his weapon. He'd killed hundreds of animals and thousands of people and no longer took advice on methodology. Jimmy appeared with two heaping plates of chicken-fried steak and biscuits in gravy and set them in front of the guests. Then he took a gulp of brandy off the bottle and scurried back to his kitchen without meeting Will's glare.

"What about your gun hands?" said Will. "They don't eat lunch?"

"They eat when they're told," said Petrovic, mouth full, devouring the hillock of sizzling meat.

Will caught movement on the ridge to the west, which offered an unobstructed view of the camp and its approaches. Luka and Marko were moving along the spine, Mausers slung over their shoulders. When they reached a reef of oak, they fanned out and melted into overwatch positions.

Petrovic shouted his compliments to the chef and placed a box of Weatherby cartridges next to his plate. "I suggest we have another drink and thank God for letting us live this long."

"You think God had other plans and changed his mind?" asked Will.

Petrovic shrugged. "I think God can do whatever he wants."

Will turned a deaf ear to the buzzed bullshit, crossed to the firepit and warmed his hands thinking about the call from Mace. Sounded like his back was against a way bigger wall than drumming up cash. And the more he parsed it, the Serbian fat cat being in the mix was an odd coincidence. Then he dismissed his paranoia as geriatric jitters, raised his eyes and checked the inbound storm. It was closing off the sky to north. Sealing him in for another rifle season.

Petrovic wiped his fingertips and loaded his rifle with five 6.5-millimeter rounds. He found solace in the click of the receiver because it signified the duality of his station in life. Hunter and hunted as two sides of the same coin that got tossed and called every day, making dawn itself an outrageous gift. Somewhere in the world a person was loading a weapon or constructing an explosive device with his face burned into their shattered heart. Hence his tactical precognition.

Like when a dark-haired young investment banker had made a bee-line toward Petrovic across a chic hotel lobby in Berlin. One hand was extended in capitalistic cordiality but his eyes burned with death and his Zegna suit was too tight around the torso. Petrovic graded these details at a glance. Pulled the subcompact Glock he carried for the same reason an asthmatic carries an inhaler and shot the man twice at thirty paces. The Semtex under the suit detonated with a clap of light, killing or maiming a dozen guests and staff but barely mussing Petrovic's hair. Certainly didn't change his dinner plans. Although he did slip into fresh clothes due to the unpleasant splatter.

But every failed attempt spawned another aspiring assassin like an endless chain reaction. Such was the unassailable debt associated with his life and times. The trick was not letting this mathematically foregone conclusion prevent him from savoring the feast of the chase. That would be cowardly. A living death. And his Colorado hunt was too anticipated to dilute with fear.

So he didn't pay much attention to the gray souls of the departed watching from the forest a stone's throw from where he sat. Hundreds of them twining through the trees like fog wearing the same clothes and gore they wore when tossed in the ground. But their vacant expressions of death were long gone. Now they watched their killer with patient amusement. As if Petrovic's posh, globe-trotting existence was the height of irony compared to the putrid darkness of their mass graves. Last year he rode his Gulfstream to Namibia to kill leopards and found an identical delegation waiting on the boiling tarmac. Some he recognized from firsthand liquidation but most were killed by men acting under his orders. Checked-off names scrawled on hurriedly made lists.

He knew they were there and always would be. Fellow travelers to the very end. A lesser monster might have put one of those blue-tipped cartridges through the roof of his mouth for dessert. But the man calling himself Petrovic wasn't the lesser kind. He was the real deal and knew suicide would leave an epitaph of weakness. So he topped off his cup and toasted his eternal followers marveling, as always, at the luminous quality of their faces.

THIRTEEN

Hazim was crouched on the edge of the cottonwoods where the mottled shade made him invisible in woodland camo. His rifle was cradled across his chest and dust devils traipsed over the scruffy hills and ravines to his front. The landscape reminded him of places he'd fought. Add some Roman ruins and barrel-bombed villages and the scenery was interchangeable.

He was watching a mob of crows harass a large bird with a limp rodent in its talons when a sound sent a jolt up his spine. A tinny howl consistent with ATVs or dirt bikes. The sound flitted in and out of range then grew sharply in clarity. He shouldered the rifle and got on the scope. If the riders kept coming and got curious about the junked Winnebago, he'd have to make an unpleasant but familiar decision. He prayed they weren't kids. It was early afternoon on Friday.

The noise ended abruptly beyond a dun-colored rise half a kilometer to the east. He rose quickly and found a tree trunk that afforded bulletproof cover and a solid brace for the forestock of his rifle. By the time he got back on the scope the wind was shaving a sheet of dust off the rise. When it cleared, two grown and sturdy men were standing on the top. They wore buffs and beanies and rifles were slung over their shoulders. Hazim was stunned. Trigger finger tingling. A search party.

He grabbed his satphone, ready to stab a number designated solely for mission-critical hazards before remembering a key instruction from the American couple. If the hostage was reported missing he'd be alerted immediately. He didn't know how they'd know this but they left nothing to chance so he stowed the phone and watched the intruders glass terrain. When they were done they walked down the back of the rise. A minute later the engine noise fired up and faded away.

Hazim splashed water on his face, wondering why so many people in this overfed, self-absorbed country looked ready to fight a war. There were no sloppy mass executions here. No Serb snipers picking off hungry men and women queuing up for bread. No streets littered with mortar-amputated limbs. Then he chided himself for his ingratitude. America's infatuation with guns was a great gift that would serve a far greater sport. The only sport that made this life worth living.

He made his way back to the Winnebago and found his prisoner in a fetal position, face turned away from the door. He laid his rifle and binos on the plastic table and slid into the breakfast nook thinking the hood must be suffocating in the cramped and squalid space. But the couple had given him strict instructions not to remove it in case she escaped before her usefulness came to an end. Then Jamie swung her legs around, sat up straight and spoke in a calm voice.

"That Arizona couple is in on it," she said. "They're not realtors."

The casual cognitive leap gave Hazim a sick sensation. Mace's involvement was the couple's decision. Once the Monster reserved the hunt they called the tactical shots. They were pricey, seasoned professionals with impeccable references. So he never questioned their judgment.

"You sent them to Will because you knew he was booked," said Jamie. "You bet he'd send them to Mace because you wanted to check him out. The mountain-lion business was a dry run."

"None of that was my idea," blurted Hazim, incredulous that he was defending himself.

"Poor baby. Kidnapping women while the fake realtors do the heavy lifting. Has to be killing someone. That's why you're here. Why else go to all this trouble? They're gonna shoot someone."

This jarred Hazim further. If she could deduce the essence of the mission while hooded and shackled in a stinking metal box, how easy would it be for the police? Or the mobile indigenous fighters he saw roaming his flanks? They could have faked withdrawing and be moving into position right now. His eyes jumped to the windows covered with rotting plywood. Then the thin aluminum skin of the RV. Might as well be paper against concentrated small-arms fire.

Jamie took the silence as a direct hit and the rest tumbled into focus. "You're hunting a hunter. Someone scary good. That's why you need Mace. Because nobody in the world could do it better."

Hazim jumped up and jammed his Beretta into her skull. Too unsettled and angry to stop himself. Jamie felt the muzzle and wondered why her life wasn't passing before her eyes.

"You better hope so," said Hazim. Then he grabbed the rifle and binos and left.

After he locked the door and went down the metal steps, Jamie did a situational recap. It was Friday afternoon. She wasn't a missing person yet. She was in Montrose County or the north end of Ouray County because of the aircraft passing lazily overhead. She was certain of this because she woke up in the toolbox before he drove out of the brush and onto gravel. A rough gauge of time and speed put them twenty-five miles east of where he grabbed her. Not far from the Adobe Hills.

She put her captor's age at near fifty. And he had an accent. Russian maybe. His instinct was to treat her with respect but his stress was acute. He was running on bedrock faith in the task at hand. Or a higher power. Her gut told her he was a combat vet. The way he moved. The quickness. The decisiveness. There were plenty on the Western Slope and she'd steered some into counseling after ER encounters. Wherever he was from, this guy was tough as nails. But she heard doubt nibbling around the edges. Her only hope was stoking his apprehensions without speeding up her execution.

She tested her restraints again, mind churning in blackness. They felt solid. She was curious about their connection to the wall of the trailer but had no way of touching or seeing it. Then she was fresh out of brave thoughts. The wind hummed around the RV and she saw Mace's brokenhearted face and wept. Cursing the monumental stupidity of leaving the love of her life to make a point. Then boots hit the stairs. The door was opened, shut and locked. For a second she worried her captor would see she'd been crying then remembered the hood. "Feel better?" she asked.

Hazim set his rifle against the doorjamb and sat at the table staring at the woman under the hood, thinking she would have made a good soldier. "No more talk."

"Oh come on. I'm never gonna see your face. At least tell me what Will's client did to cause all this? I mean, wouldn't you be curious if you were in my place?"

Hazim crossed to Jamie, lifted the hood just enough to tie a gag over her mouth and marked each word by jabbing a finger into her forehead. "No. More. Talk."

Then he backed away and fumed at himself. Putting a pistol to a prisoner's head just to make a point was sadistic. He'd fought in monthslong engagements without quarter or sleep and never done it. This woman was dangerous. She spawned second-guessing. Even worse, she made him feel like the man he was before Mecca went from distant concept to daily nucleus. The beer-loving eighteen-year-old who wanted to be a carpenter like his father. Then he reminded himself that the future was already written. Focus on guarding the fulcrum of the plan. Hold the woman until her value became nil. But she was right. Talk was irrelevant. Her fate was sealed the day she was born, just like his.

After sitting with that truth, Hazim carefully raised the hood to Jamie's nose and removed the gag. Then he stepped back, bracing himself for more caustic insight.

She wetted her lips and spoke calmly given her situation. "Kitchen still open?"

Hazim hesitated then rummaged through the bag in the ice chest, reading off labels. "Black bean veggie wrap, ham and Swiss, chicken double-smoked bacon, turkey and pesto panini."

Jamie's head went up. She was a Starbucks junkie. This bastard must have followed her all over town and watched her eat. "Ham and Swiss."

He was about to unwrap the sandwich when he saw how grimy his fingers were. He cleaned them with Purell, tore off the packaging and lifted the hood to her lips. "Lean forward."

Her mouth found the food. He waited until she'd chewed and swallowed and gave her a sip of water. He repeated the process until the sandwich was gone. Then he pulled the hood down and stood there, legs spread, bulky thighs a foot from her face. She felt the heat coming off his muscles and smelled his coppery sweat. He could do whatever he wanted. Any way he wanted. For as long as he wanted. A bolt of terror took her breath away. Hazim misread the shiver in her hood.

"Are you cold?" he asked.

"No," she whispered but the hood continued to tremble.

He stepped back feeling like an idiot. She was scared to death and the next call with her husband could come at any time. If she wasn't composed it could backfire. "How about some coffee?"

The normalcy of the question struck her as outlandish. "Sure."

Hazim made her a mug, let it cool then lifted the hood to just beneath her nose and let her drink. When the coffee was gone he pulled the hood down. Thought a second. "Do you need the toilet?"

"Yes," she said.

He unlocked the lanyard from the wall and helped her off the mattress and onto her feet. Then he removed the cuffs, guided her into the phone booth of a bathroom and turned away.

She stood there, hands blindly braced against the wall. "How about shutting the door?"

"There is no door," he said over his shoulder. "Tissue on your right."

Jamie dropped her scrubs and sat on the marine head the Winnebago rolled out of the factory with. When she was done she found the toilet paper, pulled up her pants and shuffled forward. Hazim gave her sanitizer to clean her hands, cuffed her wrists behind her back, seated her on the mattress and locked the ankle shackles to the D-ring in the wall. The sound of the lock clicking was almost even with her head. Couldn't be more than five feet away given the size of the RV. It gave her an idea. Then she turned toward the creak in the floor where her captor stood.

"I take it you're not worried about the hantavirus we're breathing," she said.

He looked at her. "What is that?"

"Virus carried by rats. Comes off their feces. Hangs in the air like dust. Causes hemorrhagic fever and renal failure. Has a fifty percent fatality rate."

"How long does that take?"

"Depends on the treatment."

"What is the untreated survival time?"

"Few days," she lied. "Just like Ebola."

He didn't doubt she was telling the truth because she was a genuine doctor. He just couldn't picture either of their lives spanning a few more days. "Then I wouldn't worry about it."

"What about my husband and my dog?" she said. "Should I worry about them?"

He limped over to the door and grabbed his rifle. "No. I wouldn't worry about them either."

Jamie registered his asymmetrical gait for the first time. The heaving thud of one leg coming down late. She'd seen hundreds of torn ACLs and bum patellas. "What happened to your knee?"

He ignored her and started out the door. Tired of her reading him like braille.

"Wait," she said, voice rising sharply like she had something important to add.

It worked. He stopped and looked back at her.

"Where did you serve?" she asked.

He almost smiled. Beneath her toughness and brains was another naïve American.

"What makes you think I stopped?" he asked before shutting the door behind him.

She waited until she heard the exterior padlock click and boots going down the steps. Put her feet together, stretched her legs and weaved her ankles around the lanyard until all the slack was gone. After that she put the soles of her Reeboks on the wall and shuffled the toes around. Didn't take long to find the D-ring anchoring her shackles. She put her feet on either side of it, visualized herself on the squat rack and shifted her quads and glutes into maximum thrust. And lo and behold the thing leashing her to this shitcan moved. No more than an eighth of an inch but it moved.

FOURTEEN

Vince woke up on the floor of the stall without knowing or caring how he got there. After eating and hydrating he barked emphatically for a while. When that failed to provoke a human response he tore into the old planks of the stall tooth and nail, demolishing his way into the barn proper. After a nose-down search, he found a rotted corner with streaks of light leaking through the siding and dug furiously. A few minutes later he squirmed into cloudy sunlight that smelled like snow.

After circling the house twice and detecting no live sounds or scents coming from within he loped down to the gate, the structure he associated with the vehicles bearing his peeps. The road in both directions was empty of traffic. More often than not, Mace and Jamie came and went from the right. So he jumped the sagging split rail and headed that direction at a purposeful trot.

He'd covered two miles when a truck bore down on him from behind at a good clip. He spun around just as a man with a rifle leaned out the right rear window thinking it was the biggest coyote he ever saw. Vince was leaping out of the way when the driver screamed about it being a fucking dog and not to shoot. Then the blue Dodge crew cab with New Mexico plates skidded to a stop.

Three men dismounted, all giddy and swaggering and barely twenty. They were buzz-cut and stout and clad in red Lobos football hoodies. They reeked of Colorado dope and nectarine vape juice. Energy drinks and binos littered the dash. Three rifles were casually stacked in the back seat, butts on the floor, barrels protruding over the left rear window. Cartridge boxes lay on the floorboard.

Vince stood his ground on the shoulder, aloof and alert. The trio of young men were mesmerized by the dog's noble demeanor. The driver, a tall Black guy with a calm power about him, took a knee and extended his arm. Vince let the strange mitt get an inch from his nose then growled. The driver pulled his arm back and stood up. "We got any of that jerky left?"

The red-haired white lug who was gonna shoot the shepherd grabbed a sack of teriyaki Jack Link's from the cab and threw it to the driver who offered a piece to Vince. The dog glided around the gift and posted up at the truck's tailgate. "Believe this shit?" said the driver. "He wants a ride."

The third guy, white with blond stubble, shoved the redhead at Vince. "Check his tag, man."

"Fuck that," said the redhead. "You wanna lose your arm, go ahead."

The driver stepped nimbly around the shepherd and dropped the tailgate. Vince levitated his hundred pounds into the bed and sat like a potentate ready to be borne away. The driver offered his hand again. Vince gave it a single, discreet lick. The driver cracked a massive grin. "There we go."

"Yo Jace," said the redhead. "You being trained."

"Called *cooperation*," said the driver. He scratched the dog's head before lifting the silver tag on the collar between thumb and forefinger and squinting at the info. "What's up, Vince?"

Then he pulled out his cell and punched the first of two phone numbers stamped in the metal.

Glenn sat through roll call in a brick building on Fourth Street in Ouray listening to the annual rifle season spiel. It's a felony to kill and abandon game. It's illegal to shoot from a vehicle or within fifty feet of a road. Hunting under the influence of a controlled substance was punishable by blah blah blah. That always got a laugh because if every hunter in the state got tested about half would fail and the elk could wear Christmas lights and graze in perfect safety. It was 2 p.m. on Friday.

After a bullshit session with colleagues about where they planned to bag their meat, Glenn climbed in his county Suburban and pondered the call he had with Mace that morning. His pal was farther along than he thought. The hunting accident was like a swarm of bark beetles eating through a lofty ponderosa pine. Sooner or later even the giants topple. When and where was the problem.

He drove north on Highway 550 out of Ouray and up the wide green-and-gold valley floor watching light traffic and thinking about lunch. The combo plate at Taco Del Gnar was reaching critical mass when his road-hawk eyes picked up the southbound truck touching the center lane one time too many. A beat-up blue Dodge with three occupants. As the distance closed, he sized them up as young and stoned but possessing enough fast-twitch muscle not to be a threat to public safety.

The guys on board sat up straight, eyes front as they whizzed past the Suburban with the lights on the roof and the big cop behind the wheel. Glenn enjoyed their scared-rigid fear until he glimpsed the German shepherd riding in the bed with its head stuck around the side of the cab.

Glenn didn't whip a U right away because there was just no fucking way. He pulled over like a regular law-abiding person, replayed the snippet of the dog in the back and then tore after the blue truck. When he caught up there was gauzy smoke coiling into the slipstream and Vince had his paws planted high and mighty on the roof of the cab enjoying the ride. Glenn tried to wrap his mind around the spectacle without success then hit the light bar, pulled them over and got out.

He hugged the mildly pleased dog while the men in the truck gawked in amazement. As far as Vince was concerned, it wasn't Mace or Jamie but close enough. Then Glenn dropped the tailgate and led the shepherd into the back seat of the Suburban. After that he pulled his Stetson low and approached the Dodge on the driver's side. He didn't mind the pot smell but the rifle barrels poking over the windowsill caused his right hand to settle on the butt of his service weapon, a Sig Sauer 9mm. The Black guy behind the wheel already had his license and registration out in his left hand.

Glenn saw none of the dazed, jerky eye movement associated with booze in the driver or his passengers but he did see three baller versions of himself from back when. Invulnerable hormones and all. "Afternoon," he said. "I'd appreciate everybody keeping their hands where I can see 'em."

The redheaded guy up front put his hands on the dash. The blond guy in the back grabbed the headrest. Glenn glanced at the bolt-action rifles. The firearms were gunked with dust as if grabbed from their grandad's Korean War footlockers. Probably explode in their unblemished faces.

"That your dog?" asked the driver.

Glenn took his New Mexico ID and registration and perused both without acknowledging the question. "Those rifles loaded?"

"Yes, sir," said the driver.

"Going elk hunting?"

"Thinking about it."

"Got out-of-state hunting licenses?"

The driver looked at his teammates. All they did was blink. "Not yet."

"But you got yourself a German shepherd that doesn't belong to you," said Glenn.

"Sure do. Found him walking down a gravel road in the middle of nowhere. We tried making friends but all he wanted was a lift. Jumped into the bed like he'd done it all his life."

"Where was this?"

The driver pointed southwest at the mass of the plateau. "Way back up there somewhere. I called the two numbers on his tag. Nobody answered so I left messages. Just waiting to hear back."

Glenn studied the guy. "Unlock your phone and give it to me."

The driver didn't move or break eye contact with what he guessed was a washed-up, pistol-packing lineman. "You can't make me do that. Not even in redneck Colorado."

"That's true," said Glenn, returning the license and registration. "On the other hand, you could voluntarily unlock your phone and do me a huge favor by reading off those numbers you called."

"Because you know who owns that dog."

Glenn liked the way he handled pressure. Cool and brisk. A quarterback, definitely. "I might."

"Then what?"

"You guys ride into the sunset and I'm not left with the impression that you're a bunch of heavily armed, stoner dog thieves."

The driver chuckled as he dug out his iPhone. "Like I said, fellas. Cooperation."

The driver read off Mace's and Jamie's numbers and Glenn sent the lads on their way with his standard don't-text-and-drive warning. When they were out of sight he called Jamie and Mace and let both calls go to voicemail without leaving a message. After that, he thumbed through his contacts and stopped at the number labeled Jamie's Mom. He stared at it before deciding the poor woman had enough shit piled on her plate courtesy of her son-in-law without him heaping on more.

Then he tossed the phone on the dash, twisted his head around and looked at Vince.

"You know what? I always wanted a canine unit."

The shepherd stared back, nostrils flaring, inhaling all kinds of data beyond Glenn's ken. And not one scintilla of it was good.

FIFTEEN

After Will spilled his hunt plans, Mace took a shortcut named Dead-horse Road northwest at a brutal clip because the quicker they got on foot the easier it'd be to avoid human contact. The track was euphemistically called high-clearance so melon-size rocks were crashing off the skid plate, socking Clay and Vanessa around like bugs in a bottle. They didn't care because they believed they now possessed the mother lode of assassin knowledge: the future location of their target.

But the good vibes waned when Vanessa failed to find the places Will mentioned on her comp map because the plateau was full of lost names before the Pyramids of Giza were even started. Utes arrived a mere nine hundred years ago speaking a dialect that irked the first ranchers so they killed a bunch, ran off the rest and relabeled all the real estate. Pithy stuff like Mailbox Branch, Telephone Draw and Blue Mud Spring. Places Mace could find in his sleep. It was 4 p.m. on Friday.

Clay saw the brow-knit scowl on his partner's face from the back seat. "What's wrong babe?"

"Not a thing," she said, shutting her laptop with a tad too much force.

Mace saw her problem from the corner of his eye clear as day. The map sure as hell ain't the territory. Then all he could see was his wife hooded and hog-tied on a filthy mattress.

They entered the lower reaches of the Cottonwood Creek drainage and Mace was looking for a place to bash off road and hide the truck. Then a fancy brown Tundra nearly clipped his left fender on a sharp turn. The driver didn't slow down. A hat obscured his features.

Mace wasn't worried because he'd never seen that particular truck before. But a minute later the same rig materialized in his dust and flashed its high beams. Vanessa and Clay pulled on their caps and sunglasses and stared straight ahead. Mace wondered who he was about to get killed.

"Who's the road rager?" said Clay.

"No idea," said Mace, eyes in the rearview. "Just stay put."

After pulling over he stood by the door. The brown Tundra rolled to a stop and Mike Horner dismounted. He wore oil-splotched overalls and a palm leaf cowboy hat over snow-white hair. His face was cherry red. He resembled a retired diesel mechanic, not the owner of a spread just a tad under eleven thousand contiguous acres. Same border collie sat in the front seat, ears cocked at the situation.

Mike laughed at Mace's horrified expression. "What's the matter?"

Mace forced himself to walk calmly over to his friend. "Never seen you drive anything but that fossilized Willys." The collie stuck her head out the window and he loved her up. "Hey, Lucy girl."

Mike swatted the air like it stank. "Some pissant desk jockey at DMV deemed it unsafe to drive on public roads. So I bought this pilgrim rig brand-new last year." He gave the truck a wistful look. "My son would have given me a raft of shit then taken the keys and never looked back."

"Nothing wrong with a roof in December," said Mace picturing Mike's son Ethan all strapping and funny and pure cowboy before a rare brain tumor took his life at age thirty-six. "Hell color is that?"

"Smoked mesquite. Got heated leather seats and a screen bigger than my first TV."

"Goddamn," said Mace. "If that ain't the end of civilization, I don't know what is."

The rancher shifted his gaze to the couple in the beat-up Tundra. "Who's that?"

"Same people I had on your place yesterday. Photographers from Phoenix. Decided to stay another day. Money's good so I couldn't say no."

Mike laid a hand on Mace's shoulder. "Good to see guiding again, even if it's shutterbugs."

Mace was forming a response to that when a door opened. He looked over his shoulder and saw Clay climb out and check for traffic in both directions. His right arm dangled behind his right leg. Mace couldn't see it but he knew the .45 was pressed against his thigh. Vanessa got out the other side and gave Mike a quick wave and a flat smile. The caps and shades hid their faces nicely.

"Hang on," said Mace, backing toward the truck. "They got ants in their pants to get going."

"Sure looks like it," said Mike, having the sense to see he was causing a hiccup in something.

Mace walked up to Vanessa and lowered his voice. "You shoot him I'm done."

"Relax," she said.

"Screw relax. Get back in the truck and let us finish our chat."

"Or what?"

"Only one way to find out."

It was a feat of self-control for her not to step back and kill him. "What about Jamie?"

"She's good as dead and you know it."

Vanessa looked at Clay. They got back in the truck and Mace walked back over to Mike.

"You wanna tell me what's really going on?" said the rancher, amused by the whispering.

Mace jerked a thumb over his shoulder. "They're high as kites on local primo."

"Who isn't?" said Mike, looking down and scuffing gravel with his boot. "But that ain't it."

Mace took a breath and lied his ass off. "They fell in love with my place, Mike. Wanna buy it. Offered big money and I'm giving it some thought. They wanted a tour of the area so here we are."

Mike shook his head in outright disbelief. "Why in the world would you do that?"

"Fresh start in Denver. Jamie's got all kinds of job offers."

"Now that's the end of civilization right there. What are you gonna do, teach taxidermy?"

Mace looked off hearing himself peddling shit. "Dammit, Mike. You screw up like I did and see if the grass doesn't look greener in every direction. You try it and get back to me."

"Maybe so," said Mike. "But selling your parents' place to strangers is just plain wrong."

"You got a better idea?"

"Sell it to me. I'll take up gardening and sit on your porch until you come to your senses."

"I'll keep that in mind," said Mace.

"Might keep something else in mind while you're chauffeuring idiots from Arizona around."

"What's that?"

"Whole lot of people up here would do anything in the world for you. Including me."

Mace wasn't ready for the raw emotion that kicked up into his throat and had to swallow a couple times before speaking. "How's Barbara doing?"

"Fit as a fiddle. And has absolutely no idea who I am."

"Sorry, Mike."

The rancher nodded with a faraway expression. "Couldn't get licensed live-in help out at the ranch so she's in memory care down in Montrose. Good food. Nice people. Probably outlive me and never know it according to the actuarial tables." Then he looked Mace straight in the eye. "So do me a favor and don't do something completely dumbass like move away."

Mace watched him climb in his shiny new rig, execute a sharp three-point turn and head downhill. After that, he walked back to his truck, slid behind the wheel, slammed the door and pulled onto the road. Then the professional killers and their guide rode in oddly comfortable silence for a bit, like old pals on a scenic jaunt.

"What'd you tell him?" asked Vanessa.

"You wanted to buy my place. I wasn't averse to the idea so I was showing you around."

"And he didn't like that."

"No he did not," said Mace, rubbing his temples against a nauseating headache.

Clay brushed Mace's ear with his Glock. "Our guide has a deeply disingenuous side."

Half mile later, the terrain flattened out into a north–south depression covered with juniper and sage. Mace turned right, dropped the truck into four-wheel low and clawed up a ravine. Few hundred yards later, he found a clearing that effectively shielded the vehicle from view in every direction. Then he cut the engine, puked stringy yellow out the window and wiped his mouth on his sleeve.

"I need to talk to my wife," he said.

Vanessa grabbed the keys, dismounted and looked back at him. "Was she happy when you accidentally evolved out of murdering harmless animals?"

Mace gripped the wheel tighter to hide the shakes. "I just need to hear her voice. Please."

Vanessa clocked the sky. The sun was a bright blob behind racing clouds. Diving barometric pressure made her ears pop. The backwoods son of a bitch was right about the weather. Then she reached in her coat and sidearmed another Tito's at his head. The throw was no-look and hard and might have put out his right eye if he hadn't one-handed it with a flickering grab.

She logged the wicked reflexes as something to account for in close quarters. Definitely not your average angst-riddled boozer. "Earn it," she said before slamming the door.

Mace pounded the vodka, climbed out, shouldered his pack and walked west toward a long bony ridge without a backward glance. Vanessa fell in behind him, Clay behind her. When they reached the timber at the base of the rise, Mace turned north and picked up the pace. Clay pulled up on the edge of the trees and glassed their rear like a man deep in enemy territory. Specks of white ricocheted off his binoculars with the continuous random motion of atoms. He didn't notice.

SIXTEEN

Hazim was standing in the cottonwoods watching the sun drop into scudding gray, vision going funky from fatigue. He braced his back against a tree, rifle at low ready trying to stay awake. His chin was on his chest when a honking noise jerked his gaze skyward. A majestic V of Canadian geese was passing overhead. The birds were fighting a headwind that wobbled their formation but never stopped their progress. Like all wild things, they knew what was coming and when to leave.

He watched them disappear south then looked back through the trees at the RV. The tarp hung limp over the door and the dirt on the steps was scuffed with his boot prints. He was making a mental note to wipe them away when a micro realignment of color caught his eye. He sank into a crouch and drew down on a lush strip of alfalfa about thirty meters away.

The yearling mule deer was reddish brown with vertical spikes. Its head and body were locked on something to Hazim's right. He looked for the threat because he didn't know mule deer possess a 310-degree view of the world. Hazim was the threat and the buck was watching his every move with panoramic ease. Then the deer rotated its head and looked straight into the man's eyes.

The animal's stare beguiled him like a child in a zoo. He lowered his weapon and the movement sent the buck bounding away in spring-loaded leaps. He watched it out of sight then glassed the western approaches to the RV. He was adjusting the focus on the Zeiss binos when he saw brain matter on the ocular. It was a memento from the past so he didn't bother to wipe it away. A remnant of the incident that had steered him all the way to Colorado. The gore was real but not in the now.

He checked the date on his watch and blinked in amazement. Today was October 5. Exactly one year later. The Koran says there is no coincidence but it does mention omens. Bad ones don't exist because they become excuses but good omens abound. And there was no mistaking this one.

Then, without prelude, he was face-down in a shell crater with bullets whipping overhead. Such craters were plentiful in the Homs Province of Syria, where he was fighting with a mélange of jihadists one year ago. Next to him was a semi-decapitated Russian soldier who had peeked over the crater's rim once too often. Hazim put a round above his ear then joined the corpse seeking shelter from the next barrage. The dead man belonged to the Wagner Group. The Kremlin's thug mercenaries. The man's skull was wrecked like a dropped egg but the superb binoculars around his neck were unscathed. Hazim was liberating the optics when he saw something jammed under the Russian's ballistic vest. Size of a loaf of bread and wrapped in heavy cloth. He tugged it free.

Inside the cloth was a filthy metallic object about twenty centimeters high and covered with knobby inscriptions. He dumped water over the mystery, wiped it clean and stared in stupefied silence. It was a chalice composed of exquisitely wrought silver and gold. A cross was embossed on one side of the bowl. A saintlike figure on the other. Greek inscriptions coated the rim. Emeralds and rubies winked in the smoky light of burning vehicles. It was looted treasure. The ancient booty of modern combat. Then Hazim's time travel was interrupted by the hum of the satphone in his coat.

He sent the all-good response and hurried back to the Winnebago watching winter weather slide over the plateau. He'd fought in snow before and hated it. He unlocked the dead bolt, pushed the door open and stopped in astonishment. Jamie's hood lay on the empty mattress. Bloody fingernails gleamed in a shaft of sunlight. The D-ring anchoring his captive was gone, torn from the fiberboard wall. He lunged for the rectangular hole above the sink that was admitting the light.

The plywood was clawed out. Then he saw it all in a flash. She'd used her legs to rip the D-ring free. Slid the cuffs under her butt, removed the hood and ripped out the window with her newly useful hands. He ran outside. Saw trampled brush and flecks of blood heading east. The road. He cut through the ravine they crossed on the way in, raised the binos and focused on the dirt track. At first there was nothing because the magnification compressed minor dips in elevation. Then Jamie's head popped up a kilometer away. Then her body. She was leaping forward six feet at a time. A standing long jump to freedom. He speed-limped after her, bad knee grinding bone, chasing down a shackled woman in broad daylight. A scenario so egregious it was laughable.

Jamie heard oncoming boots and waited until they were right on top of her. Then rotated her hips and whipped her arms around with all the rage and torque she could muster. Her double backhand nailed Hazim flush on the forehead. The impact broke her left wrist and sent her tumbling. She rolled to her feet and kept going. Screaming for help at the top of her lungs.

Hazim saw the silvery flash of handcuffs then a bolt of red then nothing. He woke up lying on his side, perpendicular to the world. Jamie was bounding away in a tunnel of light. He lurched to his feet and stumbled after her, going low this time, diving into her knees. She whipsawed backward, whacking her head on the hard-packed earth. He rolled to his feet and watched her eyes flutter. She was out cold. Then the jeopardy of the situation pierced his concussed brain. He slung Jamie over his shoulder, grabbed the binos and lumbered for the RV, weaving like a drunk.

He was almost to the cover of the ravine when a pulse of blue-white light came off a hill to the east. A tick of sun bouncing off the objective lens of a scope. The hill was almost a mile away but given the quality of modern optics, the visual equivalent was akin to being across the street. Hazim didn't see the flash because Jamie's body was blocking that quadrant of his vision. But whoever was perched on that rise, their face mashed to that eyepiece, saw all they needed to see.

SEVENTEEN

The anemic sun was nearly gone when Vanessa told Mace to find a spot with long-range views. They were on the western flank of a narrowing valley cut by forested chutes and the noisy North Fork of Cottonwood Creek. The cold was building and the snow was beginning to stick. They'd traveled five miles, half the distance to the trophy hole from where they left the truck.

Mace spotted a small gouge high on the sandstone fin of the ridge and bushwhacked toward it with the couple in tow. When he clawed through the last line of oak and rimrock he found himself on a level bench and could see for miles. Then he looked down and stood stock-still. Flaked lithic debris littered the surface. He knew immediately what he was looking at. Archaic hunters used this perch to spot prey and enemies and rework weapons for time immemorial. Now his hunter clients were continuing that tradition with a twist. They had no enemies and their prey was human.

Clay and Vanessa set their packs on the loamy ground and broke out warmer gear, oblivious to the scatter of hand-hewn stone. Clay sent a text and got Hazim's all-good reply in a matter of seconds. Then the couple began glassing terrain in every direction like Mace wasn't there. Except he knew damn well he never left the corner of their eyes. Like two mule deer with firearms.

Mace donned a hooded anorak and snow gloves and ate the elk jerky they let him bring along while studying the ground. Nothing recharged his soul like the handiwork of meat hunters gone to dust. And his soul was running on fumes. He followed the debris fan to a bristlecone pine on the end of the bench. Based on its girth, he reckoned men were hunched in its shade, eyes peeled when Christ gave the Sermon on the Mount. Beyond the pine was an overhang the size of a big doghouse.

He bent down and took a knee. The outcrop was the crown of a modest rock shelter drifted roof-high with sandy ocher soil. A virgin archeological nook biding its eternal time. He removed his right glove and gently probed the top layer of soil with his fingers. A minute later he'd unearthed two beautiful side-notched obsidian points with busted tips that either missed prey or hit bone.

"Hey, great white hunter," said Vanessa. "How high you think Stoddard'll go in the morning?"

He left the points in their dirt crypt and looked at her. "Not over nine-five if this front unloads."

"He won't wait it out in camp?"

Mace shook his head. "Not on opening day. His job is filling tags, snow or no snow."

"What's the upside?"

"Snow leaves tracks," said Mace, casually returning to his little dig. "And muffles sound."

"So we can get closer," said Vanessa.

"In theory."

"What's the downside?" she asked.

"The animals get spooky," said Mace. "And the air pressure gets funky."

This fired up Clay's onboard thesaurus. "Funky as in odiferous or eccentric or what?"

"Big temperature gradients inside storms up here. They can bump a round. Ruin a shot."

Vanessa gave him a skeptical look then took out a Kestrel 5700 ballistic computer the size of a remote and deftly worked the pad with her thumbs. Thirty seconds later she had a firing solution under existing conditions at five hundred yards. The results intrigued her. Barely. Then she looked at Mace.

"Thanks for density-altitude tip. We'll true our dope extra careful when the time comes."

Mace squinted at the gold standard of weather-integrated shooting gadgets. It was excellent technology but a crutch in his book. "You shoot in junky conditions at high altitude much?"

She put the device away and looked at him. "How hard could it be if you made a living at it."

Clay snickered and they fell into hushed conversation while Mace pushed his right hand deeper into the soil, ruining ages of archeological context before touching a polished oblong object. He got a grip and put the dimensions at five inches by three. His palm brushed the business end of the tool and it laid him open like a scalpel. So sharp it barely stung. He knew exactly what he had.

"What'd you find?" asked Vanessa, missing nothing.

Mace turned, right hand hidden and bleeding into the earth. They were both staring at him. He tugged the glove over his injured hand before he stood up. Then crossed the dozen steps to his customers, left hand extended. Lying in his palm were the two obsidian points.

"What'd I tell ya?" said Clay. "Arrowhead man's at it again."

He snagged the points off Mace's hand one at a time, studied them briefly and threw them in the snowy dirt. Then he reached into his parka, retrieved the green jasper arrowhead missing from Mace's house and held it up between thumb and forefinger. A foot from Mace's nose.

"Those are nice. But this one is still my favorite."

Mace stared at the pilfered jewel of his collection, sucker punched by the obvious. Of course they were in his fucking home. Drugging his dog. Stealing his wife. Taking souvenirs. His legs started quivering. He couldn't breathe. Shit, he could barely see. Then something touched his open palm. He looked down at the little bottle of Tito's, not knowing or caring how it got there.

"How far to their sunrise position?" asked Vanessa.

Mace unscrewed the top and drank his dose. The liquid burned down through his panic attack, flowered in his gut and set him right as rain. "Depends on where they drop into the drainage."

"How far to where we can observe that?" she asked.

Mace looked off, calibrating distance and feeling the shapely weight of the tool lurking up the right sleeve of his anorak. "Six miles maybe. If we stay in the lee of this ridge."

Vanessa nodded and moved out. Clay tossed Mace his pack, waited while he shrugged it on and fell in behind him. In seconds they were blobs leaning into a white deluge. A minute later they were gone altogether along with the light. Then the spirits and the elements went to work. Gleefully covering the lithic workshop and the empty plastic vodka bottle for another thousand years.

EIGHTEEN

Glenn stood at the foot of his squared-away bed in his prefab home on the dark side of Ouray on Seventh Avenue, nothing but boxers swaddling his jumbo girth. A radio scanner and his service weapon were on the nightstand. On the bureau was a neat stack of Louis L'Amour novels and a framed photo of twin girls who looked to be around five. Their resemblance to the axe-murdered twins in *The Shining* was unfortunate. Glenn was staring at two scoped bolt-action rifles lying side by side on top of the bed's comforter, brow furrowed in rumination. It was 8 p.m. on Friday.

The older weapon was a Mossberg Patriot with a black synthetic stock, a hand-me-down he'd hunted with forever. The other was a Savage Ultralite with a lovely blue-black finish that looked fresh from the box. Glenn had bought the Savage from a stranger in Nevada ten days ago. They connected on Armslist.com, the never-closed Walmart of anonymous classified gun ads.

Seeing the sexy Savage alongside the scruffy Mossberg made Glenn feel vaguely disloyal. Then he reminded himself the Savage was a long overdue upgrade and a life-was-short admission rolled into one. After putting the Mossberg in the bedroom closet and setting a box of 180-grain soft points next to the Savage, he went down the hall. Past Frederick Remington prints depicting cowpokes punching cattle and Kiowas putting arrows into buffalo. Then he pushed the bathroom door open. Vince was standing next to the tub facing the man. His ears were up, body rigid, an untouched plate of cut-up elk steak at his feet. The floor was completely covered with newspaper.

"Sorry to keep you cooped up in here but my yard isn't fenced," said Glenn apologetically.

Vince marched past him to the front door and looked back as in enough was enough. Glenn watched him thinking his tidy crib wasn't so lonely-guy desolate with a dog around. A woman's touch was nonexistent because he'd burned all bridges, including impregnating a fellow officer. She quit the force and moved to Denver without revealing the name or gender of the child. Unfazed, he moved his mate search down to Montrose and joined a large Methodist church. There he knocked up a Bible Belt type with twins, got married and then divorced before the girls hit preschool. Now that catastrophe dined on his paycheck like a permanent swarm of locusts.

"Here's the situation," he said to the dog. "Jamie's at her mom's being sick and Mace is out doing the dumbest thing you ever heard of. And since I have no idea how you got out and ended up hitchhiking, I don't feel comfortable taking you home. So you're with me for the duration."

Vince didn't budge so Glenn back went into the bedroom and fussed with the Savage. He'd already zeroed the gun in at two hundred yards and found its carbon-fiber lightness exhilarating. He was admiring the rifle when Vince appeared in the doorway, ears flat, shoulders hunched, giving a vivid impression of the damage he could inflict on a person wearing only cotton underwear.

"Might as well eat your dinner and get some rest," said Glenn. "You're gonna need it."

Vince doubled down on the glare and lowered his head. Glenn loaded the rifle and swung the barrel toward the animal, actually getting a bit nervous. Then he burst out laughing, threw the gun on the bed and scratched the shepherd's neck because he'd known the damn dog all its life. Vince tolerated the affection but didn't wag his tail or take his eyes off the man's face for a second.

"You need to stop staring at me like that," said Glenn.

NINETEEN

Hazim was standing on the north side of the Winnebago, rifle cradled, ears ringing from Jamie's backhand. This wasn't his first concussion so he wasn't too concerned. The others were all blast related. This one being inflicted by a pretty American doctor with her bare knuckles was almost funny. Except for the part where she almost escaped. He pulled on NVGs and the countryside popped into lime-green focus. It was midnight on Friday and the snow was downy soft but steady.

He circled south and studied the rise where he had seen the two men on ATVs. It was placid as a painting until a wild dog appeared in the foreground moving left to right. Hazim thought it was the same canine he'd seen carrying the rabbit in its mouth. Then the animal's exquisite nose detected the man standing eighty meters away in pitch dark and pirouetted instantly into nothing.

Hazim admired the animal's stealth. Then felt a fleeting comradery. Two beings alone in the world, fending for themselves. Then a freezing wind thrashed through the trees and he saw the future. Jamie would be reported missing and the cowboy cops would jump in their helos and SUVs and scour the earth like Satan's hounds. When the kidnapper was found to be a Muslim their joy would be uncontainable and he would be martyred in a burst of gunfire. And that was fine as long as the Monster was already dead because justice was the backbone of creation. The fact that nobody would mourn his passing gnawed at his heart but that ache was no different than breathing.

He reached into his parka, retrieved a laminated color photo the size of a playing card and held it near his face. The night vision's monochrome concentration of light caused the features of the girl in the picture to ripple with life. Her smile brightened and she became an angel in a dream. Then the photo trembled and tears crawled from under the technology strapped over his eyes.

Jamie lay sideways on the mattress, head hooded and hands cuffed behind her. Her feet were shackled with a tow chain running to the hole in the wall where the D-ring used to be. From there it wrapped around an aluminum joist and through a combo lock. The plywood on the window over the sink was back in place and reinforced with liberally nailed two-by-fours. There would be no more jailbreaks. She heard boots mount the steps and stop. She squirmed into a sitting position, jaw clamped against the pain jetting from her busted wrist. Then she emptied her mind and waited.

Hazim pushed inside, shut the door, dropped his gear on the table and studied his prisoner. Her plight disgusted him, clouding his mind with more doubt. He turned away, reminding himself that fortitude was the bridge to victory and checked his watch. He'd missed evening prayers. He took off his jacket, washed his face and arms and spread his rug aft of the driver's seat. He knew the RV faced southeast. Close enough for Mecca. Then began his supplications in a firm voice.

The Arabic washed over Jamie as a death sentence. She even knew the time of her execution. Mace would have the couple dialed in on Will's client no different than a nice bull. The dawn of opening day would arrive and they'd shoot who they came to shoot. Then kill Mace and call the guy praying in Arabic and he'd put a bullet in her head. She thought about how she and Mace put off having kids. Waiting seemed so sensible. Waiting for what now completely escaped her.

Hazim finished his prayer and stared at Jamie. She was perfectly still. Head erect. Other than being married to a useful man, she was immaterial to his quest. That truth clawed at his gut and he hated the two assassins he'd hired. They killed strangers for money. They were different than the Monster but no better. May they rot in hell along with their endless rules. Then he went over to Jamie, yanked the canvas hood off her head and stepped back. "That was stupid," he said.

Jamie gaped at his face, memorizing it all over again. She had seen his crewcut blondness during her failed escape but the Muslim prayer was next-level stereotype smashing. "What was?"

"Trying to get away. You could have got your husband killed."

"You mean my husband who's gonna be fucking dead in about six hours anyway? What would you have done? Sit around like a good little hostage and wait to get beheaded?"

He glanced at the prayer rug. Face flushing with anger. "I am Muslim so I must cut off heads?"

"Why not? You came all the way to Colorado to murder some hunter."

Hazim's voice rose sharply. "I am not a murderer. I am a soldier fighting in the name of Allah. I kill those who killed my family and friends. And those who would kill me. No one else."

Jamie looked around the RV. Her crypt to be. "In what wet dream do Mace and I not die?"

"I did not come here to hurt you!"

"But you already did. And you're not even close to done."

Hazim shut his eyes asking for strength. Didn't work. Then the metallic whine of ATV engines sawed through the RV's hull before veering toward the cottonwoods and abruptly quitting.

Hazim yanked his parka on, grabbed his night-vision goggles and rifle and slipped out. Jamie heard the dead bolt thud and pictured the surrounding terrain. They were not in good elk habitat. Mule deer for sure but not elk. And plenty of fools enjoyed bagging deer at night. Jacklighting was illegal as hell but easy to get away with. Then the satphone on the table vibrated with a fresh text.

Hazim crouched behind the RV's steps, scoped the cottonwoods and everything around them. Saw nothing and moved low and silent into the grove despite his bum knee. He put his back against a huge trunk where he could see 180 degrees and stayed inside its silhouette. Then raised his rifle to high ready wishing it was a Kalashnikov. After a bit he glanced up. The snow was steadier now. Hard little flakes spitting down from darkly radiant clouds. When his eyes came back to earth he saw a flicker of movement thirty paces away. A hand. It was tweaking a scope on a rifle.

The man attached to the hand was prone, aiming directly away from Hazim at the open ground beyond the grove. Hazim raised his scope to see what the guy was targeting and saw the beautiful canine he'd been commiserating with. The animal was curled up under a canopy of sage about two hundred meters away, eyes shut, blissfully unaware it was about to be shot for sheer entertainment.

The man on the ground had just started his squeeze when a rifle bore pressed into his skull.

"Are you going to eat that dog?" whispered Hazim.

"Hell no," said the man, twisting his head around to look at Hazim. "I look Chinese to you?"

"Then why shoot it?"

"Because it's a goddamn coyote. Open season year-round on the bastards."

Hazim punched the rifle barrel deeper into his head. "Not tonight."

Then a second man's voice came out of the pitch dark to his left. "Lose the gun, friend."

Hazim didn't move but his eyes cut over. Saw nothing but a black tangle of undergrowth.

"I'm locked on your chest, dumb fuck," said the second man. "And getting kinda bored."

Hazim dropped his weapon and a figure appeared, bolt-action Browning shouldered and steady.

"Nice night for it," said the second man as he closed the distance. "Whatever it is you're doing."

The first man jumped up and put his Ruger carbine on Hazim while his hunting buddy covered the stranger from the other side. They owned a muffler shop in Montrose and shared a passion for shooting inedible creatures to fill the gaping holes in their souls. They wore buffs and watch caps and GoPros. They were of medium height and solid in stature. Definitely the ATV riders.

"Actually," said Hazim, "I was stargazing."

"In a fucking snowstorm?" asked the first man. "And ready to blow my head off for shooting a four-legged cockroach?"

Hazim shrugged amiably. "It reminded me of a Malinois I used to own."

The first man poked his rifle into Hazim's gut thinking he was being pimped. "Hell is that?"

"It's a damn dog," said the second man, eyes nailed on Hazim. "Take off those fucking NVGs."

Hazim dropped the goggles in the grass and studied his opponents. They weren't military or law enforcement but they definitely knew how to handle a weapon. And they were getting nervous.

The first man squinted at the stranger with the odd accent. "Where you from? Mars?"

"Belgium," said Hazim. Then he indicated the Winnebago. "I'm renting that trailer."

Both men glanced at the abandoned RV then reset on the oddly confident foreigner who didn't seem to mind rifles aimed at his chest and head. Indignity and confusion gave way to alarm. Their shooting grips tightened and they inched backward in tandem but not quite far enough.

"Since when?" said the second man.

"Since last week," said Hazim. "I'm on holiday."

"So you're renting that shitcan from Wade Gruner?" said the first man. "Is that right?"

"That's right," said Hazim. "Did it online. Never met Wade in person."

"Probably because Wade's been dead going on five years."

"Three-packs-a-day cancer," added the second man. "Ask me how we know that."

"How do you know that?" said Hazim, enjoying himself now.

"Because I'm his nephew and the guy with the other gun aimed at your lying ass is my cousin."

Hazim let his arms drop to his side and lowered his head slightly. "My condolences."

Then came a moment of hyper stillness. The big blond guy was all wrong and the ATV riders knew in their hearts they should kill him now because there was something insanely dangerous about him. But being slayers of furry animals not hardened warfighters, they made two mistakes. Hesitating to do what their instincts were screaming to do and standing too close to the stranger.

Hazim lunged right, bum knee no match for muscle memory, crushing the cousin's throat with his elbow. Then he batted the nephew's rifle aside as it discharged, drove a boot into his chest and fell on top of him, mashing the gun into his throat. The nephew pulled a knife and slashed at his attacker's face and arms without effect before suffocating in mid-gurgle. Hazim got to his feet, heard something and spun around, Beretta up. The cousin was on his back, madly bicycling for air and making a hacking sound. Then he died with the same startled expression as his relative.

Hazim pulverized their cells and GoPros then thoroughly covered their guns and bodies with brush and rocks. After that he unlocked the

Silverado's toolbox, grabbed Jamie's red trauma case, limped back to the RV and pushed inside.

Jamie hadn't moved. She jerked her head at the satphone. "That thing's been going off."

He saw three texts, sent the all-copacetic code, stripped off his parka and layers, threw them on the floor and examined his arms. Both had deep cuts running from elbow to wrist. A couple were deep enough to see muscle and bled copiously. He went to the sink, poured water over the lacerations then popped the trauma case, dug out gauze and staunched the bleeding.

"I heard a shot," said Jamie.

Hazim didn't respond, too busy tending his wounds.

Jamie noted the cuts on his forehead. Some very near his eyes. "Who did that?"

"Doesn't matter. They're gone."

She frowned. "They cut you up and just left?"

He shot her a look. Eyes dilated with hand-to-hand adrenaline. "What do you think?"

Jamie got his drift and recoiled. Hazim doused both arms with anti-septic and grabbed clamps and sutures with curved needles. Then sat on the floor and set his left arm on his knee, caught the needle, punched it through the flaps of the worst cut, knotted the suture and bit off the excess. He did this repeatedly until the gash was snug then closed the deepest cuts on his right arm the same way. After that he dabbed antiseptic on his facial cuts and taped them over by feel.

Jamie missed none of this. "You've had some practice."

He looked at her. Saw her face was pale with pain. "What hurts?"

"Think I broke my wrist on your skull."

He uncuffed her hands, washed the blood off her fingertips where she mangled the nails tearing out the plywood and smeared them with Neosporin. Then got a SAM splint from the kit and carefully molded it around her purple and bulbous left wrist.

"You have a hard head," she murmured.

"And you're a very violent doctor."

He gave her Tylenol and water and gently cuffed her hands behind her back. Then he pulled his parka back on, slung the rifle over his shoulder and left. Jamie was staring at the bloody EMS trash scattered across the floor when something else caught her eye. It was lying against the mattress. She twisted her torso, bent over backward and eventually snagged the thing with her fingertips.

Hazim made a big slow loop around the grove. Found both ATVs, ran them into the thicket of understory and covered them with limbs. He was walking back to the Winnebago when he passed through a pocket of warm air and something softly touched his face. He turned but there was nothing near him. He tried to nurture the sensation without success. Then reached into his parka and found his vest pocket empty. He retraced his steps at a run as far as the dead men and their machines, flashlight cupped to contain the glare. But the laminated photo he kept near his heart was gone. The weight of the loss was instant and unbearable.

Jamie set the photo on the mattress and studied the woman in the picture. She had lush raven hair and slanting brown eyes. Her smile was teasing and wise. She was in her mid-teens but already breathtakingly beautiful. The back side of the color snap had a date scrawled in ink: DECEMBER 6, 1991. When Jamie heard boots on the steps she twisted sideways, grabbed the photo and hid it behind her back. Then Hazim burst in, dropped to his knees and began frantically searching the floor where he had thrown off his parka. Jamie sat silently on the mattress watching her kidnapper melt down because his angst was too satisfying to interrupt right away. Only when he gave up in abject despondence did Jamie twist around so he could see what was in her cuffed hands.

"Looking for this?" she asked.

TWENTY

The man was around forty and remarkably serene. His dark eyes followed a bulldozer blading the earth around him smooth as shag carpet but only his eyes because he was buried to his chin. His high forehead and strong jaw were classic Balkan. The collar of his blue jacket was visible under muddy brown hair. Red leaked from his nose and mouth. Clothed human appendages sprouted in every direction. The clanking treads came closer with every pass like a combine at harvest time.

A much younger version of the man calling himself Petrovic stood on the rim of the mass grave. He wore spotless fatigues and the green-and-gold commander's cap of the Bosnian-Serb Army. A pearl-handled Walther P99 rode his hip. He'd just supervised the placement of a single round into the occipital lobes of several dozen fighting-age Muslim males and watched their bodies rolled into the pit. Except the man in the blue jacket was only paralyzed by his bullet. The Monster was initially annoyed by the oversight and but now deeply grateful for the exquisite private theater.

The doomed man's eyes found the spiffy officer spectating from the verge of hell and they had a moment of mutual fascination. Then the man's lips began to move as if to speak. The Monster waved the machine to a stop and strolled over because in his experience last words were always diverting. But all the poorly executed fellow did was hawk gory mucus onto his executioner's shined-to-death boots. The Monster stepped back and applauded the man's flair. Then motioned the bulldozer forward and watched a wall of dirt and ten tons of steel squash the head from view.

The Monster tried to wipe off the rosy gunk with a handkerchief but the harder he scrubbed the faster it spread. Over his boot tops and up his legs like gooey tentacles. It reached his waist, mushroomed over the insignias on his chest and wrapped around his neck with strangling power. Then pulled him down into the earth until he was cheek to cheek with the man he just suffocated.

The Monster lurched off his cot inside his insulated Swedish hunting tent, gasping for oxygen like a large pale fish dumped onto a dock. The same pearl-handled pistol lay on his nightstand alongside a copy of the Koran, the bible of his enemy. He was used to nightly visits by a rotating pack of revenants but this trip down memory lane felt different. He dressed quickly and checked his Patek Philippe Nautilus. It was 3:40 a.m. on Saturday. The first day of rifle season had arrived.

Ten yards away, Will stared at the bowed roof of his tent and felt the compressed stillness of heavy snow. Petrovic was drunk when he woke his guide at midnight to praise the gods for ideal tracking conditions. A gross simplification that Will didn't bother to correct. He watched his client stumble back to his tent, half hoping the man would trip and be frozen stiff come dawn. When the odor of bacon penetrated his ruminations, Will pulled on Gore-Tex overalls, waded over to the chuck tent and pushed inside. Jimmy was clanging pans and spatulas over a four-burner propane range. Pancakes, eggs and hash browns were piled high on steaming platters.

"Fuck the snow and fuck all the global-warming cocksuckers," said the cook.

Will nodded amiably, got coffee, sat at the table and chewed an Aleve. The Monster entered a minute later. He wore camo snow gear and his eyes were slit and mean like a prematurely roused bear. He sat opposite his guide and Jimmy brought him a piping-hot mug with obsequious speed.

"How'd you sleep?" asked Will.

"I haven't slept since Clinton was president," said the Monster.

Will waited for him to make light of the statement. Then watched him pour brandy into his java with a rock-steady hand and realized it was the casual and absolute truth. "What about pills?"

"They eat pills like candy."

"'They'?"

The Monster waved a dismissive hand. "Creatures from the past courtesy of sleep deprivation."

Will sipped his coffee and studied his client. "Heard you put away some bad people who knew how to carry a grudge."

The Monster shrugged. "A man who doesn't adore revenge doesn't know how to live or screw."

Will leaned back thinking this shit was borderline mental but he'd swallowed the hook and there was no getting off. "That why you brought soldiers with assault rifles on a hunting trip?"

"Former soldiers," corrected the Monster.

"Because you're worried these people will come after you."

"If I were them, I would hunt me to the ends of the earth."

After a queasy stretch of silence, Will changed the subject. "This weather's gonna make the animals jumpy. They don't like not being able to see what's coming. They'll probably hold in timber until there's a break."

"So we work at close range?"

"No. We wait for a clean shot. We don't have a clean shot we don't shoot."

"And who decides what is a clean shot?"

"You're talking to him," said Will.

The Monster raised his mug and downed it. "So much for American democracy."

Then Luka and Marko entered and piled their plates high with food. Stefan came in last, grabbed coffee and sat next to Will. All of them wore the same camo parkas and pants.

"I forgot my skis," said Stefan.

Will didn't smile. He was looking at the mercs. "I need you to translate something for them so there's no misunderstanding."

"My pleasure," said Stefan before airily repeating that phrase in French, German and Italian.

Will got to his feet and tapped his mug with a spoon until he had all the eyes. "I'm running this hunt. That means nobody chambers a round or takes a shot until I say so. Everybody clear on that?"

Stefan spoke in Serbian. Marko and Luka glanced at the Monster expecting a countermand but their leader was silent so they went back to shoveling down food. The air got thicker.

"Tell 'em we leave in thirty minutes," said Will. "And all rifles ride unloaded in the bed."

Stefan told them. Luka stared at Will and muttered something in Serbian. Marko laughed.

Will looked at Stefan. "What'd he say?"

"Something about asexual reproduction at an advanced age."

"As in go fuck yourself old man," said Will.

"Loosely," replied Stefan.

Will stopped at the gun hands' table on his way out of the tent. "Either of you got something to say to me, say it in English next time."

"Why?" asked Marko. "You writing a book?"

Will grinned. "Turns out I am. It's called *Meeting Ignorant Assholes from Faraway Places*. I'll autograph you a copy when it comes out."

Half an hour later, the red F-350 was churning into darkness. The Monster had the front passenger seat, Stefan and the mercs were in back and all rifles were in the bed. They hit Government Springs Road and cut west toward Old Highway 90. Will checked the rearview and saw everybody in the back seat texting like teenagers. Then he turned north on the same BLM road he took on his scout.

When they got to the trailhead, a blue Cummins Dodge 3500 was sitting there. A large grizzled man and his two twentysomething sons stood by the Dodge with scoped rifles cradled. They wore felt cowboy hats, wool scarfs, muddy anoraks and high winter boots. They looked homegrown to the killing ground. A white Jeep Grand Cherokee sat empty ten yards from their truck.

The Monster started to dismount but Stefan put a hand on his shoulder and stopped him.

"Do you know these men?" he asked Will.

"Known 'em since the flood. That's Charlie Gustafson and his boys. They ranch south of here and don't give a shit who you guys are as long as you stay off their ground."

"What flood?"

"The one Noah rode out in his yacht."

"Of course," said Stefan. Then he pointed at the white Cherokee. "And who owns that vehicle?"

Will squinted at the Jeep. "No idea. Those are Denver plates."

Then he told his clients to sit tight, walked over to the ranch clan and shook hands all around.

"Got yourself a busload of customers," said Charlie Gustafson, eyeing the men in the red pickup as they eyed him right back. "They know they need to get out of that rig to fill their tags?"

"Probably scared of you survivalist types," said Will.

Charlie's sons laughed. Then Luka and Marko dismounted the red F-350, popped the bed's hardtop, removed their Mausers and glared at the armed locals. The Gustafson boys read the energy and caressed the safeties on their rifles with their thumbs.

"They look like interesting people," deadpanned Charlie.

Will followed his gaze. "That's one way to put it. You see who came in that white Jeep?"

"Nope. Here when we got here."

"Well good luck."

Charlie stared at the two mercs another second. "You too."

Will watched Charlie and his brood move quickly and quietly into cover and disappear.

"You must know everybody in this beautiful place," said the Monster.

Will turned. His client was right behind him, loading his Weatherby and taking in the scenery.

"Pretty much," said Will, grabbing his pack and the lever-action Model 94 Winchester out of the bed. After stuffing shells into the rifle he snagged the keys from the ignition and shut the door.

Stefan pointed at the venerable Winchester with the worn leather sling. Had a buttstock shell holder carrying six 150-grain Remington 30-30 cartridges in addition to the six in the tube.

"When was that made?" he asked.

"Nineteen fifty-nine. Belonged to my dad."

"Are you going to hunt with us?"

"Nope."

"Then why bring it?"

"Habit," said Will.

Then he went around to the bed and unlocked the steel toolbox nestled against the cab. "Every cell phone and two-way gets locked in that box until we get back."

Stefan smiled but not in a good way. "Why in the world would we do that?"

"Devices distract people and spook animals and I don't allow them on my hunts. Period."

"And what if someone gets hurt? How do we summon help?"

Will pulled out a black and yellow ResQLink locator beacon. Size of a stocky smartphone with a spring-loaded antenna. "We get in trouble, people come running. Helicopters and all."

Nobody moved until the Monster spoke up. "Do as he says. Let the chef cook."

Stefan and the mercs dug Garmin two-way radios from their coats and put them in the box with their phones. The Monster spread his hands indicating he was clean of devices. Will locked his own cell in the box and pulled on his dayglow cap and vest. Then handed four more sets to his guests. Luka and Marko stared at the vivid orange gear that would make them insanely easy targets.

"All about hunter safety," said Will. "Nobody goes without it."

The boss donned his hunter safety gear without a word and his men followed suit. After that, Will tossed a canvas bag at the mercs' feet. It landed with a heavy metal clank.

Marko ran a hand through his hair with a surly expression. "What is this?"

"Bone saw, rib-spreader and shears," said Will. "We don't waste meat up here."

With that he headed up the trail. Stefan and the Monster fell in behind him.

The mercs watched them disappear around the first bend, in no rush because they couldn't conceive of assassins lurking in the frozen, air-starved landscape. After that, Marko took his time strapping the field kit onto Luka's pack. Then both stood silent, captivated by the vertical panorama of the earth's crust rammed skyward and chiseled into mountains. Their insignificance was jarring.

Then the sensation of being watched by a gargantuan sentience leached into their heads. The geology itself became slyly alert and predatory. A Creation-size crocodile submerged under miles of rock, waiting patiently for prey to wander near its maw. Then both men chambered rounds in the same breath and ran after their meal ticket, drifts parting around their legs with a reptilian hiss.

TWENTY-ONE

Mace was breaking trail on the western flank of the drainage where Will had said he would hunt when he started picturing the shot. He was stalking a man not an elk but the drill was the same if not easier in some respects. A trophy bull was a brick shithouse. A round had to be placed just right to knock it down. A human was a flimsy sack of organs. One high-caliber hit above the waist would ruin a person's day forever. The shock alone was usually lethal. They might crawl some but they weren't gonna run for half a mile like a belly shot rack. It was 5 a.m. on Saturday.

The trick would be spotting the bull first then guessing where Will would position his client for the shot. Once that trigonometry was done, the couple's long-range murder would be on autopilot. Mace looked up, grading the snow pummeling his face. The dump was still in its busy prime. There wouldn't be any first light. Just a pasty leaden glow. Clay was right behind him and Vanessa had the rear. Then Mace saw it. A steady yellow shimmer three hundred yards to his right down by the stream.

He kept moving, eyes front because he didn't want to believe what it had to be. He side-eyed the flicker again and saw a modest fire tucked in thick alder. Then nearly tripped over a foot-high block of pink salt. It was licked smooth and surrounded by deer and elk tracks. He turned toward his minders, about to point out the problem but both already had their binos up glassing the flames.

"Fuck me," sighed Clay.

Mace got his Leicas up and saw four gutted elk hung head down from tripods made of aspen saplings. A horse pawed the ground beyond the flames. "We need to keep moving," he whispered.

"Too late."

"Why?"

Clay jerked a thumb at Vanessa. She'd set her rifle aside and dropped into a crouch.

"Dead animals," he said. "They do it every time."

Mace moved toward him. "I promise you whoever is sitting around that fire is way armed."

Clay put his silenced Glock on Mace. "Roger that. Now shut up and take a knee."

Mace did as ordered. Vanessa dropped her pack, palmed a combat knife from her right boot and glided catlike down the slope toward the light. Clay watched her go with a wistful smile.

"Long-ass story, bro. But this is kinda how we met."

The poacher vaping by the fire wore a bloody hooded parka and grew up in Nucla just to the west. He was thirty-seven years old with matted black hair, sunken eyes and sharp cheekbones. He had a malnourished quality, not unlike a thousand tintypes of Confederate soldiers. His brains were weed and crank fried but he excelled at killing animals and didn't believe in laws or seasons. Blew his feral mind when a pretty young woman strolled out of the icy dark with a nice smile on her lips.

"I must be goddamn dreaming," he mumbled, jaw hung and not moving.

Vanessa stopped three steps from the guy, not worried about the bolt-action rifle across his knees because she was way too fast to worry. "Did you enjoy shooting those lovely creatures?"

The poacher's name was Terry. He looked at the hung meat then back at the woman. "What?"

Vanessa exhaled. Sliding closer. Picturing the blade hidden behind her right hand flashing through firelight and severing his throat so fast the creep barely felt it. The image was so deeply pleasing it tunneled her superb tactical awareness just enough. The knife was off her hip, sweeping toward thin skin and arteries when she registered two more horses in the gloom. And saddles. Then a white mass T-boned her sideways so hard she was out cold before she hit the snow.

Terry and his pal Norris and the latter's sibling Cobb rolled Vanessa onto her back. Terry slapped her face but her eyes stayed shut. The brothers were red-bearded, sumo-size lugs holding scoped crossbows and wearing gore-splashed white overalls. Each bow held a razor-head bolt and a terrifying load of energy cocked in abeyance. The bolts were aimed at Vanessa's nose.

Cobb, the one who clobbered her, caressed her jawline then ran his hand under her parka and over her breasts imagining her buck naked in the tent. "Tell you what. There is a God after all."

"Shut up," said Terry, rifle at high ready, scanning the night with quick swivels. There was a level quality to his voice. A seasoned tracker's patient focus. "She was huntin' trouble."

Norris shrugged. "Meth heads love trouble. Hell's bells, why look a gift horse in the mouth?"

"That's no tweaker," said Terry. "She snuck up on me all calm. Real cocky."

"Okay," said Norris. "Shrooms then. Or acid. Lotta good acid floating around these days."

Terry shook his head. "No way. This bitch was dying to open me up for a reason."

Cobb kicked Vanessa's boot. "How 'bout it lady? You high or psycho or what? Spit it out."

Vanessa slitted her eyes and scanned the three men before locking on Terry because his rifle was aimed squarely at her chest and he was hyper-alert. The two fat ones were just staring, lips parted. Their crossbows were already drifting off target away from her face.

"Where am I?" she asked, shaking her head and moving her right hand toward her torso.

"Step on her arms," snapped Terry.

The brothers stomped on her elbows. Terry knelt down, unzipped her parka and reared back.

"Fuck did I tell you morons?"

Then he lifted the Glock 9 from its nylon web holster and held it up. The dull black weapon looked venomous in the flickering light. The brothers gaped. Then someone coughed. Twice.

Cobb and Norris gave little jerks then blood ran from their noses and Cobb shot a bolt through his left foot up to the fletching. Both were brain-dead on their feet. Terry was still processing their frozen expressions when Vanessa snatched her pistol back and shot him twice in the face.

All three poachers were sprawled in the snow when Mace walked into the glow of the fire. Clay stepped from behind him, sidearm extended. Then pulled Vanessa to her feet, brushed a lock of hair from her face and kissed her on the forehead. "Can we put a pin in the PETA stuff for now?"

She stared at the corpses, wishing there was time to eviscerate them just like the elk. "I guess."

Clay motioned at Mace. "Bro. Gimme a hand with the trash will ya?"

They tossed the dead down a timbered gully draining into the creek. Mace squinted at their final resting place thinking critters would have their way and by June they'd be rags and bone. And unless he pulled some immaculate miracle out of his ass with professional killers two steps away and more than happy to waste him so would he. Vanessa saw his brow-knit machinations, jammed a bottle of water into his hands and watched him pound it while recalculating his best-by date.

"Why bother with these guys?" asked Mace.

"Too many coward-piece-of-shit sportsmen in the world and not enough wild animals."

He looked at her, thrown. "Wait a sec. You're after Will's client because he's a hunter?"

For a moment she couldn't tell if he was kidding or further gone than she thought. "Get a grip. We're running a business here. Someone wants that guy dead for some old war stuff."

"What war?" asked Mace.

She looked at Clay, delicious grin spreading over her face. "Hear that, honeybun? He wants to know in what war the guy we're gonna waste did the shit we're gonna waste him for."

Clay grimaced like he was doing a math problem. "Wasn't it the Peloponnesian War?"

"Wait what?" said Vanessa. "Thought it was the War of the Roses."

"That or the Trojan War," said Clay.

"Or maybe the Hundred Years' War."

Clay snapped his fingers. "Now I remember. It was the French and Indian War."

Done riffing on Mace's ignorant civilian reasoning, Vanessa slapped him twice. One full-bore blow per cheek. Her version of a wake-up call. She let his eyes stop spinning before speaking.

"Fuck difference does it make what war it was? One's as good as the next. Just do your job."

Mace looked down. Her hand was out. A white tablet lay in her palm. "What is that?"

"Nalmefene. Blocks opioid receptors. Reduces booze cravings. Keeps your wife alive."

Mace ate it then stood there stiff and quivering. "Got any weed?".

She produced a professionally rolled joint with a magician's finesse. Fired it up, took a solid hit herself and stuck the wet end between his lips. "Got whatever keeps you operational."

After ingesting enough skunk to clobber a moose, Mace got a bearing off his compass and headed north at a steady stride. Clay fell in behind him humming "The Star-Spangled Banner." Vanessa hung back, studying her guide's gait and carriage closely. Crossed her mind Mace was faking being so diminished. Hard to tell with so much practice. She slipped her Glock from its crib under her parka and held it against her thigh like a pacifier, reminding herself that familiarity breeds contempt. And hand speed like Mace's could get you killed. After that she holstered the pistol and moved out.

TWENTY-TWO

azim sat at the table holding the photo of the girl with both hands, satphone at his elbow. Snow ticked off the RV's skin. Jamie was asleep, stuck in a dream where Vince was licking an empty bowl with a cracked and swollen tongue. The shrill vibration of the phone woke her. She looked at Hazim. His million-mile stare stayed on the pic. Like it was a fire and he was freezing.

"Hey," she said, sitting up. "You got a message."

He glanced at the screen, thumbed the correct reply and went back to the picture.

She checked the gaps in the wood over the windows. Still pitch-dark out. "Who's the girl?"

Hazim knew what she was doing. Trying to connect and put off the inevitable. Make it harder to put a bullet in her head even if he had no choice. "Doesn't matter."

"That's horseshit. And you wouldn't even have that picture if it wasn't for me."

He set the photo down and looked at her. Her resilience made him feel old. He reconsidered the gag or sedatives or both. "No matter what I tell you or you tell me, the end will be the same."

"You mean the end where you kill me?"

The lie crawled from his mouth and they both knew it. "That is not set in stone."

"Great," said Jamie. "So what's the harm in chatting until it is?"

Hazim briefly shut his eyes. His prisoner was right. "The girl is my little sister."

"What happened to her?"

"She died in Bosnia," he said. Being a connoisseur of geopolitical illiteracy, he gave her time to draw a blank before filling it in. "Across the Adriatic from Italy. Between Croatia and Serbia."

"Died how?"

Jamie's question was no different than flicking a switch.

Hazim tumbled into darkness landing on his knees in the same brooding forest where he saw his father running for his life. Now the trees were bare and a dusky sky spit rain. The girl in the photo dangled from the limb of a colossal beech tree on a thin white rope that used to be a clothesline. Her arms hung limp at her side and her long black dress twirled modestly in the breeze.

She wore a red knit sweater with big pockets. Her feet were bare and bluish. Hazim looked up at the corpse, AK-47 in his hands, filthy combat fatigues clinging to his eighteen-year-old frame. He was too gaunt and ravaged to cry even as he cut the rope and cradled her body. After laying her on the ground he noticed the small hardback volume sticking from her sweater pocket. He opened it and saw a lined diary with a chewed ballpoint pen lodged in the binding. The book overflowed with his sister's meticulous handwriting. He fanned the pages and read the last entry. It was dated two days previous. Same day he heard from his cousins that she'd been missing for a week. Same day he set out to search the secret wooded places only he and she knew from childhood. The impulse was irrational but prescient and all too late. She'd already decided what she could not live with.

"She was raped," said Hazim. "Every day. For days and days. She was sixteen."

The statement took Jamie's breath away. "And then that person killed her?"

"No," said Hazim. "That person let her go when he got bored. Then she hung herself."

There it is, thought Jamie. Grief that stays hot and poisonous forever. "When was this?"

Hazim down looked at the photo. "November. Nineteen ninety-two."

Something pinged but barely. Long before her time. "There was a war or something over there."

Hazim smiled because the understatement was so rich. "Or something."

"And that's why you're here? To get this guy?"

"Yes."

She shook her head, exasperated by her shit luck. "Why wait so fucking long?"

"God had other plans for me."

Then Jamie made the big leap. Saw the whole point of the madness. "Will's client killed her."

"The Monster killed as many of us as he could. It was his calling."

That designation threw her. The medieval feel of it. "Why come all the way to Colorado?"

"He thinks he's safe here. And I couldn't afford it until recently."

"Meaning what?"

"I found a chalice," said Hazim. "A Byzantine chalice. Late sixth century. On a Russian pig."

Jamie missed the import entirely. "So what?"

"A dealer in London gave me five hundred thousand pounds for it. I gave most of that to some open-minded Serbs I used to drink with. They specialize in killing people anywhere in the world. And they don't care what god the customer prays to."

"So they found the couple."

Hazim shrugged. "They outsource."

"Why not do it yourself?"

Hazim scratched his stubble. "I got too damaged and too old."

"How come no one else has gone after this guy?"

"Many have. From up close and far away."

"So he's lucky," said Jamie.

"There is no such thing as luck. He is fortunate to be alive because Allah has preordained it."

"What if Allah preordains his health right through rifle season? Then what?"

"Then so be it," said Hazim. "Allah creates all our destinies down to the minute and the hour."

Despite the fear brimming through her body, Jamie found that soothing. "Tell me your name."

He got up, went to the door and pushed the tarp aside the width of his hand. The sky was milky black. Snow drizzled straight down in the stillness. Three inches coated the ground. "Hazim."

Jamie frowned. Didn't fit his Slavic face. Her preconceptions dashed again. "Hey, Hazim."

He turned, struck by his given name coming from her mouth. Sounded unnervingly normal.

"Were you always this religious?" she asked.

The question caught him by surprise. He'd burned the old version of himself. "No. But when people you've known all your life decide to kill you for being a Muslim that becomes all you are."

Jamie looked down at her shackles. "And knocking off two Americans who were little kids when some bad shit happened in a place they never heard of is just the way the cookie crumbles."

Hazim had never heard that phrase but he could visualize it. A brittle world coming apart. Huge burning chunks falling where they may. The chaos of war as pastry with bodies mixed in like raisins. "Ajna," he said softly. Like it was the antidote to everything and too precious to waste.

"What?" said Jamie. Not quite catching it.

"My sister's name was Ajna."

TWENTY-THREE

Glenn stood on the porch of his home in Ouray drinking coffee in the darkness and wearing dayglow orange over winter camo. His silver 2007 Dodge Ram idled in the driveway, windshield brushed clean of snow. Up and down the street hunters were loading their gear into vehicles with primordial concentration because opening day did that to people. Like they'd just hopscotched over Bering Sea ice floes, ditched their mammoth skin for North Face and their spears for firearms.

He waved at a passing truck full of guys he knew and clocked the sky. The storm wasn't anywhere near done. He went inside, rinsed his mug and grabbed a length of rope tied to a choke chain off the kitchen counter and knocked on the bathroom door. "Rise and shine," he said.

When he pushed it open Vince was standing as far away as possible. The dog's eyes went straight to the rope. The plate of elk steak was licked clean. "How 'bout a walk?"

Glenn led the shepherd out to the truck and put him in the back seat, which was covered by a plastic tarp. Then he set his pack and new rifle up front and hopped in. He wasn't a dog person but he was an anthropomorphist who dabbled in psylocibin. He believed shooting wild animals was part of a cosmic bartering scheme the animals fully embraced, preventing them from suffering pain when being killed. His decision to take Vince on his hunt wasn't nearly as nutty. He was watching over his friend's beloved pooch during a family emergency. Gave him a Good Samaritan buzz.

He drove north out of town on Highway 550, caught a red light outside Ridgway and had time to think about opening days gone by. Succumbing to melancholy, he punched a number on his cell and drove on, following the down-cutting Uncompahgre River on his left. Rang four times before Mace answered. He sounded winded. His phone was on speaker, picking up boots on snow.

"What's shaking, officer?"

"About to go fill my tag," said Glenn. "Just making sure you weren't curled up in a ball beside the trail like a glazed donut because the snow feels so warm and cuddly."

"Okay by me. My guests are pain-in-the-ass triathletes. Gonna kill me just keeping up."

"Heard from Jamie?"

"Not a peep," said Mace. "Holed up at her mom's far as I know."

"She's not answering her phone."

"Would you?"

"Probably not," said Glenn. "Anyway, Vince got out."

Mace's brain, lungs and everything else stopped. Like a plug was pulled. "When?"

"Yesterday. He's fine but something weird happened."

"You mean after he got out?"

"Yea. Near as I can tell he got picked up by some college kids out on the road up by your place. Just dumb luck I saw him joyriding in the back of their rig. You leave him locked in the house?"

"Sure thought I did," said Mace.

"Well buddy, I think dicking around with tourists and Jamie taking a powder tripped you out."

"Maybe. What'd you do with my dog?"

"He's in the back seat. Gonna leave him in the truck while I hunt. No more Houdini shit."

There was a stretch of scratchy silence before Mace spoke. "Where you hunting?"

"West of Colona around McKenzie Butte. Where're you?"

"Working our way up Shavano Creek," lied Mace. "Lotta alder and willow. Good bull parking."

Glenn watched flakes slanting through his high beams. "Hell's going on, partner?" he said quietly.

Mace held his breath again. "What do you mean?"

"You babysitting tree huggers on opening day and me chauffeuring your dog around."

"Definitely strange times."

"Tear in the fabric of the universe if you ask me."

"You gonna get all weepy?" asked Mace.

"Not till I get my meat."

"Good. Save me some chops."

"You got it," said Glenn, killing the call. Then he checked the rearview. The shepherd's eyes gleamed like wet rocks directly behind his head. "Lighten up."

Vanessa was in front of Mace. Clay was ten paces behind him. Mace gave his phone back. She stared at him, wind playing with her hair. Tickled by the chaos theory churning in their wake. Because she could do anything she pleased. Make him stand on his head naked and piss in his own face. He was the hemophiliac in the razor store. Any false move was fatal. Then she unzipped her coat to stow the cell and Mace ripped her pistol from its holster and spun her around in a blur.

By the time Clay got his sidearm up, Mace had Vanessa's Glock rammed into her right ear and his arm locked around her neck. The accelerated reality of Mace's quickness left all three stunned and frozen by their new predicament. Archly posed figures in a vault of whipping snow.

Vanessa knew Clay was focused solely on the kill shot so she kept her head erect and her shoulders squared to shield Mace as much as possible. And give herself time to lay out all the options before there were brains splashed on the snow and she was short one highly irascible but gifted guide.

"Anybody mind if I toss out a few scenarios?" she said.

Nobody answered so she let fly.

"Number one. You kill me. Clay kills you. And mystery man kills Jamie. Number two. You kill Clay. Then you and I do the death match thing for my gun. And mystery man kills Jamie. Number three, which is more certainty than scenario, Clay puts a slug in your cranium and clips your motor skills in mid-squeeze. And mystery man kills Jamie. See the through line in all this?"

Mace processed that keeping his head tucked behind Vanessa's and watching the concise weave of Clay's pistol as it tracked his noggin for the cleanest shot. Mace couldn't find the tiniest crack in her reasoning. Even the highly unlikely best-case scenario left him alive and everyone else dead. He eased the Glock out of Vanessa's ear and stuck it out butt-first in front of her. She took the gun and walked over to Clay without a backward glance and held up Mace's cell phone.

"Obliterate this."

Clay took it, sidearm locked and steady on Mace. "What about mountain man?"

Vanessa turned. Surveyed Mace standing there head hung like a bull-whipped mutt then checked her watch. "Two minutes. Don't get carried away. And leave his eyes and legs alone."

"Roger that," said Clay. Then he moved toward Mace with an expectant leer.

TWENTY-FOUR

Glenn turned east off the highway onto county gravel with barbwire on both sides and pulled over. He grabbed a hammer off the floor and got out. After checking for traffic, he lowered the tailgate, set his cell on the steel and smashed it to pieces along with the SIM card. Then he tossed the debris in the ditch and kept driving. Few miles on, the elevation was lower and the snowfall lighter. When the wire fell away into public land, he put the Ram in four-wheel low and eased off the road in a northerly direction. After negotiating a stretch of boulders and gullies, he reached a derelict fence line and killed his lights. He set a bowl down in the back, filled it with water and motioned at the tarp covering everything. "You gotta go, you gotta go," he said to the dog. "Don't sweat it."

Then he grabbed his rifle and pack and was pushing the front door open when Vince arced over the seat like a splashless ten-point dive and hit the ground running. Glenn lunged for the rope, landed on his face and got nothing but a fine view of the shepherd's ass hightailing into darkness.

He screamed the dog's name a few times then got up wiping muddy snow off his hands and cursing himself. Shoulda tranked the son of a bitch and left him locked in the bathroom. After waiting a minute to see if the dog had second thoughts, he shouldered his gear and walked north. He tried shrugging off the slipup as minor but couldn't because he was an omen enthusiast. Vince started out as a beautiful gift but now he wasn't so sure because the animal saw right through him.

After striding through low hills for an hour, Glenn reached a line of juniper and willow marking a seasonal spring that petered out to the west. He followed the riverine fold in the ground in that direction until he reached the base of a smooth rise. There he reconnoitered for tracks, head bent to the ground in the dark making sure no other hunters had the same idea. Nothing worse than slapping on a fake smile to work out opening-day etiquette with trigger-happy armed strangers.

Finding nothing but pristine white, he scooted up to the crest. There he unlimbered his rifle and got prone amid clumps of grass and sage ideal for disrupting silhouettes. He didn't need to check his watch. In an hour or so the sun would rise behind him providing a skybox view downrange. The terrain and everything in it would be lit in great detail. There'd be no excuse for anything less than a one-shot kill. None whatsoever. The dog wasn't really his problem anymore.

TWENTY-FIVE

Mace broke trail into the upper reaches of the valley Will had warned him to stay out of using a sturdy six-foot tree limb as a cane. His stride was labored as if he'd abruptly aged. If he had to guess, he'd suffered a fractured rib and maybe a ruptured disc. Icicles of blood hung from his nose. Clay and Vanessa were right behind him, vigilant as cats. Their rifles were assembled, neoprene scope covers in place. The drainage itself was a V-shaped slab of rough ground topped by a monolithic granite dome with a near vertical face. Snow was coming down in fat undulating waves.

"What's the long-ass story?" asked Mace in a regular voice because the dump muffled sound.

Clay glanced back at Vanessa. "Babe. You good with me telling him how we met?"

She didn't answer right away. Like she might say no. "Why not."

"So we're employed abroad in a completely different milieu," said Clay. "Think Dune without all the metaphors. We're taking fire and call in some iron but the strike goes long and hits this dinky farm. Turns the farmer family and their cows into jelly with hair. All except this one calf. His insides are liquified by the overpressure but outside he's still cute as a button. Vanessa shows up with another team and starts crying and cursing and I meander over to introduce myself, thinking she found some child turned to steak tartar because there were plenty of those lying around. But that wasn't it. She was bawling over that dead calf. Didn't give a damn about all the splattered people."

Mace shook his head. "Wow. A genuine Hallmark card moment."

Clay smiled. "Oh yea. I was irreversibly and irretrievably smitten. What about you and Jamie?"

"What about us?"

"How'd you two meet?"

Mace kept walking, mind grabbing for anything to block the answer to the question from cracking his heart and wrecking his wits. "Let's circle back to that when you're bleeding out."

Clay picked up the pace and leaned into his ear. "Whatever happened to civil discourse?"

Vanessa tapped Clay's shoulder and they swapped places. Mace listened to her bootsteps and pictured the ground ahead. Come dawn the bull would be on the western flank where the sun hit first. Will would be on the east rim glassing for his rack while the couple was glassing for their target. He wondered if they needed proof. Like DNA. In which case they would kill Will for sure.

"How far out are we?" asked Vanessa.

"Couple miles."

She checked her watch. "Sunrise in seventy-nine minutes."

Mace studied the flat-bottomed dark overhead. "And shooting light comes ten before that."

"Even this socked in?"

"Yep. Just no shadows so no depth perception."

She cocked her head. "Is this some psyops jerk-off about being perpendicular to the target?"

"Just doing what you brought me along for."

"Remind me again," said Vanessa.

"I've hunted this plateau in all kinds of nasty and seen every fuckup known to man. You think you're all squared away but you never worked this high on a junky day."

"That's some serious self-esteem for a guy who picks up garbage instead of going to prison."

Mace kept walking and talking. "You going for a head shot?"

"Why?"

"You might be shooting from way out. You miss or wound him and his bodyguards get wind of what's happening, they're gonna unload."

"So what?" said Vanessa.

"Lot of hunters up here now. Always some off-duty cops mixed in. They hear a shoot-out they'll come running. Or call it in."

Vanessa sighed before speaking. "Was that jarhead the first person you ever killed?"

"You could say that," said Mace.

"You could do a lot more than say it. You called the shot. Shit the bed and got him dead. So you've killed exactly one person your whole life. Accidentally."

"You're not wrong."

"So shut up and learn something. His operators won't unload unless they have a target. Which they won't. And the cabeza is overrated. You bagged that Marine with a random ricochet through the chest. We don't do random. But we do love the thoracic. Let shock and exsanguination do the work. But to answer your question. If I get a head shot inside six hundred, I will go for style points."

Mace was thinking the scary bitch was right on when a stupendous growl split the gloom and rose to a demented violin shriek that pinballed around the drainage. Vanessa and Clay jerked their rifles to high ready. Heads twisting in every direction. Dumbstruck by the power of the sound.

"Fuck is that?" said Clay.

"That's a bull elk in rut," said Mace. "Called bugling."

"Why is he doing that?"

"Wants to get laid. Letting his harem know he's coming in hot."

Another bull challenged the first with bellowing coughs and grunts. Then the coyotes joined in, beckoning the whole pack because where there were cows there were calves. Then the hunting and breeding cacophony subsided. Mace got out his Leicas and scoured the rim of the opposite slope. Saw a filmy glow in the sky to the east. A barely discernible blush was spreading over the world.

"What are you looking for?" said Vanessa.

"The forest service trail that tops that ridge. Will's gonna glass everything from up there to make sure his bull is holding. We need to spot the animal first. Then find a spot within range of where they'll likely shoot from before the sun clears that lip. Or Will is sure as hell gonna see us."

"Think one of those bulls we just heard was the one they're after?"

"Probably."

"How far away?"

Mace made a lackadaisical gesture toward the top of the watershed. "Hard to say really. Up in that black timber maybe. All this snow makes them nervous because it messes with sound."

"Black timber?" she said, squinting where he indicated.

"Trees so thick there's no light on a sunny day. Bull that big and smart might just stay there."

She processed his pointedly vague tone. "Say what you mean."

"Either I talk to Jamie right now or my services end here."

Clay leveled his rifle at Mace's tummy. "I'm super amenable to that."

Vanessa looked off then at Clay. Didn't say a word. He lowered the gun, took out his satphone, punched a button and put it on speaker. "Comm check," he said. "You feeling me, Lima-Charlie?"

"Yes," said Hazim in a sullen voice.

"Put her on," said Clay.

When the hooded hostage was on-screen against the black drop cloth, Clay passed the phone to Mace and he brought the screen even with his face. "So what's for breakfast where you're at?"

The hood shifted, getting a bead on the voice. "Eggs benedict and cappuccino with extra foam."

Mace smiled, blinking hard. "I definitely got the wrong end of the stick here."

"Oh yea," said Jamie, cuffs clinking. "I landed in the freaking Four Seasons."

"Listen. I love you. I love you and I'm sorry I was so blind about what I was doing to us."

"Shut up. I should never have left. Should've stuck with you."

"You are with me," said Mace, quickly wiping his eyes. "Hey. Remember how many times I said the scumbag factor in guiding couldn't get any worse?"

"Probably a few hundred."

"Well, turns out I was wrong."

Jamie was silent a few seconds. "I know they need you to help them hunt down a hunter."

Mace looked at Vanessa then back at the screen. "How do you know that?"

"What else would they need you of all people for? So just do what you do best, my love. Get it done and come home to me. No matter what. Okay?"

Mace stared at the screen. Jamie's hooded head was motionless, her mind melding into his. Her guts and calm spreading through him like liquid resolve. "You got it, darling. No matter what."

Then the call was cut and the device yanked from his hand.

Hazim put his satphone away and took the hood off Jamie's head. He expected to see tears but her face was dry. Her eyes were far away and so was she. *With her man*, thought Hazim, *on a frozen mountain doing a task that should be his.* The task he committed one sin after another to accomplish. Then he sat at the Formica table and reflected on countless days of desperate combat. He remembered precious few souls with Jamie's courage. He'd kidnapped a warrior. And a martyr.

Mace was still staring at his empty palm when a long-gone buzz swept over him. He could hear the intricate innards of the storm passing overhead. His skin and eyes were measuring wind speed and direction with digital clarity. Opening day was here. His day. Even if this one was his last.

Vanessa recognized a predator at ease with his fate. "Check out the rabid dog under still water."

"Yep," said Clay, backing up a little. Rifle tight on Mace. "Gone and got radicalized on us."

"Remind me not to pet him," said Vanessa.

Then both dug out hooded camo snow suits and took turns pulling them on while the other covered their beat-up guide. After that, Vanessa dug out a third suit and underarmed the garment into Mace's gut at highway speed. Screw biathlon, he thought. She had a Big Ten softball arm. He yanked it on and zipped it up. The material was smoky white and creamy to the touch. Engineered to melt silently into cover like gauzy mist. Ideal for slaying big-brained hominids on a blizzardy day.

"Let's hunt," said Mace.

TWENTY-SIX

Back home on the Danube at twenty-three hundred feet above sea level, the Monster rode his Peloton and lifted daily with his Austrian trainer and that regimen had sufficed. But the Uncompahgre Plateau pissed on dilettante conditioning with bone-cold air containing far less oxygen than he was used to. Hence his sloppy stride as he passed through ninety-five hundred feet with visions of a popping fire and shots of brandy. His guide was breaking trail and Stefan was at his heels. Luka and Marko brought up the rear, rifles at ready carry. They were taking turns walking backward and checking the sky. They'd dealt with drones before and seen their godlike lethality up close. It was 6:15 a.m. on Saturday.

Soon enough an icy rock escaped the Monster's gassed attention and jetted his boot sideways. He landed hard on hands and knees, smearing snow on his rifle. Stefan helped him to his feet and wiped the gun clean with a glove. Will watched this in silence and kept climbing, a strange unease filling his gut. He'd honchoed plenty of hunts with jackass clients but this felt different. Like he was out of his depth doing what he was put on earth to do. Turning back was becoming an irresistible idea. But he didn't know how. Then Stefan pulled even with him. He looked worried.

"Perhaps we could take a breather soon."

Will didn't slow down. "So the big chief back there doesn't pass out on his feet?"

Stefan glanced at the Monster huffing along tens steps back "And a fire if at all possible."

Will shot him a look. "You gotta be kidding me."

"With all due respect, Mr. Stoddard. It is his hunt."

"Read the fine print. His money. My hunt. I can put this circus back in the barn anytime I want."

Stefan savored another new idiom. "Back in the barn means go home, more or less."

Will kept slogging. Finally shook his head. Disgusted. "I got a spot up ahead oughta work."

Stefan gave the outfitter a grateful, exaggerated bow then conferred with his boss in Serbian. Luka and Marko didn't give a shit what the sanctimonious male secretary was sucking up to their boss about. They possessed an encyclopedic understanding of kinetic carnage and slogging up a white incline wearing orange was begging to be blown to bits. They had no idea the ground they walked on was once the bottom of a vast inland sea ruled by colossal carnivorous amphibians that made great whites look cuddly. But they knew ideal ambush terrain when they saw it.

Will was cussing the light edging across the sky when they reached a rock overhang that kept a few square yards of earth reliably dry. He set the Winchester aside, gathered twigs, set them alight and squatted to nurture the combustion. The mercs stayed on their feet, combing the forested slopes on all sides and muttering about the death-wish quality of their tactical situation.

Stefan moved away from the others, raised the Benelli and practiced sighting in on distant rocks of a certain stature while applying the training he received at an elite firearms academy in Poland. The training covered handgun and rifle accuracy and occurred on weekends over several months prior to the Colorado hunt. He kept his self-improvement regime a secret, hoping to surprise his boss and colleagues with his vastly improved marksmanship should the opportunity arise.

The Monster sat by the fire, Weatherby across his lap, eyes shut, heat baking into his face. Then something scratched his neck and a whiff of lavender hit his nose. His eyes shot open in alarm. It was the dark-haired beauty his men had found in a shell-blasted cellar in Kozarac. The one he briefly made his child war bride. She had never joined his traveling troop of executed cadavers because she wasn't executed, merely detained. When they brought him the lanky teen she was unscathed but fading like an orchid severed from light and water. He gave her a bar of lavender soap, made her bathe then took her at his leisure for nights on end. She was the flawless treat he looked forward to after a grueling day of cleansing bucolic hamlets. His special reward to himself.

But their assignations became increasingly lifeless so he finally shooed her out into the world he destroyed and forgot about her. He didn't even know she was dead until the visitations began months later. Fingernails dragging across his neck stinking of cheap soap. While eating. While putting bullets in heads. While desecrating other pretty Bosniak girls. But those visitations had ceased decades ago. Now dread entered his ruminations because he didn't believe in coincidence. Why would she return to taunt him in this place after all that time? A remote and wintry escarpment in North America on the hunt of a lifetime. He tried to remember her name but couldn't.

"Hey," said Will. "You requested a breather. Not a damn sleepover."

The Monster surveyed his guide sitting across the fire and wondered why he felt so comfortable with someone he hardly knew. "Do you believe in God?" he asked.

Will picked up a stick and poked at the flames. "I'm not in the habit of baring my soul to people I set eyes on day before yesterday, Mr. Petrovic."

"Please. Call me Dragan."

"What happened to David?"

"That's the anglicized version of my first name. For business. I was born Dragan."

"Dragan it is," said Will.

The Monster looked around. "But doesn't a landscape this exquisite argue for God's existence?"

Will stared at the snow-drenched forest and the distant wall of peaks. The storm was a painter's brush, turning the Sneffels Range into immense white serrations that blurred in the wind. "I'd say it's more of an open-and-shut case than an argument."

The Monster rubbed his hands vigorously over the flames. "And what about souls?"

Will marshaled his thoughts, amazed he was chatting around a fire instead of sneaking up on the goliath trophy he saw yesterday. The revelation had a dreamlike quality. Made him wonder if the son of a bitch hadn't hypnotized him. "Most of us have 'em. But it's up to us how we use 'em."

"And the rest?"

"They just don't come with one. Not even their fault. Trick is spotting 'em ahead of time."

"And then what?"

"Since killing 'em ain't quite legal, staying way the hell away is about all you can do."

The Monster nodded thoughtfully. "You must be very good at spotting them."

"Used to be," said Will. Then he got to his feet, shouldered his pack, grabbed his Winchester and looked down at the rifle lying across his client's lap. There were fat beads of condensation on the barrel and receiver due to its proximity to the fire. Crossed Will's mind to point this out but the thought passed. He didn't know why. "You want a shot at that rack it's now or never."

"Like everything else," said his client. "But first, nature calls."

The Monster waded around the overhang into ponderosa, dropped his pants as if to defecate and took a metal tube from his pocket. The kind that holds a fine cigar. He unscrewed the cap and removed a syringe with a needle guard. The plunger was drawn and the barrel full of clear liquid. He aspirated the syringe and injected himself in the right buttock. He wasn't diabetic. He was shooting up with his personal cocktail of speed, prednisone, testosterone and tramadol. Bodybuilders called it stacking. The Monster called it better big-game hunting with big pharma.

His bronchi dilated before his pants were up. He was gulping air laced with pine when a huge bird banked silently through the treetops, wings canted like sails. A red-and-brown hawk with a blazing white chest. He tracked the sacred messenger out of sight, gratitude filling his heart. The raptor was prophecy. A gauntlet thrown down at his feet. The bout of trepidation delivered by the malignant Bosniak girl was demolished. She was a harmless invention of his own mind. A carnival sideshow peddled by gypsy psychics. A figment. Nothing capable of interfering with his hunt.

Will was antsy about trophy hour but the fire was a narcotic against his legs. He was sorely tempted to sit back down then stopped himself and kicked snow over the flames. The wind was dead calm and the hissing white smoke piled straight up. The heat in the column of twirling particulate generated ice crystals as it penetrated ever colder air. Then the rising sun refracted off the ice producing a dazzling halo in shifting shades of silver and blue the size of a beach umbrella.

Stefan watched the blinding orb rise into the dawn with a fascinated expression. A voracious reader with a scientific bent, he correctly surmised that the phenomenon was hot smoke hitting frigid air.

Luka and Marko didn't have such cerebral hobbies. They were pure soldiers and thus slaves to superstition. They saw a dazzling harbinger of doom. Proof the alien world they'd invaded was dialing them in with merciless precision. Their jaws went slack with the same thought.

They were going to die in this place.

TWENTY-SEVEN

Running below the rim of the western flank of the watershed targeted by both hunting parties was a thicket of Gambel oak that had survived drought and fire for a century or more. A person could walk right up to the hedgerow of snowy branches and not discern the people within because winter camo made them invisible. All except the eyes. Three unblinking pairs staring due east.

Clay and Vanessa were ten yards apart and Mace was between them. The sun was below the horizon but a dull luster was oozing over the valley. Then a blazing nimbus breached the opposite ridgeline and halted on a dime, as if tethered to the ground. Three pairs of binoculars jerked up. The object glimmered through incandescent shades of yellow and red then vanished without a sound.

"That a flare or what?" asked Clay.

"Sun dog," said Mace. "Someone put out a campfire. Smoke freezes. Bends the light."

Clay peeked past Mace at Vanessa. "Man's a wellspring of rough-hewn knowledge."

She kept glassing the jagged outline of the crest. "So that's gotta be our guy on the other side."

Mace checked the time and tried to imagine why Will would stop and build a fire on a stalk on opening day. All he came up with was a client suffering hypoxia or hypothermia. Will might let him rest and warm up and still be coming instead of ditching the whole hunt. "Most likely."

Vanessa looked at him. "So it could be someone else?"

"Doubt it. Will believes his animal is in this drainage. So he's coming."

"What about more evolutionary dead ends like the three we disposed of earlier?"

Mace saw the poachers lying on their backs in the snow, soggy halos of blood spreading around their heads. "Pretty sure that species has been hunted out for now."

"Shame," said Vanessa. "They were a blast."

They stayed put in the thicket until a string of elk emerged from cover to the north and walked through gloom to a south-facing meadow where the dead grass was thicker. Mace glassed the animals until he was sure they were all cows, got to his feet and headed in that direction.

"Gotta stick with the ladies," he said over his shoulder.

After fifteen minutes of hugging cover and gaining elevation he stopped five hundred yards from the same meadow. His minders crouched on either side. The cows were pawing at forage, heads lazily scanning for trouble as they chewed. Heavy timber lined the far side of the clearing.

"How come no bulls?" whispered Vanessa.

"They hang back at dawn," said Mace. "Let the females transition first."

"Define *transition*."

"The ground between where they bed down and where they feed."

"Why let the girls go first?" she asked.

"Survival math. See if any of them get shot."

She thought on that a sec. "You saying the bulls know when elk season starts?"

Mace kept glassing the cover beyond the cows for the rack in charge. "Why wouldn't they? The weather changes and the shooting starts. Big-ass bulls don't get that way by accident. They know gunfire is all wrong and their nervous systems adjust accordingly. Learn quick or die."

Vanessa nodded, thinking he could be talking about the man they were hunting. He was a wily, sought-after trophy. The analogy gave her a decisive high she associated with microdosing acid. Then the crack of a rifle echoed up the drainage from the south. Seconds later another gun decided not to wait for legal light and pulled the trigger off to the west. She and Clay looked at Mace.

He graded the reports. Shook his head. "Too far away to push our bull out of his comfort zone."

Then he shifted his glass to the ridge opposite and focused on wild cards. Like Will and his guy dropping over the rim unseen and losing track of them until they took the shot. And the sun dog. If Will was building fires he might let that merc team come right on up. Let them lay low on that rim with the sun at their backs and clean shots at everything. Dirt-nap time just like Clay said. Then he ditched the might and maybe and focused on what he knew to a certainty. If things went sideways, Clay would shoot him. If things went smooth, Clay would shoot him. Either way his value to these creeps was dissolving by the second. He lowered the glass and saw Vanessa reading him like a large-print book. Calmly. Like they were lying on a sunblasted beach.

"Lot to consider," she said.

Then something in her expression revealed a truth he'd been looking at for days but not seeing. Vanessa wasn't accounting for the depth of her transgressions. Not really. She was so accustomed to getting away with snuffing lives that the hazards associated had been neutered in her mind. Hence her faint fucking amusement at his doomed misery. Because when it came to slaying folks for money, she had never encountered anything but smooth sailing. Mace took careful note of this shortcoming because it was probably the only one she had. And his only chance. Then he got back on the glass trying to spot his old friend and help this smug bitch murder his client.

TWENTY-EIGHT

Will was breaking trail through shin-high snow toward the ridgeline he'd spotted his money bull from. Clouds were still charging overhead and the light was crap but the rate of accumulation had dropped. He wore glacier glasses under his orange cap. The philosophical rest stop had left him disoriented and sluggish. Never in his life had he gotten a hunt off to such a late start. The thud of distant rifles was now intermittent, never quite dying away and pissing him off further.

Nine seasons out of ten his clients were field dressing their kills before the sun got this dumbass high. And more often than not remarking on the beauty of the creature lying destroyed at their feet. Exalting in the sanctity of the so-called fair chase even if their euphoria was secretly tempered by shame and confusion over what they'd just done. Feelings they would quickly bury until next year.

Will could hear the four men strung out behind him on the steep and skinny trail but he had to listen close. They were watching where they stepped and nobody was sucking for air. Will wondered what the man now calling himself Dragan had done behind that rock to magically ramp up his conditioning but it didn't matter. All that mattered was filling his tag and going home.

He stopped a quarter mile below the ridgeline where the trail dropped into the next valley, the last place he saw the giant bull. He swiped snow off a flat rock, sat his butt down and took a long drink of water while Dragan and his retinue formed up around him expectantly.

Luka and Marko's eyes were hidden behind Oakleys but their body language was wired tight. Their Mausers were at ready carry, trigger fingers snagged around the guards as they scrutinized the terrain front and back with tight little head movements. Reminded Will of two Dobermans.

Stefan peeled off his Ray-Bans and moved closer to him. "How much farther?"

"Not far at all," said Will. "In fact, this is as far as you and your gun hands are going."

"Why?"

"Because that bull would hear us coming like a gravel truck. Be just me and Dragan from here."

The use of the Monster's actual given name startled Stefan. His boss was taking stupid chances left and right. "I have no problem staying here as long as Marko and Luka are able to observe."

"In case some of those people with long memories happen to be hiding in that next valley?"

"I know it may sound overly cautious but . . ."

"Doesn't matter how it sounds," said Will. "You three aren't coming."

Stefan looked at his boss and waited for this notion to be squashed. The Monster said something in Serbian that landed like a slap. The mercs snickered but kept their heads on swivels.

"So," said Will. "We're good?"

"Whatever Mr. Petrovic says is good," said Stefan, eyes averted.

"Okay then. Nobody wanders off and nobody builds another damn fire. Stay put even if you hear our shots. I'll come back over the ridge and give you a wave when we need you."

Stefan pointed up to where the game trail notched over the rim. "Right there, I assume?"

Will followed his arm and nodded. Then he looked back at the men he was leaving behind and realized every one of them was carrying a pistol under their coat. Didn't know how he knew that but did as surely as he was standing there. Wasn't jack to do about it now but make a suggestion.

"Another party shows up, say the next valley is private and being hunted and leave it at that."

"Where else would we leave it?" asked Stefan.

"Good question," said Will, slinging the Winchester over his shoulder and heading up the slope.

The Monster fell in behind him, his customized medley of narcotics shearing years off his gait.

Stefan watched them out of sight then heard a spattering sound at his heels. He jumped and turned. Saw yellow snow. Luka and Marko had their rifles in one hand, dicks in the other and matching malignant grins. Then they zipped up and practiced their English on the Oxford man.

"So Stefanie," said Marko, using the feminine form. "How was shooting school in Poland?"

Stefan knew his private life was under surveillance. But extracurricular firearms training was nothing sinister for an employee required to conceal carry on the job. "Excellent actually."

"Did you kill lots of paper targets that look like men but don't shoot back?" asked Luka.

"I did," said Stefan. "It was very instructive. I got rid of some bad habits."

Both mercs lit cigarettes and chuckled at this pussy boy nonsense. Being thirty-nine years old, never married and flitting between Belgrade and London cultural scenes on his days off, Stefan knew what was next. Ten seconds later, Marco blew smoke past yellow teeth with a withering expression.

"Tell the truth. Were you in Poland to shoot better or teach Polish boys how to load your pistol?"

Stefan smiled at their Cro-Magnon predictability. "Your English is really coming along."

"What'd you tell your man back there?" asked Will without breaking stride.

The Monster looked around. Intoxicated by the view. "This life is but a sport and a pastime."

Will recited that under his breath, taken by the elegance. "Real life begins when this one ends."

"That is exactly right."

"What's it from?"

"The Koran."

Will glanced back in mild Protestant alarm. "You're a Muslim?"

"Christian. But lately I mix and match. Both have very useful concepts."

Will thought on that. "Mixing religions that people kill each other over sounds kinda tricky."

"Not really," said the Monster. "Both worship one all-knowing deity. Both revere Noah, Abraham and Jesus. Both believe in Satan and heaven and the end of the world. And every few centuries, both swarm from their nests to massacre the other. Sounds like a perfect fit to me."

They slogged in silence a ways before Will spoke. "But sooner or later you gotta pick a team."

The Monster felt a surge of affection for his guide. This living breathing puritan artifact with his quaint rules about killing things put on earth to be killed. "I am my own team."

"Sounds like a one-man cult," said Will.

The Monster laughed and clapped him on the shoulder. "Best religion of all."

Will kept climbing and thinking the man tagging along behind him was a novel genus of primate. Something nurtured in twilight off to the side of the evolutionary tree. He was wrong of course. The Monster was an outlier but nothing particularly new. And even though Will killed fetching animals for a living, he was in fact obscenely sheltered from real darkness. Because truly malevolent creations didn't usually sign up for guided hunts on the Western Slope. If ever.

They scrambled up the last stretch of trail into the same stunted stand of juniper Will cut through on his scout. After they got tucked in, Will motioned the Monster to stay put and worked his way through branches to the fin of the ridge and glassed the drainage beyond. Saw a bunch of cow elk on the western side where the weak sun was already landing but no racks. Didn't mean the bull wasn't there but it gave him a nagging feeling he'd missed the boat. Then he reminded himself running late wasn't the end of the world and kept scouring the meadows opposite.

Back in the juniper the Monster was sitting on a rock, rifle across his lap. The dull light was dreamy in the lee of the trees. He was hydrating when he saw them. Dozens of scruffily attired people standing on a huge flat-topped boulder a kilometer to the north. Like a ghoulish sculpture garden. Normally the manifestations preferred to observe him at close range. Close enough to see their faces. Close enough to chat if either side of the abyss felt the urge. But today was different. They were hanging back. As if they wanted the hunt to proceed without any distraction or delay.

He raised the Weatherby, aimed at his eternal followers and got behind the scope. He swept their faces but the dark-haired Bosniak girl was not among them. Then something slithered through the trees at him from the left. He swung the rifle around and thumbed the safety off.

The brim of Will's cap was low and kept him from seeing the muzzle aimed at his forehead. Or the day would have ended then and there one way or another. The Monster cradled the rifle across his chest, barrel pointed at the sky. As if he hadn't been a squeeze away from decapitating his companion. Will crawled out of the trees and sat beside him, catching his breath before checking the cloud cover. The snow had dialed back to flurries but his nose told him that was just a tease.

"Did you see my world record?" asked his client.

"Nope. But I saw his harem. So more than likely he's still around."

The Monster took a swig off his flask and offered it to his guide. Will hesitated before pounding a good gulp and handing it back. He was wondering why he did that when the brandy warmed his gut and sanded down his worries. Then he led the crawl to the fin of the ridge where both men got flat and glassed the dozen cows feeding directly across the valley. A chunk of windy silence passed. Long enough that Will started chewing on plan B, as in backtracking and coming up the drainage from the south. Try to spot that smaller bull he saw yesterday. A consolation prize but better than getting skunked. His mind was drifting when the Monster sucked in his breath.

"Is that him?" he whispered. "Above the others. To the right."

Will adjusted his glass and felt a wave of awe. There it was. The enormously endowed animal he glimpsed not twenty-four hours ago, hugging the shadows beyond the cows. Even at two-thirds of a mile, the animal was a copper-brown goliath with a rack for the ages. He put the weight at near a thousand pounds and the reach of the bull's main beams at a freakish five feet. Its damn head reminded him of a quarter horse. The phrase world record flitted through his mind. He tried to dismiss it as magical thinking but the longer he looked the more he knew it was a Christ Almighty fact. The capstone of his career. Hell, any guide's career anywhere on the planet. He lowered the glass and studied the ground they had to cover absolutely unseen and unheard to have any chance whatsoever of success. Then he looked at his client. The Monster's eyes were bugged and he'd swapped his orange cap for a Soviet-style fur hat with flaps. Looked good. Like it was made for him.

"Gonna be a hard hump down to the shot. Don't talk. Stay in my tracks. And above all, do not kick anything loose. You're never gonna see a trophy like that again. And neither am I."

The Monster stared at him. Captivated by his certainty. "How can you know that?"

Will glassed the animal one more time. Saw the bull's singular size and perfection. Felt the oncoming day wheeling overhead, embossing the watershed with glossy light. How many times had he watched the same sublime spectacle and counted himself blessed beyond reason.

"Not sure," he said finally. "But I do."

Then he stowed his binoculars and slipped noiselessly over the lip of the ridge. His boots landed in a ravine on a narrow game trail he'd used innumerable times. He stayed in a crouch, leading loosely with his hands to deflect contact with the noisy brush crowding the path. The Monster followed at five paces. Mimicking his guide's every move except for regularly glancing over his shoulder to see if his eternal followers were tagging along. They were not and that pleased him. He wanted to kill the majestic beast in solitude. Unincumbered by the annoying debris of the past.

TWENTY-NINE

Off to the east, not far from the Adobe Hills and thirty-five hundred feet lower in elevation, Glenn was prone behind ice-caked bunch-grass, Savage snugged into his shoulder, forestock resting on his pack. His right eye was on the scope. Downrange was swirling nothing top to bottom because fog had rolled in after the snow eased up. A blunt white wall that reminded him of a curtain across a stage. He gulped a grape 5-Hour Energy and was admiring the rifle's blued finish when he heard a crack somewhere down the hill behind him. Minuscule and clean but clear as a bell in the freezing air. Just one then not a peep. A hoof or paw or boot finding a branch under a few inches of snow.

He got to his feet, slung the rifle over his shoulder and pulled his sidearm. Then he crept downhill following his own barely discernible tracks. When he reached the bottom he froze, pistol snapping up. Fresh sign paralleled his route to the base of the rise until abruptly reversing course out of sight. He moved closer and stared at the tracks. Wolves were long gone from Colorado. And they didn't make coyotes that big. The snaky drag line made by the rope leash was the clincher.

He looked around thinking Vince was trying to find him and gave up because scents aren't worth shit on fresh snow. He was tempted to yell for the dog but knew that was dumb as hell and out of the question. He studied the tracks again. Judging from the U-turn, the shepherd was headed back to the truck anyway. He was a smart animal all right. Little too smart for his own good. Ten to one he'd be posted up by the Ram shivering and grateful when his new best friend returned.

He briefly wondered if Mace and Jamie would ever forgive him if Vince never turned up. Mistaken for a coyote by idiot varmint hunters or clobbered by a semi crossing the highway toward home. Probably not. Then the fog tore away in ragged hunks and bright sun spilled over everything. Glenn speed-crawled back up the rise. Dropped behind the same cover, braced his rifle on his pack and watched the terrain beyond his perch unveil itself. Rising from fallow pasture was a grove of giant cottonwoods, a cluster of dilapidated wooden structures and a toppled windmill.

Parked amid the ruins was a mangy white Winnebago with a canvas tarp hung over the door.

THIRTY

Thirty-nine miles to the west, Mace watched the same gust of daylight flood the plateau and immediately glassed the ridge opposite. Took thirty seconds to spot what he feared most. A gash in the snow where something skidded down off the rim into brushy cover, disturbing the powder down to dirt and rock. He'd missed it before because the light was crummy and the shade too deep.

He bore down on the binos, saw a sign emerge from the bottom of a ravine and tweaked the focus. They were goddamn boot tracks. Two pair veering toward the creek before disappearing into the oak and juniper that ran all the way down. These weren't knucklehead trespassers. These were careful guns who knew what they were doing. He made himself breathe. No doubt in his mind now. Not a fucking shred. Will and his client had spotted the bull and were getting into position.

"See something?" whispered Clay, registering the hiccup in Mace's sweep.

Mace eyeballed Will's probable route down to a shooting perch on the far side of the creek for a flash of orange. Saw zip. Then the burst of sun was gone and the snow resumed. "Not sure."

He rose to his feet, put his back to a squat spruce to hide his silhouette and searched the high ground on his side of the drainage. Saw several clearings beyond the big meadow he hadn't seen before. Small pockets of open ground farther back in the timber. But he was too low to get a clean angle on them. He looked uphill. He needed another forty yards of elevation to see what Will saw.

"I gotta squirrel up there a ways," he said, pointing.

"Why?" asked Vanessa.

"Get eyes on the animal they're after."

She glanced at Clay. He shifted around and shouldered his rifle. Vanessa braced hers against a rock, palmed her sidearm and motioned Mace to move out. Clay watched them worm their way higher with his crosshairs nailed on Mace's back. When they found a spot with good cover and adequate angle they stopped and glassed the maze of openings north of the cows. After a minute, Vanessa lowered her binos and stared at Mace. He could feel her eyes but didn't blink.

"What'd you see on that rim to the east?" she asked.

"Saw where two people came over the ridge this morning."

"Will and our guy."

"Most likely."

Vanessa looked at the ground across the creek. Even in full light, it was clogged with trees and rocks and endless variegations of shade. Easy to never be seen. "So they're getting set right now."

"Yep," said Mace, focusing on a clearing half a mile away, slightly above them and to the left. It was screened by heavy timber but the Leicas weeded out the stray light and kept the resolution sharp. At first he thought he was looking at the desiccated limbs of a toppled fir, except they were too dark and tapered. Then they moved and he saw a colossal bull with a rack to match. The one-of-a-kind specimen the vast majority of elk hunters would never see much less get even a shitty shot at.

The animal scanned the terrain in every direction then disappeared into cover but not before Mace got a good look at the headgear. Based on that fleeting assay of point and beam length, mass and inside spread, he was certain he'd just seen a 450-point animal. At least. He reminded himself of the range at which he was air-judging but still, by any measure the bull was extraordinary.

"Fucking hell," he muttered. It was the golden ring of his former profession.

Vanessa clocked the bearing of his glass and shifted her binos. "How far out?"

"About eight hundred yards. Right side of that big dead fir back in the aspen."

She probed the timber. At first she couldn't see anything because of the contrast gain from luminous snow to arboreal gloom. Then something huge eased forward and became the tan flank and dark shoulders of a bull elk. Its rack dipped into a shaft of full sun unveiling superb symmetry.

"Holy shit," she muttered.

"More like the Holy Grail," said Mace.

Then he combed the ground across the creek at the base of the opposite ridge looking for where Will would set up. After a few sweeps he came back to an irregular chunk of flat ground. A bench no bigger than a driveway. Just above the creek and in the shadow of the towering dome. The feature acted like a catcher's mitt, snagging rocks eroding off the face. The debris lay in random knee-high piles encased in oak. If the bull kept grazing downhill at the same angle that bench of rocky brush would provide a perfect blind and a clean uphill shot. Call it five hundred yards at thirty degrees.

Vanessa still had eyes on the bull, mesmerized by its grace. How the antlers avoided contact with foliage as if they had eyes of their own. Then it was gone. "How old do you think he is?"

"Nine or ten. Winter coats get lighter with age."

"Takes that long to grow antlers that big?"

"Takes five or six months. He'll shed in March if he's not dead. Grow 'em back by August."

"Exactly the same?" she asked.

"Yea. Just bigger."

She thought about that. "Why not pick up his old antlers and let him live?"

Mace studied his gloved hands. They were dyed dark with the blood of many a fine and sentient creature murdered in their prime for a souvenir. And Vanessa's question was excellent. It cut to the heart of opening days everywhere and every species killed for no reason other than Homo sapiens' randomly determined perch on the food chain. "No brush with omnipotence," he said.

Vanessa heard her drug of choice plucked from thin air. Crossed her mind she married the wrong guy but only for a second. "Where would you kill him from, back in the day?"

Mace pointed downhill. "From that bench above the stream with the scree piles."

She glassed the spot picturing the target prone behind the low mounds of rock. Head and neck might be all she'll have to work with. "And where will we be?"

Mace made a chopping motion toward the spot where they last saw the bull. "Farther up this side. About two hundred feet above their position and five hundred yards from the guy you need to kill."

Vanessa broke off a branch of oak, stripped away the stems and leaves, handed it to Mace and pointed at the fresh snow overlaying the black rock they crouched on. "Show me," she said.

Mace drew a skeletal version of the valley and the location of all pertinent parties at the moment of truth. Then added arrows for bullet paths. The drawing resembled a crude, inverse blackboard.

Vanessa was absorbing the sketch when a distant shot echoed up the valley from the south. Then two more. She turned and studied the timbered ground in that direction. Mace followed her gaze visualizing rifle-toting men humping the public land they'd crossed the night before.

"That the unwashed masses?" she asked.

"Yep. Bunch of regular joes roaming around amped up and shooting at anything on four legs. But that's what you were counting on, right? Meat hunters camouflaging the professionals."

She looked at him through driving snow. She liked how he reminded her there was a good chance they'd run into more armed locals. And in turn, how they might need him to validate their harmless presence. Might. He never stopped running angles, even on the razor edge of the abyss.

"I'm gonna miss this," she said.

"What's that?"

"You biding your time. Grinding on ways to kill us."

Mace stared back. Serene. Nothing to add.

"Sure that's the bull your buddy is after?" she asked.

"Only thing I am sure of," said Mace.

She watched him scramble back down to Clay, weighing the moving parts. The horny bull was mobile. The weather was great for cover but a net negative on ballistics. And the target carried at least two high-quality marksmen whose current location was unknown. Still, even at five hundred yards it was a stationary plain vanilla shot. Fairly unfuckupable compared to Oswald's Dallas motorcade work. She waited until Mace was fully occupied glassing the ridge opposite and caught Clay's eye. Then drew a quick finger across her throat. Clay gave a tiny nod, pulled out his satphone and sent a text. There was no reason to postpone critical housekeeping any longer.

THIRTY-ONE

Hazim dozed in the Winnebago's driver's seat, satphone on his lap. Sunlight leaked through the plywood over the windshield and a riot of magpies and meadowlarks greeted the day. Then the phone vibrated, jerking him awake. He saw two banal words on the phone's screen. *CLEAN UP.* Astonished by this, he jumped to his feet and read them again. Meant dispose of Jamie and evac ASAP. He sent a text for confirmation. The reply was instantaneous. *RECIPIENT UNAVAILABLE.*

He called Vanessa's number then Clay's. Got the same synthetic voice describing both as no longer in service. He looked around the RV hoping it was a nightmare but it was real. His hostage was slumbering in a shackled ball with her hood off as before. He was wide awake and the test had come. The ultimate proof of his resolve. He grabbed his pistol off the table and stood over Jamie watching her sleep. He'd lost sight of how pretty she was. Now it was all he could see.

He raised his right arm until the Beretta itself mercifully obscured most of her face. Then aimed at her forehead until the gun became barbell heavy and dropped away. He wiped the sweat off his face and raised it with a two-handed grip, praying she would slip from this life to the next in a dream. When the sights got on target the gun bucked stubbornly as if electrified. Unnerved by the power of his doubt, he bore down on the two-and-a-half-pound weapon with all his strength. Pressed the muzzle into the bridge of her nose and started his trigger squeeze. Then Jamie opened her eyes.

She saw the Beretta's barrel against her skull and willed herself not to blink or look at her killer. She wanted to see the last millisecond for herself. The jump to nothing. Then came a moan. Low and horrible. Someone receiving news that left them wrecked and void of purpose. The pistol fell away and Hazim stood over her, face covered by one quivering hand. Like a huge mortified child.

"Forgive me," he whispered.

"You talking to me or God?" asked Jamie.

He took his hand away and looked down at her. "Both."

Then a high, unearthly shriek pierced the RV's hull. Hazim rushed to the door and shoved it halfway open with his boot, pistol up and ready. The tarp swayed gently in the breeze. The bird concert continued unabated. Jamie sat up. Eyes still locked on the weapon that nearly killed her. Then the cry came again. Shrill and eviscerating and rich with animal agony. The birds fell silent. The wind stopped. The stillness was deafening. Hazim looked at Jamie, totally baffled.

"That was a rabbit," she said.

"Why would a rabbit make that sound?"

"Just got killed. If it was a real one."

"Why wouldn't it be real?" he asked.

Jamie replayed the two shrieks in her head. "They don't usually take that long to die."

"So what was it?"

"Game call maybe. Makes a dying rabbit sound. Brings coyotes in close enough to shoot."

Hazim grabbed his rifle and started to leave, thinking it was more idiots on ATVs.

"I wouldn't do that," said Jamie.

He stopped, one foot out the door. "Why not?"

Jamie looked around. Saw snowy daylight cutting through the cracks in the boarded-over windows. Trophy hour had come and gone. Now she knew for sure. "They're not hunting coyotes."

Hazim stared at her. Some fundamental miscalculation whispering in his ear. "Then what?"

"Wake the fuck up," she snapped. "Whoever's out there bet you wouldn't know what that sound was. That you'd go out to see what's what. Then they shoot you and make extra sure you'd shot me. Because it doesn't matter if they got the Monster or not. That couple needs us both dead."

Her truth made him lightheaded. He looked at the tarp beyond the door. The shooter would have it locked in. He looked up. There was a roof hatch he might fit through. But he'd be a chunky target on a pedestal. He looked at the windows. Way too noisy and too exposed. Sitting tight was suicide. All they had to do was soak the hull with cans of gasoline like he had in his truck and cremate them in place. Or cut them down as they stumbled outside choking and burning.

"So what's the plan?" asked Jamie evenly.

Hazim didn't answer. Too busy studying the scummy gold carpeting on the floor. Then he paced in small circles, throwing his weight into every step until he located the RV's steel chassis beams. Didn't take long to find a spongy area. It was aft of the galley and across from the head. Looked just big enough for his shoulders. He dropped to his knees, pulled his combat knife and started hacking out the carpet in big jagged hunks and flinging them aside.

Glenn was much closer than he was on Friday afternoon when he watched Jamie hopping for her life in cuffs and shackles. All because the blond bastard named Hazim got sloppy. Not surprising with Jamie being so hot and smart at the same time. Probably wore his guard down. But the way he tackled her and slung her over his shoulder like a Hells Angel on his honeymoon didn't sit right. Who knows what nasty stuff he did to her in that RV and who could blame him. Christ. He might be having his way with her right now. Over easy. Sunny side up. The whole deal.

According to Clay, the guy with the enemy-combatant handle was one of the last people in the world to fuck with. A stone-cold mercenary burnout. Glenn backed off the scope, dropped Visine into both eyes and wondered how Clay knew that. He'd ask him tomorrow when they rendezvoused in Moab. Just before he shot the asshole dead along with his bossy but way-cute Mexican wife. Glenn had never killed anyone before but he had no choice so he wasn't worried about being up to it. Besides, he was about to bust that cherry big time in a matter of minutes.

He glanced at the Flextone predator call in his hand. Had a hard plastic mouthpiece and a soft rubber sound chamber. Looked like a miniature flute and Glenn was a maestro with it. He started to blow it a third time then stopped and tilted one ear toward the RV. There was some kinda noise coming from inside. Chopping maybe. Not with an axe but definitely with something metallic.

Whatever it was, no sense in overdoing the dying rabbit. He put the game call in his coat, got behind the scope and put the reticle back on the tarp hanging over the RV door. Then he waited for the foreign dude to come out dying of curiosity or looking to take a piss. He didn't care which as long as he came out blinded by the low sun coming from the same direction as the bullet.

THIRTY-TWO

M ace powered through sideways snow, aiming for a spruce covered promontory that looked down on the rocky bench across the creek where he believed Will's client would shoot from. The boot tracks dropping over the opposite ridge seemed headed for the bench but at this point it didn't matter. It had to be Will's shooting perch because he was all out of hunches and failure was fatal.

When he reached the steep ravine clogged with deadfall just below the point he stopped. Clay and Vanessa pulled up on either side of him. She indicated the outcrop Mace had in mind.

"That our spot up there?"

"That's it." said Mace.

She skidded into the ravine, clambered up the other side like a goat, dropped prone, crawled onto the overlook and glassed downrange. When she was satisfied with her field of fire she signaled Mace and Clay to come on. Then all three bellied up the lip of the point with Mace in the middle. Vanessa studied the bench across the creek with her naked eye then extended her left arm, made a fist and squinted over her raised thumb. Twice she rotated her fist down then back up so her thumb aligned with the bench. "I make it four hundred ninety-five yards at twenty degrees," she said.

Mace had seen plenty of shooters fisting inclines, a serviceable method when technology failed or was absent. But none with such unerring confidence. He put the Sig Sauer to his eye. The display settled on 501 yards at a nineteen-degree incline. The lady could dope a shot in her sleep. He turned the rangefinder her way so she could see for herself. "Losing your touch," he said dryly.

She noted the data, cleared the ground beneath her elbows, broke out the Kestrel and got her own trajectory validation. Then set the Remington's forestock on her pack and put her shoulder into the butt. After tweaking the optics she melded into the weapon. Right hand on the firing grip, left arm running under the stock so her left hand was resting on her right biceps. She got behind the scope and let her entire body settle into the ground. Her eyes became wide and placid. No different than a 150-pound cobra waiting for a warm-blooded meal to wander into striking distance.

Mace measured the erratic wind patting the side of his face. He guessed it was running up to twenty mph. He turned his head and watched flurries spill over the northern rim and corkscrew into the confines of the drainage. The uptick in velocity was appreciable. He wondered if the Venturi effect would register on the Kestrel where they were set up under the spruce. Then he side-eyed Vanessa and realized none of that esoteric ballistic crap mattered. Given the gnat's ass grouping she put up at the uranium mine, she could splash the first shot and put the second in the guy's ear without mussing his hair. As usual, all that really counted when it came to killing things far away in bad weather was good eyes, good nerves and a rifle you knew as well as yourself.

Then Clay scooted ten paces back from the lip, got to his feet and looked around for something serviceable for what came next. Mace twisted his head, watched him study the timber at the mouth of the ravine they crossed then thumb a text. After squinting at the screen, Clay put the phone away and looked at Mace like he knew he'd be watching and shot him a thumbs-up. There was a whiff of theater to the whole thing. Sent a chill through Mace's spine. Here we go, he thought.

"All good on the home front," whispered Clay, not moving from where he stood.

Then he raised his silenced Glock, put it on Mace and motioned him to come with.

Mace waded through drifts a few steps ahead of Clay willing his legs not to shake enough to notice. When they reached the trees at the top of the ravine, Clay pointed at a large aspen.

"Put your back against that and your arms behind it."

Mace complied. Clay zip-tied his hands and slapped gaffer's tape over his mouth. Mace felt a wave of irrational relief. Why bother with a gag and ties if they hadn't decided to keep him alive for the trek out. Then answered his own question. Unless that was their intention. To keep him hoping and behaving. Then Clay yanked a hood over his head and mashed the pistol into his skull.

"You know what the word *equanimity* means?" he asked.

Mace racked his vocabulary, found nothing and shook his head.

"Composure and evenness of temper in difficult situations."

Mace waited for more. Heard nothing but flakes bouncing off his hood so he nodded.

Clay caressed the bulge of his nose with the gun's muzzle. "I suggest you get some."

Then he walked around the tree twice, making sure there was nothing a man in Mace's situation might find useful lying nearby before scrambling back up to Vanessa. After dropping prone to her right, he glanced over his shoulder and confirmed he had an easy twenty-five-yard shot on their guide. Then broke out his spotting scope and got busy looking for their payday.

Mace let himself skid down the trunk until his butt was in the snow and his knees up by his chin. Then he ditched all the magical thinking. The couple had him on ice in case they needed a do-over. Which they wouldn't. And when they were absolutely certain Will's client was dead, Clay would put a bullet in his head. There wouldn't be any evac accompanied by an infamous guide to bullshit other hunters. What's another body come spring anyway? After ditching their weapons in the intricate vastness of the plateau, the couple would hike out to a fresh vehicle and head for parts unknown. Then get busy planning the next murder on their playlist.

The only angle left was a few seconds of hushed chat before Vanessa squeezed the trigger. Whispers that might or might not carry and tell him when every shred of their attention was focused on killing the man they'd targeted for months. And if he hadn't pulled his little magic trick by then, a bunch of search and rescue people he'd drunk beer with forever would find his frozen hooded carcass tied to a tree. A grisly detail that would be rehashed for years around late-night campfires.

Out of nowhere an image of Vince in all his glory bounded past Mace's eyes and the power of their bond nearly crushed him. For a minute he agonized over what would happen to the shepherd if he and Jamie ended up under matching headstones in the near future. Then it came to him.

Thank God for Glenn.

THIRTY-THREE

Will and the Monster were halfway down the east side of the drainage opposite the bull, following the same game trail that dropped toward the rocky bench above the creek. Will knew the way by heart because he'd filled more than a few tags from the same spot. When he reached a clump of juniper he eased his binos through the whorls of green and glassed the animal again. Still over nine hundred yards out. Then it occurred to him that his client's marksmanship was purely anecdotal at this point. He'd never seen him shoot a single round. Never thought about it until that second.

Normally a guest arrived forty-eight hours prior to the hunt and sighted their rifle in at camp, giving Will a good look at their skill set. The man behind him arrived late, started drinking early and brought trigger-happy companions. He watched the guy overoiling his weapon but never fire it. He'd blanked on the most basic of outfitter due diligence because the whole party got under his skin from the get-go. He wondered what else he was letting slide. Then got a tap on the shoulder.

"See him?" whispered the Monster.

"Yea."

"How far?"

Will turned around. Saw a strangely confident guy dying to use his pricey gun. "Too far."

Then he ducked low and kept descending toward the bench at a soundless clip. He knew his client was right on his tail because he could hear the faintest rustle of outerwear. But other than that, Will couldn't detect a speck of noise. The spooky son of a bitch could move as quickly and quietly as anybody he'd ever hunted with. Got him thinking he might be a pretty fair shot after all.

Hazim tossed the last piece of carpet and rubber padding aside and saw healthy plywood underneath. He stabbed the blade into the seam, pried the sheet up, got both hands around a corner and tore it out. Below that was a foot-thick layer of Styrofoam insulation sandwiched between ten-by-two wooden stringers. He ripped the foam away and saw the steel-plate belly of the RV. Each plate was a yard square and riveted into the Winnebago's undercarriage. He needed better tools.

He grabbed his flashlight, opened the door below the sink and jumped back as two obese rats zipped past his boots and vanished under the dinette. Then he dug around coffee cans full of nails and screws and buckets of paint until he hit a metal box. He dragged it out, unlatched the lid and sorted through gunk-caked tools until he found a chisel and a claw hammer. After wiping them off on his pants, he went over to the mattress and raised his knife. "Back up," he said to Jamie.

She did and he sliced the mattress cover into pieces and wrapped them around the butt of the chisel and the business end of the hammer to dampen the noise. Then got on his stomach, wedged the chisel under the head of a rivet and gave it a whack. The sound was minimal so he hit it harder and it sheared off. After cutting off five more, he set the chisel aside and used the hammer claw to pry up the corner of the plate. Then planted both legs, got his hands under the metal and hauled back. The plate gave way and he set it aside. Now there was a big square hole in the floor. Nothing but dirt and dead grass below that. Hazim lowered his head through and looked around.

The corrugated-steel skirt around the chassis was intact. Nobody could see what was happening under the vehicle. He pulled himself back in, took keys from his jacket, unlocked Jamie's cuffs and shackles and helped her to her feet. Then they stood there, face-to-face. Like a normal couple on the verge of goodbye except for being in a junkyard RV with shackles and guns lying around.

He held his combat knife out. "In case I don't kill the person pretending to be a rabbit."

"You gotta be shitting me," she said, struck by how steady his hand was.

Hazim tapped her neck with his forefinger. "Go for the carotid if they come through the door."

She swatted his finger away and took the knife. "I know where the fucking carotid is."

"And do not come outside unless you hear me tell you to," he said.

"Why can't I go with you?"

"Two people are twice as easy to spot."

He cradled his rifle and dropped through the hole. When his boots hit the earth he looked up. She was gripping the knife handle with both hands, knuckles white. "Peace be upon you," he said.

Jamie shook her head in disbelief. "From the jerk who was gonna shoot me in my sleep."

Hazim shrugged. "Wasn't your time."

He dropped from sight and she ran to the trauma kit and tore through the contents. She found the carboard box with an N95 mask pictured on the side. The box she used to hide the thing Mace got her after a nurse friend was sexually assaulted on a backcountry road a few years ago. Then she dumped the masks on the floor and a Smith & Wesson .38 caliber Airweight clattered out last.

The revolver was silver with a black synthetic grip. She snapped the five-round cylinder open, saw it was full, snapped it shut and extended the gun using a thumbs-locked, two-handed grip. She thought she was gonna puke but didn't. Instead a dormant target range proficiently flickered to life. She looked for a place to shoot from and decided to wedge herself between the two front seats.

After dropping into a crouch, she extended the pistol aft. She tried to picture Mace or her mom or her long-gone sweet dad to give her strength but all she could see was the gun. Then for some idiotic reason she thought about the Hippocratic oath and revised it on the spot. Do no harm that doesn't drop the shithead with the game call for good. Her professional experience made the bull's-eye a no-brainer. Go for the chest. Put two rounds between their tits and ask questions later.

Will and the Monster reached the back of the bench above the creek and sat in the oak glassing for the bull. Neither saw it but Will wasn't worried because he could see cows parked ten stories above their position. He also knew the slope opposite was cut with brushy ravines that could hide an ice cream truck much less a humongous rack. He pointed at the brow of rocks in the center of the bench and they wormed over and tucked in. Then the snow kicked and they hydrated in silence.

Ten minutes later the sky brightened enough to throw hard shadows. Will motioned his client to set up on the left end of the rocks for the shot. The Monster slid over, set the forestock of the Weatherby on his pack and ran the bolt. Never crossed his mind that he might be exposing himself to a superb marksman perched high on the western flank of the drainage. He'd banished that brand of paranoia when he'd made his secret truce with fate and fate had been more than happy to oblige.

Vanessa was thrown by the furry thing nudging into her field of view. Didn't make sense. Then she discerned a three-inch strip of forehead behind a scope and put her reticle just below the brim of the goofy animal pelt hat. "Right side of the rocks," she said.

Clay shifted his glass. Saw what she saw but no orange and no guide. "Sure it's him?"

Her eyes weren't but her gut was so she started her squeeze. "Has to be."

"Wait," said Clay.

He wasn't the insanely elite shot she was but he excelled as spotter so she hesitated. Interrupting her trigger pull with exquisitely calibrated nerve control. Then a powdery blast of white slapped visibility down to nothing and the opportunity for a one-and-done clean kill was gone. The round that would have sheared off a meaty hunk of the Monster's head stayed cold and still in the chamber. Neither Clay nor Vanessa had the faintest notion that one pesky gust of wind had just sealed their fate along with that of a few others.

THIRTY-FOUR

Hazim crawled to the east side of the Winnebago's underbelly because he knew the shooter's first choice would be good light on the door and what sun there was to their back. When he reached the corrugated skirt he found a two-inch gap by the stairs. He put an eye to the opening and saw a grim, socked-in sky. Didn't matter. The day of days had come. Whatever outcome was in store, no more waiting. He shifted his view left and right. Saw the cottonwood grove and the greenhouse but neither would be his choice. Then he focused on the low hill to his front. About three hundred meters away and topped with scraggly vegetation. Ideal for shooting someone coming out of the RV.

There was nothing discordant along the rim and that was to be expected. The person lying up there behind a scope had hours to get perfectly settled in cover. He moved to the far side of the Winnebago and found another narrow break in the skirt. He saw tall weeds and brush on the other side. More than enough to hide his movements once he got out. He set his gloves on the dirt, his rifle on top of them and muscled the skirt apart until the space was shoulder width. Then he slid through the gap with the rifle strapped across his back and slithered toward the cottonwoods.

When he reached the great trees in the center of the grove he lay still a minute then rose to a crouch keeping a massive trunk and dense bramble between him and the sun. He eased the rifle around the bark and scoped the low rise to the east again. Nothing moved or stood out.

Then a flicker of movement off to the right caught his eye. He slid the rifle around the tree and brought it to bear. Saw the same reddish-brown yearling grazing with a companion. Another young buck with vertical spikes. The deer were sixty meters away, eyes and ears locked on the man hiding in the grove. Hazim had no idea a seasoned hunter could mark his position by watching the bucks.

He pulled back behind the trunk, let his heartbeat normalize, snaked the rifle around the same side of the tree and scoped the pasture beyond the RV. More bright snowy nothing. Then he rose from his crouch to check the cover around the fallen windmill. And that's how he missed the spark of light coming off the nape of the rise. The slug arrived less than one-third of a second later.

When he was a child, Hazim watched a farmer kill a tethered cow with a sledgehammer. The man was famous for his single-blow precision. He raised the sledge high and slow then brought it down on the animal's skull with terrible, unerring force. The bovine dropped so fast its knees didn't have time to buckle. That image crossed Hazim's mind as he spilled onto his back, strings cut. There was a roaring waterfall nearby and his right hip was gooey and warm.

He wished he'd given Jamie his pistol.

THIRTY-FIVE

f it hadn't been for the two mule deer, Glenn would have given up staring at the tarp hanging over the Winnebago's door and shifted his position closer. His perch was perfect for dawn but not midmorning sun. Too easy to get silhouetted. He would have eased down the back side of the hill, circled around and set up in the shade of the old greenhouse. Or maybe that tumbledown windmill. And if he had made that move, Hazim would have killed him an hour ago. No maybe about it.

But the deer saw something in the trees and Glenn saw them give whatever they'd spotted somber scrutiny. Then it was just a matter of shifting his optics to their point of concern. He expected to see a coyote since he'd been working the Flextone. Not some pain-in-the-ass deer hunter trying to fill his tag when everyone and their mother was humping the plateau for elk. And that's exactly what he thought he was looking at until he got a good look of Hazim's face and about shit himself. Just wasn't possible this guy was out in the cottonwoods and not in that RV.

Then he remembered the funny noises. Indistinct but industrious. It was this bastard exiting the vehicle. Cutting a hole in the damn floor. But why would he do that? What made him so afraid to walk out the front door that he tunneled his way out of the fucker? He wondered if the game call had somehow backfired but he couldn't fathom how. Then he shoved the questions out of his head and waited to see enough of this mega tough guy to warrant taking a shot. Didn't take that long.

Hazim let a chunk of his torso drift out from behind the tree and Glenn pulled the trigger at the same instant the son of a bitch decided to straighten up. Glenn knew right away he'd jumped the gun and sure enough the .225-grain bullet plowed into the guy's right hip instead of his right chest cavity. But the hellacious impact still twirled him away and out of sight like a lumberjack ballerina.

Glenn ran the bolt without taking his eye off the scope. The rifle's beefy boom rolled all over so he sat tight giving any curious eyes time to give up spotting the source. On the bright side, he definitely got a chunk of the blond fella with the Arab name. Maybe shattered his pelvis. The impact alone would do the job. He might crawl off but he was done walking. No rush now. None whatsoever. Let one of the last people in the world to fuck with bleed out. Then get inside that RV and do the hard part. Because he had serious doubts the man he just shot had wasted his hostage.

Jamie heard the crack of a rifle to the southeast. One jarring report. The sound dissipated into silence and she knew in her heart the person working that game call had shot Hazim. And for one wildly stupid second she thought maybe it was a police sniper. Then five minutes of silence passed and the birds started up with a joyful cacophony and she knew the shooter wasn't a cop. He or she was watching the RV closely. Not sure Hazim was dead or still trying to figure out how he got outside unseen. Then she saw Hazim's gear by the Yeti. Crawled over and ransacked his stuff for a phone but there wasn't one. Then she parsed her options. Going out was suicide. Plan B was a gunfight in a can. So be it. She got behind the driver's seat, put her back to the dash and practiced shifting the Airweight's sights from the door to the hole in the floor in case the shooter found it.

She reminded herself the revolver had a long pull and solid kick and tightened her grip accordingly. Then she noticed Hazim's burgundy-and-gold prayer rug rolled up on the passenger seat next to her. She put her left hand on the rug and sent a lapsed Christian's prayer skyward, thinking any port in a storm would do. Then she heard his voice. Didn't surprise her. Dump enough adrenaline down your veins and you hear what you want. Except there it was again. Hazim saying three faint words over and over. She put her eye to a crack in the wood over the windshield.

The aperture was tiny so it took a second to get a bead on him. He was fifty feet away. Dragging himself toward the Winnebago through wet snow leaving smears of red that caught the light like fresh paint. His rifle was cradled to his chest. He was pasty with shock and his progress was slowing to nothing. Then his head hit the ground and he lay still.

Jamie snugged back down behind the driver's seat and reviewed what she just saw. Hazim was hit in the right lower torso. Maybe the hip. A jackpot of vessels, bone and nerves. He was definitely exsanguinating.

Add shock and bitter cold and he was down to minutes without attention. *Peace be upon my freaking ass,* she muttered. She pulled on her jacket,
stuck the Airweight in her pocket, dropped through the hole in the floor
and crawled toward the big opening in the skirt. When she got there she
stopped and got the pistol out and up. Then she heard Hazim's voice again.
Clearly now.

"Jamie," he yelled hoarsely. "Stay inside."

THIRTY-SIX

Stefan put his binoculars on the notch in the ridge where Will said he'd signal from for the hundredth time and saw nobody. There was a steady drip of faraway gunfire but the lofty terrain knocked the sound around like billiards. Range and direction were muddled. It was impossible to tell if any of the reports came from the valley just over the ridge. He checked his watch again. His boss and guide had been gone three hours. The snow was tapering off and time was running out.

He moved back down the trail to where he could see Luka and Marko in their rock-shielded firing positions, Mausers trained on their rear. They were conversing in Serbian and spewing matching plumes of cigarette smoke. Stefan slung his rifle over his shoulder and kept walking until he was ten meters away and directly behind the two men. His mouth was too dry to swallow.

"Maybe we should move up the ridge," he said in English. "Make sure everything is okay."

The mercs looked at him as if he'd just suggested a naked group hug, turned away and kept chatting. Stefan checked the notch in the ridge one more time and extended his HK45 with both hands just the way he was taught in Poland. Then he shot Luka once between the shoulder blades. Marko was leaping to his feet jaw hung, rifle almost shouldered when a round punched through his nose and out the back of his head. He dropped inertly in a gauzy puff of white.

Stefan circled the face-down forms with his sidearm at low ready. The snow and wind were covering the red mess with pleasing speed. He checked each man for a pulse, found none then walked to the verge of a sheer drop north of the trail and looked at the .45 in his gloved hand. He was about to hurl it into the abyss then reconsidered. He'd have to dump the beautiful bolt-action Benelli soon enough. That made the pistol too useful to discard until the airport was in sight.

He holstered the gun, tore off his dayglow-orange vest and cap and cradled his rifle. Then he headed up the ridge, coaching himself about the shot to come. Exhale. Squeeze. Follow through. Run the bolt with authority. Put another round in the target to be absolutely sure then go baby go.

He hadn't gone far when he stopped and reached into his pocket to confirm that the remote for the white Grand Cherokee parked at the trailhead was still there. It was. The consequences of such a banal slip made him shudder. No going back now. No seeing his parents or his sister or his corgi Alfie ever again. No doing anything microscopically connected to the affable, overeducated man pictured in his Serbian passport. He took off uphill feeling immune to the altitude. His previous bonds to earth were cleanly severed. He wondered if the rest of his obligation would be so easy.

THIRTY-SEVEN

Clay and Vanessa turned toward the two crisp pops bouncing up over the ridge. Being deeply versed gunfire aficionados, they instantly identified the reports as coming from one handgun.

"Who hunts elk with a fucking pistol?" said Clay, brow furrowed.

"Not our problem."

"You don't think that was a tad incongruous given the circumstances?"

Vanessa snugged into her weapon and got back on the scope. "Shush."

Clay looked over his shoulder. Saw Mace slouched in a heap, head caked with ice and felt a sudden urge to check his zip ties. Or better yet, kill him right now. Those pistol shots were all wrong. Like a whiff of smoke in a bone-dry forest. Time to shed baggage that slows you down.

"Eyes front," said Vanessa with the hard edge of a superior.

Clay tore his gaze off Mace and glassed the blurry figures prone on the bench near the base of the opposite slope. They were almost clear one second, blobs the next. Wind gushed through the spruce overhead, bending limbs, imploring caution. "Maybe we should let them kill the thing first."

She blinked. Cranked her around and squinted at him. "Do what?"

"Let the guy kill his elk. They'll have to come up this way to get the horns, right? Saw its head off or whatever. They'll be a hell of a lot closer. Pumped up and distracted. Turkey shoot time."

"What about the two pros he brought with him? You don't think they'll tag along for that?"

"I'll take care of them," said Clay. "You take the big dog."

Vanessa shot him a scary look then got back on the scope. "Nobody's gonna shoot that bull."

Will registered the same two shots and lifted his head. "Hear that?" he whispered.

"Yes," murmured the Monster, lips barely moving, eyes on the scope.

Will rolled onto his back and glassed the ridgeline they just came down.

Saw nothing through the driving snow then put his mouth close to his client's ear.

"I know your people are carrying pistols."

"So?"

"Think they're stupid enough to use 'em while we're on a stalk?"

The Monster turned into Will's face. Cold-blooded calm. "Never."

Will saw a demented certainty and hesitated. "Well someone sure did."

"So what," said the Monster, getting back on his glass. "This is all that matters."

Will's eyes shifted to the smear of frost on the rifle's receiver. The icing on the cake of the man's arrogance and again he said nothing to warn him. But now he knew why. He wanted him to fail at the most critical juncture. Wanted to smash the psycho confidence off his face with the butt of the Winchester but blowing the shot would more than suffice. And seeing the finest bull he'd scouted in decades wander off unscathed due to malignant self-esteem would be beautiful. Then he chided himself for succumbing to unprofessional emotional bullshit. Get the man his rack before you do something you can't live with. He pointed at the frost. "You got ice on your rifle."

The Monster rubbed off the white glaze with his gloved thumb and got back on the scope.

"Better unload and swab out the action just to be sure," said Will.

"How about you do your fucking job and I do mine," said the Monster.

Will started to suggest using the over-lubed weapon as an enema, scope and all. Then bit his tongue and went with something a tad more civil. "Works for me."

Mace heard the reports in the dark under the hood and plotted their bearing and range as they faded. Sounded like a pistol. Came from the east in the vicinity of where Will's client would have parked his retinue prior to the stalk. And just like that, he was certain someone just got shot to death because that was the norm over the last forty-eight hours of his life. And whoever did the killing was coming over that ridge and they weren't coming to save anybody. He had no clue who it could be.

He ran his gloved left index finger over the zip ties mashing his wrists together to make sure he had their alignment clear in his head. Then went back to working the glove off his right hand.

The great bull was upwind of both hunting parties hiding in the drainage but that wind was stiff, blunting the animal's otherworldly senses just enough. It heard the pair of sharp cracks lofting over the valley and discerned them as alien but not imminent threats. Then it scoured the terrain in that direction with eyes that could detect a fully camouflaged man turning his head at half a mile. Not seeing or smelling any of the five humans concealed in the watershed below, the two shots fell into the neutral zone of opening-day noise. Worrisome but not get out of Dodge quite yet. The bull did another scan of the world and went back to hyperalert grazing. But any further aberration in the environment, no matter how tiny or ostensibly organic, would be red-flag time.

THIRTY-EIGHT

Other than scoping the area around the tree Hazim was hiding behind, Glenn hadn't moved. The brush was thick under the cottonwoods but the man went down so hard he wasn't worried. He did wonder how long it would take a person to bleed to death. He'd shot plenty of large animals but never a person. He figured the latter took longer for some reason. Then his thinking drifted back to where he'd go when today played out. He'd checked out Canada and Mexico because he could drive but settled on Anguilla because it was crazy beautiful. And no income tax and lots of Americans. Assuming he didn't bail on everything he'd signed up for and be the hero for once.

Say he was acting on a hunch or a tip. Say some dirt biker said he saw something suspicious going on inside a junked RV south of Montrose. Or even better, the dirt biker thought he smelled a meth lab. That shit plagued the Western Slope and gunfight busts happened with regularity. But the more he ruminated on the knight-in-shining armor option, the more holes he found. Like the Winnebago being in Montrose County so why didn't he alert Montrose PD. Not to mention the Muslim fucker was from some dump on other side of the world. Probably lonely as hell and then gets cooped up with a hot witty female for days on end and gets chummy. Entirely possible he told Jamie everything, including how the pair from Phoenix bought a local cop to bat cleanup.

And that's how the mess would play out. He'd be the golden boy for a few hours then Jamie would nuke his life right down to the studs. Multiple counts of murder and kidnapping and conspiracy to commit God knows what else. Turn eighty in prison writing to his public defender in crayon. Nope. Jamie had to go. Goddamn shame but there was no wiggle room in the matter.

Glenn checked his watch and was surprised to see thirty-five minutes had passed since he pulled the trigger. He grabbed his pack and moved downhill with his rifle at high ready. When he got to the edge of the grove he stopped, listened hard for a bit then kept going. Twenty yards later he reached the blood-splattered tree. There was a torn-open green plastic pouch lying at its base. Size of a bag of chips. The writing on the pouch was incomprehensible. Russian maybe. Couldn't tell what had been in it. Then he headed west through trees and wheatgrass, following the drag marks.

Three minutes later he found Hazim lying on his side, thirty feet from the front of the Winnebago, rifle clutched to his chest. For a second Glenn thought he was dead. Then the downed man grunted, shoved himself forward with his legs a few more inches and lay still again. Glenn tossed Hazim's rifle aside, frisked him, found the Beretta and pitched that away too.

After that, it being broad daylight on the first day of rifle season, Glenn did a thorough scan of his surroundings. His gaze lingered on the RV, picturing Jamie bound and gagged. Satisfied with the lack of eyes, he shoved Hazim onto his stomach and jammed a knee between his shoulder blades. Then palmed his crewcut skull like a bowling ball, using the eye sockets for holes and yanked his head back. The blade of his Buck knife was parting skin on Hazim's throat when Jamie eased around the driver's side of the RV with the .38 Airweight extended with both arms. The revolver was steady and her stance was correct but her face was contorted in horror and incredulity.

"What are you doing?" she asked in a small voice.

Glenn let Hazim's head plop in the snow and stood up. He snapped the knife shut and put it in his pocket. Then let his right hand dangle by the sidearm on his hip and broke out a relieved grin.

"Jesus Christ, Jamie. You all right?"

"Am I what?" she said, still thunderstruck.

Glenn moved forward, eyes ticking from her face to the gun aimed midway between his nipples.

"Did that bastard hurt you?"

"Stop," said Jamie with a rattled inflection that stalled his advance.

Glenn chuckled. "Careful with that thing. Might be puny but it'll sure kill a person."

"Like you were being careful with that knife?"

"Now Jamie girl. You need to listen to me right now. You're not thinking straight and that's normal for what you've been through. And I know the knife thing looked messed up but that's an armed-and-dangerous criminal right there. And I damn sure wasn't gonna use my sidearm and give away my position until I knew how many of them were inside there with you. Understand?"

"But you already shot him with that rifle."

Glenn threw his hands up, trying on righteously pissed. "Hell's wrong with you? We knew these guys were armed and freaking dangerous. You rather me chat him up first? Read him his kidnapper rights?"

"We?"

"Montrose and Ouray County sheriff. SWAT teams. Dogs. Whole world is looking for you."

Jamie fought the urge to look around and check the sky and kept the pistol dead center on his ample chest. "But you're the one who got lucky. All by yourself."

"'Bout time, huh?" said Glenn, switching back to jocular. "Main thing is you and Mace are alive."

Jamie gave a start. "Mace is okay?"

"Safe and sound," he said, easing toward her again. "And so are you."

She saw the scary dark in his eyes and backpedaled. "Then put him on the phone."

"No can do. He's on a medevac right now. Just gimme the gun and let's get you to a doctor."

"Glenn," said Jamie, hunching her shoulders into the grip. "You really oughta stop right there."

He did, right hand clamping down on the butt of his pistol. "I gotta say, I can't believe you're actually thinking about shooting me."

"That makes two of us."

Glenn looked over at the man he shot and realized he had no more faces to try on and relaxed.

"Old Hazim there was supposed to kill you before I killed him. But I had a hunch he wouldn't hold up his end and I was right. I also figured he told you about my part in this. So here we are."

Jamie managed a grin despite tears spilling down her cheeks. "Well Glenn, guess what?"

"What?" he said, looking at her.

"He didn't."

Glenn was surprised. "I'll be damned. I figured being cooped up with someone like you would make any man have second thoughts and spill his guts about stuff he shouldn't."

"Someone like me."

"You know. Great-looking with a big brain."

"As in fuckable but able to carry a conversation," said Jamie.

Glenn heard the flatness in her voice. Saw the unwavering grip. The solid stance. The range was about to go hot but he forced himself to wait for his chance. "No offense," he said.

"None taken. But I need to know why you did this before the real cops get here."

He cocked his head. "Oh yea. Who called 'em?"

"Me. I found Hazim's phone."

"No you didn't. Or they'd be here by now. But to answer your question, I did it for the money. About five times what I'd have if I wasn't a screwup and retired at sixty. Believe that shit?"

Jamie took a deep breath, eyes narrowing as she exhaled. Glenn curled his right index finger into the Sig Sauer, raised his left hand as a misdirect and pointed at her revolver.

"Mace and I were wondering where you stashed that sweet little piece."

"Wonder no more," said Jamie. Then she pulled the trigger.

Glenn moved quick for a big man. Had his weapon clear of the holster but not quite laid on Jamie when the .38's stocky slug caught him on the right shoulder. The round sent his pistol flying and him sideways. A normal-size person would have dropped. Glenn spun with the impact like any good defensive lineman and kept his legs churning and his shoulders down. Then he drove Jamie headfirst into the frozen ground with a soggy whack that knocked her into a dream where she couldn't breathe. When she woke up, Glenn was astride her waist. There was a little hole in his parka by his collarbone. Blood was fanning out fast, soaking everything but he didn't notice.

One of his hands was clamped around her windpipe. The other was raising the Buck knife even with his ear so he could drive the blade through her heart and get on with his life.

"I'm sure sorry," he said, almost sounding like he meant it.

Jamie was resigned to Glenn's fanatical expression being the last thing she ever saw when Vince collided with the side of his head like a fanged cruise missile and tore half his face off.

The scream that followed wasn't human.

THIRTY-NINE

Stefan pushed through the juniper beneath the fin of the ridge, dropped to his knees and scrambled up to the notch Will had used to drop into the drainage below. Then he slung the Benelli over his back, crawled to the lip, planted his elbows and glassed the timbered valley beyond. It was cut by a meandering stream layered with ponds created by a system of mud and limb dams. Stefan knew all about beavers but never saw their superb engineering skills firsthand. He would have been enthralled for hours if he weren't focused on the mechanics of shooting his employer.

Killing Will wasn't part of it. He enjoyed the American's company and if he had a clean shot from a concealed position he'd take it and leave the guide alone. Slaying Luka and Marko was oddly easy and emotionally satisfying. Killing Will would be grotesque and unnecessary. Unless the guide actually saw him do the deed. Then there would be absolutely no choice in the matter.

He spotted some elk in a meadow opposite but none had antlers so he studied the brooding rock dome at the top of the valley. It struck him as emblematic of a realm crawling with armed people driving giant trucks. And now a disgruntled novice sniper hunting a billionaire war criminal. Paid a life-altering sum of money by Dragan's business partners to unclog the bottleneck at the top of the food chain. And stranger still, more afraid of success than failure because of Dragan's sons.

Jovo and Milan ran drugs and arms across Eastern Europe in the tribal shadow of their father. They were wealthy ogres in their own right, partial to making snuff films starring snitches and competitors. Savants with blowtorches and dental drills, they used block anesthesia to prolong mind boggling agony and carried their terror tools in aluminum attaché cases wherever they went. The energy applied to finding their dad's killer and anyone remotely involved would be demonic.

Invigorated by the hazards of his future, Stefan studied the far side of the valley again and saw a huge creature on the verge of the same meadow.

A giant elk with magnificently complicated horns. He dug out a Leupold laser rangefinder and put it on the bull. The LED display clocked in at 1,029 meters. He ranged the distance to the stream. Came in at 564 meters. The difference was a doable shot from the slope beneath him. And that was where he would find Dragan and his guide.

He peeked over the rim into the windy white void. It was the most godforsaken moment of his life. Then something he read a long time ago popped into his head. Written by an American named Emerson. How a hero is no braver than an ordinary man. Just brave for a bit longer. He grabbed the Benelli, cycled the bolt and seated a cartridge. The steadiness of his hands surprised him. For one childish moment he wished his mother could see him. Then over the edge he went.

FORTY

Man and dog tumbled sideways in a howling blur until Glenn managed to grab the rope leash with the choke chain and throttle the animal inert. Then he got to his feet, unaware his entire nose and right cheek were dangling below his jaw suspended by a thread of mucos membrane. He saw his Sig 9mm in the snow twenty feet away and lurched over thinking plain vanilla police work sounded pretty goddamn good right about now. He was reaching for the gun when Vince crashed into his knees, knocked him flat and commenced shredding his calves like a blender on purée.

Glenn was already in shock so his legs getting butchered didn't stop him from grabbing his sidearm and aiming at the dog's chest. His thumb was still fumbling for the ice-slick safety when the barrel of Jamie's S&W .38 touched his right temple. The revolver bucked, excavating the far side of his head in a ruby eruption of dura and parietal bone. He flopped onto his back, weapon aimed at the sky, brow knit as if supremely baffled by what just happened. Vince didn't notice the deputy was deceased and kept right on rending appendages with righteous abandon.

Jamie stared at the pistol she was holding in a gory one-handed grip, thinking they didn't teach that stance at the gun range out past the drive-in in Montrose. She stuck the weapon in her waistband, pulled Vince off the corpse and hugged the dog saying good boy over and over. Then Hazim groaned, reminding everybody that he wasn't dead yet.

FORTY-ONE

Jamie ran into the Winnebago thinking Hazim was way too big to move and grabbed the trauma kit and prayer rug figuring the latter was the cleanest surface around. Back outside, she rolled him onto the rug, yanked his parka and layers aside and saw chalky gauze on his right hip. She got a whiff of fresh clay and knew the gauze was impregnated with kaolin. She couldn't help being impressed. The warfighter carried QuikClot like most people carry a wallet. And it saved his life.

She gloved up, peeled off the gauze and saw a through-and-through gunshot wound even with the pelvis. The entrance was neat and clotting, the exit jagged and bleeding. The round nicked some muscles and nerves but missed the salad-bowl-size bone of the ilium so he could probably walk. The real problem was the mud that got under the gauze. Like all soil, it naturally carried enough pathogens to kill a horse much less a man in hemorrhagic shock. Fun things like tetanus, anthrax and botulism.

She cleaned the entrance and exit wounds, irrigated the bullet tract, covered both holes with hemostatic dressing and taped them over. Then she injected five hundred milligrams of cephalosporin against the microbial army marching through Hazim's body. Being out cold, he had no idea how lucky he was that Jamie, like most docs in remote locations, carried a first aid kit on steroids in their personal vehicle. A first-responder level of meds and instruments because of the lead time to a hospital.

When the autopilot part was over Jamie craned her head around. Saw Glenn lying in the snow with his head blown out like a hairy paper bag. Saw Vince crouched behind Hazim, targeting the inert stranger just in case. Then she noticed the money belt velcroed around Hazim's waist. She ripped it off, saw four compartments and started tearing them open. The first contained bound packs of dollars and euros. The second, British and Belgian passports. The third, SIM and credit cards. The fourth, a Samsung Galaxy S22 still in shrink-wrap. She tore off the wrap, hit the power button, held the cell up and briskly slapped Hazim's face. "Hey. I need the passcode."

His eyes fluttered open. After that, he jerked his head sideways and vomited. Jamie cleared his airway with her fingers and grabbed a plastic chair from the weeds. Then she unbuckled his pants, elevated his legs, set his boots on the seat, jammed the phone in his face and raised her voice.

"You're not gonna die but you need a hospital. Give me the passcode for this freaking phone."

Hazim squinted at his former hostage. Her cheeks were spattered with bloody goo and there was a revolver stuck in her pants. He wondered where the gun came from. Then he saw something new and hard in her eyes. "What happened to the man who shot me?"

"He's dead," said Jamie. "Now gimme the fucking code."

Hazim shut his eyes. Took a breath. "If you call for help the police will look for your husband. And when the couple hears the first helicopter they will put a bullet in his head. For sure."

"What makes you think they didn't kill him already?"

"They fought in deserts. Not snow. Not mountains. They might keep him alive to get out."

Jamie tried to think but her throat and head were brutalized by Glenn's assault.

"Here's the thing," said Hazim, teeth gritting against the pain. "They think we're dead."

"So what?"

"We can still save your husband."

This threw her. Pissed her off actually. "Why would you wanna do that?"

A grin creased his face. Like it was obvious. "Good deeds wipe out evil deeds."

Jamie picked a shiny marble of Glenn's temporal lobe from her jaw and flicked it away. "That's horseshit. You just want to shoot Will's client yourself if they didn't get him yet."

"Why not both?"

She looked at Highway 550 a few miles to the west. She and Vince could walk over there and hitch a ride. Put one foot in front of the other until she was standing on pavement. Say she had no memory of the past seventy-two hours and the injuries to prove it. Or search her kidnapper for his truck keys and just drive home. Let Hazim sink or swim on his own. But none of that would help her husband.

"Is Allah gonna send us a map showing exactly where Mace is?" she asked.

"We don't need a map and we don't need blasphemy."

"Why not?"

"We're hunting a hunter," said Hazim. "You said nobody in the world could do it better than Mace. And you know him better than anyone. So maybe you already know where he is."

Jamie started to scoff at the idea. The implausible needle in a ginormous haystack frailty of it compared to the vastness of the plateau. Then a snippet of conversation floated by but didn't stick. She shut her eyes and waited until it glided by again and held on. Saw Mace standing by the highway, hungover and hating himself. Mad at the world he no longer inhabited. Saying Will didn't need him because he'd been leasing the same ground forever.

"The trophy hole," she said quietly, surprising herself.

"What is that?" said Hazim, still having no idea the shepherd was crouched right behind him.

"Place we fished. Same place Stoddard likes to hunt. North Fork of Cottonwood Creek."

"You know how to get there?"

She nodded. He kicked the chair away and rolled to his knees. She started to help him up but he brushed her off. The light in his eyes was scary. Do or die primeval shit.

"I have fentanyl citrate," said Jamie. "Good as morphine but quicker."

"And makes you stupid."

"So does pain," she said.

He looked around. Jaw clenched. "No time for that. Where's my rifle and pistol?"

"No idea."

Then he took a tremendous breath, pressed his hands into the ground and deadlifted himself to his feet. His face paled from the pain but the sheer power of his quest kept him upright. Then Vince decided he was a threat to Jamie and went ballistic. Zero to mayhem in one leap.

"Down!" she yelled, stopping the shepherd in mid-launch.

Hazim threw his arms up, astounded. Knew it was Jamie's dog. Had no idea how it got there.

"What's the matter?" said Jamie. "Never seen a miracle before?"

He shook his head. Face regaining color and implacable faith simultaneously. "Not until today."

Hazim found his weapons where Glenn threw them, made sure they were clean, holstered the pistol and slung the rifle over his shoulder. Then he grabbed the prayer rug and the money belt and stuck his hand out at Jamie. She gave him the phone and watched him limp off into the trees thinking he was a brick shithouse on a mission. Seconds later, the burgundy Silverado bashed out of the trees and skidded up at her feet.

Hazim tossed her the parka and snow boots he took from the Rubicon, grabbed a plastic tarp from the truck bed and spread it on the ground. After dragging Glenn's body onto the tarp, he gathered the deputy's firearms and knife, set them on the corpse, rolled up everything and sealed the ends with rope. Then he dropped the tailgate and looked at Jamie. "Give me a hand."

She helped him lift the corpse into the bed and stepped back. "What are we gonna do with it?"

He slammed the tailgate. "I don't know yet. Get in the truck."

Jamie and Vince climbed in the cab. Hazim ducked into the Winnebago, stuffed his pack with food and water, took the trauma kit, ran out and threw it all in the back seat with the dog. Then he took one of the two gas cans from the bed and a flare from the glove box and soaked the inside of the RV. He looked around one last time. Saw his satphone on the table and left it there. Saw Jamie's hood and stuck it in his coat. Then stepped outside, ignited the flare, tossed it in and shut the door.

The gasoline erupted and the Winnebago shuddered. Flames belched from the roof hatch and licked out the windows. A pillar of molten black smoke marred the cloudy sky. When Hazim was certain the inferno was unstoppable, he climbed in the truck, dug a vial from his pack and dumped three chunky brown tablets in his palm. He gulped two and offered Jamie the third. She stared at it.

"What is this?"

"Lebanese speed," he said. "Every fighter's daily bread."

Jamie ate it thinking the person she was two days ago was deader than Glenn. "Now what?"

Hazim threw the truck into gear and cut a rooster tail of mud and snow around the burning motor home. "Kill everybody but your husband and his friend."

By the time they reached Buckhorn Road and sped west, the crank had detonated in Jamie's empty stomach and twisted her dopamine spigot wide open. Her limbs felt charged, her thoughts nimble as spiders. Her headache was gone and her vision had regained its normal keenness.

"What about your side?" she said suddenly. "They didn't murder and rape innocent people?"

"I am not my side," he said.

"But you didn't answer the question."

Hazim stared at the blacktop running through pastoral white hills. Saw bloated corpses lining the road as far as the eye could see. Soldiers and civilians. Men and women. The leaking refuse of war and depravity that he carried around in his head like the devil's unerasable porn.

"Whoever creates the most grief wins."

Jamie thought about this. "So who won that Bosnian thing?"

"No idea."

They crossed the Uncompahgre River and she looked down at the storm-swollen water charging north to be swallowed by the Gunnison like it never was. "So nobody wins."

Hazim didn't argue.

FORTY-TWO

Will was getting glimpses of the bull grazing downhill when it stopped, looked around then veered leisurely south and disappeared into snowy cover. Wasn't a sharp departure from its regular transition but enough to screw the shot from where they lay. He lowered the glass and visualized the slope opposite like a steep and cluttered chessboard. The way it eroded into brushy gullies toward the bottom. Offering several routes for a wary bull to rendezvous with his cows.

"What's wrong?" said the Monster, sensing his guide's unease.

"We gotta move. He picked a different fall line. No shot from here if he holds it."

"Move where?"

Will referred to the topo map in his head again. Extrapolated. "Left about thirty yards."

Then he led the crawl to a heap of granite on the south lip of the bench and they got prone side by side again. Will to the right in spotter position. After glassing uphill, he pointed at an opening in the oak midway down the slope opposite but still high above their perch. "See that clearing?"

The Monster set his pack on a rock, elevated the Weatherby and sighted in on the spot. "Yes."

"He should pop out right there. That's four hundred and seventy yards give or take at twenty-five degrees."

Will saw hesitation when the man tweaked his scope. Made him wonder. "You know gravity doesn't care about angle, just sea level distance. Bullets tend to hit high going uphill or downhill."

The Monster took a petulant pause before answering. "Of course."

Will cussed himself for not covering this two days ago. Son of a bitch didn't know jack about high-country ballistics. Probably bagged all his trophies on flat ground in game preserves.

"Look at me."

The Monster turned, eyes bright with bull fever, Cossack hat caked white.

"His heart and lungs ride low," said Will. "You need to put that round two inches behind the shoulder and halfway to his belly. Figure being four inches high from here. You got me?" He approximated that distance with his gloved thumb and forefinger. "Four inches at least."

"Aye-aye Captain Stoddard," murmured the Monster, putting his cheek into the stock.

Will watched his client caress the safety wondering what stripe of goat-fuck he'd walked into.

Hazim drove west on Highway 90 until he saw a gorge through the snow to his left. He pulled over, got up in the bed and scanned the world in every direction. Found it trackless as the day it was created. He hopped down, leaned into the cab and looked at Jamie. "I need my knife back."

"Why?" she asked.

He stuck his hand out. She gave it to him. He dropped the tailgate, grabbed the tarp, slid the body out and dumped it in the powder. Then he slogged for the gorge, dragging the shrouded corpse behind him like a misshapen toboggan. Jamie and Vince caught up with him a minute later.

"What are you gonna do?" she asked.

He stared at her, breathing hard, face glazed with sweat. "Go back to the truck. Please."

"Fuck that. I'm the one who killed him. Now you're saying I can't handle this part?"

"I know there is nothing on earth you can't handle," said Hazim. "Because I've seen it with my own eyes. But watching what I'm about to do will take a piece of your soul and never give it back."

Jamie opened her mouth to bicker further then a ghoulish inkling of what Hazim had in mind shut it like a trap. She grabbed the shepherd's collar and retraced her steps toward the truck.

Hazim reached the lip of the gorge, dropped his cargo and studied the thick layer of sedimentary rock rimming the sheer drop. It was serrated with bottomless black fissures from meter wide to coffee mug size. Then he unrolled the tarp and went to work with grim concentration.

Took a full minute to decapitate Glenn's corpse because hacking through the Winnebago's floor had dulled the blade considerably. Took

half that long to cut off both his hands. Then he rolled the body he'd inoculated against dental records and fingerprints into a dark slit and listened to
it slither and tumble. Eventually it thudded into basement rock ten stories
below where he stood and stopped.

After that he dropped Glenn's head and hands, his firearms, the tarp and
the snow-wiped knife into separate and equally deep fissures. He thought
about offering a prayer regarding the butchered deputy but drew a blank
on anything applicable and speed-limped back to Jamie and the dog.

The more Vanessa bore down on the scope, the more her abnormal acuity told her the target was no longer prone behind the same line of rocks
and gnarled trees across the creek. The snow was blowing left to right in
creamy waves producing a shimmering and compacted perspective of objects downrange. And just as their guide predicted, depth perception was
junk. But none of that mattered. When her eyes and gut sang the same
song she listened. "They're gone," she murmured.

Clay was scouring the same spot but wasn't so sure. "How do you know?"

She looked over her shoulder at the man zip-tied to the big aspen above
the ravine. "Because they're not there anymore, honeybun. Stay on the
glass."

Then she scooted downhill and stood over Mace with her rifle at parade
rest. "Got a sec?"

Mace raised his hooded head and waited, hands hidden under smooth
mounds of fresh powder.

"They left the location you said they'd shoot from. They were there
then they weren't."

She was calm and matter-of-fact. Like she missed a bus and needed to
know about the next one.

Mace clocked the snow drumming into his hood. Visibility must suck.
"You saw them leave?"

"No. But I know they're gone."

"So this is a hunch."

"No. Not really. What do you think happened?"

Mace listened to the wind rattle branches. Pictured the bench low on the
opposite slope facing gullied terrain and heavy cover. No way Will would
drag his guest all the way down there if he didn't know where the bull normally transitioned. Probably filled a sack of tags from the same perch over

twenty years. But a king-size dump three weeks before Halloween wasn't normal. And a trophy animal improvises from long experience. But not dramatically. "I think they're still there."

"Why?" she asked.

"We saw that bull two hours ago. It's not leaving this drainage in this weather and neither are Will and your guy. The animal probably strayed laterally on the way down and Will had to move to get the shot he wants. Dice some range off. But he didn't go far. You just missed it in the mess."

"Sure they didn't quit and go home?"

Mace caught a tiny whiff of anxiety in the question. Surprised him. "Will would never bail on bagging record headgear because of a little snow. And neither would I."

Vanessa studied him thinking poise in a pickle was sexy as shit. "Spoken like a dying breed."

Then she climbed back up to her shooting perch, congratulating herself for being so open-minded and not killing him sooner.

FORTY-THREE

Stefan was moving carefully, knees bent against the frozen incline, head below the scrub oak. The boot tracks he'd been following were erased so he was dead reckoning downhill. The weather was toggling from blizzard to pure white calm then back to full-bore alpine blast. The sheer speed of it was amazing and distracting. He'd slipped twice already and pitched shoulder first into forgivingly quiet snow. He was careful to keep his rifle barrel high so the bore stayed clean.

When visibility spiked, he'd take a knee and scope the lower portion of the slope. Eventually he caught a dash of dayglow orange and saw two figures lying behind a low mound of dark rock. It was them. Just above the stream and to his right. Will on his binoculars. Dragan on his rifle.

Unfortunately, range-wise, they were still beyond his comfort zone. Then Stefan noticed both were focused on an area midway up the far side of the valley. He raised his head and scoped the same densely forested ground. He caught movement in the trees and saw the same enormous bull through a gap in the foliage. It was walking slowly, ears and horns rotating in decisive sweeps.

Then the animal stopped and seemed to focus directly on Stefan's nose with laser precision. At first this unnerved him. Then he dismissed the notion as absurd given the animal was at least a kilometer away and continued his descent with an urgency he would regret.

Hazim gunned the Silverado through rows of bumper-high drifts and stopped at the trailhead. The blue Dodge truck, the red Ford F-350 and the white Grand Cherokee were encased in bulky slabs of snow like abandoned relics of the petroleum age. The world was now glacial in all directions, devoid of any indication of warm-blooded life.

Hazim stared at the vehicles. "I don't see your husband's truck."

Jamie looked around picturing the couple as hyper careful killers. "Because they probably hid it and hiked in." Then she pointed west up the trail. "The trophy hole is that way."

Jamie grabbed essential supplies from the trauma kit then watched Hazim dump a can of gas in the cab and the bed. After that, he ignited flares and turned the vehicle into a glass-popping cauldron. Happened so fast it took her a moment to process. "How are we supposed to get off this mountain?"

He shouldered his gear and motioned her to lead on. "Doesn't matter. We were never here."

She started to ask what that meant then knew. He was planning for the future. Hers in particular. Destroying all evidence of the kidnapping along with his very existence. She headed up the trail with Vince at her side. After a ways, she looked back. Saw pain contorting Hazim's posture and gait. She stopped and offered her arm. He shoved it away without a word and they kept going.

FORTY-FOUR

Vanessa was snugged into her rifle and Clay was on the spotting scope. Ice crusted their suits from hood to boot. They were scouring everything within a reasonable lateral crawl of where they'd last seen the target. Snow was coming in fine sandy showers, degrading visibility enough to make a five-hundred-yard shot a rather sporting proposition. Even for a shooter of Vanessa's ilk.

Then Clay got still and tweaked his glass. "I got orange."

"Where?"

"Scoot due south. Hundred feet."

She slid her scope over. Saw a patch of dayglow peeking over a pile of granite chunks. Saw half of a man's face under an orange cap, lean and grizzled with graying stubble. He was gripping binos with gloved hands, looking at something below and to her left. "That's Stoddard."

"Roger that," said Clay. "Fur cap guy is peekabooing to his right."

Vanessa glimpsed the man she almost killed two hours ago just as he dropped from sight. But it didn't matter. She had him. Now it was purely a matter of visibility. When it got sufficient he would expose his head to take the shot. Had to. And she'd be ready. She pulled her eyes off the scope to brush snow off the receiver and caught movement on the slope opposite. Something large moving downhill at a shallow angle. She shifted her weapon. Combed the spot and saw nothing. Played the snippet over in her head. Could have been an animal's snowy flank. Or winter camo.

Clay's eyes were glued to his glass but he noticed. "What'd you see?"

She reminded herself distraction was poison. Got back on her scope and put the reticle on the rock the fur gap guy was lying behind. "Something moved over there."

"Where?"

"Straight across."

"Man or critter?"

"Couldn't tell."

Clay pulled a glove off with his teeth and brushed her cheek with his bare hand.

"Tranquillo. Almost done."

She kissed his hand, snuggled into her weapon and the second-guessing fell away. The shot would unfold when it was ready. No different than a flower. Then she settled into the flow state that made her so lethal. Twice the snow parted but she had no clean look and the lull was too quick to shoot. First time, she glimpsed the antique rifle with the iron sights strapped over the guide's shoulder and wondered why he brought it along. Second time, she glimpsed a dime-size dark spot on the left temple of the man she needed to kill and made that her bull's-eye.

Stefan crouched behind the charred stump of a lightning-struck spruce, unaware that he'd been ever so briefly spotted by an elite shooter clear across the valley. The tree was snapped at waist level and the blackened shards of trunk offered a nice V-shaped brace for the Benelli. He depressed the barrel and scoped the fuzzy forms of the two men prone behind the rocks down by the creek. Then got on his rangefinder and despite the vexing snow, eventually got a valid distance of 420 meters, well within his skill set. After that, he scoped the two men's respective positions again.

His boss was closest, Stoddard lying a meter beyond. Due to the steep angle, the guide appeared to be well above the line of fire. Stefan found comfort in this because the shooting school in Poland was on flat ground and didn't teach mountain marksmanship, omitting concepts like the difference between true distance and map distance and the effect of gravity on a bullet traveling downhill.

After a cursory scan for the trophy bull, he settled into his rifle and waited for a clean shot. He tried to clear his head but his thoughts kept tumbling into stressful minutiae because he'd forgotten entirely about regular hydration at altitude. He was practicing his breathing exercises to no effect when his adrenaline drained down to nothing and cramps burned into his parched quads.

He set the rifle aside, stayed low and braced his back against the trunk. He was stretching his right leg when his heel nudged a rock the size of a softball. It started rolling then picked up speed before hanging up in the juniper below. The snow-hushed clatter lasted all of three seconds so he paid it no mind. Neither the hunting party below Stefan's position nor the accomplished assassins set up on the opposite slope heard the noise. And that was good but they didn't count.

Nearly three-quarters of a mile away, the bull fixed its marvelous senses on the faint dither of one loose stone because it didn't get that majestic by ignoring the little things. The animal promptly deemed the noise aberrant and foreboding and the rest was inevitable. The bull pivoted on a dime, displaying unearthly agility for a half-ton critter before loping west at a stately gait. Hauling its pendulous balls and the premium genes encased therein out of harm's way. And that, in terms of adding a flawless and colossal rack to this year's record books, was that.

FORTY-FIVE

Hazim and Jamie reached a drifted patch of scrub oak flanking the trail and stopped to rest. They had no idea they were standing over human remains until Vince got agitated and unearthed two bodies and two rifles. Jamie pulled the dog off and frantically brushed the faces clean making sure one wasn't Mace. Except for the black entrance wound where Marko's nose used to reside, both mercenaries wore strangely contented expressions. As if being shot to death was the only fitting conclusion to their innately violent lives. "Friends of yours?" she asked.

Hazim stared at the dead bodyguards. Saw soldiers like himself. "They protected the Monster."

"Looks like hard work," said Jamie.

He looked away. Gauged the position of the cloud-covered sun and put it near midday prayer. There was no time for supplication but the thought of it gave him comfort. Jamie read his mind.

"Need to pray?" she asked.

"No. Do you?"

"What would I pray for?"

He shrugged. "Making sure the right people continue to die."

"Doesn't seem like something you ask God's help for."

"Men pray for evil the same way they pray for good."

"Because men are stupid," she said then pointed up at the ridge. "That's where we're headed."

Hazim squinted at the objective and took the lead, slogging uphill favoring his wound and bad knee like a listing ship. Vince and Jamie trailed at his heels until she couldn't take the spectacle of his misery anymore and threw an arm around his waist. He recoiled and gave her a harsh look.

She cinched up her grip and took his weight. "Get over your fucking self."

He grudgingly laid an arm across her shoulders and they plodded on. They'd hadn't gone far when a canyon of blue raced overhead, dragging a swath of perfect visibility across the plateau.

"Are you blind?" hissed the Monster, trigger finger coming off the gun and pointing at a broad meadow far above the gap in cover they'd been watching. "He's getting away."

Will slapped glass to his eyes and saw the bull's massive rump and rack floating uphill at a good gallop. He put the distance at nearly a thousand yards and growing by the second. The Monster saw the same thing, got on the scope and settled in for the shot.

"He's out of range," said Will, feeling a wave of relief that surprised him with its power.

"Not yet," said the Monster, aiming for the back end of the bull's spine thinking he could cripple the beast then get up there and finish his prize up close. With or without his guide.

Then he exhaled and squeezed. The Weatherby emitted a sharp dry click.

The absence of a deafening report was itself deafening. The Monster peeled his cheek off the stock, astounded. After viciously cycling the bolt he snugged back into the rifle and got on the scope. Saw nothing but steep, inscrutable terrain. Like the bull never was. "What happened?"

Will looked at him and laughed. "Exactly what I told you would happen."

The mocking levity jerked the Monster's eyes over to his guide. Then another membrane opened like the third eyelid of a lizard and Will saw the unvarnished abomination lurking beneath. He wanted to scramble away. To run from this creature but his limbs were bad-dream frozen.

One second later, the business end of three hunts collided in a quirk of triangulation and chaos theory. Stefan had his reticle parked tight on the right ear of his boss and pulled the trigger. The Benelli's bark shattered the stillness like a vast pane of glass. Clay said send it at the same instant and Vanessa started her normal silky squeeze. And her shot would have been impeccably placed per usual if Stefan's discharge hadn't slapped her ears and made her yip. Disrupting her follow-through by a microscopic sliver of pressure. But that misguided caress was all it took.

Stefan's slug went high by three inches, creasing the Monster's skull and knocking him unconscious but missing his brains altogether. Then the round continued on its supersonic journey, passing through Will's neck and cervical vertebrae like cotton candy. Took him a second to register his ruin and face-plant in the snow. Took another thirty seconds for his heart to pump the rest of his life out through a yawning exit wound. But not before he saw himself saying goodbye to his wife Lucinda three days ago. He was telling her about his irrational kernel of fear that this, whatever this was, would happen. She shushed his worries with a kiss and reminded him to take his meds.

Vanessa saw her shot splash wide right and cycled the bolt. After years of reliably shooting people dead at much longer range, this was a galling outcome. She bore down on the scope in disbelief. The target and Stoddard had dropped from sight and visibility had tanked. "Talk to me."

"Well," said Clay, laconically as an air traffic controller. "Somebody whacked the guide."

Stefan saw his round hit Dragan's fur-hatted head then rip through the American's neck in a geyser of red. He was briefly horrified by the ballistic snafu. Then elated. He'd killed both men with one bullet. Which was rather fantastic really. No loose ends. No witnesses. Nothing left to do but pull his meticulously planned intercontinental vanishing act. He rose slowly to his feet. Rifle still shouldered. Savoring the most consequential act of his life with a beaming expression.

Vanessa spotted the mystery shooter standing tall on the opposite slope right away. She was mesmerized at first then ice-cold rabid. Cocky bastard screws the money shot then fully exposes himself, grinning like he hit a home run. She stood up, wrapped the rifle sling around her left elbow, dead reckoned range and wind and put the crosshairs on the man's chest.

"Hola, dipshit," she whispered.

Then snapped off the best unbraced shot of her homicidal career.

The round tore through Stefan's breastbone and aorta and kept going. Flat on his back and cocooned by warm snow, he watched a jet cross a fissure of blue sky dragging a silver contrail. Then he was inside the aircraft looking for his seat. Passengers toiled on laptops and stared at their phones despite oxygen masks dangling wildly over their heads. For the life of him he couldn't remember the plane's destination. He was about to ask a flight attendant who looked eerily like his mom when his brain ran out of dissociative imagery and he died. Center-chest shot at 613 yards.

FORTY-SIX

Clay saw the shooter eat the slug. Recognized him right away. Then went back to glassing the bench because he saw the target get his head grooved but not popped. Vanessa dropped prone beside him. He glanced at her. "The dude you just deleted works for the target."

"What was he shooting at?"

"His boss."

She processed. "That explains the pistol shots."

"How?"

"He was doing the mercs."

Clay followed her reasoning, getting annoyed. "So there's a line to kill this old asshole."

Vanessa snugged into her scope and rifle. "Not anymore."

Clay squinted over his shoulder. He'd forgotten about Mace in the heat of battle. He was slumped over, arms tight around the tree exactly as before. The picture of quit. But now it struck Clay as somehow hinky. The son of a bitch was too hardcase to just sit there and hope for the best when he knew there was nothing but a bullet coming. He had to be up to something. Had to be.

"Eyes front," said Vanessa. "If our guy's gonna dip it's gonna be now."

Clay yanked his gaze off Mace and scoured the ground around Will's body. Saw another pair of legs and boots scooched up against the line of scree. "Still behind those rocks. Looked like he got nicked on the cabeza by the round that got Stoddard. Probably sleeping it off."

"*Pobrecito,*" Vanessa purred.

Jamie and Hazim were a quarter mile below the notch in the ridge when Stefan's shot rolled overhead. They were arm in arm and moving at a snail's pace, too exhausted to speculate what it meant. She wiped the snow off her eyebrows and gauged the last stretch against Hazim's infirmity. The incline was steep and blown out by drifts. It would take them an hour at this rate. Maybe more.

"How's your heart?" she asked.

"What?" he said, sucking on thin air.

She looked at him. "You ever have heart trouble?"

He shook his head. "No."

"Good. Gimme your pack and rifle and pop some more speed. I'm gonna break trail."

He squinted at her. Hypoxia making him slow and belligerent. "Why?"

"Because you're the guy who's gonna get us both killed and I don't want to be late for my own fucking funeral. Now give me your gun and pack, eat your crank like a good little terrorist and step where I step. Think you can you do that?"

He scowled at her. Fumbled his pack over but kept his rifle clutched to his chest in a death grip. She shouldered the brick-heavy load and high-stepped up the grade with Vince in her wake. Hazim watched her progress, stunned by her stride and stamina. Then he gobbled two of the fat brown tablets and went after her, head bent in concentration, filling her boot prints with his own.

The heavy boom of Stefan's rifle jerked Mace's head up. Split second later he heard Vanessa's suppressed shot. A minute later she fired again. Could've been putting a make-sure round in Will's client. Or in Will. Or somebody else entirely. That would explain the new gun. Then he heard Clay and Vanessa murmuring. Parsing indiscernible options. Seemed impossible she missed. But that lone unsuppressed shot was a massive wild card. Wasn't from down by the stream. Came from much higher on the slope opposite. Maybe from one of the mercs. But what were they shooting at? And why just one shot? None of it computed. Unless the mystery gun made Vanessa flinch and the rest devolved into a hot ballistic mess. Mace's inadvertent forte. He lowered his head. Eyes bugged and blind in the pitch dark. Focusing on tiny, tactile machinations. Now or never.

FORTY-SEVEN

The Monster woke blinking blood, befuddled by the lead skimming his skull. His first thought was that the cartridge exploded in the chamber then he remembered the misfire and turned to Will. Saw his guide face-down, neck in tatters and flattened himself in the snow. After ripping off his orange vest, he dug the ResQLink beacon from Will's parka, slung the Weatherby over his shoulder and waited. When a flurry raked his position, he sprinted for the oak to his rear, weaving with vigor. Two rounds snapped past his head. One tore his left earlobe off. The second grooved his neck. He noted the shots made no sound and that the shooting was very consistent, given the conditions.

Then a third round hit him high on the left side of his back, nicked his deltoid and punched him to the ground. He saw huge boulders ahead and dove through a cleft into gloom. After rolling to his knees, he drew the pearl-handled Walther P99 and aimed at the light leaking in behind him. He'd been shot before. More than once. So he knew the blood seeping down his back wasn't arterial. And his right arm was functional. Meaning essential bones and nerves were spared.

His partially shot-off ear, slug-seared neck and dented scalp were on fire and that was divine. Even better than his former mistress, cocaine. Meant he was alive. Meant he would survive. Again.

When no one came bursting in after him, he field-cleaned the Weatherby cursing himself for his sentimental lapse in judgment regarding security. As if his enemies ever stopped dreaming of roasting his severed head over a crackling fire. And the more he dissected his latest opponent's tactics, the more he admired their ingenuity. Hunt him while he was hunting elk in a remote corner of the Rocky Mountains. When droves of ordinary men carrying high-powered rifles in plain sight was the norm. A truly inspired scheme. Then a whiff of lavender jerked his head around.

It was the annoying Bosniak girl whose name he couldn't remember. He wanted to tell her to go away and be dead like everyone else he ever liquidated but his voice might carry. So he ignored her fragrant manifestation and focused on getting his weapon ready. Fuck his naïve infatuation with the enemy's fatalism. He wanted to fondle Russian models until he was too old to remember life without diapers. But first, his favorite sport and pastime beckoned. Let them come.

Vanessa seated a full magazine and cycled the bolt. "Okay, boomer. You still got some moves."

"You ruined his serve with number three," said Clay. "But no goodies. Doubt he bleeds out."

She kept her reticle nailed on the target's hidey-hole. "Give him a sec to shit himself and run."

"Doesn't strike me as the defecating type. What if he finds a back door?"

"To where? He chugs up that slope I'll clip his spine before he gets ten yards."

"Yea you will," said Clay. "Assuming we see him before he hits cover."

Vanessa took that in. "Okay. Three minutes. Then we go down there and dig him out."

Clay checked his watch and got behind the spotting scope. Then the wind died and downrange became a photoshopped winter wonderland. All they needed were Christmas carols and a sleigh. Then a feathery alarm tickled Clay's nuts like icy fingers. Happened all the time in his previous incarnation when he wasted indigenous shooters in dusty faraway places before they wasted him. He firmly believed the tickle had kept him alive to this day. That it was a sacred portent and never to be ignored. He whipped his head around, jumped like he was electrocuted and pulled his Glock.

"Pernicious son of a bitch," he whispered.

Vanessa followed his pistol's aim. The big aspen was empty. Mace was a mist. She had to admit she loved their guide's sneaky grit. Kinda the cream of the whole gig. A wrecked soul who knew his shit inside out. And surly rugged hot on top of that. What a waste. Then she got back on her scope and locked on the dark gap between the boulders.

"Go kill his ass and get back here," she instructed with no more ceremony than ordering coffee.

FORTY-EIGHT

Clay slung his rifle over his back and took off, sidearm at high ready. Saw Mace's hood on the ground and boot tracks making for the timbered ravine where it dove into the valley. He followed the sign in a two-handed stance, sweeping his front and flanks. Snowy debris messed with his footing and sight picture but he wasn't worried because he wasn't the unarmed rabbit. No sir. Mountain man was leaving a sloppy, scared-shitless swath a blind man could follow. Then the gulley narrowed and steepened into a deadfall-choked crevasse. Clay shifted to a one-handed grip. Started using his left hand to grab branches and keep from skidding into the bone-breaking clutter of trees and rocks below. Then he dug his heels in and stopped. Pistol up and rigid in disbelief. There was nothing but pristine powder in front of him. Mace's progress ended as if he'd levitated.

Clay pivoted, pistol sweeping the tangle of spruce and pine up down and sideways. He wanted to believe Mace had backtracked on him and kept running another direction entirely but his testicles didn't buy it. The story about the bear hunter coming upon his own tracks overlaid by the bear's flitted through his mind. Then his head was yanked back and something stung his Adam's apple.

He whipped around but Mace had already snagged his gun wrist and laid his face open from eyebrow to chin with the same object used to cut his throat. But that didn't immediately negate Clay's mass and muscle advantage. They tumbled down the ravine, Mace getting destroyed by punches and headbutts until Clay realized the jetting blood was all his. He let go of the weapon and they rolled to a stop, Clay on his back, hands pressed into his neck as if choking himself. Mace stood over him. Glock in one hand. Lovely ovoid of sculpted stone in the other.

Clay couldn't take his eyes off the Ute knife Mace had found in the rock shelter and stashed up his sleeve. It was lavender with flecks of amber, five inches long, two inches wide and made from moss agate. Its razor belly was devoid of the tiniest nick because it was designed to skin and disarticulate bison. So slicing a human down to bone was akin to carving through Jell-O wrapped in toilet paper.

"Know how they got it so sharp?" asked Mace like a patient teacher with a slow student.

Clay frowned, larynx sliced in half. "How?" he squeaked.

Mace leaned down close to his ear. "They had all the time in the world, bro."

Clay nodded then died staring at the thing that killed him. Mace made sure the pistol had a round chambered and was trying to muscle Clay's 225-pound carcass off his rifle when he heard the swish of boots cutting fast through snow at the top of the ravine. He hurled himself down the centerline of the draw, leaving the rifle where it was. After a hundred feet of uncontrolled sliding, he cartwheeled over a one-story face and briefly knocked himself senseless. He roused himself and clawed the knee-deep snow for the Glock but it was gone. And he'd completely spaced on taking Clay's satphone. Then a primal howl of grief soared over everything and he plunged downhill again, thinking that if nothing else, fear had made him so dimwitted he richly deserved to die.

Vanessa was on her knees cradling Clay's head. His syrupy hands were clinched over his throat and flakes had piled up in his sockets like matching bowls of salt. She brushed the snow away and saw his hazel eyes were open and vaguely expectant like he was in transit to a better place. She kissed him on the mouth and noticed his shoulder holster was empty. The missing handgun complicated things but not that much. This wasn't gonna be close work. Then she moved down the ravine until she reached the little cliff that Mace took headfirst and paused. Halfway down the drop she spotted the muzzle of Clay's Glock sticking from the snow and almost burst out laughing. The man who promoted the riskless slaughter of animals with the equivalent of a sniper rifle was naked prey running for his life. The irony was so delicious it made her teeth ache.

She left the pistol where it lay and followed Mace's tracks with a radiant expression. As much as she loved Clay, her sorrow was dwarfed by a rising karmic roar. Even if she'd waxed the old war criminal, the emotional orgasm would have been fake compared to hunting the guide in his own domain. She reminded herself to be patient. To kill him in little pieces. Scrupulously avoiding any vital organs until the very end. Then send one through his navel. That way they'd have plenty of time to chat while his intestines and pancreas dangled from the exit wound.

FORTY-NINE

The Monster checked the full box of Weatherby Magnum cartridges in his pocket. Counting the five in the magazine that put his ammo supply at twenty-five rounds, more than enough for a fighting withdrawal. Then he crept to the mouth of the cleft and looked around. He had no view of the ridge above but to the south he saw downhill ground and forest. That was the obvious escape route and his pursuers would have it covered. They'd botched the long-range option and were waiting to see if he bolted. But they wouldn't wait long. He knew all this because he'd hunted people with great success. They were highly predictable when terrified. Except he wasn't and his plan was simple.

Activate the ResQLink. Elude his pursuers until rescuers found him and transported him to the nearest hospital. Assume the Gulfstream was disabled by his enemies and contact the Serbian consulate in Denver. Instruct them to fetch him via helo and have a private med flight waiting at Denver International to whisk him back to Belgrade. Stefan and Luka and Marko barely crossed his mind other than making a note to fire them if they weren't already dead. The only variable was terrain and tactics. Then the soaring dome on the north rim of the drainage caught his eye.

Specifically the avalanche chute running down the face of the monolith. The last thing his would-be killers would expect. A fully exposed seven-hundred-meter climb up a narrow rock channel just shy of perpendicular. What better way to burnish his legend? Enthralled by his plan, he activated the ResQLink beacon. A strobe popped on and a signal intended for search and rescue networks began to beam skyward. He covered the light with an extra glove, clipped the device to his pack and crawled to the entrance of his hidey-hole. But a nagging question delayed his exit. Why had the dead Bosniak girl followed him all the way to this lonely chunk of Colorado? Why show up after all these years? Then it occurred to him, quite strongly, that she had come to see him die.

He looked over his shoulder and whispered a quote from the Koran just in case she was still lurking. One of his favorites. "Only those who are patient shall receive their rewards in full."

Then he slung his rifle over his back, slithered out of his burrow and into a reef of Gambel oak that ran all the way to the granite dome lording over the world.

Mace ran through drifts and scrub until his lungs screamed stop or else. He was bent over sucking icy air when a slug skimmed his right arm like hot grease chased by a faint cough. He lunged behind a tree and peeked uphill. There was no goddamn way she could spot him through all that timber. Then he saw the sign he was cutting through brushy snow. Shit. Maybe she could hear his branch-popping progress and was dead reckoning his position. Then he realized that was more magical thinking. He just butchered her partner. No way she'd kill him quick. She absolutely saw him with those freakish eyes and was hitting exactly where she aimed. She was toying with him. Like a cougar with a fawn. His heart was thumping hard enough to make his vision shimmy.

"Try not to die of fright," he muttered then took off staying so low he was crawling.

Jamie and Hazim reached the patch of juniper below the notch and rested in the same spot Will and the Monster had their final brandy. Vince watched the rear while they oxygenated then Jamie led the way up to the rim. Hazim handed her his binos and got behind his rifle and scope. After that, both got prone and scoured the blizzard-socked watershed until Jamie froze and gasped.

"Oh no," she whispered. "Oh please God no."

"What is it?" asked Hazim.

She stabbed a trembling finger at what she was looking at. He put the scope where she pointed. Found the bench above the stream with the face-down corpse and discerned the weapon strapped across the dead man's back. Even dredged in white, the shape of the rifle was recognizable.

"That is not your husband," said Hazim. "That is the Monster's guide."

She looked at him. "How do you know?"

"The rifle. It's the old gun he keeps in the window of his truck."

Jamie saw Will's wife Lucinda getting the news. Saw her toppling to her knees, head in hands. "You think the couple did that?" she asked.

"Absolutely."

"Why?"

"Practicality."

Jamie kept staring at Will's body. "We're definitely gonna kill them. Right?"

"Most definitely," said Hazim.

Then he scoped the area around the dead man wondering if the Americans blew the shot and hit Stoddard by accident. Or confused the guide with the Monster in the storm. Both possibilities seemed highly unlikely given their experience and discipline. He gauged the amount of snow piled on the guide's back and guessed he was killed an hour ago. So the Monster could still be hiding nearby. And very much alive because that was his gift. The possibility made Hazim's heart sing.

FIFTY

Mace splashed up Cottonwood Creek, dove into the alder and squirmed through a basket-weave of branches to the lip of a beaver pond. He squinted up the eastern slope. Saw the notch where the trail dropped in. Knew the cover was thick all the way to the fin of the ridge. Once he got up and over he'd haul down the other side and find hunters with cell phones. But then what. Call the cops. Get Jamie killed if she wasn't already dead. A noise to his rear made him turn. A creak of brush. Then a round clipped his left side chased by another splat. Felt like a bear claw dipped in sriracha.

He scrambled onto the beaver dam. Ran low along the mesh of wood and mud, slipped into the next pond up and waded out the far side leaving a large gap in his tracks. After that, he cut uphill and tucked behind a large rock to reconnoiter. The mouth of a timbered draw was right above him. She might track him in there but she'd never get a clear shot. He peeked downhill. Figured it'd take her five minutes to circle both ponds, pick up his sign and keep coming at a terminator pace. And that was all the head start he was gonna get. He scrambled into the safety of the draw, glanced downhill one last time and saw the bench by the creek. Then the body behind the low line of scree. It was caked with snow and he assumed it was the man the couple was hunting.

It even crossed his mind that Will was hiding nearby waiting for help, wondering what the hell he'd stepped in. Then he studied the dead guy again, dissecting what was breaking his heart long before his brain processed it as fact. That was a lever-action rifle across the corpse's back. So it wasn't the client. It was his lifelong friend lying down there. And his dad's. Then all that miserable prey behavior clogging his gut shit itself out leaving nothing but clean cold rage. No more rabbit.

Vanessa followed Mace's tracks to the creek, hit the dense alder, cradled the rifle and brought her pistol up. She circled the ponds like a bloodhound and picked up his sign again. Followed the tracks to within sight of the tree-filled ravine running up the ridge and knew his plan. Keep cover between him and a rifle round until he got over the top. Then lose her in open country and find help. Her choice was now binary. Go after him and hope to get within crippling range. Or go back across the creek, gain elevation and wait for a long kill shot. Then the decision got made for her.

Before he bolted, Mace calculated it would take her at least three seconds to get the rifle up and the scope tracking. Three seconds max and then dive for cover. Then he took off. But he was wrong. Two seconds later he heard the Remington's splat and felt the slug simultaneously. The round grooved his left quad and kicked his leg sideways. He crumbled into brush, rolled to his knees and kept clawing downhill praying the trees would spoil the next shot.

By the time Vanessa got over her surprise and on target she had to squeeze fast or not at all. Then she ran uphill and found the disturbed snow where Mace had sluiced downslope. She followed the mess at high ready, listening to the clatter of rocks and breaking branches he was making. Then it stopped and ringing silence ensued. Her instincts screamed break contact and find cover but her hands were gummy with Clay's blood and that was all that mattered. She crabbed forward, rifle shouldered. When she saw the bench through the oak she took a knee and scoped Mace's tracks. They went around Will's body and dropped out sight toward the creek. But now there was something different about the corpse. Something missing. She scoped it again. The old cowboy gun was gone. This fact registered simultaneously with the arrival of a 30-30 soft point.

The round plowed clean through her sternum, punctured her right lung then splintered her spine and stopped. The energy expended knocked her on her butt. She never heard the beefy crack of the Winchester but the rolling echoes told her what happened. She was surprised how little it hurt.

Mace levered a fresh round, caught the spent casing and moved in a wide circle to come up behind her. He heard her hacking before he saw her. She was sitting up, Glock extended with both hands. He waited until her head lolled and the pistol dropped then ran over and kicked her flat on her back. After that he grabbed her sidearm and rifle, tossed them and dug into her parka with gloved hands. Found her satphone, couldn't unlock it and dropped it. Found his Tundra keys and stashed those in his coat. Then she groaned awake and saw Mace standing over her. He raised the spent casing and wiggled it until her eyes made sense of the thing. "That's for Will," he said.

She grimaced up on one elbow. "Wasn't me. But it's the thought that counts."

Mace squatted low and scanned the skyline, worried about the unknown gun. "See who it was?"

"Oh yea," she said, face briefly brightening. "He was hard to miss."

Mace looked at her replaying the flurry of gunfire. Now it made sense. The couple had competition. "He hit Will by mistake. You yipped. Then killed the shooter with your second."

Vanessa ducked her chin. Saw the bubbling hole in her chest and the pair of legs and boots she knew were hers but couldn't feel and nodded. "Fucking limp dick amateur hour."

Mace cupped her face. Jerked it into his. "Where's Jamie?"

She frowned at him. Puzzled. One foot out the big door. Mace grabbed her by the shoulders and shook her, grinding wrecked vertebra and lumbar nerves. She shrieked in a garbled falsetto and passed out. Mace yanked her up by the hair and waited until she came to hacking blood.

"Tell me where my wife is," he said quietly.

"Or what?" she slurred through pink teeth. "Gonna shoot me again?"

He let her head flop in the snow and watched her fight for air. Produced less pleasure than he imagined it would. Then her eyes locked on the blizzard's belly and her face went slack as if some huge bird of prey was swooping down. Made Mace think of Robert Martinez. The cool serenity in his final gaze compared to Vanessa's jaw-hung terror. After that she shuddered hard and died.

Mace got to his feet seeing Jamie's shackled body in some down-and-dirty grave he'd never find and it broke everything inside him. He was rubble with skin. Not worth killing as his father used to say. After a minute something came to him and he fumbled under his anorak and dug out the wadded-up note Jamie left on the kitchen table. The one reminding him of what had to be done and how much she loved him. He was reading it for the fourth time when the vibration leaking up through the snow finally registered. He put the note back where he found it, pawed Vanessa's satphone out of the powder and wiped it clean. There was a missed call from an unknown number.

He was staring numbly at the screen when the phone vibrated again. Same number. He peeled off a glove, swiped the green icon and put it to his ear. Someone was breathing hard on the other end. A man's deep-throated rasp. Mace opened his mouth then bit his tongue wondering what the guy on the other end might do if he didn't hear Vanessa or Clay's voice. Then he decided the downside was nonexistent at this point and started speaking in a conversational tone.

"This is Mason Winters. Vanessa can't come to the phone right now but she got the guy you were after. Nice clean kill. Shot half his head off. So I'm thinking we're done and I did my part. Just tell me where Jamie is and go. I won't call the cops. Won't go near her until you tell me to. Just don't hurt her. And bear in mind I'm better off dead without her. So chasing you and anyone you ever cared about to the end of the earth would be a fucking paid vacation. What do you say?"

Static hissed from the phone. Mace's tears were turning to slush as fast as he made them.

"Tell her yourself," said the caller.

"Do what?" said Mace, certain he hadn't heard right.

FIFTY-ONE

Hazim gave Jamie the cell phone, shouldered his rifle and scoped the man at the base of the slope to the south. He was holding the guide's carbine. The woman called Vanessa lay at his feet.

"Turn around, my love," said Jamie, binos to her eyes. "And look up the ridge behind you."

There was a sound of recognition from the other end. Guttural and inarticulate. Then Hazim took the phone back, pulverized it against a rock and scattered the shards into white nothing.

Mace wheeled north. Squinted up the incline toward the notch but the snow was a shimmering curtain. He yanked his anorak open and grabbed the Leicas he'd forgotten were around his neck. Got them dialed in on the blurred specs atop the ridge and nearly buckled at the knees. The smaller spec was Jamie and she was waving both arms. A man was standing next to her. A large man. He had a bolt-action rifle aimed right at his nose. For a second he thought he saw Vince standing between them. But that was impossible. All of it was completely impossible.

Hazim and Jamie stumbled on the corpse of a man halfway down the slope. He was on his back, arms flung as if making a snow angel. A swank Italian rifle lay near the head. Hazim brushed the snow off, recognized Stefan and kept moving. Jamie didn't bother asking who it was. Vince gave the black goo clogging the cadaver's nostrils a sniff then caught up with Jamie, fur riled and ready.

When they reached Vanessa's body, Mace was gone. Fresh boot tracks disappeared into alder. Vince caught the scent and followed them at a lope. Jamie yelled for him to come back but he paid her no mind and vanished. Hazim handed Jamie his rifle and clapped his hands behind his head.

"What are you doing?" she asked.

"Trying not to get shot twice in one day."

She cradled the rifle and they waited. The snow intensified and the invisible shepherd started barking and whining until falling silent on a dime. Two minutes passed. Then Mace materialized behind them with Vince at his side. The Winchester was locked on Hazim, hammer thumbed back.

"Get away from him, Jamie."

She did and Mace moved forward. Jamie slid under his arms and buried her face in his chest while he kept the big guy nailed at point-blank range.

"Where is Clay?" asked Hazim without turning his head.

"Resting," said Mace. "Who the fuck are you?"

"I kidnapped your wife."

Mace took a deep breath, about to shoot the guy then and there until Jamie laid a hand on his arm.

"His name is Hazim," she said. "He also saved my life."

Mace eased her aside and jabbed Hazim's neck with the barrel. "That true?"

"No, it is not," he said. "We saved each other."

Mace glanced at Jamie, getting sick of surprise answers. She nodded. He stabbed Hazim with the Winchester again. "You packing a sidearm like every other asshole around here?"

"Under my coat. Left side."

Mace found the Beretta and lobbed it downhill into the creek. "Look at me."

Hazim turned around, hands on his head. Jamie saw Mace was still inclined to shoot him.

"Glenn was in on it," she said by way of putting off the execution.

Mace winced. As if she'd bounced a rock off his head. "In on what?"

"Everything. The couple paid him to kill Hazim and me after they killed Will's client."

"How could you know that?"

"Glenn told me after he shot Hazim. Then I blew his brains out with that .38 you bought me."

The Winchester sank along with Mace's jaw. "You blew Glenn's brains out."

"Sure did," she said. "Then I remembered the trophy hole. And here we are."

Mace stared at the new Jamie. The calmly matter-of-fact murderer. Tried to slow it all down. The roaring deluge of crazy inexplicable shit. "Just to rescue me?"

Hazim gingerly took one hand off his head. Pointed north at the dome. "Among other things."

Mace followed his finger. Saw a shape moving up the avalanche chute. Took a step back and glassed the thing. It was the bastard everyone and their mother was trying to kill. He was moving at a snail's pace with his rifle over his shoulder but getting it done. Made no sense. Unless he thought he was still being hunted. And the most unlikely way out of the drainage was the best. He looked at Vanessa's snow shrouded body then at Hazim and the bigger picture snapped into focus.

"You're the son of a bitch behind all this. You paid the realtors to kill that guy up there. Now you have to do it yourself."

Hazim nodded. "With Allah's blessing."

The Islamic mantra threw Mace. A layer of outlandish smeared over the whole extravaganza. He glanced at Jamie. Her eyes were on the man scaling the dome. Like he was the mother lode of the whole misbegotten mess.

"He's getting away," she said.

"So what?" said Mace.

"So we can't let that happen."

Mace looked at her kidnapper. Saw the blood caking Hazim's right hip and figured that was a bullet hole. Saw knife cuts all over his face. Wondered how he stayed upright. Then jerked a thumb at the fellow on the granite massif. "What'd he do to you?"

"I'll leave your education to your wife," said Hazim. "May I please have my rifle back."

"Hell no."

Jamie heaved the gun at Hazim in one clean thrust. He caught it like he knew it was coming, careful to keep his fingers away from the safety and trigger. Eyes daring Mace to shoot him.

Mace kept the Winchester laid on Hazim even as he looked at Jamie. The phrase Stockholm syndrome flitted through his head. "You lose your goddamn mind? He caused all this."

"I know," she said, unfazed. "Now let him hunt."

Hazim saw rage and confusion in Mace's body language but no lethal threat. He moved closer and spoke quietly. "Get rid of the dead woman's satphone. Dump anything connected to this."

"Why would I do that?" said Mace.

"Maybe to grow old with your beautiful wife."

Mace was incredulous. "And forget you put her in chains and got my friend killed?"

Hazim's eyes slid over to the dot moving up the chute. Calculating the distance to reasonable range then slant and bullet drop. "How many people did you kill today?" he asked.

Mace shrugged, still seeing red. "Two. But the day is young."

"And Jamie killed a policeman. You think that will be easy to explain in your American court?"

Mace looked at her. Saw a fateful calm bordering on madness. Then Hazim shifted his rifle to low ready, snicked the bolt and made sure a round was seated. Mace heard the oiled clack and turned to face him. Saw an innate familiarity with firearms. Nothing for show. A soldier for sure. Occurred to him the guy called Hazim could have shot him dead from up on that ridge a while ago.

"You really think you can walk away from a goatfuck this big?" he asked.

"Never planned to," said Hazim. "But you and Jamie might."

With that he headed for the dome with a listing stride. Just before he hit cover he looked back at his former prisoner. They had a raw moment. Then a howling flurry smeared him from view.

FIFTY-TWO

The Monster had traveled two hundred meters up the chute when he paused for a vertical recon. His route followed a wide stone gutter into roiling clouds. He checked the ResQLink and confirmed the signal was good. But flying conditions were junk and being plucked off the face was problematic. Plan B was to reach the top and drop into the next valley. Find shelter, build a fire and come dawn find people not trying to kill him. Then the brute cold stuck a knife through his parka and paranoia followed. He scanned his rear and sure enough saw movement in the trees below. Someone was coming after him. Their gait was odd. Not unlike a wounded animal. He got on his scope.

There was a good reason the Swarovski glass cost five thousand euros. The clarity and color balance were sublime. He followed fresh boot tracks into heavy timber, scoured the far side of the cover and saw none. Then he waited, finger on the trigger, right eye unblinking even though the range was prohibitive. Whoever made the tracks was sitting tight and probably glassing him right back. Then the Monster noticed the dying quality of the light. The October day was slipping through his fingers. He shouldered his rifle and resumed his ascent with a keenness born of growing unease.

Mace was breaking trail south along Cottonwood Creek when he looked back and saw Jamie had stopped a good ways behind him. She was frowning down at the snow with a stricken expression. Vince stood beside her, not going anywhere until she did. Mace retraced his steps at a lope. By the time he reached her, she'd turned toward the dome. He got in her face and blocked her view of the hunted man relentlessly working his way toward the top of the chute.

"That is not our problem anymore," he said.

"Maybe. Except it's all for nothing if he gets away."

He cupped her face. Saw the scary fire in her eyes. "Listen to me. We walk outta here right this second all we ever have to do is tell the truth. And that is not nothing."

"You're right," she said. "I just don't think I can live with it."

Mace stepped back. Braced himself. "What exactly don't you think you can live with?"

She shook her head. Like he was being obtuse about the obvious. Then raised her arm and pointed at the distant dot that was the Monster. "Hazim will never get that fucker by himself."

That fact fizzed through Mace's brain, making him lightheaded because he knew what it meant.

"So you want me to guide your new best friend? Help him harvest that guy up there on the cliff? For what? Not getting both of us killed already? You know how bat-shit crazy you sound?"

Jamie nodded. "Yep. Guess it's my turn."

Mace eyed the dome again. Realized it was the perfect place for this misbegotten mess to end. A billion-ton beast offering a hundred ways to die on a balmy June day much less coated with blue norther ice. Then he searched Jamie's face for the woman he married. She was still there but brand-new in a way that couldn't be altered. She'd been thrown into the fire and crawled out reborn.

"And what about us?" he asked. "What happened to no matter what?"

Jamie didn't flinch. "This is it."

Mace blinked and looked around. Saw Vince the eternal guardian reading his thoughts before they formed. Saw the river of snow barreling overhead, entombing mountains and bodies with indifferent ferocity. Saw the whole world balling by with or without him. She was right. This was it and there was no going home. Not yet. He dug the satphone from his coat and stared at the gluey smear of Vanessa's blood on the keypad. Then tossed the thing in the creek and stuck his hand out.

"Gimme the pistol."

Jamie didn't move. "Why?"

"They call it rifle season for a reason."

She pulled the revolver out and gave it to him. Mace couldn't help but notice the oatmeal spray of brain gunk on the barrel as he pitched the gun into the deepest, darkest pool he could find.

FIFTY-THREE

Hazim didn't hear Mace and Jamie until they were on top him. He twisted around, rifle leveled at blurred apparitions, ready to unload before the sight of the dog snapped his combat trance.

"Go back," he said, incensed at their recklessness. "Go back now."

Mace stopped in his tracks, cradled the Winchester and snagged Vince's collar. Jamie walked right up to Hazim, smacked the barrel of his gun aside and pointed at her husband.

"See that guy?" she said. "You got zero chance of bagging the Monster without him."

Hazim parked one massive palm an inch from her nose as if shutting down a willful child. "Just for once be quiet. And go home. I will not put you in danger again."

Jamie bashed his hand away, voice rising. "I am motherfucking home. And I've been in danger since you showed up."

"Hey, Hazim," said Mace. "I got a question."

Jamie and Hazim turned like they'd forgotten he was there.

"Ever shoot that rifle in a snowstorm at ten thousand feet?" asked Mace.

"I won't miss," said Hazim.

Mace gauged the sickly sun and the stiff breeze. "You won't get a chance to miss unless you get position and nail the drop and windage."

Hazim was digesting that when he saw a slender female figure emerge from driving snow beyond Mace. Her hair was lush and billowed like black fire. Vince growled at the apparition but neither Mace nor Jamie took notice. As if the figure was beyond the realm of their senses. Then the shape turned and melted away and Jamie's hand was resting on Hazim's chest.

"You wanna kill that son of a bitch?" she asked. "Or freeze to death while he gets away?"

Hazim stared at her then at Mace. Flakes stung his eyes until the second miracle disguised as two brave Americans revealed itself. The power of it bowed his head. "Kill him," he whispered.

Jamie slugged him on the shoulder. "Now you're talking."

Mace broke trail keeping dense scrub oak between his party and the dome. Hazim was right behind him and Jamie and Vince brought up the rear. He was heading for a runoff cut ravine that curved skyward along the east side of the drainage. The feature was carved in bullet-stopping scree and might cut range and elevation down to something under fat chance. He glanced back at Hazim without breaking stride. Saw the true-believer glow and a load of pain under that.

"What kinda rifle is he carrying?"

Hazim had to suck air before answering. "Weatherby Magnum."

"What kinda glass?"

"Swarovski."

"He any good with that high-dollar gear?" asked Mace.

"Very."

The Monster was making steady progress when the snow paused and the light swelled, throwing his shadow against bleak rock. He dropped behind a piano-size slab lodged in the chute and scanned the sky. Shooting conditions were suddenly ideal. He raised the Weatherby and glassed his rear. Took less than a minute to spot three people moving carefully behind snow-draped trees about fifteen hundred meters from his perch. He started to smile thinking it was his crew coming after him. Then he saw the shepherd and nearly jumped for joy thinking it was a search and rescue team. After that, all the magical thinking fell apart. The trio was adroit about cover and not bothering to signal because they were maneuvering into range. He was looking at a stalk and he was the trophy.

As he watched, the hunting party veered into a gully that rose sharply toward his position. He studied the gash in the slope and saw their tactic plain as day. Gain altitude, close distance and pick him off at their leisure. He checked his flanks. The moraine on both sides of the dome was scrolled with deep drifts. If he left the chute he'd be a slow, flailing target. A hot dose of panic rammed his heart. Then he calmed himself with a simple ballistic truth. If he was in range, the enemy was in range. If he stayed behind the slab and was judicious with his fire, he could keep his pursuers at bay until dusk. Maybe kill one or two of them before finishing his climb in full dark.

Pleased with his plan, he hydrated with brandy, set five rounds on the rock by his elbow, got on the scope and waited. Then a popping noise made him look up the chute. A skirmish line of his eternal followers waited on top of the dome. Twenty or thirty of them. The noise was their raggedy burial clothes snapping in the wind. They seemed highly entertained by his situation. Ghastly grins creasing each and every face. He laughed, flipped them off and got back on his scope.

FIFTY-FOUR

Mace reached the ravine, motioned Jamie and Hazim to stay put, bellied up to the lip and glassed the chute. Saw a head pop up behind a big slab, snug into a scoped rifle and scour the length of the ravine before disappearing. The man did it quick and clean. Like he knew they were coming. Mace put the range at a steep eight hundred yards. He looked up the cut. It seemed to curve into a mound of glacial debris some distance above his position. Just might work. Then he slid down off the lip and moved uphill hugging the ravine's sheltering wall with Hazim, Jamie and Vince behind him. The madness of putting his wife and dog in greater hazard with every step was a squirming blade in his gut.

When he got near the mound, Mace crawled up to it by himself, found a notch and studied the slab again. He'd shaved off a bunch of range. As he watched, the man in the chute appeared, scoped his hiding place with creepy accuracy and dropped from view. The bastard was guessing right every time. Then the blizzard resumed its gale-force punch as if tired of piddling around.

Mace scooted down to his new client. "Think he'll sit tight till dark and keep climbing?"

Hazim thought on that a second. "No. He will do his best to kill us now."

"What makes you so sure?"

"That is what I would do."

Mace pointed at his rifle. "What'd you zero that in at?"

"Three hundred meters."

Mace did the math. "Okay. You're looking at a five-hundred-meter shot at twenty-five degrees. Wind's a bitch from left to right. Not gonna be any drop. You're gonna hit high. Understand?"

Hazim nodded and looped the sling around his left biceps with disconnected calm. Mace checked his watch. Sixty minutes of shooting light left. Tops. Then he moved Jamie and Vince behind a boulder that could stop a semi and cupped her face. "Don't even stick your head out until I say so."

She kissed him. Nice but nothing special. Like they were standing on the porch and he was off to guide some country club neophyte toting his first big-boy rifle. "Don't miss," she said.

Mace and Hazim scrambled up to the mound of rubble and paused. Mace motioned at the right side of the pile where it was laced with slits and holes like an Anasazi ruin. Hazim scooched over and found an aperture to his liking with room for his scope and forestock. Then he rose to one knee and slid the barrel through the opening. Mace found a wide enough slot for his binos to Hazim's right and both got busy glassing the chute. Visibility fluctuated between fair and none due to the whirlpool of flakes in the lee of the dome. Then a wobbling roar crashed by on the wind. High up and some distance away. Mace's first thought was thundersnow. Upward sheering pockets of ice getting electrically charged like a summer rain. Thunder and lightning resulted. It was rare but he'd seen it more than once. Then the sound echoed away to nothing and he got back on the Leicas.

"See that sideways slab two-thirds of the way up?" he asked.

Hazim shifted his weapon a few inches. "Yes."

"He's behind it."

Emboldened by alcohol and rapidly fading light, the Monster hitched his right shoulder and scoped the mound of rock at the top of the ravine to the east. His gut told him his pursuers would settle in and shoot from there and his gut had never been wrong in these matters. But he saw no sign of them. Thinking he might have overestimated their progress, he rose a bit higher to sweep the lower approaches, unwittingly exposing the upper half of his torso.

Mace saw the man in the chute's mistake at the same instant he heard a deep thud bearing down on their perch. Wasn't thundersnow, it was rotor blades. He looked left. Saw Hazim was starting his squeeze and tackled him before the firing pin went home. They landed in a heap as a red Bell 407 with a basket on the skids screamed out from under the clouds directly over their heads.

The chopper banked over the dome, yawing and bucking in the wind. The Monster jumped to his feet, waving the beacon with its dazzling white light. Hazim saw his target fully illuminated, shoved Mace away and shouldered his weapon. His reticle was locked on the Monster's heart when Mace ripped the rifle from his arms, jammed the muzzle into his stomach and bellowed in his face.

"They can't drop a basket and they can't land! They're gonna call ground teams and split! But if they see us now we're all fucked! And I swear to whatever god works I will kill you right here!"

Hazim lay there hyperventilating. Eyes on the muzzle stuck in his navel. Then nodded.

Mace thumbed the safety on and gave the rifle back. "And you better goddamn shoot straight."

The Monster couldn't believe the efficiency of America. Hit a button and a big beautiful helicopter spirals out of a snowstorm into frozen wilderness to haul him off to a warm hospital. One minute he's DiCaprio in *The Revenant* and the next he's in the lap of high-tech medicine. Then the chopper leveled out into a wobbly hover twenty meters away and even with his position. A barely discernible crewman slid the bay door back and waved at him through the whiteout. The Monster waved back and the crewman made a flattening motion with both hands. As in stay put. The Monster shook his head and yelled something obscene and incredulous. Then the bay door slammed and the helo clawed up into the gloom, red-and-yellow nav lights blinking bye-bye.

By the time Mace and Hazim got reset behind the mound, the Monster had stowed the beacon and dropped behind the slab. The snow was steady and dusk was sucking light away by the second. Then the top of a fur hat eased into view on the left side of the slab. Hazim and Mace both saw it as a ruse to give up their position and sat tight. A minute later, on the far right side of the slab where shadows pooled down the dome, something slid into view with snakelike caution. Mace tweaked his Leica's. Discerned a rifle barrel. Then a scope. Then the vaguest suggestion of a human head behind the glass. The Monster was combing their position like they were his.

"See him?" said Mace. "He's all the way on the right."

Hazim shifted and bore down on the scope. But thousands of sunblasted days straining to see the enemy before they saw him had taken their toll. "Yes," he lied, amazed at Mace's acuity.

"Get ready. And do not pull that trigger until I say so."

Lucky for Hazim, Mace was counting on frustration and arrogance to make the man high on the rock face careless. To expose more than a dim portion of his head. And not a minute later the Monster got antsy and rose almost a foot. Just high enough to offer the upper reaches of his lungs.

"Send it," said Mace.

Hazim saw the anatomical gift clear enough and squeezed. Half a second later the 150-grain slug passed six inches above the Monster's right clavicle before pulverizing itself against the chute.

Hazim cycled the bolt and brass chimed.

"Wide left and high at two o'clock," said Mace.

"I know," said Hazim.

The Monster dialed in the flash and fired simultaneously with Hazim's second shot. Casings clattered and the slugs passed in the ether. Wind nudged the Monster's round left, blasting flecks of stone into Mace's face and knocking the binos out of his hands. Hazim's number two passed just left of the target's neck where it enters the torso and splashed rock. The Monster ran the Weatherby's bolt without flinching at the shock wave of debris. Then put his reticle on the face of the man out to kill him and exhaled slowly. Hoping his eternal followers were paying attention.

Mace got his glass up, blinking away blood. Saw the Monster drawing down on Hazim's muzzle and the head behind the gun. He was about to shout a warning when Hazim squeezed first and the Monster vanished like a deleted photo. There one second, rifle shouldered. Click. Gone the next.

Hazim cycled his weapon and stayed on the scope. Mace wiped his eyes and looked down. Saw the spent brass from Hazim's third shot lying at his feet and picked it up. The cartridge was warm to the touch. A thread of white smoke tore off in the wind like a caricature of a tiny soul.

FIFTY-FIVE

The round passed through the Monster's upper-right chest, socking him backward. He bounced off the rock wall, landed face-down and unconscious until demolished nerves stabbed him awake. He rolled over and gaped at the monolith overhead. He had no idea what happened because high-caliber gunshot wounds induce a fugue state common to head-on collisions. He saw a rifle nearby and dragged it over. The sight of his beloved Weatherby unclogged his short-term memory. He was hunting elk in America. But something had gone horribly wrong and he was unspeakably cold.

He craned his head around, teeth chattering violently, thinking maybe he fell off the cliff rising above him. Except he would be dead. Eventually he noticed his own blood, gobs of it, dashed on icy granite with Pollock-like abandon. Then he found the small dark hole in his parka and concluded he'd been shot. It occurred to him that whoever did the shooting might be on their way to finish the job.

He tried to shoulder the rifle but it was incredibly heavy. He remembered the Walther P99 in the holster under his parka but his fingers couldn't operate the zipper. Then he blacked out again.

Mace was crouched two stories below the slab, Winchester at high ready. Hazim was five yards below him and Jamie below that gripping the dog's collar. All three were tucked behind boulders in the main channel of the avalanche chute. Deep snow was lathered and corniced all the way up.

Mace looked over his shoulder and whispered, "He carry a pistol?"

Hazim frowned like it was a dumb question. "Of course."

Mace thumbed the hammer back and scrambled straight up until he saw an arm and a leg flung out on the right side of the slab. They were slack. He steeled himself, swung around the left side and saw the downed man had his back and head braced against the rock. His eyes were closed, his hands open and empty. The Weatherby lay beside him, thinly veiled in white. Mace kicked the rifle away, dug a swank semiauto out from under the guy's parka and backhanded it into space.

The Monster opened his eyes. Saw the old scopeless carbine Mace carried. "Well done."

"I'm not the one who shot you," said Mace, waving at the others to come on.

Jamie and Vince climbed into view first then she went back and helped Hazim up the last steep stretch. He immediately leveled his rifle at the Monster as if he might need another round. Jamie saw a hypothermic gunshot victim circling the drain and shook her head. "Don't bother," she said.

Hazim set his rifle aside and took a knee. The Monster squinted at him, shivering nonstop.

"What do you want, soldier?" he asked sternly, knowing the breed at a glance.

Hazim stared at the torn-up old man as if he were a mythical beast fallen from the sky. Saw his body emptying out by the second. Settling into rock and snow like the mummified climbers littering Everest. Then he dug out the laminated photo and held it close until the playful gaze of the dead burned through the Monster's befuddlement. His head reared back in amazement.

"The girl from Kozarac," he whispered.

"Yes," said Hazim. "Do you remember her name?"

"No. Do you?"

Hazim bowed his head. Jamie laid a hand on his shoulder and felt sobs running up her arm.

"Ajna," Hazim said at last. "Her name was Ajna."

The word flowered in the Monster's mind and he saw the raven-haired beauty become flesh and blood and console the weeping soldier. Jamie watched the Monster gape at her in astonishment and wondered what his dying brain saw. Then Hazim cupped his chin and aligned their eyes.

"I am her brother," he said.

The Monster saw the shattered heart of his assassin and gasped. He had no idea a brother existed until that moment but knew their fate was indivisible. Two lives arcing across the decades toward a preordained, zero-sum collision on a nameless Colorado mountain. Ancient enemies squatting in the gory rubble of their past. Their trajectories now complete. The symmetry exquisite.

"How does it feel?" asked the Monster, no longer cold or confused. The world and everything in it making perfect, familiar sense. An eye for an eye and a tooth for a tooth. Always and forever.

Hazim got to his feet and took the deepest breath of his life. "Good enough."

The Monster swirled that answer around in his mouth with a smitten expression. He was a connoisseur of payback and this particular vintage was aged to earthy perfection with a brash but harmonious finish. Then his eyes landed on the line of luminous creatures waiting patiently on the rim of the dome. His face darkened and he shouted something succinct in Serbian. After that, his blood-filled lungs cut him off and he died with a gargling snarl congealing on his lips.

Jamie followed his gaze upward. Saw harsh ramparts and sideways snow. Nothing else.

"What'd he say?" she asked.

"Here I come," said Hazim.

Jamie was about to check the Monster's pulse out of habit when a fluttering sensation seeped through the soles of her boots. She looked at Mace and Hazim. They were both watching Vince. The dog's ears were cocked skyward, registering what the humans could not. A swarm of minute cracks was emanating from the McMansion-size cornice crowning the chute. The mass of snow and ice was bowing to an untenable angle of repose made worse by the helicopter's pounding blades. Fissures were fanning out and propagating, weakening the snowpack's precarious hold on the dome by the second. Then everything in every direction broke free and charged downhill.

Mace shoved Jamie and Vince behind the slab, clutched them to his chest and wrapped his hands and arms around their faces to form air pockets. Hazim landed on top of him, bear-hugging everybody. Then the 100 mph avalanche hit and the world cartwheeled into darkness. Hazim was torn away like a toy and a lung-squashing mass no different than cement settled on Mace's back.

When the impact faded to petrified silence, Mace couldn't move a finger or an eyelid. Powered by pure panic, he freed his hands and cleared space around his wife and dog's mouth. Then bucked and clawed his way up through a yard-thick sheath of friction-hardened snow until fresh air poured in. A minute later he hauled Jamie and Vince into the bitter night and they looked around like snowmen with their snowdog. Aside from the slab, the slide had swept the chute clean as a whistle.

The runout zone ended a mile away in the watershed below. They stumbled downhill screaming for Hazim until but it was akin to yelling at a cemetery. They were halfway across the avalanche track when Vince began to bark and tug at something. Mace saw a boot heel and yelled for Jamie. They dug until an ice encased head appeared. Jamie cleared the nose and mouth while Mace freed the torso and legs. Hazim gasped in panic, opened his eyes and let Vince lick his face with the wondrous expression of a man declared dead then lifted alive and well from his coffin.

Mace and Jamie looped their arms around his waist and they all followed the avalanche track downhill. A bit later, they came upon a tubular object sticking out of the snow and enameled in white. Mace lifted the Winchester's barrel clear, brushed the rifle off and slung it over his shoulder.

Hazim squinted at him. Concerned by this decision. "That's a dangerous thing to keep."

Mace scanned the night and kept moving. "Compared to what."

They continued three abreast with the dog roaming their flanks. Every five minutes Hazim's knees would buckle and they'd let him oxygenate and lurch on. They were just twenty yards from the safety of undemolished timber when two hard beams of light speared the darkness to the east. Then two snowmobiles crested the ridge trailing plumes of powder and stopped, engines idling.

Mace made everyone drop to the snow. He couldn't see the riders but knew they were the tip of the spear. A massive search-and-rescue effort was gearing up. Will and his client must have been reported missing hours ago. Throw in Glenn and the four men Clay and Vanessa murdered for giggles and the rodeo would be on steroids by dawn. He was wondering what the people on the machines were waiting for when the answer slapped his bone-tired head. They were combing the avalanche track with night vision and checking their receivers for a beeping rescue beacon.

Then the snowmobiles fired up and screamed down the slope, headlights blasting the debris field.

Mace and Jamie dragged Hazim into the pitch-dark spruce praying the searchers wouldn't cross the dog and boot tracks before the wind wiped them clean. Because that would be game over.

When they reached the Tundra it was an angular mass submerged in white. Mace got the engine going, dug a tarp and a spare pair of insulated overalls from the toolbox and tossed them to Jamie. She spread the tarp over the back seat and they lifted Hazim in. She redid his dressing and slammed him with more antibiotics. Took both of them to pull off his bloody pants and coat and wrestle him into the overalls. After that, they got rid of the tarp and Vince jumped in beside Hazim and Jamie took shotgun. Then Mace busted out of the woods and drove east on Dead Horse Road worrying about the quarter-tank on the gas gauge. Couple miles on, Jamie got tired of Hazim grunting in pain with every jounce of the truck and almost lost a finger ramming a fentanyl tablet down his mouth. Nobody noticed the constellations sparkling through ragged clouds. The blizzard was done.

FIFTY-SIX

A helicopter passing low overhead finally yanked Jimmy Temple from his alcoholic slumber. He groaned off his cot and out of his bag and peeked outside. Saw deep snow piled on the G-Wagon and his Explorer. Will's red F-350 was nowhere to be seen. This struck him as weird but not catastrophic. After that he got dressed, waddled over to the chuck tent, made coffee and got his supper fixings out. Then the caffeine hit and an inkling of disaster breached his marinated brain. He checked his watch and cursed in disbelief. It was fucking 2:29 a.m. on Sunday. Saturday supper had come and gone eight hours ago. He checked the thermometer outside the tent. Read five degrees Fahrenheit. Took a few seconds for the disastrous implications to sink in. Then he dug out his cell and stabbed 911. Oblivious to the lavish head start he'd given Mace and Jamie and her kidnapper.

After dropping off the plateau, Mace looped through Placerville then cut south on 145 and got behind a snowplow clearing Lizard Head Pass or they wouldn't have gone anywhere. An hour later they hit Cortez and pulled over in the dark across from a Chevron station. Mace took his Visa from his wallet before realizing how terminally dumb that would be. He stuffed the card back and saw exactly eleven dollars in cash in his wallet. "Shit," he said, looking at the gas pumps across the street.

"What's wrong?" asked Jamie.

"We use a card we're done."

She reached in the back, relieved the out-cold Hazim of his money belt and gave Mace a sheaf of C-notes. He grabbed a cap and scarf from the console, covered most of his face then snagged a big jerry can from the bed and walked over to the station. After filling it with gas and loading up on Red Bull, jerky and water he loped back to the truck and fueled it up. Then they rolled south on Highway 491. Just past Chimney Rock, he pulled over and climbed up in the bed with the Leicas. The road behind him was empty black but he couldn't shake the queasy feeling of being prey all over again. The Winchester was under the back seat with five rounds in the tube but that didn't make him feel any better. He glassed the pavement to their rear one more time and drove on.

They crossed the Ute Mountain Reservation and the New Mexico line without incident. After grabbing more gas in Gallup they ran through tiny communities named Fence Lake, Buckhorn and White Signal. Then they traversed the volcanic fields of the Mogollon Mountains looking like a postapocalyptic Toyota commercial. At Lordsburg they jumped onto the 10 Freeway and merged with a river of semis hauling east into predawn darkness. Ten miles later, Mace spotted a pair of headlights weaving lazily through big rigs. It was not a truck. Eventually the vehicle settled in thirty yards off his stern and hung there. A minute later a light bar erupted in blue and red.

Mace signaled and pulled over to the shoulder. The cruiser stopped two lengths back, high beams hosing the Tundra blind. Hazim stirred and cranked his head around.

"What is this?" he asked.

"Cop," said Mace, rolling his window down.

The cruiser opened and a lanky man wearing the Smokey Bear hat of the New Mexico state police dismounted. He walked up to the truck, right hand resting on his service weapon then stopped at the driver's window and ran his flashlight over the occupants. Only the dog looked unscathed by barroom violence. Being New Mexico, this wasn't uncommon in the wee hours. What struck the trooper as weird was the lack of booze or dope fumes. He shifted his full attention to the driver.

"Good morning, sir. License and registration please."

The officer was a crewcut Latino in his mid-forties. He had a lineless face and bullshit-cured eyes that stayed glued on Mace's hand as it popped the glove box and grabbed what he asked for. After a cursory inspection of Mace's credentials, he handed them back and looked at Hazim again. The deep cuts on the big guy's face and overall thrashed condition were too evocative to let slide.

"You doing okay, sir?"

Hazim gave him a woozy thumbs-up. "Excellent. Never better."

The cop graded the off-key answer and odd accent, weighing if he gave a shit. Turns out he didn't. Not this close to the end of his watch. He reset on Mace. Noted the gash on his temple.

"Where you headed?" he asked.

"Las Cruces. Thought we'd get out of the snow a while."

"Know why I stopped you?"

"Not yet," said Mace.

"You're driving with expired tags."

Mace stared off. Saw Glenn sitting across the booth in the Grit, fork speared through a chunk of gravy-laden meatloaf, head turned out the window toward the Tundra's plates. "I am?"

"By half a year. I don't know how you do things in Colorado but down here you can get cited."

"Do what you gotta do," said Mace, eyes front, both hands on the wheel.

"Well I sure appreciate you giving me the go-ahead on that. Because what I'm gonna do is encourage you to address this issue when you get home."

Mace looked at him. "Thank you."

The trooper nodded. Then couldn't help meeting the shepherd's hyper-alert stare. "Who's this?"

"Vince," said Jamie.

"Beautiful animal. You folks have a safe day."

He tipped his hat at Jamie, climbed into his cruiser and killed the light bar. Then whipped around the Tundra and accelerated into the chalky glow of the oncoming sun. Mace checked the rearview and saw Hazim watching him with an oddly emotional expression. Like he might choke up.

"What now?" asked Mace.

Hazim tilted his head back. Shut his eyes. "I'm beginning to love this country."

Mace drove east another hour then turned south onto a two-lane highway running through scrawny desolation. Signs reared from the gloom bearing silhouettes of rifles and pistols with red lines slashed through the weapons. Sunday dawn was igniting the razor wire on an infinite east–west fence when they reached a cluster of metal buildings. Several green four-by-fours were parked out front with Homeland Security emblems stamped on the doors. A huge American flag waved over the line of vehicles flowing between nations. Foot traffic and vendors coiled in both directions. Otherwise, the Antelope Wells Port of Entry could pass for an aging mid-century gas station.

Mace parked in the lot farthest from the crossing. Hazim lifted Vince's head off his lap and everybody got out and stood there staring south like they'd reached the rim of the earth. A fair size town named El Berrendo was visible on the Mexican side and the Sierra Madre Occidental Mountains hung hazy and enigmatic beyond that. Jamie handed Hazim the money belt and hugged him so hard he froze. Then she backed away and Mace and Hazim squared off in wary admiration. For a second it looked like they might shake hands or even hug but neither could muster the will.

"Better do what the cop said," advised Mace.

Hazim frowned. "Remind me."

"Have a safe day."

"Safe?" said Hazim, head cocked. "What is that?"

"Beats the shit outta me," said Mace.

This caused them both to laugh so hard they had to brace themselves against the Tundra's hood to maintain their balance. Like safe was the funniest concept ever conceived or uttered. When the gallows humor ran dry, Hazim grabbed his pack and limped toward the border. A dozen paces later he stopped suddenly like he forgot something and retraced his steps. When he got back to the Tundra he leaned in and hugged Vince before continuing on his way without a backward glance.

After using his Belgian passport to cross into Mexico, Hazim angled toward a taxi stand. He reached a dusty Camry and looked back at America. Mace and Jamie were buried in a fierce and oblivious embrace. Only Vince was watching him. Head stuck out the window making precise little adjustments to keep his new friend in sight. Hazim waved at the dog, shocked by the tightness gripping his chest. He barely knew the man and woman he'd gone to war with but dreaded never seeing them again. Then he climbed in the cab and disappeared down a teeming street.

Mace and Jamie were back in the Tundra and all buckled up before they saw the laminated photograph of Ajna resting on the dash. And the prayer rug rolled up tight in the back seat.

FIFTY-SEVEN

It was dusk when the Tundra rolled through the gate into the yard. Mace got out with Vince and the Winchester. They checked every room and closet before he waved Jamie inside. After that they lit the wood stove in the charred kitchen, made instant coffee and fed the dog. Then all three stood on the porch and stared at the darkness trying to imagine what fresh hell might be coming home to roost. Night fell and the cold intensified but they barely noticed. Jamie jammed her hands deeper into her pockets, felt something and pulled out a wad of black cloth. A souvenir from a nightmare.

"What's that?" asked Mace.

"My hood. Hazim wanted me to keep it."

"Why?"

"Proof I never saw anything."

Mace ran his fingers over the fabric thinking he should have killed the kidnapper when he had the chance. Then the more he thought about it the more he wasn't so sure. "Right nice of him."

"Yea. Except I see myself putting a bullet through Glenn's head every five minutes."

"What'd you do with the body?"

"He didn't want me to see that part."

"Good," said Mace.

He wrapped his arms around her and they watched the road together until the wind stung their faces numb. Then man, woman and dog went upstairs and slept like the dead in the same bed.

Mace was snowshoeing across the meadow toward the cabin his parents built when Monday poured brassy blue over the horizon. A hard plastic long gun case and a shovel were over his shoulder along with a trash bag full of ripe clothes he and Jamie had worn four days straight. The October dump didn't surpass the forty-one inches left by the Thanksgiving storm of 1919 but it clobbered the plateau with over two feet of powder and hip-deep drifts where the wind curled around the timber. He was sweating like a pig and dying for a drink and a joint but kept right on slogging like he wasn't.

After burning the clothes in the firepit behind the cabin, he went deeper into the woods and dug an oblong hole in the frozen ground. He placed the long gun case in the hole, popped it open, took the Ute knife out of his pocket and laid it beside Will's carbine. He stayed on his knees a minute, staring at the two weapons made centuries apart but equally efficient. Then he put the knife back in his parka, locked the gun in the case, buried it and retraced his trail.

When he got home he got online and read about a sprawling search for a missing hunting party led by a well-known guide. Then Jamie came downstairs wearing scrubs under a parka and snow boots and held up her spare Rubicon keys. They drove off with Vince in the bed and went left at the gate. Thirty minutes later they crossed Roubideau Creek and Jamie told Mace to stop. Both climbed out. She studied the willow-lined curve leading to the bridge. Saw the motorcycle on its side and the rider lying on his back. Then felt a chill that had nothing to do with the brutal cold.

"It was here," she said. "Right here."

Mace eyed the heavy cover off the right. "If I had to hide a vehicle in a hurry, it'd be in there."

No sooner had he said that than two Ouray County search-and-rescue trucks blew by hauling trailered snowmobiles. Mace waved and they waved back then he followed Jamie and Vince through the willows into pine and aspen. When the timber got too thick for a vehicle, they turned around and zigzagged toward the road until they saw a squarish mound with foliage piled on top.

The Rubicon started right up and Jamie bashed it back onto the road with Mace and Vince following on foot. She cupped his face through the window and felt the twitchy heat and rapid heart rate of delirium tremens through her palm. His gaze was bloodshot but steady.

"It's only gonna get worse. Sure you'll be good till I get home?"

"Unless you got a better idea," he said, kissing her hand.

He watched her drive off and the day they met dropped in front of his eyes. Glenn had busted his ankle bad enough to show bone while hunting on Red Mountain south of Ouray. Both were covered with elk viscera and Glenn was conjugating the word *fuck* ad infinitum when Mace helped him into the ER. Then Jamie took over, all lanky and gorgeous and jaded competent in snug teal scrubs. She stabilized the break and suggested Mace take a kerosene bath and find friends that didn't have drag marks on their knuckles. Then she wheeled Glenn away for X-rays leaving a puddle of a grown man wearing a lovesick grin. They were engaged before the ankle fully healed.

Jamie bought two prepaid phones at the AT&T store on the way to work. She passed through the ER waiting room and saw the local news on the flatscreen mounted high on the wall. The Montrose County sheriff was being interviewed near a burnt-out Chevy Silverado at a trailhead full of emergency vehicles. He was describing the challenges of a crime scene covering tens of thousands of acres. Then she pushed through the double doors into the sheltering bustle of exam rooms. Colleagues kept stopping her and asking how she was feeling. She said great every time.

FIFTY-EIGHT

The cadaver dogs hit the jackpot, finding six bodies in forty-eight hours, all but two scattered along the North Fork of Cottonwood Creek. Five were gunshot victims and one had their throat cut. All six homicides occurred in Montrose County but San Miguel and Ouray counties joined the party because of the brute manpower required. Not to mention the mother lode of telegenic publicity.

The godawful gore led to Will's camp and a G-Wagon with a safe full of automatic weapons and passports matching four of the dead men and one for a David Petrovic. The latter remained missing. Paper copies of a flight plan found in the same vehicle led to the crew's cell numbers, which led to a pair of dumbfounded British pilots killing time at the Hampton Inn. They led authorities to a fully fueled Gulfstream sitting at Montrose Regional Airport. Which in turn led to security cam footage of the jet's passengers disembarking in the bright fall sun the week prior.

When no one claimed the white Grand Cherokee parked at the trailhead, the vehicle was hauled off and searched. Three passports were found inside, each bearing the same man's photo but different names and countries of origin. Those being Peru, Cameroon and Argentina. The face on the passports matched the stiff packing the Italian rifle, which only made the mess more inscrutable.

Jimmy Temple suffered a nervous breakdown while being interviewed by detectives and went straight to a bar afterward. Four hours later he was admitted to Montrose Memorial with severe alcohol poisoning. Being of stout constitution, the cook survived without adding to the body count.

The icing on the mayhem was Glenn Frazier. The Ouray County deputy went hunting on opening day like he always did and thoroughly vanished. The collective anxiety created by a generational murder spree coinciding with the disappearance of a cop was reaching critical mass.

Mace and Jamie spent Tuesday morning following developments online like arsonists tracking their handiwork. Then she left for the ER and

Mace and Vince went to Ridgway to buy groceries and gauge the uproar. Roaming town, Mace passed through pockets of flimsy speculation about the murders. Wasn't until he dropped by the Cimarron Coffeehouse that he heard about the officially missing deputy. Sounded like a fuse burning right up to his door. When he got near home and saw a silver Ford Expedition at his gate, he knew he was looking at the dynamite.

The vehicle had a push bumper, a whip antenna lashed down on the roof and exempt Ouray County plates. Mace dismounted and the man behind the wheel climbed out and walked toward him, cheerless and alert. He was fifty-two years old, clean-shaven and wore jeans, work boots and a moss-green fleece jacket. He looked worn but robust with short brown hair and eyes that bore a perpetual squint like everywhere he looked was straight into the sun. He could be in any number of trades that required close attention to tiny details. But Mace had already narrowed his trade down to one.

"Afternoon," said the man. "Raymond Honeycutt. Ouray County Sheriff's Department."

Mace shook the offered hand and let it go. "Have we met?"

"Nope," said Raymond, producing a card. "Always admired your work. Just couldn't afford it."

Mace stared at the word *Investigator* printed under his name. "Any word on Glenn?"

"Not a thing. Missed roll call yesterday without excuse so it's all hands on deck."

Mace put the card in his pocket, unlocked the gate and swung it back. "Instant coffee okay?"

"I'm an instant guy all the way," said Raymond, eyeing the shepherd in the Tundra's back seat.

"Don't worry," said Mace. "He just looks like he's gonna rip your face off."

Mace set mugs on the coffee table in the living room, sat on the couch and watched Raymond browse his arrowhead collection. Vince stood by the front door, mesmerized by the visitor in all the wrong ways. Then Mace realized too late he'd left something irresistible lying on the mantel. The investigator picked up the moss agate knife with both hands, beguiled by its beauty and utility.

"Found that in a rock shelter out by Horsefly Peak," said Mace.

Raymond turned it in the light. "Looks brand-new."

"I'm pretty sure it was ceremonial."

"Why?"

"Utes don't make a tool that perfect then bury it unless it's for something special."

"Like what?"

"Cutting umbilical cords. Sacrificing important enemies. Stuff like that."

Raymond set the knife on the coffee table and pulled up a chair. "Bet it worked like a charm."

Mace waited for Raymond to produce a notebook but none appeared. He just leaned back, laced his fingers across his lap and let go with an unwavering gaze and a brisk delivery.

"When's the last time you talked to Officer Frazier?"

"Saturday morning," said Mace, thinking the guy already knew that.

"Seem like something was eatin' on him? Something off in the way he talked?"

"Nope. Sounded the same way he always sounds on the first day of rifle season."

"How's that?"

"Like it was Thanksgiving and Fourth of July rolled into one."

"Would it be an exaggeration in any way to call you his best friend?"

Mace hesitated. Caught off guard by the peculiar phrasing. "Not a bit."

"Kinda odd him not checking back in if he filled his tag."

"Odd either way now that you mention it."

Raymond sipped his coffee. "Understand you're not guiding anymore after that thing last year."

"That's right. Lost my taste for it."

Raymond appeared mildly disappointed then pressed on. "Found your friend's Mossberg in his bedroom oiled and unfired. Found his Ram this morning, east of Highway 550 in fallow pasture."

"Just sitting there?"

The investigator glanced at the German shepherd. "With a tarp and a plastic bowl of water in the back seat. And the tech guys say his phone has been deactivated. As in probably destroyed."

Mace frowned at the floor so the guy couldn't see his face. "Then something is way wrong."

"Yes it is. So anything you might remember from that call, no matter how trivial, could be incredibly important." Raymond said this carefully, as if teasing a critter out of its hidey-hole.

Mace registered the tone and looked up. Found the investigator's slitted eyes waiting for him like a double-barreled polygraph. "Nothing comes to mind but if it does I'll let you know."

Raymond nodded, finished his coffee, considered the dregs then let his eyes rove around the room. There was a rolled-up rug on the floor in the corner. Bit bigger than a bath mat. The Kaaba in Mecca was woven into the burgundy-and-gold fabric. "You or your wife a Muslim?" he asked.

Mace blinked. "No. Why?"

Raymond pointed at what caught his attention. "You got a prayer rug over there."

Mace turned. Squinted at the thing. "Oh yea. Jamie found that at a swap meet in Ouray. Loved the colors. What makes you so sure it's a prayer rug?"

"Walked all over 'em with muddy boots in a place called Fallujah."

Mace was in the process of forming a question when Raymond gave him the answer.

"First Battalion, Eighth Marines."

Then the investigator's phone rang and he excused himself and went out onto the porch.

Mace watched him through the window. The cell was mashed to his ear. His eyes were fastened on the mountains to the south with a grim expression. When the call ended he came back inside but didn't sit down. Just stood there studying Mace like he was sifting their chat for fabrications.

"They found a torched RV three miles from Officer Frazier's truck. Probably just another meth lab gone bad but you never know. They got the dogs out there now and they don't miss a thing."

"How can I help?" asked Mace.

"Don't go anywhere."

Raymond almost patted Vince on his way out but something explosive in the animal's stillness made him stuff his hands into his pockets and keep them there until he reached his vehicle.

FIFTY-NINE

Grandview Cemetery south of Montrose offered a fine view of the snow dunked San Juans that hinted at eternity but Jamie didn't notice. She was sitting behind the wheel of her Rubicon in the graveyard's full parking lot. Vince was in the back seat and she was glued to her phone reading the online edition of *The Denver Post*. The headline running over the pictures of the dead and missing was vaguely reassuring: NO ARRESTS IN OPENING-DAY KILLINGS.

The photos came from various sources. The Serbians had their passports scanned. Will's pic was from his sixtieth-birthday party. Clay and Vanessa's blank mugs came from their bogus Arizona driver licenses. The blurb about David Petrovic said he was last seen by a search-and-rescue crew high in valley struck by an avalanche shortly thereafter. Given the unusually harsh high-country conditions, his body wasn't expected to be found until the spring thaw, if then.

Will was identified by his wife and the bullet that killed him was recovered and matched to Stefan's rifle so his funeral was first in line. The bevy of gunshot Europeans and the dead American couple were all on ice at the coroner's office. The foreigners were waiting on positive ID and repatriation of remains. Being stiffs of growing interest to law enforcement across several states and countries, the fake realtors would remain refrigerated guests of Montrose County indefinitely.

Then Jamie swiped to Glenn's full-uniform photo under a separate headline: OURAY COUNTY DEPUTY STILL MISSING. She combed the article below his smug face for any solid connection to the slaughter on the plateau but found nothing. After that, she climbed out wearing a black dress under a long wool coat. Took her a minute to find Mace standing in the oldest section of the graveyard. He wore a blazer and jeans and was reading the eroded headstones of pioneers and their barely born children with a gaunt expression. They joined hands and merged with the flow of shell-shocked mourners heading for the pile of fresh earth and the burnished wooden coffin.

The preacher's eulogy was succinct and wry and sounded eerily like Will himself. When it was over, Mace asked Lucinda Stoddard if that was the case and she said it was. He wrote his own eulogy after a physical revealed his heart wasn't as bombproof as he imagined. Something called ventricular tachycardia. Mace and Jamie hugged her for a long time feeling like grotesque frauds.

When everyone ran out of platitudes and tears, Jamie and Mace drifted back toward the Rubicon in a head-down funk. So they didn't register Vince's barking or see the two men lounging against the Jeep until they were almost there. The older guy was fifty-three years old, square-jawed and substantial with a brushy mustache. His dark hair was buzz-cut and he wore a blue parka over a white button-down shirt. A S&W 9mm rode his right hip. His face bore a pleasant but dogged skepticism. The younger man was rangy, brown-haired and thirty-three years old. He wore a black parka, a flat smile and the same sidearm as his boss. Both wore badges on their belts, silverbelly Stetsons and work boots. Mace laid a finger over his lips, pointed at Vince and the dog fell silent on a dime.

"Morning," said the older man. "Detective Stan Ludwig. Montrose County sheriff."

"My face on the wall at the post office or what?" asked Mace offhandedly.

"Nah," said Ludwig. "Mr. Stoddard's widow was kind enough to point you two out." Then he indicated the younger cop. "This here's Doug Mathews."

Mathews nodded politely but his grin remained drum tight.

Ludwig dissected the hollow-eyed pair thinking they looked like they'd been dragged to hell and gone. "Hate to ambush you folks burying a friend but your phones are no longer in service."

"Kitchen caught fire last week," said Jamie like it happened a lot. "Phones were on the counter."

"Well that explains it," said Ludwig but his eyes didn't stop drilling into their faces.

"What else is on your mind?" asked Mace, sticking with the helpful nothing-to-hide tone.

"That couple that ended up dead after you took 'em on a mountain-lion photo expedition."

"You mean those realtors from Phoenix?" said Mace, wondering how the fuck he knew that.

"Unless you're in the habit of guiding realtors from elsewhere."

"Nope. They were my first."

"When's the last time you saw 'em?" asked Ludwig.

"Thursday night at my place. I got paid and they drove off. Didn't say where they were headed."

"Remember what they were driving?" asked Mathews.

"Black Beamer. The X5 with Arizona plates."

"You find 'em a puma?" asked Ludwig.

"Sure did," said Mace.

The sheriff smiled, impressed to no end. "Kinda long-shot deal sneaking up on one of those."

"Got lucky."

Ludwig parsed Mace's gunfighter eyes and taciturn modesty. "I doubt that."

Then he swiveled his head and watched a backhoe drop dirt onto Will's grave. "Here's the thing. Week ago Friday you called Will Stoddard. Turned out to be the last call he ever got. Week ago Saturday, Deputy Glenn Frazier called you about dawn. And that turned out to be the last call he ever made. Correct me if I'm wrong but I'm guessing that was before your kitchen burned up."

Mace resisted saying anything ornate. Like he'd known both men most of his life and opening day was the acid test of their bond and existence and commiserating was normal. "So what?"

"Gets worse," said the detective.

Mace filled his lungs and let his body go loose and limber like a fighter entering the ring. He and Jamie were alive. It was all cake from here on in. "Let her rip," he said.

Ludwig held up both hands, fingers spread. "Picture ten people. Two Arizona realtors. Four guys from Belgrade. One huntin' guide. One Ouray cop. And you two. All ten know each other directly or have a connection through someone else in the group. All ten are alive and well on Friday. Come Sunday, six are dead of highly unnatural causes and two are missing, one under a slide and the other just plain up in smoke. Everybody but you folks extremely out of pocket."

Mace slipped his arm around Jamie's waist and they stared at the cops until Ludwig pointed at the unmarked blue Tahoe parked tight behind the Rubicon to make sure it didn't go anywhere.

"Would you mind following us?" he asked.

Wasn't really a question.

SIXTY

Mace and Jamie sat in a third-floor conference room in the sheriff's office on North Grand Avenue. They were facing Ludwig and Mathews across a fake-walnut table messy with paperwork but no recording device. There was a nice view of the parking lot and beyond that the plateau.

"You two comfy without a lawyer?" asked Ludwig.

"Why wouldn't we be?" asked Mace.

"Good question. Know what a ResQLink is?"

"Sure. Rescue beacon."

"One registered to Will Stoddard was activated on opening day. Stoddard was probably dead already. We think his client, guy calling himself David Petrovic, was the person who set it off."

"What do you mean 'calling himself David Petrovic'?" asked Jamie.

Ludwig tapped some scanned documents. "Mean he had good reason. He was a war criminal. Supervised the murder of a few thousand Muslim civilians. Got a slap on the wrist in some international court. Left a lot of folks who'd love to punch his ticket. Real name is Dragan Kordic."

"What war?" asked Mace.

"Bosnian."

Mace leaned forward, elbows on the table. "What does that ancient history have to do with us?"

If Ludwig was caught off guard by the cut to the chase he didn't show it. "Didn't say it did. Just having a friendly chat based on your circumstantial relationship with a bunch of deceased people."

Mathews caught Mace's eye and cleared his throat. "That bull Stoddard was after must have had some royal headgear if he saved him for a client with bodyguards and a jillion-dollar jet."

Mace nodded. "If it wasn't a top end six-by-six-trophy, Will wouldn't have bothered."

"Why'd you call him a week ago Friday?"

"Got bored sitting on my butt when he was out with clients getting ready to fill tags."

"Sitting on your butt where?"

Mace saw Clay unlock his iPhone and change the settings so it couldn't be tracked and hoped the son of a bitch knew what he was doing. "At home with my wife who was down with the flu."

"What'd you and Will talk about?"

"Mostly it was him giving me a hard time for guiding cameras instead of guns."

Mathews absorbed all that, expressionless. "Why'd Officer Frazier call you on Saturday?"

"Standard stuff. The weather. Where he was gonna hunt up around McKenzie Butte."

"No kidding," said Mathews. "That's where I filled my cow tag last year. What do you think Frazier was doing in that dusty country way out by the Adobes where they found his truck?"

"No idea," said Mace.

Ludwig shoved his chair back, went to the window and took in the view. "So your best buddy tells you he's gonna be hunting on the plateau but his truck ends up thirty miles east of where he said he'd be. In crap habitat where there's more giraffe than elk and you have no idea why."

"That's right."

Ludwig turned around. "Think Officer Frazier was part of all this?"

"Part of all what?" asked Mace, pulse spiking to a shrill buzz.

"This whole clusterfuck. Plus a Department of Energy guard and three convicted poachers from Nucla missing over a week. Kinda wildly coincidental otherwise, ain't it? Respected officer with ten years under his belt takes a permanent powder on the same day we get our first mass murder."

Mace cocked his head as if the idea was beyond ludicrous. "You mean my friend who loved being a cop more than anything in the world and wanted to be one since he was eight?"

Ludwig sat down. Drummed his fingers on the table. "Wanna hear my overarching theory?"

"If you can't help yourself," said Mace.

"There were two hunting parties up there. One hunting elk. One hunting this guy Kordic."

"What makes you say that?"

"The trail of bodies leading up to that valley, everybody packing like they were going to war, including your realtor clients. And if and when Kordic's carcass ever turns up, I'd bet my badge a rifle got the job done. What else would make him climb that dome in a blizzard other than being hunted down like a rabbit. And whoever pulled the trigger, in my hypothesis, got clean away."

Mace leaned back. Met Ludwig's stare. "You really think I had something to do with it?"

"Not sure. But a top-shelf local guide like yourself would sure be handy to have in the mix."

"So would a local cop like Glenn," said Jamie. "Where do you think he is now? Hypothetically."

Ludwig grinned and looked around the room. "Well if I had to guess, I'd say he's having a cold beer down in Panama or being spit out of a wood chipper not fifty miles from here."

The preternatural depiction of the truth left Mace and Jamie with matching blank expressions until she snapped the spell with an icy non sequitur. "Then there's the assholes from Arizona. Anybody bother to find out who they really were? Or does that just happen on cop shows?"

Ludwig glanced at his partner. "Might as well toss that greasy meat on the fire."

Mathews got on his iPad. "Guy calling himself Clay Brewer was Robert Styder, age thirty-four, born in Gainesville, Texas. Played tight end at Baylor. Woman calling herself Vanessa Delgado was Silvia Carrillo, age thirty-two. Born in San Pedro, California. Softball star at Nebraska. Both joined the Air Force right outta college. Both deployed to Afghanistan with Close Precision Engagement Teams. Both did two tours. Came back engaged. Got hitched in Hawaii."

"Wait," said Jamie. "They were pilots?"

"Ground security. Countersniper stuff. Protected forward flight lines. Wasted a bunch of bad guys and punched out four years ago. Two all-American sweethearts with no criminal record."

"How'd you find that out?" asked Mace.

"Couple of clicks. All branches of the military take biometrics and fingerprints on the day of enlistment. Prints go to the FBI for inclusion in the national database."

Mace stared at his hands seeing the gloves the couple never took off. Now he knew why.

Ludwig asked if anyone needed a coffee break. Nobody did so he played his hole card. "There's one other thing I'd be remiss if I didn't mention. Dragan Kordic has two sons. They're on their way here right now. They sounded highly motivated to find out who offed their old man."

"I don't blame 'em," said Mace. "But we don't know any more than what we told you."

"But they don't know that," said Ludwig.

"Meaning we're supposed to be worried or what?"

"It'd make me pucker. Cops over there called 'em animals. Said they ran drugs and guns all over Eastern Europe. They also dabble in extortion and use acetylene to fry up folks who get on their nerves. When they find out you guided two veteran snipers into the area where their dad disappeared, which they will find out because it's all over the Internet, they're definitely gonna look you up."

Jamie slapped both her hands down on the table with a tremendous whack that made everyone jump. "Why don't you just do your fucking job instead of trying to scare us?" she said quietly.

Ludwig leaned back. Twiddled his thumbs a moment. "What do you make of that idea, Doug?"

"Food for thought," said his partner.

"Show 'em the point."

Mathews shoved an evidence bag across the table. Had an exquisitely fashioned green jasper arrowhead inside. "Coroner found that beauty on Robert Styder, otherwise known as Clay."

"The one with his throat opened from ear to ear," added Ludwig.

Mace stared at the Middle Archaic point lifted from his collection. Saw the moment he found it after a drenching August monsoon. Washed clean and bright. Sitting on a rain-sculpted pedestal of soil. Waiting for him and him alone. He was sure gonna miss it. "What about it?"

"Raymond Honeycutt described you as a serious arrowhead guy," said Mathews.

"So?"

"Said you had a real nice collection. All framed up and everything. We were just wondering if that one ever belonged to you."

Mace looked at the point one last time and pushed the bag back across the table. "You don't have the faintest goddamn idea what you're talking about do you?"

Mathews shrugged amiably picturing his fist colliding with Mace's jaw. "So enlighten me."

"Something that perfect never belongs to anyone but the hunter who made it."

After Mace and Jamie left the room, both cops went to the window and watched them cross the parking lot to the Rubicon. Jamie climbed in behind the wheel. Mace stood by the vehicle staring at the purple dusk settling over the plateau until he felt eyes on his back and turned. He saw Ludwig and Mathews watching him and studied them right back. Something in his expression gave the lawmen the nasty sensation of being downrange. Then Mace got in the Jeep and they drove away.

"That woman strike you as homicidal?" asked Mathews, following the taillights out of sight.

Ludwig plucked a cigarette from his shirt pocket and ran it under his nose like a fine cigar then put it back to prove he could. "In a pinch."

Mathews looked at him. Head tilted. Dubious. "Dragan Kordic's boys really on their way?"

"I mighta jumped the gun on that. But you never know."

"They really barbecue people on a whim?"

"Supposedly," said Ludwig.

"And what about Mason Winters?"

Ludwig replayed Mace's stainless-steel composure under pressure. Never flustered. Never not knowing exactly what he was gonna say. Catching their questions like soggy telegraphed punches before they arrived. As if he'd thoroughly scouted the ground they were gonna cover in advance.

"I think those Air Force guns picked the wrong guy."

SIXTY-ONE

Mace went to every window, upstairs and downstairs, testing latches with Vince on point. Then checked the dead bolt on the back door, went into the living room, parted the curtains and looked outside. He'd parked the Jeep and the Tundra facing the gate, rear bumpers close to the porch in case they had to leave in a hurry. But they were still sitting ducks thirty miles of bad to impassable road from help. Montrose County jail suddenly sounded like the Holiday Inn with twenty-four-hour guards.

"Remind me why we're doing this," he said.

Jamie was lying on her back on the couch, eyes shut, fully clothed, boots and all. "Doing what?"

"Not going with the truth."

She squinted at the ceiling, composing her answer in chunks. "Because if we tell that detective I gunned down a cop. Then throw in you killing two veterans. And Ubering my kidnapper down to Mexico after helping him shoot Will's client. A bunch of scumbag lawyers will end up owning our home. And we'll be out of prison about the time we're eligible for Medicare. Maybe."

"Still feels crazy."

"What does?"

Mace stared at the starlit peaks framing the black hulk of the barn. A view he loved forever now coiled and full of peril. "Sitting here empty-handed with all kinds of psychopathic shit running around out there in the dark."

"You worried about what Ludwig said about the sons?"

"If half of it was true, we'd be stupid not to."

Jamie considered this and sat up. "Where's Will's rifle?"

"Buried it."

"Why?"

"Jimmy Temple."

"Who's he?" she asked.

"Will's cook. No way he didn't see Will take it with him on opening day."

Then Jamie noticed the stone blade on the coffee table where Honeycutt left it. "What's that?"

"Ute knife I used to kill the guy calling himself Clay."

She stared at the thing. Not remotely tempted to touch it. "And you're gonna keep it."

Mace nodded, mind elsewhere now. "Might not be done with it."

Then he pulled the curtains tight and punched a number on his new cell from memory.

SIXTY-TWO

S unday's dawn was a milky smear to the east and Jamie was sound
asleep in their bed when Mace came downstairs dressed for serious cold, truck keys in hand. Vince followed him to a window where he
checked his watch before parting the curtains and scanning the yard. Then
he cupped the shepherd's muzzle and they had an eyeball-to-eyeball mind
meld before he spoke.

"Your mom told me what you did to Glenn. Anybody but me tries to
come into this house, you do the exact same thing. And don't stop working until they stop moving. You got me?"

The dog absorbed these instructions with unblinking concentration
then Mace went out the door and locked it behind him. Vince bounded
over to the window, nudged the curtains aside and watched the Tundra
drive away. After that, he posted up at the bottom of the stairs leading to
the bedroom, clocking every creak of the timbers like the zombie apoca-
lypse was rolling up outside.

Mace drove out the gate and secured it behind him. Then got in the truck
and sat there, one hand on the shift. He meant to drop it into drive but the
routine perfection of the dawn-washed terrain prevented him. Because
routine was gone. Eventually his eyes landed on a stand of pine atop a knoll
across the road to his right. It was on his neighbor's acreage. He knew it had
a fine view of his place because he'd hunted arrowheads there in his youth.
Cursing himself for burying the Winchester, he turned right and drove until
he saw what he feared. Then dropped the Tundra into four-wheel low and
followed fresh tire tracks where they left the road and ran toward the pines.

He was a hundred yards from the knoll when he saw the vehicle hidden
behind the trees facing his gate and hit the brakes. Then he recognized
the silver Expedition with the whip antenna and push bumper. When
his nerves settled to a dull crackle, he drove up to the Ford, got out and
rapped on the driver's window. Raymond Honeycutt rolled it down with

an inconvenienced expression. He had a thermos in his lap, binoculars in his hands and a black Colt AR-15 clamped to the dash.

"Morning," he said as if they were neighbors standing in their respective driveways.

"I take it I'm some kinda person of interest," said Mace.

"Take it any way you want," said the investigator.

Mace nodded. "How does this work? You follow me around or just sit here and drink coffee?"

"Kinda up to me."

Mace stared at the semiautomatic rifle. "Can I ask you a favor?"

"You can try."

"I gotta run an errand. Would you mind staying put until I get back?"

"And do what?"

"Watch over my wife and dog."

Raymond shook his head, mildly amused. "When the going gets weird, the weird turn pro."

"You come up with that pearl all by yourself?"

"Hell no. Hunter Thompson."

"What does it mean?" asked Mace.

"Means I don't blame you for asking given the circumstances."

Mace glanced at his home on the far side of the road. All his blood and treasure under one roof. "I shouldn't be gone more than an hour."

Raymond fiddled with the AM radio in the dash until he found an all-news station then poured himself a cup of coffee like the confab was over.

"So we're good," said Mace.

"Not really. But I'll probably be right here enjoying the view for an hour or so."

Mace looked at him thinking he must be a killer card player. "Gonna ask me where I'm going?"

Raymond gave him a sideways squint. "You really want me to?"

Mace drove west pushing his luck speed wise and didn't slow down until he saw the shiny brown Tundra parked on an empty stretch of Government Springs Road in the heart of the plateau. The driver was leaning against the hood. Mace stopped on the opposite shoulder, climbed out and met Mike Horner in the middle of the gravel. Then both men stood there, hands stuffed in their pockets staring off at white peaks and silvery-blue sky like they had a serious bone to pick.

Mike Horner spoke first. "No questions asked, huh?"

"Least give it a try," said Mace.

Mike crossed to the bed of his truck and gruffly shoved a load of fence posts aside revealing a canvas rifle case and a shoebox. "Okay. The hardware store is wide open."

Mace picked up the rifle case, unzipped it and slid out a bolt-action Remington Model 700 with a Leupold scope and sling. The weapon was far from new but clearly a prized possession in pristine condition. Then he saw the initials *EH* engraved on the stock forward of the bolt and reared back.

"Of all the freaking guns lying around your place you had to bring me Ethan's?"

"Was gonna do it anyway if you hadn't quit hunting. Nothing my boy would've wanted more."

Mace stared at the rifle, seeing Ethan Horner in all his brawny, precancer glory. Riding horses and bulls like a damn Comanche and harvesting elk by bow and gun with equal, eerie precision. He was the gold standard of bred-in-the-bone ranch scion, right up there with Mace's father Randy in the pantheon of backcountry legends. When all that poignant footage had run through Mace's skull, he caressed the dead man's initials with his thumb like they were an epitaph on a tomb.

"He was a better shot than you and me put together. Just born in the wrong century."

Mike chuckled. "Well hell. Who wasn't?"

Mace slung the rifle over his shoulder. Pointed at the shoebox. "What's that?"

"Rattlesnake," said Mike. "Isn't that what you wanted?"

Mace flipped the lid off. Saw a black Ruger .45 ACP and two boxes of federal ammo. The sidearm was streaked with mold and looked like death personified. "Hell did you find this?"

"Had a top hand who kept getting DUIs. Finally ran him off. Found that under his mattress."

Mace racked the slide. Dropped the magazine and shoved it back. The gun's guts were crispy.

"Thought you hated pistols," said Mike.

Mace stuck the sidearm back in the box and the box under his arm. "Changed my mind."

Mike studied his friend a moment. "Same way those two realtors from Phoenix who got their pictures in the paper changed their minds about buying your place."

"Something like that."

The rancher got into his truck, slammed the door and stuck his arm out. There were three boxes of 7mm Remington Mag cartridges stacked in his hand. Mace took the rifle ammo and Mike stared at the man he'd just armed to the teeth. "You know what Ethan would say right about now?"

"Yea. But tell me anyway."

"Looking for trouble is the best way to find it."

Mace grinned, eyes sweeping the road in both directions and creation in general. "Thank you for the tools, Mike. But I'm pretty sure trouble's gonna find me, no problem."

Then they shook hands and Mike drove off leaving him backlit by a blazing husk of rising sun.

After loading the rifle and racking it in the rear window, Mace loaded the Ruger and stuck it in the console. Then he sat there a minute, eyes flicking from the windshield to the mirrors before making a U-turn and heading for home at the same good clip. A few miles on, where spruce and aspen crowded the road like a tunnel, something huge and fast broke cover on his right. He didn't get a decent look until he skidded up on the shoulder. By then the creature had stopped and bladed its massive atypical rack toward the truck as if gripped by the same revelation as the driver.

Mace climbed out and walked toward the animal, not believing his eyes. He counted nine antler points on the left beam and twelve on the right then counted them again just to be sure. After that there wasn't a shred of doubt because tine length, inside spread and mass were as singular as a fingerprint. He was looking at the same bull elk he told the directional driller from Tulsa to shoot in a long-ago life. The animal betrayed nothing but regal patience so Mace treaded lightly through undergrowth until he was fifty paces away. Close enough to see the gunshot right antler had regenerated what was lost to perfection. An object lesson in healing and maybe even forgiveness.

Clobbered with relief and wonder, Mace raised his empty right hand as if the beast might recognize a gesture of penance. After a brazen communion the animal wheeled with a flourish and vanished into a cathedral of powder-draped timber. The silence that followed was immaculate.

It was the end of all coincidence.

ACKNOWLEDGMENTS

My thanks to Mike Horner, Matt Horner, Randy Johnson and Morgan Pihl for generously sharing their backcountry experience and knowledge.

To Tim Kelly, Dan Kelly and Walker Kelly for their brute love and irrational faith.

To Nancy Heritage, my refuge and frontline reader.

To Bruce Hermann for invaluable and mostly gentle reality checks.

To Emily Bestler for her courage, prowess and patience.

To Sloan Harris and Anthony Mattero for their unshakeable chill.

To Matthew Snyder for believing so completely and opening so many doors.

And to Joe Ide, who lit the path I could easily have missed.